A NOT-SO-FRIENDLY WARNING

I was pulling the key out when cold touched the back of my neck—not a cold breeze or a cold drip of water, just . . . cold. The cold was followed by a soft whisper that crawled right up into the back quarters of my brain.

"You need to stay away from the Alden job."

I slid the keys into my pocket and wrapped my hand around the miniature spray bottle I keep there.

The nightblood stood about two feet away from me. He had hollow cheeks, dark hair, and a very long, narrow nose that, together with his high cheekbones, gave him a vulturelike appearance.

Suddenly, turning down Chet's offer of a sympathetic shoulder and brotherly escort didn't seem like such a great idea, family quarrel or no family quarrel. If I got drained in my own alley because I lacked the cojones to make up properly with my own brother, neither one of us would ever forgive me.

"Sorry—you are?" I kept my thumb on the spray bottle's trigger. Having been attacked in an alley before, I had developed this nervous habit of going around armed. In this case, the armament was a light but effective mixture of garlic-infused holy water.

"Jacques Renault." The vampire tilted his chin so he could look yet farther down that long nose at me. Not that he had any right to. It was a seriously high-class expression coming from somebody dressed as an undead slacker. In a departure from the rest of his overdone blood family, Jacques wore loose khakis and a button-down shirt, its tails untucked, over a black T-shirt. He also smelled of fresh onions, which was not your normal nightblood perfume. "And I will say it again, Charlotte Caine—you need to stay away from the Alden job."

Also by Sarah Zettel

THE VAMPIRE CHEF NOVELS

A Taste of the Nightlife

Let Them Eat Stake

A Vampire Chef Novel

SARAH ZETTEL

OBSIDIAN
Published by New American Library, a division of
Penguin Group (USA) Inc., 375 Hudson Street,
New York, New York 10014, USA
Penguin Group (Canada), 90 Eglinton Avenue East, Suite 700, Toronto,
Ontario M4P 2Y3, Canada (a division of Pearson Penguin Canada Inc.)
Penguin Books Ltd., 80 Strand, London WC2R 0RL, England
Penguin Ireland, 25 St. Stephen's Green, Dublin 2,
Ireland (a division of Penguin Books Ltd.)
Penguin Group (Australia), 250 Camberwell Road, Camberwell, Victoria 3124,
Australia (a division of Pearson Australia Group Pty. Ltd.)
Penguin Books India Pvt. Ltd., 11 Community Centre, Panchsheel Park,
New Delhi - 110 017, India
Penguin Group (NZ), 67 Apollo Drive, Rosedale, Auckland 0632,
New Zealand (a division of Pearson New Zealand Ltd.)
Penguin Books (South Africa) (Pty.) Ltd., 24 Sturdee Avenue,
Rosebank, Johannesburg 2196, South Africa

Penguin Books Ltd., Registered Offices:
80 Strand, London WC2R 0RL, England

First published by Obsidian, an imprint of New American Library,
a division of Penguin Group (USA) Inc.

First Printing, April 2012
10 9 8 7 6 5 4 3 2 1

Printed in the United States of America

To Alex Guarnaschelli and Christopher Lee

ACKNOWLEDGMENTS

No book is ever created by a single person. I'd like to thank the Untitled Writers Group, who read it first; my husband, Tim, who was patient throughout; my agent, Shawna, who never quits; and my editor, Jessica, who is always right.

I

"Charlotte! He left me!"

The kitchen door banged open and a blur of color hurtled past the hot line.

"The wedding's in ten days!" The intruder—whose name, incidentally, was Felicity Garnett—shouted over the hyperactive drumbeat of thudding chef's knives. "Ten days and he left me alone!"

Being grabbed and shaken by a hysterical woman in a designer pantsuit is never a good thing. Just then it was particularly bad. For starters, I had a fish knife in my hand and a lovely fillet of sushi-grade tuna on my board that needed my attention. It also happened to be five o'clock on Thursday afternoon, so I was heading up the dinner prep for my restaurant, Nightlife.

The door from the dining room banged open again. "I'm so sorry, Chef Caine . . ." Robert Kemp, my white-haired, English maître d', rushed in, looking as mortified as I've ever seen him, but pulled up short when he saw our intruder had me in a death grip.

Felicity ignored him. "You can't say no." She shook me for emphasis. "You're not going to say no! If you say no, it's over!"

Now, it's one thing when random passersby have hysterics on the street. I mean, that's just New York City. It's totally different when those hysterics erupt in a confined space full of knives, fire, and massive pots of simmering stock. My crew members were busy at their stations, chopping the components for their *mise en place*, seasoning soups, checking the temperature of the ovens and making sure the containers of fresh ingredients and garnishes were in place for when we opened at eight. I had to get Felicity out of the middle of the hot, fragrant, noisy, frenetic action before somebody and her new spring Donna Karan pumps got hurt.

Knotting my fingers into her jacket collar, I spun Felicity around to face the door.

"No!" she wailed. "You can't! He left . . ."

"You. Yes. Got that. Zoe, Reese, keep it moving in here."

"Yes, Chef," Zoe, my petite, eagle-eyed executive sous, replied calmly from the dessert station.

Reese, on the other hand, is an ex-drill sergeant with a manic SpongeBob laugh that would have given Alfred Hitchcock goose bumps. "Hear that, slackers?" he boomed. "You're mine now!"

"It's . . . !" Felicity began again.

Robert held the door, allowing me to shove Felicity bodily out of the bright kitchen into Nightlife's dim, cool, and much, much less hazardous dining room.

"But . . . !"

"Felicity!" I spun her back around, put my hand under her pointy chin, and pushed her jaw closed. "Cut it out!"

Felicity's tears shut off as if she'd thrown a switch somewhere, and her wide, wild amber eyes narrowed in raccoon-masked fury.

"Cut. It. Out," I said again, to make sure she fully understood the nuances of the phrase. "Are you going to cut it out?"

Felicity's chin trembled against my palm, but she nodded.

"Okay." I let her go. Felicity drew in a deep, shuddering breath, and I had my hand ready again, just in case. She held up her own palm in answer. I nodded, then waved back Robert, who was hovering just out of Felicity's field of vision.

Of all the professional acquaintances I might suspect capable of total disintegration during dinner prep, Felicity Garnett was not one of them. Far from being a bride left at the altar, Felicity was one of the highest of the high-end event coordinators in Manhattan. She regularly stage-managed the Big Day for discerning daughters of Fortune One Hundred families. I had personally seen her face down a bride who had been slipped an extra caffeine dose in her triple-mocha latte, gotten hold of the cake knife, and threatened to carve up the room unless the flowers were switched from golden dawn peonies to summer azure delphiniums *right now.*

We'd sort of lost touch since she shot up the ladder in her chosen profession, and I . . . stalled. Well, maybe not stalled, but there had been a few setbacks. The biggest had come last fall when my restaurant, Nightlife, experienced a murder on the premises, a takeover attempt that could charitably be described as hostile, and the departure of my vampire brother, who had been part owner of the establishment. All little things, of course, but they did raise eyebrows in certain circles.

"I'm sorry, Charlotte." Felicity brushed at her black jacket and tried to adjust the collar of the plum silk blouse underneath. "But he . . ."

"He walked out on you. You said. You want to tell me who 'he' is?"

"Oscar Simmons."

The name hit me with a dull thud. What Felicity was to

event planners, Oscar Simmons was to executive chefs, except Oscar got way more time on the morning talk shows and the foodie networks. Oscar and I also had what gets called "history." Unfortunately, it was the kind of history that involves barbarian hordes and burning cities. "Felicity, do not tell me you hired Oscar for a high-pressure event."

"I know, I know. But he's one of the most talked-about chefs in Manhattan . . ."

"There's a reason for that."

"And he just won the Epicurean Award . . ."

"He was sleeping with a judge."

"Saucer of cream with that attitude, Charlotte?" Felicity's eyes glimmered as anger waded back through her private swamp of desperation.

"That attitude is why I'm not the one running around on a Thursday evening like the proverbial chicken with its head cut off."

"Maybe we should just go back in the kitchen so you can have one of your cooks rub extra salt into the wound." Felicity pushed a lock of copper-highlighted hair off her cheek, and her fragile confidence wavered again. "Oh God. It's all over."

Now it was my turn for the deep breath. Starting round the bend of another weepy conversational circle was not going to get the story out of Felicity, especially not before opening time. Intervention was clearly necessary.

"Want a drink?"

Felicity looked at me as if I were an angel descending from on high. "Please. Coffee. Black."

If I hadn't known things were serious before, I did now. Felicity was strictly a skinny half-caf cappuccino kind of woman. I pulled two mugs of coffee from the industrial-sized urn we keep hot for the staff and gestured Felicity over to table nineteen. Around us, Nightlife's long, narrow dining room held the hushed anticipation of a stage before the curtain goes up. We open a little later than most dinner places, because Nightlife's specialty is haute noir cuisine—that is, we cater to both human and paranormal customers and tastes. This is a big job in Manhattan where the magically oriented minorities are growing faster than scandals around a reality show star, and finding a place where a mixed party can share a meal without anybody getting hurt can still be a challenge. At the moment, the warm golden track lighting was turned down low, bringing out the highlights in the antique oak bar that runs along the wall. Our tables were perfectly laid out with gold under-cloth, white over-cloth, and settings of pristine white dishes. Clatter and bustle drifted nonstop out from the kitchen, but it sounded thin and far away.

"What kind of wedding has got you this wound up?" I asked Felicity as I handed across the coffee.

"Vampires versus Witches, to the tune of five hundred thousand dollars."

I allowed a moment of respectful silence for the dollar figure. That alone was worth getting dramatic over. Even with this level of promised payoff, though, coordinating a wedding between vampires and witches took guts. There's a lot of fuss made about the supposed rivalry between vampires and werewolves, but the deepest hatreds run between vampires and witches. And for heaven's sake, don't get either side started on how this came about. It's worse than a bar fight between Red Sox and Yankees fans. Most people think it started with the Five Points Riot in the 1980s, but some feuds go back centuries. If they involve one of the big witch clans, such as the Maddoxes or the Coreys, they can rack up serious body counts and gallons of—excuse the expression—bad blood.

Felicity gulped down the hot coffee as if it were ice water. I watched, eyebrows raised.

"You'll get a stomachache."

"Too late." She gasped. "Give me a Tums, and I can tell you what vintage it is."

"Join the club. Felicity, I'm glad you like the coffee, but if you want my help for something, you need to get a move on." My front-of-house staff would be arriving soon. We had family meal to serve, prep to finish, and, based on the reservations list Robert had shown me, a decent-sized dinner crowd on the way.

"Okay, okay. Back in November I got a call from Adrienne Alden." Felicity paused and looked at me.

"Adrienne Alden!" I exclaimed.

The corners of Felicity's mouth flickered upward. "You have no idea who she is, do you?"

"Robert," I called over to my maître d', who was busy with the computer at the host station. "Who's Adrienne Alden?"

"Mrs. Adrienne Alden, married to Scott Alden," replied Robert without hesitation or even looking back at me. He has a social register in his brain that is the envy of restaurateurs throughout Manhattan. "Scott Alden is CEO of North Island Holdings and oldest son of the very prominent Alden family. Mrs. Alden is on the board of several important charities and galleries, and lunches with a highly exclusive group of similarly connected ladies."

I turned back to Felicity and translated this into my own terms. "Adrienne Alden gets a good table on Saturday night, and possibly a complimentary appetizer."

"She's also got a daughter named Deanna," said Felicity. "Last year, Deanna Alden got engaged to Gabriel Renault, a nightblood originally from Paris, or so he says."

"Nightbloods"—that is, vampires—have been known to get a little cagey about where they're actually from. It's way more romantic to be Nightblood Victor from "Paree" than plain old Vampire Vic from Hoboken.

"So, groom's the vamp, and the bride's the witch?"

Felicity frowned. "Well, the mother's a witch. I'm not entirely clear on the daughter."

This was one of those times when discretion was the better part of sarcasm.

"Anyway"—Felicity took another swallow of coffee—"Mrs. Alden decided Deanna and Gabriel were going to have the wedding of the decade." She paused. "I would have called you to do the catering right away, you know." Felicity seasoned her earnestness with that special blend of tension that comes when you realize you may have already screwed up. "But back in November things . . . weren't going so well for you."

"You mean back in November I was standing in front of a jury while recovering from smoke inhalation and trying to explain that I shouldn't be sent to jail for burning down a vampire bar." A situation that, incidentally, had been the direct result of a clash between the aforementioned Maddox witch clan and some vampires, one of whom happened to be my brother, Chet.

"That qualifies as things not going so well."

"They did get better." Kind of. Mostly. Except for some little holdover issues, such as how my sort-of-kind-of-yeah-okay dating Brendan Maddox had not endeared me to some of the more hard-line members of that particular magically oriented family.

Focus, Charlotte. "So, you called Oscar Simmons, even though you know he's the restaurant world's biggest prima donna. A title for which there is hefty competition, may I add. What were you thinking, again?"

"The society page of the *New York Times*," said Felicity to what was left of her coffee. "And did I mention five hundred thousand dollars?"

"You've seen both before."

"I know, I know." Felicity wilted down until her chin was in danger of dipping into her mug.

A very unpleasant idea settled into my brain. "You're not sleeping with Oscar, are you?"

"What do you take me for? I don't sleep with chefs. No offense."

"You're not my type."

"Besides, he's with somebody else right now."

"Oscar's always with somebody else. Being unavailable is supposedly part of his charm." This is to me one of life's great mysteries. What is attractive about a guy who is ready and willing to walk out on his current relationship at the drop of a toque? Especially if you stop and think for just one second that the same guy could just as easily walk out on you.

"So, if it wasn't personal, what pushed Oscar over the edge?"

"That's the problem. I don't *know*. I spent hours on the phone with him yesterday. I went over to Perception and camped out on his doorstep. All he'll say is he's pulling out of the Alden-Renault wedding, and he's stopped returning my calls."

"Sounds like he's trying to up his fee."

"He returned his fee."

"Oh." I sipped coffee while the gears in my head ground hard to keep up with this new conversational turn. Part of the reason Oscar was so successful was that he was an Olympic-level penny pincher. "What about his staff? He must have a sous who . . ."

"He told them he'd fire them all if they took over the job."

This was hardly reasonable, but at least it sounded like the Oscar Simmons I knew. "And you've really got no idea what brought this on?"

"I swear, Charlotte. I've tried to find out, but no one will tell me anything." Felicity leaned toward me, and I realized at some point in our conversation she'd stopped blinking. "This was supposed to be the biggest paranormal event since the vampires came out of the coffin. Now, the client's talking about postponing, the bride's talking about eloping, I've got no caterer and only ten days until the zero hour. You have got to help me."

"Felicity, I don't know. Nightlife's on shaky ground, and I haven't got a full staff . . ."

"Did I mention the hundred thousand dollars?"

"That's the food budget?"

"That's your fee."

It was a long moment before I could answer, because I had to concentrate all my energies on not leaping to my feet, or starting to drool. Felicity clearly found hope in my hesitation. She was blinking again, and color returned to her ravaged face. She was also jumping to conclusions, probably fueled by rapid caffeine intake. Something was missing in her story. It poked at me like a pinbone under my fingertips.

"Felicity, tell me what this job entails. Exactly."

"Wedding day catering includes breakfast and lunch buffets, hors d'oeuvres, a sit-down five-course dinner, plated dessert, plus the cake. Besides that, you come out to the house and act as personal chef for the family and guests until the wedding."

I let all this sink in next to the internal spreadsheet all executive chefs carry deep within them.

"One hundred thousand," said Felicity again. "Over and above the budget for food and staff. Pure profit after taxes. You can plow it all straight into Nightlife."

I took a deep breath. "Felicity?"

She leaned forward. "Yes?"

"Two hundred thousand."

2

This was how I found myself in a cab hurtling through the early-evening traffic, headed for Brooklyn Heights.

I love Brooklyn. Brooklyn has texture, flavor, and color, and you shouldn't turn your back on it for too long, because it will get up to something. A quick smartphone-aided Google on the address Felicity rattled off for the cab driver got me a real estate listing talking about the beauty of the "double-width Italianate mansion in the heart of one of the city's most historic neighborhoods." It left out the part about most snooty. Brooklyn Heights has families that remember President Roosevelt back when he was still Little Frankie.

All of this made me very glad I'd taken the time to grab a clean jacket.

Felicity and I were not alone when we climbed out of the taxi in front of the sprawling brownstone. Much to Felicity's consternation, I'd insisted we stop on the way and pick up another member of my team. Marie Alamedos—better known to one and all as Marie-Our-Pastry-Chef—stepped out of the cab with all the dignity of the Queen Mother stepping down from a carriage.

In a kitchen well stocked with short, round women,

Marie's the shortest, the roundest, and the oldest. Her third grandkid had been born just six weeks earlier, but if you met her in a dark alley, you'd never peg her as anybody's adoring *abuelita.* At sixty-five, she has arms like a longshoreman from hefting sacks of flour and masses of dough. Her jaw and neck are scarred down the right side from the time she took a direct hit with a spray of hot sugar. Years of watching apprentices has given her black eyes the hard glitter of a security guard at Kennedy airport. At the same time, concert pianists would sell their souls on eBay to have the delicacy and precision in her fingers.

And, believe me, if Marie Alamedos ever gets called "the Cakeinator," it happens where she can't hear.

Marie did not wear kitchen whites. She wore a black knit twinset and a single strand of matched pink pearls. With her personal portfolio tucked under her arm, she nodded to me and Felicity.

"I am ready."

"Thank you, Mrs. Alamedos." Now that Felicity had an answer to her crisis, the Hysteric had been given her pink slip and a swift kick. The Felicity in front of us was smooth and sophisticated, and she didn't waver even slightly as she mounted the broad steps of the brownstone mansion to ring the bell. Marie walked up beside her, equally at home. I, on the other hand, looked at the stained-glass fan light, the carved wooden doors, and the ornamented window frames, and tried not to feel as if I should be headed for the servant's entrance.

The door was opened by a tall, rail-thin woman in a neat black work dress.

"Good afternoon, Ms. Lyons," said Felicity. "Mrs. Alden's expecting us."

"She's in the living room." Ms. Lyons's gaze slid past Felicity to assess my and Marie's status relative to the rest of the people in her house. "Wipe your feet. I just finished the mopping."

Marie narrowed her eyes. The effect was a little like a laser scope finding its target. Ms. Lyons narrowed hers back. I swear I heard that *clack-clack* sound you get in the movies when somebody's working the pump action on a shotgun.

I wiped my feet.

Ms. Lyons led us up an oak staircase that would have done Scarlett O'Hara proud, down a narrow hall, and into a living room roughly the size of Nightlife's entire dining area. Everything from the original artwork on the stark white walls to the Victorian-era mahogany furniture looked down on you from the perch of well-aged money. A tidy line of bell jars decorated a black marble mantelpiece, each covering a single antique; a gold knot work necklace studded with garnets, a silver pocket watch, a wrist cuff of etched bronze, and, at the far end, a tiny, oddly delicate-looking silver pistol.

In the middle of it all sat a woman who could only be the mistress of the house. Felicity walked over immediately to shake her hand. "Mrs. Alden. As you can see, we have our new catering team." With professional smiles all around, Felicity made the introductions.

"How do you do, Chef Caine?" Mrs. Alden held out her perfectly kempt hand to me. "Thank you for coming on such short notice."

It takes practice to achieve perfect simplicity of appearance, and Mrs. Alden had clearly put in her time. Not one detail was out of place, from her neatly coiffed black hair to her lavender twinset, tailored white slacks, and pristine white designer flats. She looked so much as if she'd been custom created for the house around her that I got this strange idea that if you took her out of there, she'd start to wilt. That, however, didn't last past her handshake. As I met my new client's blue eyes, I saw the other thing that comes to cool, poised, refined and elegant women of a certain income bracket—resolve. I also got a strong shiver of déjà vu.

"I'm sorry, Mrs. Alden, but have we met?"

Mrs. Alden gave me a long look before she replied, because she was the kind of woman who liked to be sure before she spoke. "I don't believe so. I'm certain I would have remembered."

But her voice hit the DÉJÀ VU button as hard as her eyes.

"Thank you, Trudy," she added over my shoulder. *Trudy?* The tall woman behind me didn't look like a Trudy, but then, she didn't look like a housekeeper either. She looked like an ex-Rockette who'd let her hair go gray and her attitude go bad. At that moment, she also didn't look as if she really wanted to leave.

"Oh, terrific, you're here!" The words were accompanied by thudding footsteps coming down the Scarlett O'Hara stairs. The girl who owned them breezed into the living room. "Sorry I'm late!"

"Hello, darling," Mrs. Alden murmured. "Deanna, this is Chef Caine and Chef Alamedos."

"Fantastic!" Deanna grabbed my hand with both of hers and squeezed, flashing the square-cut diamond engagement ring straight at me. "Gabriel and I have been to Nightlife, you know. The food was fantastic. It is just so freakin' awesome you're here!"

The bride-to-be had gotten her coloring from someone other than her mother. Deanna had an untidy mane of mahogany brown hair and deep brown eyes. Her skin was the kind that tanned to an even gold, leaving those of us prone to imitating lobsters every summer seething in envy. But there was a pallor beneath her natural warmth, and dark rings around her eyes. I didn't have to try to sneak a look beneath the fold of her turquoise cowl-neck top to know she'd have the distinctive, two-puncture mark that got called the "red hickey."

Note to self: orange juice and cookies for the bride.

"So now we know everything's going to be all right." Deanna plopped onto the love seat. "I mean, up until now it's been, like, this total disaster!"

Mrs. Alden smiled with bland disapproval, and Deanna rolled her eyes. "You said the same this morning, Mother, and you were right."

Total disaster? Something's gone wrong besides Oscar Simmons? But Felicity trained a laserlike glare on me in case I was tempted to step out of line and ask personal questions.

The bride wasn't pausing for breath in any case. "I'd be just as happy with something small, but Gabriel wants to have the big show." As she spoke her fiancé's name, Deanna filled with that special, misty sort of glow, that one that says the person has already passed corny-as-Kansas-in-August and is headed straight for high-as-a-flag-on-the-Fourth-of-July. It was the cue for a fond mother to smile indulgently, but Mrs. Alden just looked gracefully weary.

"Perhaps we can get started?" Felicity gestured me and Maria to chairs and took up her position at Mrs. Alden's side. Deanna curled her knees up under her chin.

"So"—I pulled the rubber band off my battered kitchen notebook and flipped it open—"I understand there are nine people dining regularly at the residence at the moment, both dayblood and nightblood?"

"Yes," answered Mrs. Alden. "Myself, my husband, Deanna, of course, Karina . . . oh no, not Karina . . ." I felt Felicity's gaze leaning hard on me. *You're not going to ask,* it said. *You are not even going to silently think about asking.* "And two of the bridesmaids, Lois Markham and Peridot Shane-West." Peridot Shane-West. Nobody should do that to a helpless infant. "Then there's Gabriel, and his father . . ."

"Sire," Deanna corrected her.

"Sire," agreed Mrs. Alden. "Henri Renault, and the best man, Jacques. They're staying with us until the wedding."

I scribbled down the nightblood names. Her ankles neatly crossed, Marie sat up straight on the edge of her chair, looking over us all as if we were unsatisfactory students at her finishing school, but I knew her mind was working through the situation methodically. Designing a menu for French vampires and very rich New Yorkers would present a world of challenges. We were all going to be earning our pay here.

"And the wedding itself?" I turned a page. "Ms. Garnett said you were expecting five hundred . . . ?"

"Yes, that's right."

"And the event space is . . ."

"The Carriger Hall," said Felicity.

I made a note. "Mel Kopekne's still the manager there, isn't he?" Mel and I were both refugees from the west side of the state. "He puts on a fantastic event."

"That's why we're using him," said Mrs. Alden loftily. "Now, as for the food. I have the menu Oscar Simmons planned for us." Mrs. Alden opened a folder on the end table and handed me a printout. I looked at it and had to struggle to keep my jaw from falling open.

This was the best you could do? This?

"Kinda sucks, doesn't it?" Deanna yawned hugely.

It *kinda sucked*? According to Oscar, the wedding of the decade was going to eat smoked salmon, beef tenderloin, spring vegetable medley, chocolate torte, and a selection of raw sauces. It was a menu you could get from any wet-behind-the-ears private chef pulled down at random off Craigslist.

"You went over this with Oscar . . . Chef Simmons? Was there an issue with . . . tradition?" Some people do not like any food perceived as "too fancy," even when they're paying four-star prices for it.

"No." Mrs. Alden was clearly struggling to keep her voice calm. "As a matter of fact, when he presented this to us, we were . . . *surprised* would be putting it mildly. He said he had been informed that this was to be the menu and that he would not stand for being constantly . . ."

"Jerked around," said Deanna darkly. "Except I don't think that was what he was going to say at first. Anyhow, when we wouldn't play, he stormed off."

"And you have no idea where this came from?" I thought about the mountain of money, the wealth of PR, and the glorious challenge of providing the food for this kind of wedding. I thought about Oscar's imperial-sized ego and the overhead at his restaurant, Perception, which was so close to that fourth star we all craved. It just didn't add up.

"I did ask a few questions," said Mrs. Alden. "I must confess that not everyone in my family is happy with this wedding. There has been the possibility of . . . foolishness."

"No one's admitted to anything." At first I thought it was just my imagination that supplied a whiff of smoke behind Deanna's words. Then I saw the white vapor leaking out of the bride's fingertips.

"Deanna," murmured Mrs. Alden. Deanna glanced at her smoldering fingertips as if checking out a chip in her nail polish, and shook her hand. The smoke dissipated. So, the bride was in fact a witch—one with control issues. Good to know.

"What Mother's trying not to tell you is Karina, my sister, is one of the 'not happy' people"—Deanna paused to make the air quotes—"and she's perfectly capable of screwing—"

"I've spoken with Karina," Mrs. Alden said, cutting her daughter off. "And she had nothing to do with Chef Simmons's departure."

"Well, she lied to you. As usual." The shrug and its accompanying slump spoke of years spent refining the sulking skills.

"That's enough," Mrs. Alden informed us all, and it would have taken more nerve than I possessed to contradict her.

I must have telegraphed my readiness to ask another

question, because Felicity spoke up, her words rich with meaning and import.

"So, Chef Caine, what are your thoughts on altering the menu?"

There was only one possible answer to that. With deliberate motions, I tore the printout into strips. Felicity stared at me, horrified, but Deanna applauded. I handed the strips to the bride-to-be. Deanna—sulk averted—let the pieces rain down into a wastepaper basket.

Now that we had Deanna firmly on our side, Marie leaned forward, ready to hook us Mrs. Alden.

"How very trying this has all been for you, señora," my pastry chef murmured to the mother of the bride, urging her to confide, matron-to-matron. "If this is the dinner menu, I can only imagine what an embarrassment the proposal for the cake must have been."

I did not imagine the flash of relief behind Mrs. Alden's eyes.

"The cake was totally pathetic, that's what the cake was," growled Deanna. "It was about eight miles past tacky and . . ."

"We do not need to discuss the cake," said Mrs. Alden. "Not the previous cake."

"No, no, of course not, señora." Marie's English is actually better than mine, except when she's being soothing. "We will make it gone. Dismissed entirely. Now, *por favor*, you might look at these." Marie opened her portfolio, pulled out three sketches, and laid them on the coffee table. "We will, of course, make adjustments depending upon Señorita Alden's choice of colors and flowers."

I was going to have to give Marie a raise. No glitzy, contest-style cakes had been allowed in there. These were stately creations, festooned with flowers and ribbons in delicate pastel shades. The best of all was a white-on-white cake with oval tiers, piping like antique lace, and a single perfect, peach-colored lily lying at the base as if it had been left behind from the bride's bouquet.

That was the one Mrs. Alden picked up. She passed the sketch to Deanna, who gave a little shriek. "Oh. Em. Gee! That is awesome!" To emphasize this, she whipped out a smartphone and snapped a picture. "I've got to show Peri and Lo!" Her thumbs flew across the keyboard. For the moment, the rest of us ceased to exist.

"Can you do this? In time?" Mrs. Alden asked Marie. Marie gave me a long, sideways, she's-mine-now kind of glance and straightened her shoulders.

"Unfortunately, with the plated dessert and other aspects of the dinner, I'd require extra staff . . ."

"Whatever you think you will need." Mrs. Alden gazed raptly at the sketch. "There's some room in the budget still, isn't there, Felicity?" Felicity was making notes on her BlackBerry, and I could practically hear the cash register ring.

"Thank you, señora. I will do my very best for you." Marie smiled. Now she also knew I had to give her a raise. "We will schedule a tasting as soon as possible." Deanna gave a thumbs-up to this without looking away from her phone.

"When can you start?" said Mrs. Alden, looking from Felicity to me. "The out-of-town members of the wedding party are arriving Saturday. We're supposed to be having a welcome dinner, and absolutely nothing is done. It's a mixed party . . ."

"There'll be vampires," translated Deanna a shade too quickly. "Gabriel, Jacques and Henri, and some friends. Say fifteen all together."

"Any allergies I should know about? Any particular preferences?"

"Something simple?" said Mrs. Alden. "My husband might appreciate a nice steak . . ."

Which settled the question of whom I was going to bring in to back me up on this job. For a beef-loving household, I needed Reese.

"We'll start on the preparations immediately," I said. "I'll begin the shifts at the house with the Saturday dinner. We'll have two staff here during the day to handle breakfast and lunch, and preparations for evening. I'll come on to assist with dinner, and I'll handle things overnight. Felicity and I will draw up the contract for you to review and approve." Felicity nodded, all smiles. I snapped my book shut. "Perhaps we could see the kitchen?"

"Of course." Mrs. Alden got to her feet. "This way."

"Have fun." Deanna waved while keeping her eyes on her phone screen. "Felicity, you stay put. We need to talk gift bags."

It turned out the Aldens' home was stately enough to have an actual back staircase. This led down to the ground floor and, through a white door, to the kitchen. I was expecting that kitchen to be nice. I did not expect to want to set up a cot in the corner and never leave.

Despite being on the first floor, the room got plenty of light from the windows over the sink and the French doors that led out to the patio and terraced garden. To the left as we came in was what amounted to the hot station; a six-burner cooktop with a built-in grill. Two wall ovens waited next to it. To the right was the cold station with a full-sized, brushed-steel fridge and a matching full-sized freezer. The counters were mostly stainless steel, a favorite choice of professional and practical cooks. The center island, however, had a white marble top, making an aesthetic statement as well as a separate space for pastry. Marie eyed it with approval. The cupboards and cabinets were all laid out so everything from pantry to utensils would be within easy reach. A swinging door led to the dining room. Another, smaller door led out to the sunken porch at the side of the house. Jackets on hooks, a Peg-Board for spare keys, and a line of boots said this was used by those who didn't want to make the grand entrance through the front.

"Do you have a regular cook?" I asked. This wasn't the

normal showpiece of a big house. The appliances were all top-of-the-line, and the dishwasher was commercial grade. This kitchen belonged to a serious food person.

"Actually, I usually do the cooking," said Mrs. Alden a little wistfully. "Especially when it's just the four of us—three of us," she corrected herself. "But with all the extra people, it's become a bit much. I hope you'll have everything you need." Mrs. Alden was glancing around at the cabinets, as if taking a mental inventory of each.

"I'm sure we will." I wouldn't have pegged Mrs. Alden for an enthusiastic cook, but food is a trendy hobby these days. Something was missing, though. I took another glance around and realized I didn't see any cookbooks or recipe binders. Well, those were probably stored in one of the cabinets. I'd have a good look around later—purely in my professional capacity, of course, not to snoop on my new clients. I'd been cured of all my latent Nancy Drew tendencies last year. No, really.

"Mom?" Deanna's voice drifted in from the other side of the swinging door to the dining room. "Brendan's here."

Brendan?

"Sorry I'm so late. There was an accident on—"

The door pushed open, and Brendan Maddox walked in. Tall and broad-shouldered with black hair and blue eyes, Brendan is a big man. When he comes into view, my head tends to start spinning, but in a good kind of way. Just then, though, he made my stomach turn over. Brendan and Adrienne Alden looked at me with matching blue eyes, and I knew where my earlier bout of déjà vu had come from.

"Holy shit!" I remarked to my new client. "You're a Maddox!"

3

"Hello, Charlotte." Brendan pulled himself together with really impressive speed.

"Um, erm, ah. Hi." Never let it be said I do not demonstrate the true depth of my social graces when surprised.

I wouldn't call Brendan Maddox my boyfriend. This is partly because the word makes me break out into a cold sweat, and partly because normal people should not become gender-prefixed friends of chefs. We work six nights a week, whether we like it or not, and we are a pack of control freaks with industrial-sized egos. None of this is good for the maintenance of a healthy relationship.

Not that Brendan is exactly a normal person. He's a warlock, as I've mentioned. He's also a high-profile paranormal security consultant. The high profile is new. Last fall, his security company landed a citywide contract to provide public spaces with paranormal protection, or protection against paranormals, which is not always the same thing. Since then, Brendan and I have been in a dead heat for the Five Boroughs Happy Workaholic Championship. This might be why we've been able to keep seeing each other. Neither of us has had the time or brain cells left over to wonder where our relationship is going, let alone whether it'll ever get there.

"Aunt Adrienne said she had some news for me," said Brendan, looking to Mrs. Alden.

Aunt Adrienne? I gaped like a fish when it sees the deep fryer.

"I'm sorry, Chef Caine," said Mrs. Alden. "I had assumed Felicity told you."

Yeah, she would, because any reasonable person would tell the caterer she was hiring that said caterer was walking into a particularly personal minefield. Last fall, a drunken warlock—one Dylan Maddox—burst into my restaurant during dinner rush. By the next morning, he was dead in my foyer. The situation eventually sorted itself out, but a certain amount of bad feeling got generated in the process—not much, but just enough that a disconcertingly large number of Brendan's relatives would be happy if my head was served up with their steak Saturday night.

"'Scuse me a second, will you?" I swung myself up the back stairs and charged through to the living room. Felicity was already on her feet. She knew. And she knew I knew.

"They're Maddoxes!" I informed her, just in case she'd missed any of the pertinent details.

"*They* are Aldens," Felicity replied with a stunningly bald-faced level of calm.

"Brendan *Maddox* calls her Aunt Adrienne."

"She was born Adrienne Maddox," said Brendan's voice behind me. "She's my father's oldest sister, and you should probably know her hearing's very good."

This was Brendan's way of telling me I might be talking a little loud. I ignored his attempt to change the subject.

"Why didn't you tell me?" I demanded of Felicity.

"Why didn't you tell me?" asked Brendan. He was smiling back there; I just knew it.

I turned and glowered at him. "I'll get to you in a minute. I'm chewing out the wedding planner right now."

"As long as I'm on your schedule." I'd been right. He was smiling. A smile from tall, dark, and handsome Brendan Maddox is a thing to warm the blood and curl the toes of any heterosexual female. I, however, was quite used to it by now. Plus, I was in no mood to have my toes curled. That my toes might have ideas of their own was of no consequence whatsoever. "But why didn't you call me?"

"No time," I answered. "Felicity showed up at Nightlife during dinner prep and dragged me out here."

"I didn't drag you," said Felicity.

"You bribed me."

"How much?" asked Brendan.

I told him. Brendan whistled. "That's a good bribe."

"Not bad, all things considered." I shrugged.

"Are you still chewing me out?" asked Felicity.

"'Scuse me," I said to Brendan. "I gotta take this."

A dangerously flippant light crept into Felicity's eyes. "Oh no, don't let me get in the way. You go on discussing bribery with your boyfriend while we're on the clock."

I turned again, much more slowly this time. Clearly, she overestimated the power of one smile. "Felicity?"

"Yes, Charlotte?"

"Do not under any circumstances act like you're the one getting the short end here. I will carve you up and serve you as event planner on the half shell."

Felicity looked to Brendan, who just held up both hands, indicating that the event planner was on her own.

"Talk fast," I said.

Felicity took a deep breath. "I didn't tell you because I didn't think family of origin for the mother of the bride was important."

"You knew how I'd react when I found out," I corrected her.

"Okay, you got me." Felicity waved one hand, maybe in surrender, maybe in dismissal. "I knew you wouldn't take the job if you knew the bride was related to the Maddoxes. I'm sorry." This last was aimed at Brendan as much as at me. "But I still need your help, and the fee still stands."

"No," I said. "It's gone up."

"Is everything all right?" Mrs. Alden née Maddox came up the back stairs with Marie right behind her. Her tired eyes were now officially worried-looking, but her voice was as smooth as when we first walked into this room. "Chef Caine? Is there going to be a problem?"

This was also when it hit me that no matter what was going on, I was in the home of a potential client. I pulled my shoulders back and smoothed down the front of my coat. It was time once again to put my social graces on display. "Well, I think we've got everything we need here. You have a lovely home, Mrs. Alden. Brendan, good to see you. Marie, we're done for now. Felicity, I'll call you tomorrow, okay? Good-bye."

Fortunately, I still had my notebook in my hand, so I could head straight down the front stairs and out the door, past a disconcertingly smug Ms. Lyons.

The street outside was quiet and treelined. The scent of the East River in spring filled the breeze, and it wasn't improving anything. I couldn't believe Felicity would *do* this to me. No, I could. What I couldn't believe was that I'd been so dazzled by the potential payout that I hadn't asked some really basic questions. That was the real problem. Felicity hadn't just played me. I'd played along.

Footsteps sounded on the concrete stoop behind me. I turned, expecting to see Brendan, but it was Marie, wearing her best Cakeinator face.

Not that I even thought that.

"We also have a few things to discuss, Chef Caine." You know that feeling you get when your mother calls you by your middle name? Marie could produce it by calling me

"Chef Caine." I opened my mouth to say I was getting us a cab, but Marie held up her hand. "I wish to visit the market. I will call you later, and you will tell me how you plan to proceed." She tucked her portfolio more firmly under one wrestler's arm and started briskly down that treelined street.

The worst part was she was right to be miffed. I was supposed to be a professional. Professionals asked questions and followed up on their suspicions before they put their employees in awkward situations.

It's amazing how far you can kick yourself down an empty block in Brooklyn without moving a single inch.

I heard yet more footsteps on the stoop and gritted my teeth. This had better not be Felicity trying to talk me back into the house. It wasn't. This time it really was Brendan.

"Not now, okay?" I said to whatever he might be thinking about telling me. I knew I should add something to demonstrate that my anger wasn't for him, but nothing inside my head would settle down long enough. I resolutely studied the toes of my street shoes. If I looked up at him, I'd start feeling better. I was not ready to start feeling better.

"How bad is it?" Brendan walked around until he was in front of me and touched my shoulder. Despite all my good intentions, that got me to look up.

"You don't know?"

"I knew Deanna was threatening to marry a vampire, but everybody was acting like it was going to blow over."

Her mother had been planning a massive society wedding since November, and Brendan somehow got the idea this situation was going to "blow over"? He could be such a guy sometimes.

"Does everybody include your grandfather?" I asked.

"Everybody except grandfather, but that's normal."

None of the Maddoxes liked vampires, but Lloyd Maddox, Brendan's politically powerful grandfather, was in a class by himself. If the FlashNews headlines were to be believed, he was at this moment lobbying Albany to require DNA samples and fang impressions to be added to the state nightblood registry, and to expand the antistalker laws, and to make even consensual bites between the living and undead into felony sexual assault.

"How did you even get pulled into this?" Brendan asked.

"The wedding planner's a friend of mine, and the original chef walked out," I told him. "How'd you get pulled into this?"

"Aunt Adrienne asked me to drop by—said she had some family business she wanted to talk over. Believe me, I didn't know it was you. Actually"—he turned his frown toward the house—"it might not be."

Perfect. "I do so love being the sideshow."

"Any idea why you?"

That would have been easy to take the wrong way, if I hadn't been asking myself the same question. Why had Felicity asked me onto this job? There was no way my presence wouldn't cause more problems.

Now, we were both staring up at the beautiful house, its windows glowing gold with the last of the evening sun.

"You do realize this situation makes no sense, don't you?" I said. That wasn't just because I had been brought in either. Vampires did not traditionally marry people they wanted to keep near them. Convert them, yes, but marry them . . . not so much. Blood children didn't do inconvenient things such as divorce their sires, and they didn't have to bother with pesky details such as prenuptial agreements. Although, according to Trish, my number two roomie who was also a lawyer, that was changing. I told her I had no desire to hear about the emerging legal field of pretransition contracts—takes all the romance out of it.

"Want me to see what I can find out?" asked Brendan.

"Oh yeah," I answered immediately. Because this was way past the question of why Oscar Simmons, one of the biggest publicity hounds in the restaurant world, had dropped this job without saying one word to the foodie blogs or the gossip columns. This was also beyond how the bride thought her sister was sabotaging the wedding. Someone had gone and deliberately involved me with the Maddoxes and their vampire troubles, again. And he, she, or it and I were going to have a very, very long talk about this.

4

After I left Brooklyn Heights, I did what I do whenever my life gets complicated beyond the grasp of a mortal woman. I went back to work.

By the time I got into the Nightlife kitchen, rolled up my sleeves, and moved Zoe from expediting to supervising the hot line, our early reservations had started to arrive. Kitchen routine folded around me like a comfortable blanket—a hot, damp, loud, fast-moving blanket that smelled of meat, spices, and onion. We had a solidly full house with very few lulls in the action. From nine o'clock on, we were going full tilt. The ticket machine went down once. We ran out of duck for the special; then we ran out of veal for the carpaccio. One of the new servers spilled raw sauce on a vampire from Altoona, and our front-of-house manager, Suchai (a werewolf when he's not on shift), had to pull the vampire back before she could sink her fangs into my guy's neck.

It was a typical night, really. I was in my groove, and after the whole throw-me-for-nineteen-different-kinds-of-loops afternoon, it felt really good.

By the time Robert finally snapped shut the lock on Nightlife's front door, my crew members were tired and swearing at one another, but in a good way. I was finally able to take off my apron, open the neck of my coat, drop into my creaking desk chair and take a long swig of water. It was standard to have a bottle or cup at your station, but on a busy night, you could literally go for hours without having a hand free to reach for it. Around me, my crew members cleaned their stations and wrapped up the remaining *mise en place* to stash away for tomorrow. Satisfaction hung in the air with the exhaustion and the fading smells of good food. Plus, if I squinted at just the right angle, I couldn't even see the stack of unpaid invoices on my desk.

"So, Chef, what went wrong in Brooklyn?"

Zoe was standing in front of my desk, with her arms folded and her no-nonsense attitude on. Executive Sous-Chef Zoe Vamadev is a petite young woman who has a critical eye on the level of Simon Cowell with a toothache. Her parents are from Bengal and Bali, and she came to the United States by way of Bangkok, Amsterdam, Edinburgh and London. She speaks more languages than a career diplomat, and she's a good enough chef to give me a serious run for my money, even in my own kitchen.

"Nothing," I told her. "At least, not much."

Zoe held my gaze a good ten seconds longer, just to make sure I understood she knew exactly when she was being distracted and to suggest that I might want to amend my answer. In another life, Zoe would have made a fabulous trial lawyer.

"So, we are doing this?" she asked.

"Who said we weren't?"

Zoe waved her hand vaguely. "You know how it is when the chef has her frowny face on. People start wondering . . ."

"My *frowny* face? Who says I've got a *frowny* face?" Because clearly there were problems with discipline on my line I had not previously been aware of.

Zoe ignored me with an ease that was truly disturbing.

"The point is, Chef, we are still doing the Alden wedding, right?"

"Yes, we are still doing the Alden wedding."

"So, what went wrong in Brooklyn?"

I decided if she could ignore me, I could return the favor. "Make sure you, Reese, and Marie are all here by two tomorrow," I said. "We're going to be doing some heavy-duty schedule reshuffling. I'll need Reese and a backup at the Aldens' until the wedding. And I'll need you to be ready to take charge here."

Zoe gave me the yes-Chef, and got back to work on the slow, detailed work of closing up a kitchen for the night. I let her go, but not without a twinge or two of conscience. I did owe her an answer. I just didn't have one. While I buried my nose in close-of-day paperwork, I turned all the events of the afternoon over in my head and came up with absolutely nothing. To make matters worse, Zoe's question seemed to have gotten stuck on infinite replay in my head. What had gone wrong in Brooklyn? Nothing major. Nothing real. Except that I was there at all.

I was able to keep myself looking good and busy until the last of the closers, including Zoe, waved good-bye and disappeared out the back door. Only then did I push my chair back and run both hands through my hair. I used to have hair down to my waist, but after that fire last year, I had to get most of it chopped off, and I still felt strangely naked without it.

There was one way to get the answers I wanted, and that was to go straight to Oscar Simmons himself. I even knew where he'd be—the same place the rest of Manhattan's chefs were at three in the morning: a crummy little bar called Charlie's Blue Plate. This was dead convenient, because if there was one thing I needed more than answers after the day I'd had, it was beer.

Happy thoughts of food and alcohol being served to me

were interrupted by a knock at the back door, followed by a familiar voice.

"Hello, Charlotte?"

"Chet!" I was on my feet and around my desk in time to hold out my arms for my undead younger brother as he strolled into the kitchen.

"Hey, C3!" Chet used my old family nickname. We hugged, with enthusiasm, but a whole lot of care. On my part this was because Chet's a vampire and consequently he's light enough for me to pull off his feet if I'm not careful. On Chet's part because, well, he's a vampire and could very easily crack my ribs.

Chet was turned nightblood at nineteen. As a result, he's an eternal and very pale college freshman; cheerful, good-looking, possessed of questionable judgment and a "why the hell not?" attitude. Despite this, or maybe because of it, he's also recently become a successful businessman in his own right.

I stepped back and gave my brother an appraising look. Chet and I share the family's light blue eyes and dishwater blond hair. Tonight, though, while I was in my stained black T-shirt, open white coat, and baggy checked pants that—trust me—look good on no one, my brother was perfectly put together in his European-styled sports jacket, bright blue button-down shirt, designer jeans and shiny loafers.

"What are you doing here?" I asked him.

Chet smirked and folded his arms. "Hello, little brother, what a surprise! How are you? Want something to drink?" He looked meaningfully at the mini-fridge under the counter where he knew there would be plastic-wrapped containers of blood left over from dinner service.

"Yeah, yeah." I waved him off, but I did ladle him out a mug of the veal blood we use for making the foam that goes on the cold consommé. "You know all that. What are you doing here?"

"I was in the neighborhood and thought I'd stop by." Chet leaned against my desk and accepted the mug.

"Zoe called you, didn't she?"

Chet shrugged. "She said you've had a weird day, and it might help to talk to family."

"I'm banning cell phones from the kitchen."

"Yeah, but you'd have to start with yours, and you'd get the shakes from withdrawal." Chet drained his cup. "So, what got weird?"

I watched my undead brother casually ladle himself a second helping of blood. What could possibly qualify as weird in a life where this was normal?

"How's Ilona?" As an attempt to change the subject, it was less than graceful, but it was all I had. Ilona St. Claire was Chet's girlfriend. We did not get along. She had views about daybloods, especially the ones who maintained relationships with their vampire relatives. I had views about vampires with gothic pretensions, separatist rhetoric, and questionable taste.

Chet's answer to my question was to shrug, sip blood, and change the subject back. "How're things here?"

"We're on target to turn a profit this month."

"Is that before or after you pay these off?" He ruffled the edge of my invoice stack.

I decided to plead the Fifth on that one and dug around for some more small talk I might have overlooked on the first pass through.

"How're things at the spa?" I tried.

"We're booked solid through the end of this year. Marcus is talking about expanding." Chet drained his mug again. "Speaking of the spa, have you thought about my offer?"

The invoices rustled uneasily. "Yes."

Chet had offered to make me a loan of twenty thousand dollars. It sounded small in the face of the other numbers that had been getting waved around today, but it was enough to clear this stack, if only to make room to start building a new one.

"Did you think about it seriously?" asked Chet.

"Very seriously."

"It'd be enough to get the food truck you've been talking about . . ."

"*Reese* has been talking about a truck." In fact, my number two sous had been talking about very little else lately. "I haven't."

"Why not? They're all the thing . . ."

"And that's why," I said. "They're all the thing. Everybody's got one. We haven't got the time, the money, or the personnel to take it on, let alone to do it right."

Chet sighed and put down his mug. His pale skin had drawn tightly over the bones of his face. "Charlotte. I can help," he said, softly, so I could hear the hurt under the words. "Why won't you let me?"

"It's not you; it's me," I said, which was true. "Besides, I've got a new gig that should take care of the backlog." Attempting to keep my voice at the appropriate level of warmth and enthusiasm, I filled him in on the pertinent details of the Alden-Renault wedding.

Chet straightened up, one vertebra at a time. "You're catering the wedding of a Maddox and a *vampire*? What's next? Setting up the buffet for the Hatfield-McCoy family reunion?"

"Not my business who's marrying who, as long as the check clears." I shrugged, smoothed the plastic wrap back in place over what was left of the veal blood, and stashed it back in the fridge. That this kept me from having to look Chet in the eye was strictly a side benefit. "As you've so helpfully pointed out, I've got a cash flow problem. Besides which, what I do with my business is not really your problem, is it?" Pride's a nasty thing. It rushes you into hot spots before you've had time to get your asbestos panties on.

"You're my sister. It is my problem," he shot back. "I helped build Nightlife. I've still got—"

I did not need to hear the end of this sentence. "You *left*, Chet! You wanted to go run your spa and get your own existence. Fine. You got it. But you don't get to tell me how I run the place you walked out on!"

"I cannot believe you are still mad about the spa." Cold lights sparked under the blue of my brother's eyes, and I had to drop my gaze, fast. "Is that why you won't take the loan? You can't stand to be reminded that I'm making it and you're not."

"I do not need you to prop me up so you can take the damned tax break!"

We were both on our feet, just inches from each other, a whole world of old arguments and old hurts swirling between us.

Chet broke first, backing up and swinging around so he could plant his hands on the edge of the counter. If he dented my stainless steel, I was going to stake him a good one.

Judging from the way Chet curled his fingers into fists and pushed himself back up, the same thought had occurred to him. "Okay." Chet dug his hands into his pockets and looked around the kitchen as though hoping somebody had left an answer lying around. "Okay. Are you heading out? Want me to walk you to the subway?"

I swallowed, hard, and with an effort set aside the argument. There was absolutely no winning it. "Um . . . it depends."

"On what?"

I don't want to say this. Don't make me say this.

"On what?" asked Chet again, slowly, in case I'd missed something the first time.

"On whether Anatole's out there tonight." Anatole Sevarin was another vampire, one whom I'd met at pretty much the exact same time I'd met Brendan Maddox, and like Brendan, he'd kind of not gone away.

"Sevarin?" As Chet said the name, he proved he had a frowny face of his very own. "I thought you were dating Brendan."

"I am. Mostly. But Anatole stops by some nights."

Chet looked down his nose at me, and I felt the beginnings of a long, slow blush. "I don't ask him to," I said, even though part of my brain was yelling at me, *Just keep quiet!* "He just stops by."

"Anatole Sevarin does not 'just' "—Chet paused to make the air quotes—"do anything."

"You barely know the man."

"I've been asking around."

"Why?"

"Because he wants to date my sister!"

A shiny new penny dropped, and I glowered at my brother. "So, what? You think I need a chaperone now?"

"Between Sevarin and the Maddoxes, I'm starting to think you need a keeper!" I watched while those words replayed themselves inside Chet's head. It must have sounded just as good the second time around, because he backed away one step. "I didn't mean that."

"Yes, you did." Anger has always brought out the honesty in our family. "And you can go now."

Chet closed his mouth and turned around, heading out the way he'd come in. I tried not to wince as the door thumped shut, and I failed at that too.

I turned away and headed for the lockers. Now I really needed that beer.

5

It takes a special kind of place to become a hangout for professional chefs. First, it's got to be open between three and six a.m., which is when most of us are out on the town, if we're out at all. Second, it's got to look so scary that tourists and reviewers will give it a wide berth. We don't want their kind hanging around when we're off shift. Finally, it's got to serve food so scary nobody in their right minds would eat it.

Charlie's Blue Plate meets or exceeds all the above criteria. Stuffed with scarred wooden tables and creaky bentback chairs, it's a pocket-sized bar that reeks of old beer and hot grease. Once upon a time it would have been filled with smoke. The streaks of ash and soot are still visible on the ceiling. In summer, the patrons take their plates outside and stand around on the sidewalk, in violation of a whole bunch of municipal codes we could recite in four-part harmony, and probably would after enough beer.

When I walked in, Charlie's brimmed with off-duty chefs and cooks, crammed knee to knee around those little tables. They were drinking hard and chowing down on plates of the house specialty: deviled kidneys with a blow-the-top-of-your-head-off dipping mustard. Mama Charlie presided over the front of the house, wedged behind the tiny bar in the corner. She was a big, gray, placid woman with a nose so crooked it must have been broken at least once. Charlie himself was a fireplug of a man with a bald head and hairy arms; he never wore anything but a white undershirt and jeans. Not that we usually saw any more of him than his beefy hands as he shoved fresh plates of kidneys or similar delicacies through the pass and bellowed, "Order up!"

It was not the kind of place an outsider would have expected to find the latest darling of the celebrity chef circuit, but there he was. Oscar Simmons sat as far in the back as the pint-sized dining room would allow, surrounded by a gaggle of would-bes and wannabes. The all-male crowd laughed at something I didn't hear and picked up hot kidneys in their fingers to dunk in the mustard before tossing them in their mouths like popcorn. This is competitive eating in its purest form. If your eyes water as you chew, you lose.

Letting my gaze slide straight past them as if they were an uninteresting part of the scenery, I pulled up a stool at the bar. "Hi, Mama. Kidneys and a Heineken." Hey, I was hungry too.

"Special for the bar!" Mama bellowed toward her husband on the other side of the pass while opening my beer bottle and plunking it on the counter.

"Yo, Chef C." Minnie Perez, a line cook I'd known on and off forever raised her shot glass to me.

"Yo, Cook M. How's it going?" Minnie was a medium tall, medium brown woman with close-cropped hair whose ancestors came about evenly from Ecuador and Haiti. We weren't the only women in the place, but it was close. The gender gap in the kitchen is closing, but it's closing slowly.

She shrugged and downed the shot of crystal clear something. "I'm quitting. I'm going back to school and getting my accounting degree."

"You've been saying that for what, five years now?"

"Yeah, but this time I mean it." She pushed the glass back toward Mama Charlie, who shook her head and filled it up again with a distinctly non-top-shelf vodka.

"You know what's up with the cock party over there?" I nodded toward Oscar and his boys. I meant it as a play on "hen party." Really. Stop looking at me like that.

"You'd know more than me."

"Aren't you going out with one of Perception's fish guys?" It's tough for a cook to have a social life. We're up all night, asleep all day, and working holidays and Sundays. Unless we're into nightbloods, we're stuck dating one another.

"Nah. He decided he was going to trade up for some pretty little thing working the door at Moody's."

"Sorry."

"Don't be. She can have him. Guy was useless. Still." She grimaced as another burst of laughter exploded from the Simmons environs. "They do seem to be having a good time over there. Wonder who he screwed this time?"

That was indeed the thousand-dollar question, but I just shook my head, and drank my beer. My kidneys arrived, piping hot and smelling richly of cayenne and cardamom. Other colleagues came up to us for an exchange of hellos and gossip. I heard from Ted that he'd been promoted to saucier at Savorings. I heard from Peter that the head housekeeper at the St. Francis had quit and management was making everybody's life hell as a result. Colon was out of work again and trying to put the moves on Minnie anyway.

All the while, I was aware of the way Oscar kept looking at me out of the corner of his famously photogenic dark eyes. I ate and laughed and drank and groused, and waited.

Finally, Oscar heaved himself to his feet and sauntered over to the bar. Or, he would have sauntered if there was room for it. As it was, to get between the tables he sort of had to turn and scoot and suck in his gut, which was starting to overhang his belt just a little. Too many good dinners are ever the professional hazard of the working chef.

"Charlotte Caine." Oscar's British accent is smooth and rich, with just a hint of the Gordon Ramsey temper waiting in the wings.

"Good morning, Oscar." I lifted my Heineken to him. "How're things on the celebrity-chef circuit?"

"It's quite good, isn't it? We're developing our own line of exclusive products."

"Congratulations."

"Branded marketing, Charlotte. It's the way of the present. I could put you in touch with people."

Those photogenic eyes made a slow and thorough appraisal of my person. They weren't looking for weaknesses exactly, more like signs of wear. If I was honest, except for the telltale softening around his middle, Oscar still looked good. The gray streaks in his hair lent him gravitas, and his square, heavy-boned face was aging gracefully. Someone would have to look hard to see this man never stopped making calculations about who he was with and what were they good for. I looked hard, every time.

"Actually, somebody's already been in touch." I popped another kidney.

"Felicity Garnett?"

"No points for that one. I guess the Aldens decided it was time to get serious about the food."

To my total and complete surprise, Oscar did not rise to the bait. Instead, he mimed tugging at a forelock. "I wish you and Felicity very happy."

"I don't suppose you'll tell me what happened with you and the Aldens?"

Oscar smiled. "Like you've always said, I'm a spoiled little boy in a big chef's coat. Who knows what I'll do next?"

An uneasy ripple strolled slowly up my spine. Oscar was into all kinds of things, but self-deprecation was not one of them. "I think you found out they couldn't pay."

His smile spread, just a tiny bit. "You would think that, wouldn't you?"

"If it's not the money, then what? The bride wouldn't sleep with you?"

"What's the matter, Charlotte? You in over your head? Again?"

There was a snicker from somewhere deep in the entourage. Of course they were listening. The entire place was listening. I was surprised one of the boys wasn't out on the street hawking tickets.

"Not me, but you clearly were. I saw that menu you put together. It looked like you were auditioning for head chef at an all-you-can-eat buffet."

The bar went dead quiet, leaving my words to hang in the air long enough for me to wonder if I'd maybe gone a little too far. I also got to watch the fascinating way the color red seeped up from under Oscar's collar to engulf his entire face.

"Oh, this is pure Charlotte Caine, isn't it?" he said, low and dangerous. "Always so sure she knows just what's going on. So keen to put the rest of us in our places. You want to know why I quit? I don't like being bribed or jerked around."

Deanna had been right. "Jerked" was definitely not the first word he'd thought to use. "You were bribed?"

He nodded. "To plant some gossip about Karina Alden in the media. It didn't matter what, just something that would get her name out in the press in a bad light."

"What would you possibly know about Karina Alden?"

He rolled his eyes in disbelief. Ah. So that was it. He'd managed to start sleeping with Karina. It did, however, raise the question of why no one had seen fit to mention their ex-caterer was also the boyfriend, or at least the hookup, of the bride's on-the-outs sister. The Aldens were starting to make my personal relationships look straightforward.

"So, who put in the order for character assassination?" I asked.

"You know, if you'd called me first, I might just have told you. But as it is, you wanted this job so bad, you can find out for yourself just what kind of mess you're in." Oscar reached down, dipped my last kidney in mustard, and popped it back, chewing. His eyes didn't water either. "Good-bye, Charlotte Caine." Still chewing, Oscar strolled back to his waiting followers.

I watched him for a while, but he wasn't watching me anymore. For the first time in our acquaintance, Oscar Simmons had dismissed me—and not just a little, but absolutely, the way you dismiss someone you've beaten.

Except I had no idea what game I'd just lost.

The uneasy ripple up my spine came back, and it brought friends.

6

Somewhere, a phone was ringing.

I dragged the covers off my face and, on reflex, tried to shove the hair out of my eyes. My bedside clock read nine twenty, which is in fact way-the-hell too early when you remembered I hadn't gotten to bed until five in the morning. Out in the living room, I could hear Jessie, my number one roommate, singing about bad romance.

I flopped backward and stuffed my head under the pillow.

My phone rang again. I lifted the pillow and glared at it. Jessie switched from bad romance to putting rings on it. The phone rang again. This had to be Felicity. I punched up the screen, ready to read her the riot act.

"I'm sorry," said a male voice while I was still drawing breath.

"Brendan." I was going to have to assign him a ring tone. Except every time I thought about it, it felt too much like making some kind of commitment.

"Good morning," he said. "I'm sorry."

"For what?" I slumped back against the wall and tried to push my too-short hair out of my eyes yet again.

"I'm sorry for not coming by last night after your shift, even though we really need to talk, and for calling so early in your personal morning now. Anything I forgot?"

"That'll do for now. What's going on?"

"I'm downstairs."

I lifted the blind with one finger and peered out. A familiar figure stood beside the half wall that ringed my building's courtyard, waving his cell phone in the air, as if he knew I'd peek, which he probably did. I'm nothing if not predictable.

"You are not expecting me to invite you up for breakfast," I said into the cell phone, just to make sure Brendan understood making me wake up before eleven o'clock was a definite relationship misdemeanor.

"I brought dosas." Down below, Brendan pointed to the white bag and a cardboard beverage tray on the wall beside him. "And coffee."

"Jessie!" I hollered toward the living room. "Hit the buzzer!"

I hung up on the sound of Brendan's chuckling.

Fortunately, my other roommate, Trish the Lawyer, had headed out to her office hours ago. This left the bathroom clear so I would be able to meet Brendan both looking and smelling civilized. I came into the dining room, wearing my usual off-duty combination of faded jeans and plain T-shirt (red today) with my hair slicked back under a red headband as a compromise between aesthetics and speed. Brendan moved around our dining nook. He, of course, looked edible, and would have even if he hadn't been setting out plates for the spicy Indian crêpes he'd brought.

"You are forgiven," I said loftily as I sat down and peeled back the lid on a very large cup of coffee.

"You may want to hold up on the forgiveness"—Brendan forked a dosa onto my plate—"at least until after we eat."

I eyed him with what was not entirely feigned trepidation as I handed across a napkin. "So, is this a bribe, or the breakup meal?"

"You're breaking up?" Jessie ducked her head out of her bedroom. "What'd she do?"

I should have known. Jessie's gossip radar was second to none. "You were just leaving, weren't you, Jess?" I frowned hard at my roommate as she emerged from the hallway.

"Not if Brendan's breaking up with you." She plopped herself down in the third chair. As usual, Jessie VanReebeck was immaculately groomed. Her heart-shaped face was spectacularly made up, and her floral-print swing dress perfectly matched her strappy sandals and dangling earrings. Jessie possessed this uncanny ability to look fun, approachable, and professional at the same time, and I tried not to resent her for it.

"Why are you breaking up with her?" She fixed Brendan with a surprisingly steely glower.

"Because I'm carrying Mayor Thornton's love child."

I snarfed a hot gulp of coffee. Jessie blinked, and Brendan lifted his soulful, apologetic gaze to her without cracking even a hairline of a grin. Not to be deterred, Jessie scooted her chair around to face me. "Why's he breaking up with you?"

"There's nothing to break up." But as I said this, my heart gave a strange and not entirely comfortable squeeze. I craned my neck so I could see past Jessie to Brendan. "You're not breaking up with me, are you?"

"I am not breaking up with you. I promise." That knee-weakening smile worked even better when he turned it on soft and low.

"There," I said to Jessie. "You can go now."

"Actually . . ."

"You can go now." I reminded her in my best being-slow-is-hazardous-to-your-health voice. Jessie, unfortunately, had been exposed to this voice enough that she was beginning to develop a tolerance. But then, it always did work better on people I could fire and to whom I did not owe rent money.

With a look intended to make me aware of the extent of her magnanimity, Jessie got to her feet and made her way to the front door, pausing only to collect her tiny handbag and large makeup case. If someone can pointedly close a door behind herself, she did.

Brendan arched his eyebrows.

"She'll try to make me tell her everything later," I warned him.

"Duly noted."

We sat in silence for a few minutes, occupying ourselves with the simple business of enjoying breakfast and each other's company.

"So," I said when the edge had been taken off both my hunger and the caffeine jones. "Did you manage to get anything out of your aunt Adrienne?"

"Not much." Brendan scooted a bit of crêpe on his plate to the right and then the left. This was something he did when he was thinking hard. It drove me mildly nuts, but I was learning to live with it. "She apologized for all of this happening now, when we're already in the news with the city contract. She said that she really had no choice and that Deanna had been utterly determined to have things her own way. Resisting or forbidding would just make her take her tantrum out into the wider world. It was better, she said, to go along so that as many details as possible could be kept strictly in the family."

"Is this a wedding or a political campaign?"

"With us, it can be kind of hard to tell."

"Did she say anything about why I'm the one who got tagged as Oscar's replacement?"

"Not really. She just said when she checked the list of possibilities Felicity came up with, you were the best available."

Which was nice to hear, but somehow in the light of Oscar's enigmatic snarking, I didn't quite believe it. I turned the paper cup in my fingers around a few times, wishing there was yet more coffee in it. "Did your aunt happen to say anything about sister Karina dating Oscar Simmons?"

Brendan's fork froze midscoot. "Karina's dating Simmons?"

This I took to be a "no." I told Brendan about my encounter with Oscar last night.

Brendan pushed his plate away. "Oy."

"Yeah. And she's ticked off somebody in the family enough that they're willing to pay for a smear campaign."

"I'd put my money on Deanna for that one. They both have their PhD's in sibling rivalry."

I thought about bubbly, bright, breathless Deanna. I could see how she might make you crazy. Not that I personally once ever resented my own sibling for being a handsome star athlete or anything.

"So, what's Karina like?" I asked.

Brendan just shook his head. "I never really got to know her. There's already a divide between those of us who lived full-time on the estate and those who didn't, but it's even bigger between the kids with magic and the ones without."

"Karina's not a witch?"

"Nope. She's a T-typ." That's short for "thauma-typical," the technical term for someone who is not a witch, or a werewolf, or undead, or otherwise inherently magical.

"A T-typ with Maddox relations. That can't be easy."

"It's not."

"Your grandfather must be having kittens about this."

Brendan grimaced. "Saber-toothed tigers, more like."

"I'm surprised he hasn't been on the talk shows with it." Lloyd Maddox had no problems taking the Maddoxes' private fights public. He had a huge repertoire of speeches about the degradation to the culture, the nation, and the human race itself caused by the Equal Humanity Acts, and he tended to pepper them with personal examples.

"Aunt Adrienne won't let him." Brendan smiled grimly.

This merited a double-eyebrow lift. "There's somebody who can keep your grandfather quiet on the subject of vampires?"

"Oh, Aunt Adrienne's special. She holds the *Popeth Arall*."

"Gesundheit."

"Ha-ha," Brendan grumbled, and took a last swallow of coffee. "The Arall's a piece of the family's power, and it's passed down the female line. The name comes from a Welsh phrase for 'in the last resort.' "

As the Maddoxes were one of the great vampire-hunting clans, I assumed this Popeth Arall was an antivampire weapon of some kind from back in the days when that kind of thing was so invisible, most people didn't believe in either witches or vamps. I thought about all the antiques neatly displayed on the mantelpiece in the living room. Could they be magical as well as old?

"And . . . ?" I prompted Brendan.

"And traditionally the secret of the Arall is passed on when the oldest daughter of the current guardian gets married."

Understanding pulled a few levers in the back of my mind, and my face fell.

Brendan nodded. "When Deanna marries Gabriel Renault, she comes into possession of some ancient, dangerous magic at the heart of the Maddox family power."

As little as I liked being able to sympathize with a man who spent his political capital trying to make it legal to put my clientele—and my brother—to the stake, I found it surprisingly understandable why Lloyd Maddox might be just a teensy bit upset by this turn of events.

I took a deep breath. Then I took pride and nerves in

both hands and shoved them behind me. "Brendan, do you think I should get out of this?"

Brendan took a long time answering. They were careful on all the big questions, these Maddoxes. "I don't know," he said at last. "On the way here, I kept trying to make up my mind . . . and now with this thing with Oscar and Karina . . . I just don't know. It's really up to you."

"Well that's all very dull and straightforward of you."

"I'm a dull and straightforward kind of guy. It's part of my charm."

"You have no idea."

Brendan smiled. His gorgeous eyes filled with hope, confidence, and something more—trust. Brendan trusted me to make a good decision, not just the one he wanted, but a good one. Whatever it was, he'd back me on it.

That shook me straight down to my toenails. I'm used to being in charge. I'm used to being both competent and confident. What I am not used to is being trusted, not really. Not by people who matter to me.

I took a deep breath, and, of course, my phone rang.

Fortunately, Brendan was also used to my acutely honed swearing abilities and was profoundly unshocked when I unleashed them now. I grabbed my phone and stabbed the ANSWER button.

"Oh my *gahd*, Charlotte!" cried the voice on the other end of my phone before I could let on exactly what I thought of this bit of timing. "Why didn't you *tell* me? You *know* I'm your first call!"

"Elaine?" Elaine West had been the publicist for me and Nightlife for three years now, and she knew darned well not to go incoherent on me before noon. "What are you talking about?"

Elaine did not seem to hear me. "It's all *over* FlashNews and the society blogs how you replaced Oscar Simmons for the Alden-Renault wedding. How am I supposed to handle your PR if you don't *tell* me when you make the news?"

"It's out already?" Note to self: Find out who invented FlashNews, Twitter, and every other form of social media and fillet them, slowly.

"I must have had fifty calls already asking for quotes."

"I was going to call you right after breakfast," I lied. "But . . ."

"No time," Elaine snapped. "The vultures are going to be descending any second. Is your fax on? I've got some draft statements here about how sorry you are about Oscar's death and what a . . ."

"Wait. Hold it! Time out! Burner off! *What*?"

Elaine paused. The pause stretched. Brendan was on his feet and coming around to stand beside me so he could hear, if she ever decided to start talking again.

She did. "Oh, Charlotte. I'm sorry. I assumed someone would have called you right away. Oscar Simmons is dead."

7

"Oscar's dead?" I had heard what Elaine said. Her statement repeated itself, word for word, inside my brain. But I couldn't understand it. It made no sense whatsoever.

"They say it must have been a massive stroke. He was found in his office during lunch prep."

"But, I just talked to him. Last night. This morning. He looked fine." It was a completely stupid thing to say, but I seemed to be cut off from my own rational thought processes.

I pushed Elaine for details, but she stubbornly insisted she had none and went back to trying to pound it into my reluctant brain that she was faxing me some statements for my approval. I hung up on her. Then I hung on to Brendan for a long time.

There's a deeply awkward feeling that comes from hearing about the death of somebody you don't like. You don't want to be glad, and you're probably not, but at the same time, you feel you should be more upset than you are. After all, that individual was somebody, and now he's not.

Brendan rested his chin on the top of my head. "What are you thinking?"

"I'm thinking I've got to get into Nightlife," I answered, which was true as far as it went. "We're supposed to be meeting about the wedding catering today, and this could make things . . . awkward."

"And they're sure it was a stroke?" he asked. He was thinking about last year, and the last body that had crossed my path. I knew he was, because I was too.

I squeezed my eyes shut. "I really, really don't want to go there."

"Okay." He kissed the top of my head, but I was sure he was already going through his mental Rolodex, deciding which of his connections he could pump for information. Brendan was the dependable type.

"You want a lift into work?" he asked.

"Yeah, thanks." I mustered a smile and went into my bedroom to get my purse. I scrubbed at my face a little and noticed how my cheeks had stayed bone dry. There was something wrong with that. A man was dead. No matter what I'd thought of him, that was worth some sign of grief, wasn't it?

That was yet another question I had no answer to.

While Brendan navigated city traffic with a skill that was the envy of many a cab driver, I called Felicity. If she hadn't gotten the news about Oscar's death, she needed it. If she had, I wanted any extra details she might have in hand. Unfortunately, my call was the first she'd heard about it. Fortunately, she was less frantic than I had expected. The only real tension came when she asked me for the third time to confirm that yes, I was still on the job, and yes, I was on my way to coordinate with my team at Nightlife about how we'd handle the catering schedule. Yes, really. Right now. In fact, I was pretty sure we'd just violated a couple of minor traffic laws in that last intersection to get there thirty seconds sooner.

Brendan very pointedly slowed down to something that might be considered a crawl, if you were the Road Runner and Wile E. Coyote was after you.

He did get me to Nightlife, however, and in one piece. When I walked into the dining room, I found Marie, Reese, and Zoe had commandeered a six-top. Marie's cake samples sat in the center, surrounded by shift charts, staff lists, and a whole bunch of open notebooks. It felt like walking into the restaurant version of the Situation Room.

Or at least it did until I noticed that everybody was looking at something other than me. Marie was looking at Zoe. Zoe was looking at a set of pages covered with notes and sketches. Reese was looking at the kitchen door as though thinking of making an abrupt exit. That was strange, because Reese was at first glance the most imposing person in that room. He has a linebacker's build, rich brown skin, cornrowed hair and the words EAT THIS tattooed on his knuckles. He swears the ink is the result of losing a bar bet, but he won't tell me what that bet actually was. I throw him the hard cases who come into the kitchen; the ones who think they know more than they actually do, or who might once in a while consider it beneath their dignity to take orders from a woman.

"What?" I asked as I sat down and pulled out my notebooks.

"Nothing," said Zoe. "We need a list of scheduled events for Alden week, and how many people are you going to need out of the kitchen?"

"Alden week?" I looked at Reese. Reese looked at Zoe. "What?" I said to Reese.

"Nothing," he said so casually, I was tempted to believe him.

I looked at Marie. The Cakeinator looked back at me over the rims of her glasses, daring me to ask her what as well. I decided to drop back and punt.

"So, I take it you've all heard Oscar Simmons is dead?" I tried.

"What?" Seeing a look of complete shock on the faces of three people who'd been trying to put something over on

you a minute before was one of life's little pleasures. It also told me that whatever subject they were avoiding, it was not the abrupt demise of a celebrity chef.

As if I needed more orphaned mysteries crowding around my door.

"So, who finally got the *cabrón*?" asked Marie.

The remark was, of course, in very poor taste, not that any of us were going to tell her that. "Nobody as far as I know," I said. "They're saying it was a massive stroke. He was found at his desk."

"Now, that is a surprise," muttered Reese.

While I was grateful to find that my dislike of Oscar was not the result of some unique personal flaw, this was not the kind of talk I cared to encourage, not when the media might come calling or knocking at any minute. Elaine wasn't wrong. With Oscar so suddenly dead, so shortly after having suddenly quit a society wedding, assorted columnists and chatty types were going to be clawing after the juicy details, and they'd figure as both replacement and ex-employee, I would have them. Nightlife had to be ready for the onslaught. Too bad city building codes did not allow for shark-filled moats.

"We are all very sorry," I said firmly, meeting each of their gazes in turn. "Oscar was a true professional and a highly respected member of the community. Our thoughts and prayers are with his family during this difficult time."

"Did he actually have family?" asked Zoe.

"Hear him tell it, he sprang full grown out of the head of Escoffier," said Reese.

"He sprang full grown from somewhere," added Marie. "I would not say it was anyplace so elevated."

"We are all *very* sorry," I repeated, because obviously my staff had not heard me the first time around. "Oscar was a true professional and a highly respected—"

"Horse's arse," announced Robert Kemp, who at that moment strode through the door, his white hair flying and suit coattails flapping. "Yes, I've heard. I would have arrived sooner, but the sodding subway had a nervous breakdown. Flowers to Perception and for the memorial, yes? Thoughts and prayers with the family during this difficult time, yes? Yes." He tossed his keys down on the host station podium, scooped up the house phone, and began to both dial and regather his trademark aplomb.

"You heard the man," I said to my three chefs. "And this is all anybody who calls wanting a statement needs to know. I don't care which channel, blog, or rag is behind them. Clear?"

"Yes, Chef," said Reese and Zoe. Marie inclined her head.

"Good. Now. What have you got for me?"

With that, we were off to the races. There is nothing like work to distract you from tragedy, especially one that's not yours and that you can do—as Robert might put it—sod all about.

If being a good cook is only part of what makes an executive chef, it's even less of what makes a successful caterer. That's all about logistics and proper staffing. What can you get to the space, what can you do in the space, how many people do you need to pull it off, and how much time do you have? This is where Reese with his army career was my ace in the hole. I swear they drink logistics down with their beer at night. Munitions or puff pastry, it made no difference. It was all stuff that needed to be gotten in place and set up.

Zoe, on the other hand, was ten pounds of creativity in a five-pound bag, and it was pretty clear none of that creativity got any sleep last night. She spread out sketches and ingredient lists for a whole series of appetizers, and full dayblood and nightblood menus. She hadn't even bothered to do cost breakdowns. *These are Aldens,* I could hear her thinking. *They can afford it.* She had grand dreams of whimsical creations: spicy prawns on spears of lemongrass served standing upright from bowls of jasmine rice; rosemary-perfumed chickpeas in lacy cones made of Parmesan *fricos*; miniature frozen cappuccino pops; a cold gazpacho, discreetly seasoned with pasteurized bull's blood; a truffle-infused cream; and an amusing little caviar-flecked savory custard. Then there was the buffet for the bridesmaids and guests while they were waiting for the ramp-up to the wedding . . .

This started Reese reminding her that all these ingredients for these elegant dishes had to be found, and purchased, and hauled, prepped, and stored, and if these were the appetizers, what was she thinking for the dinner . . . and . . . and . . .

Marie, true to form, just plucked the proposed dinner menu out of Zoe's stack of papers and started to read. What she read led her to a curt demand as to how this was going to affect staffing and budget for the sweets and was Zoe expecting her staff to bake all the savory pastries and breads she had planned in that menu? She, Marie, also had work to do.

To tell you the truth, I was mostly there to keep the three of them adding a knock-down, drag-out portion to the planning session—just another one of those little details of being an executive chef they don't tell you about at culinary school. Nothing was made easier by the fact that about halfway into it, the phone started to ring off the hook, and I could hear Robert in the background, laying the plummy accent on thick with the callers about how very sorry we were to hear of the loss of such an esteemed professional and our thoughts and prayers were with the Simmons family at this difficult time.

Except none of us was really sorry, and I'd just talked to him last night, and he was dating, or at least in bed with Karina Alden, and I didn't know if it really had been a stroke that laid him out so abruptly and completely. And none of this would get out of my head.

It took a certain amount of verbal arm-wrestling, but I got Zoe down to a dinner menu with two salads, a soup tasting, and just four entrée choices. Reminding myself we had a sky's-the-limit budget, I promised Marie that we would add a third assistant pastry chef for Alden week. We all agreed that the apricot-walnut cake with lemon-ricotta filling, the vanilla cake with raspberry, and the triple chocolate with brandied-cherry filling samples were perfect to take to Brooklyn for the scheduled tasting. This cleared the deck so I could assure Reese that I did know Mel Kopekne, the manager at the event site, personally. I would swear on my sense of taste that Mel could get us whatever we needed, and that we'd be in the space in plenty of time to check the layout and facilities.

But this was nothing compared to the horror of reworking the schedule for the Nightlife staff to adjust for the fact that both Reese and I would be missing for more than a week.

It had gone on four, and the back-of-the-house people were beginning to arrive. No matter who was getting dead or wed, we had prep to start. I dismissed my staff, but stayed at the table a little while longer, flipping over my notes and wishing I could stop thinking.

I don't like mysteries. As I may have mentioned, chefs are control freaks by nature, and unanswered questions bothered me badly. Especially when people's lives and my work schedule were going to get messed up because of them. Even more especially when I could not get rid of the feeling that I had been dragged into the middle of them deliberately and with malice aforethought.

Not that anybody who wanted Oscar off the job and me on it could possibly have known Oscar would turn up dead the next day.

Could they?

I tossed down the pen I had been toying with. The Nancy Drew tendencies I had been so sure were long gone appeared poised to make a spectacular eighth-inning comeback. I got up and I stretched my back and neck until the popping began. I looked toward my kitchen, where I should be right now, because prep was starting and it was Friday.

Instead, I walked over to the host station. Robert had found time to change into his tidy dark work suit and was going over the reservations list. The phone miraculously had gone quiet for the moment.

"How're we looking for tonight?" I asked.

"It should be another full house," he answered, without looking up. "A number of them new since yesterday. I think word of your association with the Alden wedding has leaked."

Now there was a surprise. Not. "Robert, in your précis on the Alden family yesterday, you didn't say anything about Karina Alden."

"I assumed you'd at least heard of her." He did not lift his nose in the air, but I got the distinct feeling that was due to that famous British self-control, and the fact that I pay his salary.

"Why would you assume that?"

"Because she is the K. Alden of Exclusivité."

I sighed. "Robert, please remember I don't get out much."

"Exclusivité is one of the few independent perfumeries in the world. They create custom fragrances for a highly select clientele."

"So they're in the 'if you have to ask, you can't afford it' range?"

"It would be more accurate to say they are in the 'if we don't already know your name, you need to present references to be allowed through our door' range."

"Wow."

A smile flickered on his thin lips. "Exactly."

Taking this new information with me into the kitchen, I buttoned on my white coat, tied my bandanna over my too-short hair, and got to work. I stashed Robert's newsy tidbit on a shelf in my brain along with all the other facts, fresh and stale, that I had about Oscar Simmons, and spent the rest of prep trying not to look at it.

The high-pressure dance of dinner rush shoved all the events of the day to the back of my mind. It was a relief. As long as I was in my kitchen, I was competent and in control, and if I was surrounded by things that could cut me up or burn me, at least it wasn't personal.

Naturally, it couldn't last.

"Chef Caine?" I heard my front-of-house manager, Suchai, say behind me.

"Pick up, ten! Pick up, sixteen! Order in, fourteen—two consommés, one pumpkin soup! What?" I asked, taking up the squeeze bottle of white truffle oil and dotting it carefully onto the plate of mixed summer greens with field mushrooms and balsamic vinaigrette in front of me.

"Deanna Alden and her wedding party just walked in. Robert's seating them at twelve."

Of course he was. One of the reasons we employ Robert is because he knows exactly when to roll out the red carpet.

"Okay." I focused on the composed salad in front of me, adding pinches of fennel pollen to the plate, even though a profound sinking feeling had settled into my premonition lobe. "Thanks."

"You're coming out to shake hands, right?" said Suchai gently.

"Order up!" I set the salad on the pass. "Yes, I'm coming out." I undid my apron. "Zoe, take over."

I followed Suchai into the cool of the dining room. The subdued lighting bathed us in its calming glow, and the shouts and the steam were replaced by the complex aromas of the food, the murmur of voices, and the clink of silverware against china. Well-dressed patrons lined the bar, waiting for Abe's elegant cocktails. Recognizing a pair of African American nightbloods who were becoming regulars, I gave them a welcoming nod.

I knew good and well the Alden-Renault party had no reservation. Nevertheless, Robert had seated them at table twelve, dead center in the dining room. Any experienced maître d' keeps a table or two open, just in case of a VIP walk-in. So far we hadn't had much call, and the sight of one of our best tables sitting empty on a nightly basis got under my skin, but tonight I was glad he'd done it. Customers who obviously had way more time than I did to read the papers and the gossip blogs were sneaking glances at the party of six.

Not that they'd dressed to be subtle. Deanna Alden had gone all out, a tight, bright blue dress with a hand-painted daylily splashed across one shoulder. Her hair was swept up and back to make the most of her pixie face, dangling diamond and sapphire earrings, and matching diamond choker that mostly covered the bite marks on her neck. Flanking her were two other dayblood girls—I assumed they were Lois and the unfortunately named Peridot. One had pale blond hair that had been aggressively straightened to the demands of current fashion. Her paisley silk top looked as if it had been standing too close when an eighteen-wheeler ran over the seventies. The other woman was a natural carrottop, her red hair pulled into a French twist and her summer green spandex top trimmed with smoke gray stones that matched the topaz in her necklace and earrings. She sized me up sharply as I approached the table, and I found myself wondering how I'd earned such a hard look from a bridesmaid.

"Chef Caine." Deanna had the dazzling smile of someone who had appeared in public a lot and knew how to behave when being watched. "Really sorry to walk in at totally the last minute like this, but we were *starving*."

"Very glad to see you, Ms. Alden." Here in the dining room I was very much on stage. It was game face time. "I don't think we've met . . ." I turned to the nightbloods.

"Gabriel Renault." The younger-looking of the two

nightbloods held out his cool, light hand to me. I glanced at his face just long enough to catch waving chestnut hair, almond-shaped eyes, and a strong aquiline nose. His cheekbones were high enough and sharp enough to make his pale cheeks look dramatically hollow—kind of David Bowie on the dark side. I didn't catch his eye color. Looking strange vampires in the eye is a hazardous pastime.

"Very glad to meet you, Chef Caine," said Gabriel. "Let me introduce my sire, Henri."

Henri Renault got to his feet and bowed. *"Bonjour! Vous êtes notre chef magnifique, n'est-ce pas?"*

Something people forget is that really old vampires tend to be really short. If Henri Renault was five feet tall, it was in heels. He was also what used to be described as "dapper." He wore a neat cream-colored suit, complete with a patterned silk vest and a gold watch chain, which, I was willing to bet, had an actual gold watch on the end. Cuff links, a sapphire tie pin, and a gold ring with a bright blue stone on his right hand added to this serious cache of antique bling. He had also clearly been converted before the idea "less is more" came into vogue, because his hand rested on a gold-headed walking stick, and he adjusted his monocle to peer up at me.

And yes, that was cologne I was smelling, a heavy wave of musk and cloves. Wow. Henri Renault left no detail overdone.

"I do so look forward to tasting you—pardon me—your work," Henri went on in French. He did not repeat the remark in English. I suspect that was because he didn't want the rest of the party to know he'd just made a really clumsy come-on. Gabriel struggled to keep the shock off his face. Deanna just blinked brightly as her girlfriends giggled. Evidently they weren't covering French at prestigious private schools these days. What was this world coming to?

"But of course," I answered in my best backstreets-of-

Paris French. *"And understand, Monsieur Renault, I know you're a fake."*

My first *stage*—that's kitchen-speak for apprenticeship—was in a French kitchen. I was quickly shunted over to pastry, because that's where us girls get shunted in traditional French kitchens. There, I learned three things. The first was that I was in no way temperamentally suited to pastry. The second was the rule not to date where you work, especially not the boss. That, however, is a long story and it does not make me look good, so I don't usually tell it. But the third thing was how to speak enough French to survive in a kitchen, dining room, or bar full of casually crude French guys. As a result, I could spot genuine French idiom when I heard it, and when I didn't.

Henri Renault's fang-baring, oh-so-gracious smile began to tremble around the edges. I'd scored some kind of hit. I could figure out what kind later.

"But please do not concern yourself unduly, Monsieur," I continued, still in French. *"It is not any of my business."*

"I understand you very well, Chef Caine." Renault sat and folded his hands on top of his cane, his demeanor as smooth and unruffled as if we'd been talking about the weather. He also switched to lilting English. "I am so sorry that I cannot introduce you to my other son, Jacques. Gabriel, what is keeping your brother?"

"He said he'd be here." Gabriel frowned at the door, and, because he was a nightblood, I could feel the tendrils of both worry and anger creeping out from him.

"Always late, that boy. I have tried to teach him manners, but it is hopeless." Henri waved his hand and gave a heavy sigh. "So, Chef Caine, I understand you have stepped in to assist with *la grande affaire*?

"She tore Oscar's menu up and tossed it out," crowed Deanna. "It's going to be perfect! Actually," she added, "Chef Caine was my first choice. If I'd had my way, we'd have talked to her *months* ago." Deanna beamed. The dining room whispered and smartphones were whipped out by compulsive text messagers. I struggled to keep my mouth shut. Did she not know about Oscar? Or was she trying to milk the situation? And why in the hell was this happening in my dining room where I couldn't demand to know what the hell was happening?

Think fast, I told myself. *And diplomatically.*

"Thank you so much, and congratulations again to you both. Now, I'm afraid you'll have to excuse me." I beckoned Suchai over. "I hope you'll enjoy your meal. Suchai will be taking care of you personally tonight." I met my manager's eyes. He nodded, and in turn signaled to Frederico, our most experienced table captain.

The Alden-Renault table would get a complimentary course, and some of the house special sangria for the nightbloods. They were VIPs; they'd be treated as such, whether I liked it or not, and I found I did not like it—at all.

Zoe eyed me as I stepped back into my spot at the expediter's station.

"You okay?"

"I'll tell you as soon as I know." I slotted a new ticket into place on the dupe slide. "Where are we on fifteen?" I shouted over my shoulder.

"Fifteen, two and three working, Chef!"

I don't think I looked up for the rest of my shift. I pushed myself into high gear and stayed there. But I couldn't work fast enough to silence the questions in the back of my brain. I was not the only haute noir chef in this city, or in Felicity's address book. I'd never had my name on an event this size, and I was in fact a liability when it came to the peaceful completion of this wedding. I had bad blood with the guy who had the job before me, who was now, surely coincidently, dead.

So we were back to the question Brendan asked me on that Brooklyn sidewalk—why me?

8

I was sorting through time cards and nodding toward Jose the dishwasher as he headed for the back door when my phone started playing "Bela Lugosi's Dead," the ring tone I've reserved for Chet.

I sighed and told myself I was still mad at him, but after the day I'd had, it seemed like pretty small potatoes.

"Hey, Chet." I clamped the phone between my shoulder and ear so I could keep sorting cards.

"I heard about Oscar," answered my brother. "You okay?"

I hate FlashNews. "Yeah, I'm fine. Why wouldn't I be?" Even over the phone Chet's nightblood silences could make my skin crawl. "I'm *fine*," I repeated.

"Okay, okay, you don't have to bite my head off." This was a saying you'd think a vampire would avoid, but Chet never was very careful that way. "You want me to come down there or anything? So we can, you know, talk?"

I thought about it; I really did. I was tired, I was sad, and I was disturbed by the resurfacing of my inner Nancy Drew. But at the same time, if I let Chet in now, it would only end with his bringing up the fact that I was in the middle of another Maddox mess, and that he'd offered me a perfectly adequate loan. This would make me yell at him, which would start the whole argument all over again. On the list of things I Did Not Need Right Now, this was item number one. Okay, maybe number two.

"Thanks, Chet," I said. "But really, I'm okay. If that changes, I swear I'll call."

I'm not sure he totally believed me, but he believed enough to make some small talk and hang up. I tossed my phone back down on the desk with the invoices, schedule sheets, and time cards. I stared at my dark, silent kitchen and reached one solid conclusion.

I needed to get out of there. I needed a full night's sleep and to remember that whatever had happened to Oscar, it was really none of my business. Nancy Drew could go take a flying leap.

I grabbed my stuff from my locker, tossed my chef's coat in the hamper, and headed out toward the alley. I locked the door behind me and tugged hard on the handle to make sure it was really closed. It had a bad habit of sticking open.

I was pulling the key out when cold touched the back of my neck—not a cold breeze or a cold drip of water, just . . . cold. The cold was followed by a soft whisper that crawled right up into the back quarters of my brain.

"You need to stay away from the Alden job."

I slid the keys into my pocket and wrapped my hand around the miniature spray bottle I keep there.

The nightblood stood about two feet away from me. He had hollow cheeks, dark hair, and a very long, narrow nose that, together with his high cheekbones, gave him a vulturelike appearance.

Suddenly, turning down Chet's offer of a sympathetic shoulder and brotherly escort didn't seem like such a great idea, family quarrel or no family quarrel. If I got drained in my own alley because I lacked the cojones to make up properly with my own brother, neither one of us would ever forgive me.

"Sorry—you are?" I kept my thumb on the spray bottle's trigger. Having been attacked in an alley before, I had developed this nervous habit of going around armed. In this case, the armament was a light but effective mixture of garlic-infused holy water.

"Jacques Renault." The vampire tilted his chin so he could look yet farther down that long nose at me. Not that he had any right to. It was a seriously high-class expression coming from somebody dressed as an undead slacker. In a departure from the rest of his overdone blood family, Jacques wore loose khakis and a button-down shirt, its tails untucked, over a black T-shirt. He also smelled of fresh onions, which was not your normal nightblood perfume. "And I will say it again, Charlotte Caine—you need to stay away from the Alden job."

In situations like this, when you're facing something bigger, stronger, and much, much more dangerous than you, the only immediate answer is attitude. "What's it to you?"

Jacques opened his mouth to flash fang—in case I hadn't worked out I was dealing with the lurking undead. This gave me time enough to get my bottle halfway out of my pocket. It turned out I needn't have bothered. We had company, and he brought a fresh cold front with him.

"Charlotte? How lovely to see you here."

Anatole Sevarin moved gracefully into the alley, smiling as if I were climbing out of a stretch limo in a designer gown instead of standing in stained work clothes with a strange vampiric companion. Anatole was a tall, lean man, and his pallor only served to emphasize his brilliant green eyes and the red-gold hair that swept back from his clear forehead. To top it all off, when he wanted, he could turn on a look filled with the kind of promises you don't repeat in public.

"Hello, Anatole." I ordered myself not to melt with relief. Myself declared it would take the request under advisement. “Anatole, this is Jacques Renault. Mr. Renault, this is . . .”

“Anatole Sevarin,” said Jacques. “*D’accord.* We’d heard you two were . . . connected.”

Anatole didn’t need to bother looking down his nose at anybody. He just leveled his gaze at you, and you could tell he already had a mental map of all your weak points. “I’m sorry, your name again?”

“Renault. Jacques Renault.”

“Oh yes, one of Henri’s children,” said Anatole. “I didn’t realize he let his boys hang about in alleyways. Unpleasant places, alleys.”

“And you never know who you’ll meet in the dark.” Jacques let a slow, cocky grin spread across his face. Half a heartbeat later, I was staring at empty space. Anatole swore and was gone just as fast, tearing down the alley after Jacques. I assumed. I couldn’t hear a damned thing except my own attempts to gulp down air and not scream.

I was still trying to get my fingers to loosen their death grip on the spray bottle when Anatole came strolling back up the alley, alone. He had that look a cat gets when it wants you to know it missed the mouse on purpose.

“That one is faster than he looks,” Anatole remarked. “Are you all right, Charlotte?”

“Yeah. Thanks.”

Anatole took my hand and gave me a small bow. He looked surprisingly good doing that, and I liked to watch him way, way more than was healthy for either of us. Anatole Sevarin said he was over eight hundred years old and that he had once worked for Ivan the Terrible. Shortly after I met him, we ended up saving each other’s lives—well, life in my case; earthly existence in his. Semantics aside, mutual rescues tend to give you warm feelings for someone. He also happened to be one of the handsomest men I’d ever seen, and as Manhattan is fashion-model central, there is locally an elevated standard of male beauty.

"Would you care to tell me what that was about?" He glanced down the alley.

"I've had a kind of complicated couple of days."

"If you're seeing yet another man . . ." The vast reservoir of amusement behind Anatole's words was no help at all in this situation.

"That's really not happening."

"You cannot imagine how relieved I am. The thought of yet another rival for your affections . . ."

"You can stop this anytime, Anatole."

"I can, but you blush so beautifully, I find it difficult to refrain from the temptation."

"Now you're really stretching things." I finally remembered to take my hand back and stuffed it into my pants pocket.

"He mentioned the names 'Alden,' and 'Renault,' " Anatole went on. "Have you become involved in a certain wedding of note?"

Of course he knew about that. Keeping up with the events of paranormal society was part of how Anatole earned his paycheck. The rise of haute noir cuisine and restaurants such as Nightlife had created a new job category—vampire dining critic. Anatole Sevarin was one of the first, and he was still one of the most widely read. This made him good for me to know, but kind of awkward to be dating.

Not that we were dating, not even on the sort-of-kind-of level I operated on with Brendan. There were a lot of reasons for this, starting with my warm and spinny-head feelings for that other man, and finishing with how it always looks fishy for a chef to date a critic.

"They've asked me to do the catering."

Anatole raised one eyebrow minutely. "I had heard Oscar Simmons was catering. And isn't the wedding only a week away?"

So there was *something* not on his radar. "Oscar Simmons is dead. I told you, things have gotten complicated."

All the sardonic humor drained from Anatole's expression, leaving behind . . . not a whole lot. "And you are further attempting to tell me with your eyes that you have no desire to be discussing this matter in this oh-so-fragrant alleyway." He held out his arm as if he were channeling Mr. Darcy. "May I escort my lady to her conveyance?"

I kept my hands in my pockets. Reckless I might be, but not reckless enough to continue casual contact with Anatole. "You are never going to talk like a regular person, are you?"

"Please define 'regular person.' I fear my English is not up to the idiom."

I had no snappy comeback to this one, so I just turned up Tenth and let Anatole fall into step beside me. A fresh breeze rolled down the street along with the late-night cruising taxis and rattling produce trucks. The cool air felt wonderful after the steam and scramble of the kitchen. I breathed deep and arched my shoulders, trying to work out the kinks. Unfortunately, memories of my "complicated" day knotted them right back up again.

"So," I said, hoping in vain that I might sound almost casual, "do you know the Renaults?" I would work my way back to the recent threat when my brain stopped gibbering at the thought of it.

Anatole considered this for a lot longer than necessary. "Let us say I know of them."

"Let us ask *what* you know of them."

"I know Gabriel Renault is marrying Deanna Alden, which means he's marrying into the Maddox clan." Anatole's grin had gone sharp enough to cut, and he wasn't bothering to hide the fangs.

"Well, somebody's enjoying this little development."

"I am exceedingly pleased," he admitted. "After all he has done to me and my kind, Lloyd Maddox will now have a nightblood in the family. He must be inches away from a major coronary event." Anatole's voice held far more genuine relish than I was comfortable with on a dark street.

I'd be lying if I said I didn't sympathize. When things exploded with Chet last year, Lloyd Maddox tried to use our problems to boost his antivampire cause with assorted legislatures, not to mention a few of the better-known radio talk show hosts. Grudge? Just a little for me, thanks.

"But you do know something about the Renaults?"

When Anatole's caught off guard, there's a moment when his face goes absolutely still and blank. It's a little disturbing to realize how much effort he has to expend to maintain any expression at all.

"Ah!" Anatole sighed finally. "What have I done that my lady should want to spend our precious few moments together talking of other men?"

"You were the first one here, and I have questions that need answering."

Remember that look I was telling you about? The one filled to the brim with very dangerous promises? Anatole turned it on me right then, and my reason started to melt like ice cream on an August sidewalk. "Charlotte, are you telling me I am first with you?"

I decided to prove that not only could I take it, I could dish it out. While we waited for the traffic to clear so we could cross the street, I moved toward Anatole and tilted my face up. "First, last, and only, Anatole," I breathed. "You know that."

This, in retrospect, was probably not smart. I looked just a little too long into Anatole's green eyes. They had gold flecks in them that sparkled in the streetlight, and I felt the powerful urge to look deeper. There were secrets waiting there I wanted to know, secrets he was keeping just for me.

"My heart sings," murmured Anatole, and I snapped back to myself.

"Your heart hasn't done anything in centuries," I muttered, ducking my head as I hurried across the street. There was a considerable amount of internal cursing on my part to accompany this maneuver. You do not tease vampires—even vampires who like you; maybe especially vampires who like you.

Anatole, of course, kept up with me easily.

"So, do you know anything else about Gabriel Renault?" I turned back to the original subject, more to put a little mental distance between me and Anatole than to get actual information.

Anatole sighed again. "You are a cruel mistress."

"You have no idea."

Anatole's entire expression turned warm and sly. It told me without a word that he saw the straight line I'd dropped, but he was going to be merciful and just let it lie there, for now. "Henri Renault and his sons are what might be classed as professional vampires."

"What? They're hedge fund managers?"

"Surprisingly, no. Rather, they are the polite, charming nightbloods you can invite to your parties to show your business associates and political constituents how broad-minded you are, or, alternately, to show your dinner guests how progressive you are."

"Or show your parents how rebellious and independent you are?"

"Quite possibly. As long as you can afford them, of course. The Renaults are rumored to have highly refined tastes."

"Well, Deanna Alden's plenty rich."

"Yes, but a rich witch. I will admit, I was surprised when I read the announcement in the *Times*."

"Why? I mean, if Renault's a parasite . . ." Plus, witch/warlock blood was an even more potent beverage for a vampire than regular human blood. There had to be a real attraction in having a reliable supply of the good stuff.

When did the fact that I think this way stop surprising me?

"But Henri Renault is a parasite with a very finely developed survival instinct. He has been playing this game since Lord Byron invited him out to Lake Geneva one extremely dreary summer."

"You're making things up again."

"I assure you, I am not. What is important, however, is that Renault has never stayed in a dangerous situation, let alone showed any signs of doing something so permanent as marrying into one. I cannot imagine he has not passed the tricks of the trade on to his children."

"Is there any chance Gabriel could really be in love?" It was a pretty pitiful last-ditch effort to make this situation into something less creep-inducing, but I'd tried everything else.

"There is always a chance," said Anatole. "But it would not be my first guess."

I let this settle down and season what little I already knew. Any girl with both money and looks had to have seen more than her share of pretty boys with bright smiles and good table manners. It would take way more than that to get her to tumble into the whole white wedding routine, wouldn't it? On the other hand, Deanna might be just a spoiled rich girl who was giving her family a hard time for reasons of her own. Except that cynical interpretation didn't fit with Deanna's misty glow when she talked about Gabriel.

Could Gabriel Renault have successfully put the vamp whammy on a Maddox?

"Has Brendan Maddox asked you to talk to me about this?" Anatole kept the question casual, but I felt the hard current underneath his words.

"Uh, no." In fact, Brendan would probably be really unhappy if he knew I was airing his family business, especially with this particular nightblood.

We'd reached the subway station. I stopped beside the entrance, turned to Anatole, and hesitated. Of course, he noticed, and, of course, he smiled. He also seemed perfectly content to stand there, waiting for whatever I was going to say or do. He waited as if he had all the time in the world. He waited, in fact, as he had almost every night for the past three months, for me to come out of Nightlife and not refuse his offer to walk with me wherever I was going.

"What's going on here, Anatole?" I whispered.

"I am seeing you to your destination."

"I mean, what's really going on here?"

I braced myself for him to come closer, to try to draw me into his gaze full of heat and promises. But he stayed where he was, and his expression was surprisingly gentle. "You are making up your mind, Charlotte." Now he did move forward. He took my warm hand in his cool one, and heaven help me, I let him. "It's all right. I understand. I am what I am, and whatever occurs between us will not be like any relationship you might have with a dayblood man. I want it to be very clear that each step we take is with your full consent."

My heart pounded in the base of my throat. I should back away. I should take my hand out of his. This wasn't fair, what I was allowing to happen right now. It wasn't fair to Brendan, or to Anatole, or to me either. All that flashed through my mind, and I still didn't move.

"Are you always this careful?" If he had told me the truth, Anatole was old even by vampire standards. By human standards, he was impossibly ancient. That meant there'd been a lot of . . . relationships down the years. Not that we talked about it. Actually, I made it a habit not to even wonder about Anatole's "others." You can file that under sanity preservation.

"I am never this careful." Anatole lifted my fingertips to his mouth and brushed his dry lips across my knuckles. He stepped back and gave me one of his bows, accompanied by his most promise-filled smile. Then, Anatole turned and strolled away.

It was not until he had rounded the corner and was out of sight that I finally regained the ability to breathe.

"What the hell am I doing?" I asked myself. The only answer myself came back with was that we both very much needed to go home and hide under the bed.

9

"Charlotte! Sweetie, darling, lamb chop chefy! How *are* you?"

There is exactly one person in the world who gets to talk to me like that, and he was trotting down a marble staircase toward me with his arms wide-open.

"Mel! My masculine cabbage! What is *with* the bow tie?"

We hugged and laughed and air-kissed, and, I have to admit, it was really good to see him.

Mel Kopekne was another refugee from Buffalo. We'd become friends in high school, working the closing shift at Holden's Dinner and the Rye (I had nothing to do with that name) during the summer. Probably the times we spent dancing around the kitchen to strains of "Honky Tonk Woman" coming from the cheap boom box are best left to fond and very private memory. Mel took himself off to the wicked city even before I did. Here, he had aged into a cheerful little man with lightly thinning hair, superb people skills, excellent taste in suits, but strangely questionable judgment in neckwear.

"Have you met my sous, Reese?"

"Not yet." Mel had a very precise eye for exactly how much over-the-topness someone could take, and toned the show down to a firm handshake and professional smile before he turned to Felicity.

"Felicit-tay!" Mel took both her hands in all solicitous concern. "My poor dear! I heard about Oscar. First that awful breakup and now a stroke! Such a shock! Don't worry, we have it all under control."

Breakup? What breakup? Who broke up? I didn't get a chance to ask. Felicity gave Mel a quick peck and pat on his cheek. "Mel, swear to me you are not kidding."

"I never kid about combat readiness."

"Like the new place, Mel," I said, surveying the domed and gilded lobby in front of us. "Small, but very tasteful."

"Why, thank you, my dearest one. I had it made up 'specially for you."

The Carriger Hall was a relatively new event space, but a relatively old building. A bank back in the 1900s, it had all the vaulting, granite, marble, stained glass and gilt trim you could ask for. The atmosphere was custom tailored to say this was a building for the ages and it would care for your money as long as the city stood.

Except apparently some of the executives had been taking better care of themselves than of their investors, and the bank folded in 2008. The building reopened shortly thereafter as a palace for marriages, banquets, and charity events. Somehow, while the rest of the country was looking under the cushions for spare change, Mel and his backers had managed to beg or borrow (I'm reasonably sure he didn't actually steal anything) enough to restore the gilding, painting, and stained glass to their original glory.

The joint was jumping now. As Mel explained, they were debuting a spring designer collection, and we got to see his people hanging banners, setting out flowers, laying out buffet tables and reception tables. It was the kind of controlled, loud, preperformance chaos we could all appreciate. Mel, the proud papa of a five-thousand-square-foot gilded-cage child, led us through it now, pointing out the perfections of setting, traffic flow, staffing, and all the useful spaces, both large and small.

From my and Reese's perspectives, of course, the best part was the on-site kitchen down where the vaults used to be. Nothing was worse than having to cart the food in from some outside space and try to keep it hot, fresh, and pretty. Mel stood up, proud and patient to Reese's rapid-fire quizzing about the number of staff he had booked for the Big Day. We would have to assemble only a foundation crew for the kitchen. When we finally got back to the vaulted lobby, Reese made a quick call to Hank back at the Aldens' to make sure everything was proceeding with dinner and snack prep there. Then Mel took him up to the main office to review the specifics of the service. Felicity was still firing off notes and messages from her PDA. She also showed every sign of sprinting out the revolving doors for a cab. I almost had enough mercy in my soul to let her go.

Almost.

"Let's me and you go get coffee." I grabbed Felicity's arm. "We need to go over some lists."

This did not fool her for a second, and she yanked away from me. "I knew it. You've had a gray cloud over your head since you walked in here. What's going on?"

I ignored her question and instead headed down the street toward a little café I'd spotted called Bean There, Bun That. Why did people insist on doing things like this to innocent little dining establishments? However, they roasted their own, and the guy in the black T-shirt behind the espresso machine seemed to know what he was doing as he scooped, tamped, poured and added a neat cap of foamed milk. The Danish were fresh baked too, which was a nice surprise. I bought a peach pastry for me and a cheese one for Felicity.

I set Felicity's Danish in front of her, and she looked at it weakly. "How can you eat with all this work to be done?"

"I'm a chef. I can eat anytime. You should eat too." I

pulled her BlackBerry out of her fingers and set it beside me, out of reach. "You need your strength."

Felicity tore off a corner of Danish and nibbled on it, possibly to keep from nibbling on her own fingernails. She did not, however, stop eyeing her BlackBerry. This is known as negotiating from a position of strength.

"Did you know Karina Alden was dating Oscar?"

Felicity's hand froze with another bit of Danish halfway to her mouth. "Oh. You found out about that."

I wrapped both hands around my paper coffee cup, but that turned out to be a very bad idea, because I nearly crushed it. "Yes, Felicity," I said in a tone my people would have recognized as the one they least wanted to hear at the end of a bad shift. "I found out about that."

Felicity went quiet, tearing off small bits of Danish and eating them one at a time. I folded my arms to keep from taking that lovely pastry away from her until she could promise to eat like an adult.

"I didn't know," she said softly. "I don't suppose it matters much . . . now."

"Felicity! Somebody's trying to tear this wedding apart, and the ex-caterer who was an ex-boyfriend is now an ex-human being, and you say it doesn't matter? What is your problem?"

But we both knew what the problem was. It was simple and universal. Prestige and money mess with your head, and they are very, very hard to turn down.

"God, what a disaster." Felicity slumped backward, and her elegant fingers tore another piece of pastry into little crumbs. "I never should have agreed to take this job."

"Probably not," I agreed.

"It had all the hallmarks of a gotcha marriage from the beginning. I mean, honestly, a Maddox and a vampire? It *has* to be the bride trying to pull one over on her family."

"So, why me, Felicity? What am I doing here, making things worse?"

"Honestly?" She scooted her newly created crumbs around with one perfectly manicured fingernail. I gritted my teeth and clenched my fists. I was never letting Felicity near a decent piece of baking again. Ever. "I don't know. When Oscar quit, I had to come up with a list, fast. When Mrs. Alden heard your name, she said we should get you. I knew it'd be trouble," she added, "but she said she'd heard good things about you. I mean, you were there when Deanna was going on about how much she likes Nightlife."

Yes, I was there. I just couldn't reconcile what I'd heard with the fact that they had to know that my being in the picture would make things worse. Unless somebody was deliberately thumbing their nose at Grandpa Lloyd. Or deliberately trying to sabotage the wedding.

"Anything else, and can I have my life back?" Felicity nodded meaningfully toward her BlackBerry.

"In a second." I laid my hand over her life. "That messy breakup Mel was talking about. Was that Oscar walking out of the wedding, or Oscar walking out on Karina Alden?"

"What do you *care*, Charlotte? Neither of them is in this anymore."

"But I am in it, up to my chef's whites. Which was it?"

Felicity sighed, then ate another bit of Danish. I kept my hand over her BlackBerry, just in case she was thinking of trying a snatch and dash.

"Unusually, Karina walked out on him. There was a blowup of some kind. This being Oscar, she probably found out he was seeing somebody else, or planning on seeing somebody else."

"And that's it?" I asked.

"That's all I know. I swear on my business license, Charlotte."

I pushed the PDA into Felicity's shaking hands, and she snatched it up. "I'll fax the contract to Nightlife." She got to her feet with a speed that suggested she was worried I might be thinking about another BlackBerry-napping. "We're good?"

"We're good."

Felicity gathered her things together, popped the last bite of Danish into her mouth, and left me sitting there with the dregs and the crumbs. I let out a long, slow breath and smoothed my hair down with both hands.

I'd lied to Felicity. We weren't good—at all. As already pointed out, I don't deal well with unanswered questions. Threats make me positively testy. This fresh reminder that I had been deliberately dragged into this disaster on flimsy pretenses was not making anything better.

I got to my feet, bused the table, and walked outside. I really needed to head out to Brooklyn Heights. I had a million details to organize and a million phone calls to make, and I had to get in there and back up Reese for this dinner tonight. And yet, I was only a few blocks from Perception, Oscar's main restaurant. It might or might not be open for business, but I knew down to the bottom of my chef's heart, somebody would be in there, no matter what. There'd be strategies to plan, press releases to argue over, territory to stake out, backers to reassure. That all took staff on the ground, and without Oscar around to issue his own set of threats, one of them might even be willing to talk to me, even if Felicity wasn't.

I turned east and started walking.

There are few things as sad as a restaurant closed up on a Saturday. It was sadder somehow because Perception's facade was made to boast a lively clientele. The street-level entrance was all sparkling glass and brushed brass. The outdoor terrace up above sported an art deco railing and a scalloped canopy in that particular shade I always think of as fleur-de-lis blue. The place somehow looked Parisian retro and modern New York chic at the same time.

Apparently, I wasn't the only one with a need to say

good-bye. The first thing I saw when I turned the corner of Perception's building was a small, round-hipped woman standing stock-still on the sidewalk. Her chestnut hair tumbled loose from a sparkling clip to curl around the shoulders of her stylish red Jackie O. dress.

I'd never seen her before, but I knew her. She had her sister's hair and coloring and something of her mother's steel around her jaw. This was Karina Alden.

Karina stared at Perception's door, oblivious to the people stepping around her. Her whole attention centered on the black-bordered sign that had been Scotch taped to the glass. It featured an eight-by-ten glossy photo of Oscar, his smile displaying teeth as white as his chef's coat and tall toque. Who the hell managed to look so at ease in a toque? Beneath the photo were three handwritten lines:

Oscar Simmons
August 15, 1969–May 21, 2011
He Will Be Missed.

She didn't even glance sideways when I stopped beside her. We all stood there for a long time. I kept sneaking glances at Karina Alden, but she remained absolutely focused on Oscar's photo, as if willing it to speak.

"He was really something else, wasn't he?" I said finally, awkwardly.

Karina drew in a long, shuddering breath and let it all out again, clearly using the time to decide if she was going to talk to me. "Yes, he was," she said at last, still without turning her eyes away from the shiny publicity photo. "You knew him?"

"I worked for him for a while." I held out my hand. "Charlotte Caine."

She stared in surprise for a minute before she shook my hand. "You're Charlotte Caine? Didn't you . . ." she stopped. "Sorry. Karina Alden." She gave me a ghost of a smile. "I expect we've heard of each other."

"I expect we have."

But evidently neither one of us could think of anything safe to say about what we had heard about each other, because we both let our eyes drift back to Oscar's memorial photo.

"He wasn't a bad person, you know." Karina said this as if continuing some other conversation. Or maybe she just assumed because I was an ex-employee, and female, I'd have hard feelings toward Oscar. It was a reasonable assumption. "He just . . . didn't know when he had enough."

I shifted my weight, trying to find some kind of answer that didn't involve the word "greedy." "You spend a lot of time living hand to mouth when you're coming up the ladder," I tried. "Some people never get over it."

"I hadn't thought of things that way," Karina whispered so softly I could barely hear the words under the city's eternal background noise. "I suppose it makes sense."

We stood there a bit longer. I pictured myself turning toward her. *So, what do you really think about your sister marrying a vampire? Were you working with Oscar as well as sleeping with him?* When Oscar had dropped the phrases "exclusive products," and "branded marketing" the other night, I'd assumed he was talking about a line of frozen raw sauces or something. But these days, star chefs had their names on everything from knives to shoes. Why not perfumes? Never mind that almost none of us actually wore the stuff. It's simply not practical. My sense of smell is one of the major tools of my trade, and it directly affects the sense of taste. I can't be smelling of Chanel No. Zillion when I'm trying to check the seasoning on the soup of the night. But Oscar had an audience, and even I had seen the perfume bottles sporting celebrity names.

Why did Oscar really quit your sister's wedding?

I pictured any such cozy little talk coming to an abrupt end, quite probably in a storm of public shouting. I conjured up three or four alternate conversational scenarios, none of which went any better. My throat tightened. I had to do something. I couldn't just stand there. Something had to give.

Then, it did.

"Chef Caine."

I spun on my heel. A short, broad man came around Perception's corner. He wore a rumpled, blue sports coat, and had a thin ring of gray hair edging his mottled scalp. I recognized him at once, the way you do a person you've hoped never to see again.

"Detective Linus O'Grady."

"Little" Linus O'Grady was the head of the New York City Police Department's Paranormal Squadron. He looked as though he'd let himself go soft years ago, and his drooping brown eyes gave him an uncanny resemblance to a mournful spaniel. But I was past being fooled by appearances. The last time I'd been alone with Little Linus it was in an interrogation room. He'd been in Bad Cop mode, and I'd needed a lawyer to pull me out of there. Right now, though, I couldn't help noticing the dark circles under O'Grady's spaniel eyes that said he hadn't gotten a lot of sleep lately. Sympathy poked its head up through my other memories, and I lacked the strength to smack it down.

Karina Alden, however, had an entirely different reaction.

"I've got nothing left to say to you!" She hitched her designer purse strap higher on her designer dress shoulder and marched away up the street.

I could sympathize with that too. I knew all about Little Linus's particular way with the ladies, especially when he suspected them of something. This caused a new question to slide into my mind.

What did Linus O'Grady suspect Karina Alden of?

"Did you know him?" O'Grady nodded toward Oscar's memorial sign.

"I worked for him once." I was not, however, in a mood to be distracted from my own—albeit currently unspoken—line of questioning. "What are you doing here, Detective?"

O'Grady smiled ruefully. "Can't tell you. Sorry."

I stared at the sign. "It wasn't . . . Oscar wasn't . . ."

The detective pursed his mouth. He regarded me thoughtfully and for a long time.

"Actually, I was thinking I might need to come talk to you, Chef. Have you got a minute?"

No. I did not. I most definitely did not. I needed to be in Brooklyn. Hell, I could arrange to need to be in Los Angeles, if it would get me away from O'Grady.

"Or maybe you need to get back to the Aldens'?" he asked. "You took that job over after Chef Simmons walked out, right?"

This was the detective's way of letting me know he already had a lot of facts in hand, and that he was not happy with them. And, incidentally, my walking away right now would make him less happy. Was I sure I wanted to do that?

Linus was very efficient with the subtext.

"You're not going to cut me a break here, are you, Detective?"

"Nope." He started down the sidewalk.

"Didn't think so," I said to his back as I started following along behind. He didn't even look back to make sure I was there.

Linus walked me to a faux Irish bar on the other side of the street. It had a dim interior tricked out in dark-stained trim and tables that had been ordered prescarred from the supplier to give the place the carefully staged version of what somebody thought a Dublin neighborhood hangout ought to feel like. The bartender seemed to know O'Grady, though, and he nodded us over to a wooden booth in the back, which did smell authentically of old beer.

We sat down, and O'Grady pulled out his notebook. I tensed. He ignored me as he flipped through the pages. A server brought us a couple of waters and left a couple of menus. We both ignored those. I can read upside down, but O'Grady's handwriting was so cramped and crooked, it defied all attempts at deciphering. I suspected he did that on purpose.

Then, much to my surprise, O'Grady closed the book, leaned back, and studied me instead. The overhead lighting showed up the dark rings under his drooping eyes like smears of soot on his ruddy skin.

"Chef Caine, if you wanted to poison someone in your kitchen, how would you do it?"

"I wouldn't," I answered at once.

O'Grady clearly mistook my speed for fear. "Hypothetically."

"Nothing hypothetical about it. It's impossible."

"You're sure?"

"You can't poison just one person in a restaurant kitchen. Especially if it's a busy place." *Like Perception.* "Almost anything you'd put the poison in is made up in large batches ahead of time. The poison would have to be odorless, tasteless, and not interfere with the cooking process in any way, because even if you poisoned one piece of meat or fish being made *à la minute*, you'd have the expediter, the line chef, and maybe the executive chef poking at it and tasting it. If the poison's in a salad, you can add whoever's running cold prep to that list. And that's all before it gets out of the kitchen. Once the plate hits the pass, there's no way to be sure which server's going to take it to the dining room, and there're all kinds of ways it might get sidetracked on the way there. It could be sent to the wrong person, or dropped, or even sent back."

"What about if the server . . ."

I shook my head. "If you want to add the poison after the dish has been plated, you're going to have to find a minute alone with that dish when it and you are not being watched. You can't exactly take a hot plate down to the walk-in, poison it, and bring it back."

"And if you wanted to get somebody on the staff . . . ?" O'Grady prompted.

Oh no. Oh no no no. My fingernails scraped against the scarred table, looking for something to grab onto. It was not possible that Detective O'Grady was looking into Oscar's death as a murder. It wasn't.

"Nine times out of ten, the kitchen staff's going to be so busy while they're on shift, they won't have time to grab a cup of coffee, let alone eat something," I said, thinking about how I regularly went for hours without a hand free to grab a swig of water. "And you can't poison one person during family meal, because that's a big-batch meal and you eat in a group, so there'd be no chance to slip a poison onto somebody's plate unseen."

O'Grady blinked. "You've thought about this."

I could see the clouds of suspicion forming behind O'Grady's eyes, and it was strangely amusing to catch him in the beginnings of a mistake. "A friend I went to cooking school with dropped out to become a mystery writer. She wanted to work up a thriller where someone got poisoned in a restaurant. I mean, it sounds like the obvious scenario, doesn't it? We tried hard to come up with a realistic solution but just couldn't make it work."

O'Grady looked down at his notes again and tapped his pencil twice. "I appreciate this is your job, Chef, and that you're a professional, but my job's taught me nobody's that good. There's always some point when you're not paying attention, something you can't watch. That's when you're vulnerable to the guy with the plan."

"Not going to argue, but this is the food you're talking about. A chef's whole reason for being in the kitchen is to pay attention to the food."

"What did she end up doing?"

"She decided publishing was even crazier than restaurant work and moved to Vermont to raise chickens."

That got a smile out of him that might even have been genuine. "I meant in the book."

"Oh. She moved the whole thing to an underground supper club where there were a lot fewer controls on the kitchen. Named me in the acknowledgments." I stopped. "Was Oscar poisoned?"

O'Grady considered the vintage Guinness poster hanging on the wall. It showed a toucan looking unnaturally cheerful about having a glass of black beer balanced on its beak.

"How'd you say you knew Oscar Simmons, Chef Caine?"

I sighed. I should have known better that to expect an actual answer. "Oscar hired me, once upon a time. I had been working at a place called the Loft, and things were going badly." Linus waited for me to go on, but there was no way I was telling him the full story of that kitchen run by a bunch of would-be rock 'n' roll rebels who had interesting ideas about what petty cash should actually be used for. "Oscar heard I was looking to make a change, and he offered me a job as saucier at L'Aquitaine." In fact, he'd offered me the job in the middle of Charlie's Blue Plate, over a pile of deviled kidneys.

"Was that a good move for you?"

"It seemed like it at the time. L'Aquitaine had just gotten three stars from the *Times*. Oscar was hot stuff, and he was starting to develop what would become haute noir cuisine. I thought I'd be learning from the best in the business."

"But it didn't work out that way?"

It took me a surprisingly long time to form the next set

of words. How could this matter? I hadn't cared who heard this story when Oscar was alive, so why should I care now? But the whole incident suddenly seemed not just stupid but shabby and more than a little sad. "It didn't take long to figure out that the sous-chefs actually ran the kitchen at L'Aquitaine. Oscar would breeze through on his way to the front of the house to shake hands with the celebrity clients. He'd make some noise in the kitchen, then breeze out again. Probably to do an interview or sign a new endorsement deal. Well, no big deal, I thought. I was working; I was learning. I'd been yelled at by bigger . . ."

"Windbags?" suggested O'Grady.

That would do as well as any other word. "The problem with Oscar was that when he didn't feel he was getting enough PR, he'd stage a scene. He'd throw a tantrum in the kitchen and storm through the dining room, or maybe he'd order a customer out of the restaurant for asking to have the sauce on the side or something. It got old fast. The best people in the kitchen stayed around only long enough to get L'Aquitaine on their résumé and then took off.

"Then, the milkshake tasting I'd come up with for the haute noir menu started doing too well. Some of the food blogs had put my name on it instead of Oscar's. He dealt with it by blowing up in my face." It was a memorable moment. It was also the first time I'd ever seen somebody genuinely turn purple. "He stormed out into the dining room. The sous told me to go after him, and apologize. That was the script. I wouldn't even have to say anything. All I had to do was stand there for a while and take whatever variety of BS Oscar decided to dish out."

"You refused, didn't you?"

"How'd you guess?"

"Trained detective. What happened?"

"I led a coup."

That actually got O'Grady to blink. "You got people to walk out?"

"No. I got them to stay at their stations and keep right on working. The orders came in and the food went out, without missing a beat. Oscar Simmons had stormed out of his own kitchen, and it didn't make a damned bit of difference."

"So, you got him fired?"

Detective O'Grady had reached a perfectly logical conclusion there. He had also identified himself as someone who'd never worked in the restaurant business. "Are you kidding? He was the name. The owners wanted profits, not first-rate food. Oscar's floor show brought in the tourist trade. He had me kicked out in front of the entire staff as some kind of object lesson." I remembered my fellow cooks watching me, stony-eyed, as Oscar smirked and railed and informed me I was nothing, and, for good measure, that I'd never work in this town again. I remembered the glorious freedom of walking right up into his space, snapping my fingers under his snub nose, and stalking out without looking back. The applause that broke out was so worth it. Even better was the way Suchai had been waiting up front, holding both our coats so we could link arms as we marched onto the sunny street.

"The next night, Chet and I pooled our money, made an appointment to talk to the bank, and started scouting locations for Nightlife."

O'Grady leaned back and regarded me with something very close to respect. "So, when you heard Simmons stormed out on the Alden wedding, you figured it was just another performance?"

I nodded. "Until I heard he'd given the money back." I stopped, and waited, just as a sort of trial. I didn't expect to really get anything, and I didn't. O'Grady was all done looking at me. He had his notebook out again, flipping patiently through the pages and reading his tiny, crowded handwriting. He was looking more tired by the heartbeat.

"Oscar was a T-typ," I said. "Why's the head of the Paranormal Squadron asking questions about him?" Linus cocked his head toward me but said nothing. "Is this something to do with the Maddoxes?" Lloyd Maddox had connections to the kind of people able to call up mayors and police commissioners for favors. It would sure explain why Linus looked so deflated.

O'Grady closed his notebook. "Actually, if he knew about this, Lloyd Maddox would be trying to get me kicked off the squad."

Now it was my turn to blink, and swear. "Why would Lloyd Maddox care about Oscar?"

"He doesn't." Linus rubbed his eyes, read the Guinness sign, put away his notebook, and took it out again. I waited, but that was less because I was feeling patient than because I was flabbergasted by the sight of Little Linus fidgeting.

"This was murder, wasn't it? Somebody killed Oscar Simmons." I knew it. I'd been afraid of this since Brendan asked that first question.

O'Grady lifted his spaniel eyes to mine and said nothing at all. We didn't like each other, but Linus O'Grady was a fair man. He took his job to serve and protect seriously. He might not give me answers when I wanted them, but I could trust him.

"Something happened last night you should maybe know about," I said. O'Grady cocked his head. I told him about the wedding party showing up at Nightlife, followed by the nightblood Jacques, with his warning, showing up at the back door.

Linus raised an eyebrow. "And Anatole Sevarin just happened by when you needed rescuing?"

"I never needed rescuing, and he walks me to the subway some nights." Anatole did not get on with O'Grady. Actually, there were very few people of authority in the city Anatole did get on with.

"A chef and a critic?" O'Grady flipped his notebook open again. "Isn't that a conflict of interest?"

"Which is why he's just walking me to the subway some nights."

"And is none of my business at all." O'Grady was diligently not smiling as he made a few more notes in his book. "All right. So why was the prodigal Jacques Renault warning you off the wedding of the decade?"

"Somehow he never got around to that part," I said blandly. "What are you going to do?"

"Unfortunately, since he didn't make an actual threat, there's not a lot I can do." Linus did not sound happy about that. I could definitely relate. "So, I'm going to wait for the toxicology and toxithautomy report on Oscar Simmons." Toxithautomy was one of those words we hadn't needed before the Equal Humanity Acts. It turned out that curses and other bad magics could leave traces in and around the human body. Thus was a new branch of forensic medicine born. "Unfortunately, that's all going to take a few days." O'Grady tucked his notebook into his jacket pocket again. "Budget cuts," he added. "What are you going to do?" It took me a second to realize this last was an actual question, not an eye-rolling observation.

"I'm going to Brooklyn Heights and earn the biggest fee I've ever seen in my life," I said.

Linus met my gaze and held it. He was looking for something, and I let him look. I'm a lousy liar, but I'm very good at waiting. He wanted to know if I was going to start poking into this thing he was not yet calling Oscar's murder. He wanted to know if I was out of my mind. I had no intention of answering either question.

Finally, O'Grady sighed and pulled out a battered leather case. He slid a card across to me. "This number gets to me direct, at any time. Use it if you need to."

"Thanks." I took the card and slipped it into my purse. Then we said good-bye, and I walked out onto the street.

Maybe it wasn't official, maybe Linus wouldn't say anything until he had those reports, but I had already pitched my wishful thinking into the Dumpster. Oscar wasn't just dead; Oscar had been murdered, and it had probably been done by something or someone related to the Alden-Renault wedding. Now, here I was standing on the curb with my hand up, trying to hail a cab to take me right smack dab into the middle of the circumstances that had gotten him killed.

Surely, the day could not get any better than this.

10

"Hey, Chef." Reese held open the side door between the sunken side porch and the Maddox kitchen. The aroma of onions and meaty stock rolled out in a warm cloud as I wrestled my hand trolley, suitcase, and tote bags inside. Behind me, the last rays of sunlight were vanishing behind the rooftops. "Whatcha got for me?"

After my meeting with O'Grady, I'd desperately needed time to calm down and get my head back into chef space. Fortunately, I'd also needed to stop off at the Terminal Market.

There are plenty of reasons for anybody who loves good food to come to Brooklyn. About fifty of them fall under the heading of the Terminal Market. Just off East Eighty-sixth, it's filled with the best the city's food purveyors have to offer. I jostled women from Ivory Coast, Senegal, and Haiti with their bright batiks, head scarves, and discerning eyes. Hassidic women in dark wigs and modest skirts who grew up being towed down these streets now towed their own daughters along behind them. Grizzled men in stained white coats hefted crates onto their shoulders like it was no big thing and shouldered their way through the rest of the boisterous, cantankerous, crowd. The air filled with the scents of fresh greens and hot chilies, and the rumble of more dialects than I could track. Even in the middle of all my anger and doubts, the market's bustle sank into my skin, soothing and straightening my crumpled-up thoughts.

Of course, I could have placed a whole set of orders over the phone, but that takes all the fun out of it. Not to mention the fact that if you want to be absolutely sure you're getting the best product, you have to *be* there. You have to heft the fruit to see if it's heavy (a sign of juiciness), and pick through the vegetables, looking for soft spots or signs of impending wilt. You need to turn the meat over to check the marbling and look the fish in the eye. You also have to be able to look your vendor in the eye in that ancient stare down between merchant and customer, and show no fear. It didn't matter that for once in my life I had a huge budget. If I acted like a pushover now, I'd never get a decent bargain in this town again.

I parked my suitcase under the Aldens' kitchen coat rack, unearthed a package from my trolley, and handed it over to my waiting sous-chef. Reese snipped the string and folded back the brown butcher paper. Reverently, he lifted out the two-inch-thick rib eyes. Delight spread over his face, the kind most people get only when looking at their true love.

"Oh yeah," he breathed. "I can work with these."

"Did you finish the list?"

"Yes, Chef," Reese answered, but he wasn't really paying attention. He laid the steaks out side by side, turning each one over carefully and scrutinizing the marbling.

"And the housekeeper?"

"Ms. Lyons. We're ready for her."

"Terrific." I tied my red bandanna over my hair. "Show me what you've got."

Since this was a party, there had to be hors d'oeuvres. We were doing shooters of beef-broth gelée, layered with sour cream and topped with minced chive. I checked

Reese's work for seasoning and added a little orange zest to the cream, just to brighten things up. For the daybloods, we would also be serving crostini with olive tapenade or spicy hummus. For the nightbloods, I'd carted in some of Night-life's house special sangria. Our bartender, Abe, had been tinkering with the recipe, and tonight was a chance to test out his new blend.

While we tasted, prodded, discussed and adjusted, the hands on the clock above the sink touched five past eight. The world turned a little farther, and the sun slid below the horizon. Overhead, and on the other side of the swinging door, we heard footsteps and voices. The Alden household was waking up for the night.

I was just wiping down the serving trays so we could lay out the hors d'oeuvres when Ms. Lyons swept in through the door from the back stairs. Judging by the pucker around her mouth, my abrupt departure the other day hadn't improved her opinion of me. That was bad, because this woman had the power to make our lives extremely difficult if she chose. That she was also the best possible source of information about the Aldens and their in-laws only made the decision to become her new BFF easier.

Fortunately, chefs have an unfair advantage when it comes to launching a charm offensive.

"Oh, Ms. Lyons, I'm glad you're here." I gave her my best smile. "We need your opinion."

Ms. Lyons's mouth drew up a little more tightly, and she turned cynical gray eyes on me. "Oh, really?"

"I was hoping you'd taste the tapenade for me." I set a plate on the marble kitchen island. "Some people prefer things very simple and low-key, and I want to make sure we haven't made it too spicy. Maybe you could let us know what you think?"

Reese had put together a pretty little plate with samples of all our dayblood hors d'oeuvres, plus a cup holding a few spoonfuls of the blueberry sorbet and vanilla sauce we'd planned for dessert, and one of the chocolate-dipped shortbread cookies Marie had sent over.

Trudy Lyons stared hard at that plate. For a few long seconds the entirety of my faith in human nature wavered. But at last, she delicately picked up a crostini covered in the rich olive-based spread, bit, chewed, swallowed.

Her eyes widened, and her shoulders sagged for just a second before she snapped back to full attention.

"Ho-ly crap," she drawled. "That's good! What'd you put in this stuff? Heroin?"

You never heard Alice on *The Brady Bunch* talk like that. I decided that was a compliment. I also decided that however this woman had become the Aldens' housekeeper had not been the usual route. "Why don't you go ahead and finish?" I inched the plate closer to her. "We've all got a long night ahead."

"Well . . ." Trudy's gaze drifted to the sorbet and shortbread. Appetite softened her tight face and glaring eyes. Oh, goodness me, the hard-bitten Trudy had a sweet tooth. She was now mine, heart, soul, and taste buds.

She glanced over her shoulder at the door to the dining room. "Just another bite. Adrienne . . . Mrs. Alden's about ready to bust a vessel out there as it is."

Pulling up a stool, Reese gave Trudy one of his ladykiller smiles as he reached over to the waiting coffee thermos to pour her a cup. Trudy gave him a long, appraising look, and we both got to watch her decide she was probably old enough to be his much older sister. She settled back to the food, but not without a certain short but visible moment of regret.

Within five minutes, Trudy had finished her snack, the pucker had entirely left her mouth, and we were all one big happy family. I also had a tray of mixed crostini and a pitcher of sangria all ready to go.

"Reese, give Trudy a hand with these, and see if we can get a final head count for dinner before you fire the steaks.

And ask Mrs. Alden if we're going to need tea as well as coffee."

"Yes, Chef." Reese, who had worked front of house as well as kitchens in his career, balanced a tray on his fingertips. "After you, Ms. Lyons." He bowed, which is no small trick when carrying a loaded platter one-handed. Ms. Lyons tipped her head, and her eyes flashed, letting him know he was playing with fire. Oh yes, she was ours. I managed to hide my grin by ducking my head and getting back to work.

Steak without potatoes makes no sense to me, so we'd planned a basic mash; fingerling Yukon Gold potatoes, butter, and shredded Parmesan. Reese had gotten the water boiling and the cheese prepped. I pulled the paring knife from my roll and started in peeling little round potatoes.

Footsteps sounded on the back stairs. I glanced over without slowing my knife work. Henri Renault, in full evening dress, gold cane in his hand, and monocle gleaming in his eye, entered through the back door.

"Ah, *bon soir*, Chef Caine," he said in his Frenchified English. "I was looking for my son Jacques. Have you perchance seen him?"

"I'm afraid not." Where would he have had time to get to? We weren't that far past sundown. Hadn't Mrs. Alden said all three of the nightbloods were staying here? Jacques would have been comatose with the other vampires until at most a half hour ago.

Beyond these thoughts, my attention was uncomfortably taken up by the fact that Henri Renault was not leaving. Instead, he was strolling toward me, tapping his cane thoughtfully against the cupboards. Warning flares fired up inside me.

"Was there something else, Monsieur Renault?" I asked, locking my gaze firmly on my knife and my potatoes. "I'm afraid I'm a little busy right now," I added, because I had the feeling he was in no mood to catch the subtle hint.

Apparently, he was in no mood to catch the direct hint either. In fact, he was moving closer to me. I couldn't hear his shoes on the kitchen floor as I'd been able to on the wooden stairs, but in the warm kitchen, it was easy to feel the cold vampires carry around with them. Vampires also tend to have a faint but distinct odor that can be anything from old blood to fresh truffles. Even beneath his cologne, Henri Renault's was a lot closer to blood. The skin on the back of my neck started to crawl.

What's taking you so long out there, Reese? I picked up another potato.

"You are direct, Chef Caine," Renault purred. "I like that in . . ."

My hands froze. "You really don't want to finish that sentence, Monsieur Renault."

"No, perhaps not." I heard the smile. He was charmed, and amused.

Time to nip this in the bud. "What are you doing here?"

"I am witnessing the marriage of my favorite son." Renault said, deliberately misunderstanding and blatantly lying at the same time. Oh, great, a multitasker. "I am also spending time with a beautiful woman." His voice dropped, becoming silky and inviting. Even more disturbingly, it managed to turn his personal cold front to an air of warmth.

Very carefully, I laid down my paring knife. Renault was right beside me, just out of my line of sight. I felt the pressure of his presence against my thoughts, urging me to lean closer, to yield to his persuasion. His stubby fingers traced a line down my neck. I turned toward that light touch, shifting my eyes slowly as I did, as if about to lock my fascinated gaze with his. I drew a deep breath. Renault smiled. A fang flashed in the track lighting. His dry fingertip dipped beneath the collar of my chef's coat. I hissed in a little more air and slid my palm across the counter until I touched the handle of my wooden spoon. Renault leaned in close.

I screamed like the Bride of the Creature in a B movie and smacked that spoon across his face.

Renault howled, leapt back, and slammed against the wall. The air filled with the thunder of running feet. A split second later, Reese was leading a charge through the swinging door backed by a full phalanx of Aldens, Maddoxes, and undead party guests.

I love it when a plan comes together.

Brendan shot past the others and caught my hand. I saw murder in his blue eyes. Not for me, of course, but for whoever'd caused me to take up spoons. *I'm okay,* I said silently. He read my assurance and nodded, drawing back just a little. But he didn't let go of me.

Just then, the handle on the side door rattled, and, I swear, we all jumped and turned at the exact same moment. The door opened. Brendan had his free hand up; so did Deanna and Mrs. Alden.

My not-quite-threatening vampire from the night before pushed his way through the door. "Sorry I'm . . ."

Jacques Renault saw me recognizing him. He also saw the witches in fighting stance. Then he saw his sire plastered against the wall.

"Late," Jacques finished. "What have I missed?"

11

"Where have you been?" demanded Henri in French, his voice gone high and squeaky from trying to shout and keep out of spoon range at the same time.

"What have you been doing?" Jacques slid sideways so as not to be directly downrange from the magic-ready Maddoxes.

"I'm going to bleed you both white!" growled Gabriel as he shoved his way through the pack of my other would-be defenders. "It's all right. Please," he said in English as he pushed Deanna's hands back down from the witch equivalent of *en garde*. "It is all right, *n'est-ce pas, Chef?*"

"Yes, yes, yes. I'm so sorry!" I apologized to the world at large, but I locked eyes with the senior Renault. He needed to know I had no fear of him, or his vamp whammy. "You startled me, Monsieur Renault."

"Not to worry." Renault stayed pressed up against the wall as if he hoped it would open at his back and get him a little farther away from me.

"It's not a good idea to come up behind a chef," I went on pleasantly. "We get lost in our work." I pulled away from Brendan and started to stir the boiling water with my wooden spoon as if there were something actually in the pot. I also ducked my head to hide the complete lack of shame on my face. "Sorry again, Mrs. Alden. Dinner will be ready shortly."

"Yes, of course," said Mrs. Alden stonily from her position by the swinging door.

"Henri," said Deanna. "Let's go out front." Her tone was even more pleasant than mine had been, and just about as genuine. I also noticed her rub her fingertips together as if they itched. Was it possible the bride-to-be did not get on well with her future sire-in-law? "I'll get you a glass of sangria."

"Yes, yes." With an effort, Henri Renault moved away from the wall and bent down to retrieve his cane. He kept his eyes on me the whole time. "Sangria. An excellent idea."

"Jacques, you're coming with us?" asked Gabriel, but there was most definitely an order supporting that question mark.

"Sangria with angry Maddoxes." Jacques was working very hard on not looking at me. "Delightful. In here?" He was through the swinging door into the dining room almost before I could see him move, and way before I could come up with anything clever to say in front of his present-and-future family about how nice it was to see him again.

And that was pretty much that. Henri bowed to let the ladies precede him out. Gabriel hung back long enough to make sure his sire left with the rest of the party. Brendan, on the other hand, stayed right where he was.

"What actually happened?" Brendan beat Reese to the question by a finely diced second.

I grimaced, thought about telling them about my previous encounter with Jacques, and thought about the delay the explanation would cause in getting the food out to the clients. It'd probably be best to stick with the basics right now. "Turns out Henri Renault is a hands-on kind of nightblood."

"I'm surprised he still has hands," said Reese. I'm sure it was just coincidence that he picked up his big chef's knife right then.

"I considered it, believe me. I'm *okay*," I added to Brendan, who was contemplating the door to the dining room. Henri was lucky Brendan's self-control was a lot better than Deanna's, or we'd have been sweeping nightblood ashes off the floor. "Renault thought he could roll me, although I'm not sure why he'd bother."

As I said that, I realized how good a question it was. Why *would* he bother? Maybe there was no reason. Maybe he was just the kind of vampire that treats the ability to walk freely among the living as an invitation to a 24/7 buffet. But taken with Oscar's all-but-official-paperwork murder, and Jacques's warning from last night, his actions took on both meaning and import. Oh, joy.

"You're sure you're okay?" Brendan was lowering his mental hackles, but it was taking a lot of effort.

"I'm sure." We did need to talk. I had lots he needed to know, but I couldn't tell him any of it now. I trusted Brendan, truly I did, but it was not reasonable to expect anyone to be able to keep calm ten seconds after learning somebody at the dinner table with him had probably offed the last chef. Besides, my potatoes were going to turn brown if they didn't get into the water real soon. "You get back up front, make nice with the family, and don't start a fight."

"Not even a little one?" I swear to God, he sounded exactly like a disappointed twelve-year-old.

"Are you trying to get me fired? Go." I folded my arms at him, but at the same time all I wanted to do was hold on to him, because I was not one hundred percent certain I was as okay as all that.

I suspect Brendan knew this, but he just gave me a peck on the cheek and headed out to join the rest of the party. I turned on Reese, but whatever he'd been watching a second before, all his attention was now directed at his precious steaks. I decided I could let his ghost of a shit-eating grin pass without comment, just this once, and only because we had to get this dinner finished.

I'd found some garden peas at the market. You don't mess with fresh peas any more than strictly necessary. We just blanched them with a little mint and a little sugar and let them be the wonderful thing they are. So Mrs. Alden wouldn't start wondering if she was paying out all this money for plain home cooking, we also put together a salad of roasted fennel bulb and Jerusalem artichoke with tangerine vinaigrette. After the steak and potatoes, the sorbet with sauce and Marie's shortbread would complete the meal for the daybloods. For the nightbloods, Reese and I had settled on a cold veal consommé for starters. It was already in bowls in the fridge, beautifully clear and delicate. Reese had also made up some curried liver pâté (a private wink to Charlie's kidneys, only much milder and much, much classier). A slice of that would go in the center of the consommé. Then, while the living had their steak course, the nightbloods would enjoy a Polish soup made from duck blood. The base for the blueberry sorbet made a flavorful dessert beverage when combined with whole milk, homemade ice cream, and more orange zest and mint. It maybe wasn't quite up to Marie's standard, but it was awfully close.

The sound of conversation reverberated through the swinging door, indicating people had gathered around the hors d'oeuvres. The clock read nine—dinnertime. I set out the consommé for Trudy to take to the guests, keeping one eye on the potatoes while Reese lovingly dried and seasoned his steaks. Then, on the other side of the door, the sound of voices stopped dead.

I looked at Reese. Reese looked at me, and the door, and at me again.

A man's deep voice said something. A woman's answered. The man spoke again. Brendan said something I couldn't catch.

I will not go listen at the door. I adjusted consommé bowls. *I will not go listen at the door.*

"And you won't either," I said to Reese, who was looking at me again.

Reese didn't even pretend not to know what I was talking about. "No, Chef."

Neither one of us was surprised when Mrs. Alden pushed through the swinging door.

"Charlotte, we have one more for dinner." She did not look thrilled. In fact, she looked as if she needed to quickly and efficiently disassemble somebody into his component parts. "Can you take care of it?"

I deferred to Reese, who mentally portioned and plated beef before nodding. "That will be fine, Mrs. Alden."

"Thank goodness. I can't imagine . . ." She cut herself off with a frown not meant for either Reese or me. "Thank you." She walked out again. The door swung silently shut behind her, and I smelled smoke in her wake.

"That's not good," I said.

"Somehow, I'm bettin' whoever showed up is not her best girlfriend."

"No bet." Voices sputtered to life out in the dining room. China and glass clinked, but slowly. It was a lot harder to turn away from that door and its inviting little diamond of a window than it should have been.

"This isn't going to turn out to be one of those happy homes housing dreadful secrets, is it?" Reese held his palm over the grill to check the temperature. "Because if it is, I want time and a half."

"Cook the steak, Reese. I'll deal with the crazy rich folks."

"That's why you get your name on the jacket." He started laying steaks on the fire. If there is a more delicious scent than the first cloud of steam rising to accompany the sizzle of good beef, I don't know what it is. "But I'll tell you, there's something weirder than usual going on here," Reese went on as the last steak joined its brothers. "I mean, you've seen what's weird about this kitchen, right?"

"Aside from the fact it keeps collecting vampires and witches?"

"Everything in here is brand damned spanking new. I mean everything. Dishes, appliances, glasses. There's nothing in here older than a couple of months."

"Huh. Well, maybe when Mrs. Alden was changing her closets for spring, she decided to change her kitchen over too."

"Nobody goes clean sweep on a kitchen. Everybody's got something they keep; old coffee mugs or the family recipe books, *something*. This place, it's like being on the movie set of a kitchen. I'm telling you, it's *weird*."

I agreed it was weird, primarily so he would close down and focus on the steaks. Reese is from Chicago, where beef is a sacred thing, and he had prepared the rib eyes according to his most stringent standards. With Reese, you do not put anything other than a sprinkle of salt on beef lest you sully the purity of the meat, and you do not cook it one second longer than is utterly necessary. In fact, ideally, you show the cow a Bic lighter, and dig in.

Reese whistled under his breath as he stood before the grill, coaxing his steaks to their grandest height. I plated salad and ladled duck's blood soup into bowls. Out front, the conversation rumbled on at a better pace. I started to relax and let the scent of cooking steak fill me with optimism.

Too damned soon as it turned out.

Movement caught the corner of my eye. Out past the patio lights, something flitted through the Aldens' terraced garden. I jerked my head around and stared at the shadowed bushes. The silver and gold lights of Manhattan glowed against the night sky like distant fireflies, and I saw nothing, except some waving branches. Somewhere, a car door slammed. Then, the house door slammed. Voices shouted. Reese froze, tongs raised.

Gabriel Renault, with brother Jacques right on his heels, barged through the swinging door in a cloud of cold and frantic fear.

"They're after us!"

12

"In here." I yanked open one of the empty cupboards under the sink.

Gabriel ducked down, knotting himself up with the kind of speed only nightbloods and yoga masters can manage. Jacques stared for one split second and lit out the French doors.

Running footsteps and outraged shrieks sounded in the dining room. I swore and kicked the cabinet door shut. The slam barely had a chance to fade before two bulked-out men in matching blue suits burst into the kitchen to find me stirring potatoes, and Reese bent over the sizzling steaks.

"Where'd they go?" shouted the taller of the suits.

"What the hell . . . !" Reese demanded.

"This is *your* fault!" screamed Deanna from the other side of the door. "You called them!"

"Where'd they go?" The shorter suit bellowed. Reese raised his tongs as if to point, but I held up my hand.

"Who's asking? And what're you all doing in *my* kitchen?" I am a chef. All kitchens I cook in are my kitchen. This is a rule.

"Deanna, *control*," said Mrs. Alden from the dining room. "We need—"

"We do not *need*! I'm sick of this!"

"Oh, fer chrissakes." The shorter suit yanked an ID wallet from his pocket and flashed it in front of my face just long enough for me to read IMMIGRATION AND CUSTOMS ENFORCEMENT.

ICE was chasing after undocumented nightbloods in a witch's home? At some point, this was going to be funny.

"You can't do this!" Trudy banged into the kitchen from the dining room and planted her hands on her hips. "If you've got a warrant, I want it on the counter, now!"

"And it's another one!" Taller Suit yanked a sheaf of papers out of his jacket and tossed them to Trudy, who caught them as they smacked against her chest. He turned back to Reese. "Where are they?"

"Came and went about ten seconds ago." Reese pointed his tongs toward the door to the side porch. Not that either one of us has ever dealt with ICE raiding a kitchen before. Yes, that is my story and yes, I'm sticking to it.

The ICE guys swore. Taller Suit yelled something into his sleeve as he slammed open the side door and vanished outside. I stared after them.

The cupboard door rattled.

"He's got a passport!" Deanna was shouting. "They're both registered! They'll be out before morning!"

"That's not all they've got, Adrienne," said that man's deep voice. Memory told me I'd heard it before, but it didn't tell me where. "They've also just robbed your house."

"What?" cried a whole Greek chorus.

What!

Feet thundered across wood, out in the dining room at first, and then overhead. I leaned a knee up against the cupboard. The door went still. Trudy was looking from the warrant to me, to the warrant again. I met her gaze. She could give the whole thing away right then. But she just marched back out into the dining room, papers in her fist.

"Well, ain't this just a hoot and a half," muttered Reese.

"Yeah."

Feet tromped down the stairs again, a whole parade of them.

"I don't believe you!" shrieked Deanna

"As your mother pointed out, Deanna, you need to get control . . . ," said the man.

"That is enough." Mrs. Alden's words were colder than a vampire's touch.

"Now look . . ."

The door to the dining room swung back hard as Deanna pushed her way through, tears streaming down her outraged face. I grabbed her arm, firmly. "Is everything all right, Ms. Alden?" I asked loudly for the benefit of the ears listening from the dining room. For Deanna, I jerked my chin down toward the cabinet.

Deanna's eyes flipped open. I nodded.

"No! It is not all right!" She pulled away from me and shouted so her family could hear every word without having to make an extra trip into the kitchen. "My grandfather had my dinner party raided, and now Henri and Jacques have taken off, and we've lost . . . something valuable!"

Grandfather? Now it was my turn to freeze, and I did so, with my hand in the air as if it were looking for something to clutch. *Grandfather?*

I didn't have much time for fear and shock to really set in, because just then, the taller of the ICE suits shoved open the porch door again, letting in spring breeze and traffic noise.

"You!" Deanna's hand went up. A fireball the size of an ostrich egg burned in her palm. Power thrummed through the kitchen, and her hair stood out from her head, crackling with energy.

"Holy sh . . . !" Shorter Suit slammed against Taller Suit's back just as Taller Suit shoved his hand under his jacket in a gesture familiar to everyone who's ever watched a TV cop show.

I snatched up the nearest bowl of duck soup and dashed it in Deanna's face.

"Bitch!" she screamed.

"Calm down!" I roared back. "You do not try to set fire to ICE!" Yes, I said it. I was having a bad night, okay? "And you!" I rounded on the Suit brothers. "Why aren't you out chasing vampires?"

Shorter Suit swore and holstered the flashlight he was carrying. Reese swore and pulled steak off the grill. I swore and handed Deanna a dish towel to help with the rivers of reddish broth pouring down her cheeks and dripping from the ends of her hair. Then, I swore and dumped potatoes into the colander. Fortunately, they were going to be mashed; otherwise I'd have to get *really* mad at somebody because they were now thoroughly overcooked.

"You sure he went through here?" Taller Suit asked me and Reese. Innocent as an ex-army enlisted lamb, Reese nodded. I dumped the potatoes from the colander back into the pot, so I could keep my face averted. "Okay. If he circles back, you're going to tell us, right?"

"Yes, sir," I said. Fortunately, he didn't stick around to register my lack of poker face.

Deanna mopped broth off her face, taking a layer of rouge and mascara with it. She glowered at Shorter Suit as he pushed past me to disappear back into the dining room. I smelled smoke and warming broth. I gripped the bride-to-be's hand and shook my head hard, at the same time wondering what I'd do if she actually turned her internal flamethrower on me.

But all Deanna did was wipe her eyes one more time. "I'm going to wash off," she informed me, her voice very low and very tight. "When I get back, no more games—do you understand?"

With an icy calm that would have done her mother proud, Deanna walked straight through the door to the back stairs.

My head fell back. "Anybody else?" I demanded of the universe at large.

"Um, Chef?" said Reese.

The dining room door was swinging open one more time. My heart swelled painfully in the base of my throat and, slowly and reluctantly, I straightened up.

That was how I got my first look at Lloyd Maddox in the flesh.

13

I'd spent a fair amount of time watching Lloyd Maddox on Internet videos and assorted news shows, sort of like you watch the approaching train when you're standing on the tracks. I'd never been able to reconcile the fact that this demagogue, who had it in for my brother and his kind in the worst possible way, was sweet, funny, smart Brendan Maddox's grandfather.

When you hang around vampires, you get used to people with the ability to exude an air of menace, but even Anatole would have had a tough time matching up to Grandpa Lloyd. Age had turned Lloyd's hair white and settled his eyes deep into their sockets, but not so deep you couldn't immediately see they were still clear and sharp. Wind and sun had burned the man's skin a permanent tawny brown and creased it with an entire atlas's worth of lines. The bones underneath that weathered face, though, were hard, sharp, and strong.

"You're Charlotte Caine," he said slowly.

"And you're Lloyd Maddox." I forced my spine to draw me up to my full height and, believe me, my spine protested. It would much rather have collapsed into a jellylike heap. "Can I help you?"

Maddox looked over my head to Reese. Only when he realized there was no authority there did he lower his gaze back to me. If I hadn't already been predisposed to dislike this person, that would have done it.

"Yes, you can help me." Lloyd Maddox's attention was heavy, like a good, sharp cleaver. "You can tell me where Gabriel Renault and that other one, Jacques, actually went."

"Sorry," I said, because that word could cover a lot of ground while still remaining content-free.

Maddox looked at Reese again. I didn't want to take my eyes off Maddox, so I couldn't see what Reese was doing, but there was plenty of clattering involved. Then, Lloyd Maddox smiled, and my cowardly spine tried once more to collapse under me. He had Brendan's smile, if Brendan had suddenly decided to take a walk on the dark side. Maddox strode across the kitchen, and I wondered frantically how to create a distraction. Did I have anything hot I could spill? But he passed right by the sink and headed for the basement stairs.

Clearly, Reese had let his glance drift in a certain misleading direction. I rounded the counter to stand beside him. "Never should have doubted you," I murmured, prodding at the resting steaks with careful fingers to test for doneness.

"No, Chef."

The door from the dining room swung open again. This time it was Brendan. With him came a shorter, older, paunchier man who had to be related to Deanna.

"You okay in here, Charlotte?" Brendan asked. I nodded, and Brendan gestured for the paunchy man behind him to come forward. "This is Scott Alden. Uncle Scott, this is Charlotte Caine and this is her sous-chef, Reese Turner."

So this was where the girls had gotten their coloring from. Scott Alden scrutinized me with bland brown eyes from behind a pair of square, tortoiseshell glasses. His brown hair was fading and thinning, and his white oxford shirt was buttoned all the way up to the neck. The tie was solid blue, the cuff links gold squares, and the wedding ring on his hand was a plain, thick gold band. From what Robert Kemp and Google told me, members of Congress and foreign princes lined up to ask this man to handle their fortunes, but the image he projected was of a stolid, boring, if high-level, nerd. On the subway, I wouldn't have looked at him twice.

"Chef, I am sorry about the uproar." Scott Alden had a good handshake, nothing false or tentative about it. Now that he was putting some effort into it, I could detect a certain charm about him, the kind that came with knowing you looked like a fish out of water, and you were comfortable with the joke.

At his side, Brendan was giving me a hard look. I flicked my eyes toward the sink. Brendan understood immediately and didn't turn his head to confirm.

"We're going to have to apologize to you both," Scott Alden was saying. "As you may have guessed, we're having an emergency here, and the dinner's been cancelled."

Now, I hate wasting food, especially good food that I've put work into, but I can understand how an ICE raid puts a damper on a party. Reese, though, looked at the steaks as if he were watching a crime in progress.

"Is the family going to want something . . . ?" I tried.

Mr. Alden glanced over his shoulder toward the now-silent dining room. "Maybe in a little bit. I am truly sorry about this. My father-in-law . . ."

On cue, heavy footsteps sounded on the basement stairs, climbing up to join us without any unnecessary hurry.

"Speak of the devil," breathed Scott Alden. I bit the inside of my cheek to keep from smiling. I didn't dare look at Brendan right then, or Lloyd would have caught me laughing. As it was, when the Maddox patriarch reappeared, he ignored both Scott and Brendan and stalked right up to me. Brendan moved a half step closer to me. Lloyd Maddox's frown hardened.

"We're going to talk, you and I, Chef Caine."

I hate being loomed over, and it brings out all kinds of attitude. "Anytime." I met Maddox's gaze. This time nothing collapsed. "I'll be here all week."

"Lloyd?" said Scott before his father-in-law could get another dig in. "I think Adrienne wants a word."

"I imagine she does." Lloyd took his time weighing his options, and he made sure we all saw him doing it. Should he pick this fight now? No, we were not worth the trouble—not yet anyway. Lloyd pulled back and started for the door, but he stopped to look over his shoulder.

"Are you coming, Brendan?"

Brendan did not move. "In a minute."

The look Lloyd flashed Brendan right then made me glad I didn't have anything sharp in my hand. Fortunately, he let Scott Alden herd him out of the kitchen before I could remember exactly where I'd laid my paring knife.

"You got it in here?" Brendan murmured to me.

I gave his hand a quick squeeze. "We're good. You got it out there?"

He grimaced but nodded. "I'll be back as soon as I can."

The door swung shut behind Brendan, and the kitchen went quiet again. The scents of beef, spilled consommé, and roasted fennel hung in the suddenly quiet air. Reese scowled. "We wouldn't have had to take this gig if you'd set us up with a truck in the first place."

"Just cook, Reese. I'll deal with the clients."

"Yes, Chef. Except the cooking's done and the clients ain't eating."

There's nothing worse than a sous who's got a point. I drummed my fingers on the counter and stared out at the softly lit garden. I looked toward the back stairs and then at the garden again. Carefully recessed electric torches outlined the pathway through the neatly groomed shrubs. Nothing I could see moved out there. From the looks of it, the show was over. "All right, Reese, you head out. I'll take care of things here."

"You sure?"

"No." I glanced toward the cupboard under the sink, then turned my back on it. "But it'll give me one less thing to keep track of. Maybe you can check in on Nightlife on the way home and just give me the heads-up if there's anything I should know about?"

Reese bowed his head, clearly feeling the burden of my request. "Chef," he said. "I'd do anything for you, except spy on Zoe."

"You're not spying."

"Fine, you call her and tell her that. Then I'll stop by." Reese hung his chef's coat and apron on one of the hooks by the side door.

"I cannot believe you did this!" A voice rose from the next room. It was Mrs. Alden.

"I didn't do anything," replied Lloyd Maddox. "If ICE received an anonymous tip, it was not from me."

Reese was looking from the door, to me, and I swear he mouthed *Truck* at me before he intelligently and discreetly slid out the door.

"It was petty and spiteful and . . ." Mrs. Alden's voice was growing shrill.

"And it was not my doing, Adrienne."

"Then how did they know to come tonight, when Gabriel and his friends just happened to all be in the house?" inquired Brendan coolly.

"You've had three vampires here for over a week. Perhaps there's a concerned citizen on the block," Lloyd said, matching Brendan's cool tone perfectly. It was more than a little creepy.

"You promised you wouldn't interfere," Mr. Alden snapped. "I had your word!"

"If I had wanted to get rid of Deanna's nightblood, you can be sure, I would not have alerted the government to the fact," Lloyd replied. "I am too old to start leaving a paper trail."

So, if this freak show wasn't Grandpa's doing, who made the call? And why? My fingers were drumming the counter again. This was getting to be a habit. For one moment I wondered if it had been Brendan who called in the tip, to get Henri Renault away from me. I dismissed that. If there was one thing I knew, it was that ICE raids take time to organize. This little drama had been planned weeks ago.

And that meant whoever did put in that tip had known the date and time of the Aldens' private party.

"Where is Deanna?" asked Scott Alden abruptly.

"She ran out through the kitchen," said Mrs. Alden wearily. "I expect she'll be back when she discovers she can't cry Gabriel's way out of ICE custody."

"All right." Scott Alden sighed. "Maybe we should just all call it a night? Lloyd, we can talk about this in the morning."

"There's nothing to talk about," replied Lloyd. "You've shut me out of the entire conversation regarding this disastrous marriage. I don't see why I should agree to help you sort out your problems with a group of illegal undead."

"No one is asking for your help with anything," said Mrs. Alden. "I just . . . Never mind. Go home, Papa."

Maddox replied, but so softly, I couldn't hear the words. A moment later, footsteps crossed hardwood. Doors opened and closed. Then, Deanna's silhouette descended the outside stairway that curved from the balcony above down to the garden patio. The bride-to-be eased herself through the kitchen's French doors. She barely spared me a glance as she hurried to the sink and yanked open the cupboard. Gabriel Renault rolled out and unfolded himself. In an eyeblink, they had their arms wrapped around each other.

"He's gone," Deanna breathed. "It's okay. You're okay." She buried her head against his shoulder.

If I hadn't already believed there was a real connection between these two before, I did now. I turned away, intending to give them their moment.

"Thanks," Gabriel said behind me after what turned out to be a very long moment. "I really appreciate it."

"We appreciate it." Deanna stood close beside him now, both her hands wrapped around one of his. "Sorry about the fire and everything."

"Glad I could help." I just hoped they couldn't see me wondering if I'd done the right thing.

Fortunately, my feelings seemed to be the last thing on Deanna's mind right then. "What're we going to do about Henri?" Deanna squeezed her fiancé's hand. "And Jacques? They just rounded everybody up like . . . like . . ." Metaphors failed her. "I'm going to *kill* Granddad!"

"We'll figure something out." Gabriel kissed the top of her head.

"Um . . . ," I said, uncertain whether I was about to cross a line. "If you need one, I know a good lawyer."

"You do? Really?" cried Deanna.

"Really. Rafe Wallace."

"Rafe Wallace?" Gabriel repeated. "I've heard of him, I think."

"He's a pretty big name. He . . . did some work for me and my brother." In fact, Rafe's one of the best paranormal lawyers in the city. He's also one of the most expensive, but somehow, I didn't think his billable rate was going to be an issue for a member of the Alden family. I pulled my phone from my purse, copied Rafe's number down on the notepad on the counter, and tore off the page.

Deanna seized the paper and Gabriel's hand. "Thank you!"

"Yes, thank you." Gabriel's relief was palpable. Because he was a vampire, I mean this literally. It rolled off him in a sweet cloud, and I could feel the tension unknotting from my shoulders. "I owe you for this."

"We both do," said Deanna emphatically, but then she turned away as if I'd ceased to exist. "We should call now," she said to Gabriel.

But Gabriel hesitated. "Deanna . . . let me handle this."

"What? Why?"

"Look, *chérie.* We talked about Henri, and the past. I don't want you dragged into anything that might come up because he's tried to pull a fast one."

This was definitely not meant for me to hear. I tried not to listen, but that would have been a lot easier if either one of them had remembered I was standing right there.

"Just let me take care of it." He squeezed Deanna's hands. "You take care of your family."

"Don't tempt me," she muttered. "All right. If you insist."

I stepped away, shuffling things on the counter. Gabriel noticed and grimaced.

"Come on." He smiled gently and kissed Deanna's forehead. "Let's give the chef back her kitchen." Deanna's brow smoothed out a little, and together they hurried out toward the back stairs.

"Good luck," I said as they disappeared.

Voices still rose and fell in the dining room. I could make out Brendan's and Mrs. Alden's, and Scott Alden's. The volume, however, had dropped down to the point where I couldn't make out the words from where I stood by the cooktop. Knowing Brendan would give me the rundown later, I tried not to listen to the murmurs and rumbles. Instead, I surveyed my bowls and plates, allowing myself my own moment of regret for the wasted labor. The steaks were the worst of it. Reese had outdone himself. They were exquisite; perfectly seared on the outside, pink and juicy and full of flavor inside. They could be used as a base for something else tomorrow, but they would never be this good again.

I couldn't do it. I just couldn't do it.

I squared my shoulders and marched into the dining room. The remains of the bridesmaids' arrival party turned to stare at me.

"Look," I said to them all. "I know it's been a bad night and the party's over, but I have a kitchen full of food going to waste in here, and you all must be starving. You might as well eat."

There're forms of telepathy that belong strictly to families, and I could feel that particular current flowing through these people. Silently, balance shifted, and decisions were ceded. Mrs. Alden in particular looked for a long time at her balding husband. I noticed how she didn't speak until he'd nodded.

"Thank you, Chef Caine. I think that would be a good idea."

"Why don't you sit down then? I'll have things out in a second."

I went back into the kitchen and set to work. A minute later, Trudy Lyons appeared with a tray. Her eyes looked red-rimmed, and the pucker was back around her mouth.

"I got this." She didn't look at me as she started loading up plates of salad. It occurred to me abruptly that I hadn't seen her since she'd walked off with the warrant. And she'd have most certainly known about the timing of this little dinner party.

Now, however, was not the time to probe.

The late, much-scaled-down dinner service went smoothly. I saw nobody but Trudy. The only sounds that came back through that swinging door were the clatter of silverware against dishes and the occasional murmur of subdued conversation. Between getting the abbreviated set of courses ready, and starting cleanup, I had plenty of time to ponder the whole set of questions raised by the evening's dramatic events. I was also painfully aware there were precious few places I could go for answers right now.

When Trudy came back from serving dessert, I had two plates of steak, potatoes, and salad ready, along with a fresh thermos of coffee.

"Thought you could probably use this."

"Thanks, Chef Caine . . ."

"Charlotte. Pepper?" I held out the grinder.

"Great."

"Coffee?"

"Hell, yeah."

I filled her cup, made sure the cream pitcher was in easy reach, and settled down to my own dinner. We both ate, one ear on the dining room, alert for any sound of waning conversation.

"So, you worked for the Aldens long?" I asked, pouring another coffee for myself. It was a lame opening, but it was all I had.

Thankfully, Trudy didn't seem to notice the lameness. "Since before she had the girls."

"Must be nice to have a steady job."

Trudy shrugged. "Usually. Although lately . . ." She set her cup down abruptly and rubbed her reddened eyes. "Charlotte . . . Damn, I'm going to sound like some kind of bigot or something, but . . . you know about . . ." She made the upside-down air quotes with one hand that had come to symbolize fangs in the pop culture. "Is it true they can control people with their gaze?"

This is one of those questions that comes up a lot. That's no surprise, given the amount of misinformation about the vampire whammy flying around. "Yes, they can, but the whammy really only works for direct commands. It's somewhere between difficult and impossible for a vampire to cause someone to, say, fall in love, or change their entire personality long term."

"So, Deanna, you don't think she's doing this because that . . . vampire . . . is controlling her?"

"Well, I haven't seen them together a whole lot, but I don't think so."

"I suppose that's a relief." Trudy pushed the remaining food around on her plate, then picked up her cup, looked at the coffee, and sipped.

"Do you know where they met?"

"Not exactly. Adrienne and Kay-Kay are active on a lot of charity boards and go to a lot of dinners. Deanna goes with them sometimes." Kay-Kay? I tried to picture the Karina Alden I'd seen in front of Perception as a little girl who could have a nickname like "Kay-Kay," and failed. "I think she started seeing Gabriel around the circuit, and even at a few private homes." Which would tally with Anatole's description of the Renaults as professional party guests.

I found myself wondering where Kay-Kay was right now, how she'd met Oscar, and when they'd started going out. I wondered when and why she'd left the paternal brownstone. The departure had clearly been recent. It also occurred to me that Oscar would have had this dinner on his schedule before he walked out, and he might have shared that schedule with Karina. The question was, was the raid the cover for the theft, or was the theft just a crime of the opportunity provided by the raid? Okay, that was one of the thousand questions.

"What I don't get is why Gabriel would agree to marry her, or why she'd even want to marry him," Trudy was saying.

"Vampires need human companionship. It's not just about the blood." I could have done without the mental jump cut to Anatole's green eyes and wicked smile just then. "We give something to them that other nightbloods can't. Deanna seems nice. Maybe Gabriel wants the company."

"That should be a relief to hear, but it just seems so . . . twisted." She frowned at her empty plate.

"A lot of this is hard to wrap your mind around if you're not used to it." I tried for gentleness, but I'm not very good at that, so she'd have to settle for blunt sympathy. "I guess working for the Maddoxes, you don't get many chances to meet the local nightbloods."

Trudy gave a tight little snort through her narrow nose. "Hardly. And after all we went through . . ." She stopped herself, made a face, and got to her feet. "They're slowing down out there. I need to go clear plates." She picked up her tray.

Damn. Again, I had no choice but the direct approach. "Trudy?"

"Mmm?"

"The other chef? Oscar Simmons? He said he was offered a bribe to disrupt things with the family. Do you think Lloyd might have tried to buy him off?"

Trudy turned away without answering, but as she started toward the door she said, "No way. Not his style. But Adrienne might."

14

"How's it going in here?"

When finally Brendan reemerged from the dining room, I was on my own, stacking plates into the commercial-grade dishwasher. Trudy had hung her keys up on the Peg-Board by the coat hooks and gone home a half hour before, with barely a word to me. I was left with nothing to do but clean, and wait.

I shrugged. "How'd it go out there?"

"About the same." Brendan looked tired. On reflex, I wondered if he'd gotten enough to eat at dinner. Sitting with a group of relatives spoiling for a fight would be enough to sour anybody's appetite. "Any idea where Gabriel took off to? Deanna came back just long enough to announce she wasn't coming down anymore tonight and vanished upstairs with Peri and Lois, but we haven't seen any of them since."

Reflexively, my gaze swept all the kitchen doors. They'd developed this tendency to open at awkward moments to let in highly awkward people. This time, though, they stayed closed, so I told Brendan about giving Deanna and Gabriel Rafe Wallace's phone number.

"Thanks," he said softly. Then he straightened up,

visibly trying to shake off what had turned into a very long night. "Aunt Adrienne said you're staying here for the duration. I'll show you your room." Brendan picked up my suitcase from where I'd left it with the coats. He also grabbed an old-fashioned doctor's bag I'd never seen before.

Well, I thought. *That's iiiiinteresting . . .* My stomach started doing strange fluttery things. Nothing between Brendan and me had yet involved his needing a change of clothes. "I suppose you just happened to ask your aunt which room is mine?"

"Just happened to." He should have smiled when he said it, one of his long, slow, lazy smiles. But he didn't. The strange fluttery feelings died an early death.

Brendan led me all the way up the zigzagging back stairs to the fourth floor, right under the roof. Probably this attic space had once been servant's quarters, but somebody had done some remodeling. The scarred door Brendan opened led to a lovely, airy bedroom with a sharply sloped ceiling. White pillows and handmade quilts covered a brass bed. The dresser and nightstand were bird's eye maple. A chair with embroidered cushions stood in front of a pint-sized fireplace with a landscape painting hanging over its plaster mantel. The shades of blue and cream swirling in the Persian rug on the floor matched the colors in the curtains and the cushions on the window seat.

"Whoa," I breathed.

"Aunt Adrienne wanted to make sure you'd be comfortable." Brendan just about filled the tiny room as he squeezed past to lay my suitcase on the bed.

"I may never go home." I had to lean down to push the window curtains back, but when I did, I found I also had a spectacular view of Manhattan lit up across the river.

A distinct warmth moved up close behind me. A moment later, I had the familiar weight of Brendan's hands on my shoulders. "Charlotte, this really isn't how I wanted you to meet my family."

"There probably weren't any good ways to introduce me to your grandfather. At least it's out of the way now." I turned. Brendan was very close, not that there was any other way for him to be in this room. The ceiling was so low, he had to slouch. He looked bashful and boyish doing it. Another time I would have noted how unbelievably cute it looked, but right then I was too worried about how worried he looked.

"Brendan? I'm going to ask this once. What the hell's happened?"

"Something got stolen."

That much I'd heard. "What was it?"

"You must have seen it on the mantel in the living room—that little silver gun."

"Crap." I thought about all those antiques neatly lined up in that black and white living room. When I'd walked in that first day, I'd wondered if they could be magic. Now I wondered if one could be this thing Brendan had talked about, the Arall.

"And, of course," muttered Brendan, "we can't find two of the nightbloods who were here, so . . ."

So of course everybody was all set to assume they stole it. The problem was, it was a reasonable assumption. "I don't suppose anybody's going to do something smart like call the cops?"

"What do you think?"

I'd already said what I thought. But I had other thoughts. In fact, I had a whole lot of thoughts. "You call them."

Brendan shook his head. "I can't."

"Brendan!"

"I know! I know, and believe me I don't like it either. If it were anything but the Arall, I'd have Linus O'Grady down here right now."

"So, that gun *was* the Arall?" Who kept the family secrets on the mantelpiece? The most feared vampire hunters this side of the Atlantic, that's who. Why? Who knew?

I sure didn't know, and clearly the man in front of me didn't know, because he was slumping his shoulders even more now.

"You are not going to believe this," said Brendan.

"Try me."

"I don't know if the gun is the Arall or not. I've never seen the Arall."

"How can you have never seen it?"

"It's a *secret*, Charlotte, and like the name says, it's a last resort. I know it exists, but that's it."

"So, this stolen pistol—it could be the Arall, or the Jimmy Hoffa murder weapon, or anything."

"Right. But Grandfather and Aunt Adrienne don't want a fuss made about it going missing."

"Really? How's that working out for you guys?" I regretted the words as soon as I'd said them. "I'm sorry, Brendan. I shouldn't have . . . It's just turning into one of those nights."

"Tell me about it, and you're not wrong." He lifted his head as far as he could without bashing into the ceiling. "I never should have let you get into this."

"I'm a grown chef, Brendan. I knew I was jumping into a mess, and I could have said no." I smiled, but Brendan was very clearly not going to play along with my attempt to lighten the mood. My stomach bunched itself up and tried to hide somewhere in back of my spine. "Brendan, what's really going on here?"

"I don't *know*." He threw out his hands. One slammed against the wall, and he winced. "But I'll tell you what. I'd give a lot to find out what ICE is doing raiding for vampires after dark."

"What?"

Brendan looked at me as if I'd just achieved a supernatural level of density. It was not a look he'd repeat often, if we both knew what was good for him. "Come on, Charlotte. Who chases down vampires when they're awake? You wait until daylight when they're out cold, and *then* you go get them."

I opened my mouth. I closed it. I slowly but silently enumerated all the kinds of idiot I was. You saw it all the time in the movies and on TV. Cops, or FBI agents, or other Good Guys burst in on the vampire hideout, stakes in hand, and a fight ensued with lots of blood and flying dust. But, of course, that wasn't what really happened. Despite evidence to the contrary, cops and government agents aren't stupid. If they know where the vampires are, all they have to do is wait for sunrise.

"Those badges were real," I said weakly. "The warrant looked it too." At least Trudy thought so, and she seemed to know what she was talking about.

"It was real. I checked." Of course he had. It was the kind of thing a professional security expert would do. "And I made a call to a friend of mine at Immigration. He said those two agents are on the books, and on shift. But this 'raid' was staged."

"So somebody could get his hands on that gun in the confusion?"

"Sure looks that way." Brendan made a fist, pressed the side against the sloping ceiling, and leaned in. It was the slow-motion version of punching the wall.

"Is this about the wedding?" I asked. "I mean, they'll have to postpone the event, right? Maybe that was the point."

"It could be," said Brendan slowly. "But this just doesn't feel like my family with a mad on."

"Why not?"

"Too clumsy. If anybody in our clan was going to put together something this big, you wouldn't be able to see the seams. And when we go in after the vampires, they do not get away." He said that the same way he'd say the sun would rise in the morning.

"Could it have been a warning shot of some kind? Somebody trying to scare somebody?"

"I think it must have been. But who?" Brendan started pacing, without seeing a thing in front of him, including me. "Who? Who? Who?"

"Do you think it has something to do with this particular set of vampires?"

"Or a particular Maddox." He stopped in front of the mantel and glowered at the innocent landscape as if it were withholding evidence. "There are other clans who know about the Arall's existence and are really worried about this wedding. One of those ICE agents might have been a warlock, and maybe he took the gun to keep it away from the Renaults. Could this get any more complicated?"

"Um . . . yes." I told him about how I'd met up with Linus O'Grady outside Perception and what had happened afterward. Then I told him about how Jacques had introduced himself in the alleyway.

They invented the word "thunderous" to describe the expression that settled over Brendan right then. Jacques was very lucky he wasn't anywhere in the house. If he was smart, he was nowhere in New York State.

"Do you want to go home?" Brendan asked, his voice terrifyingly even. "Just say so, and I'll take you out of here."

His hands were clenched hard enough to turn the knuckles white. I stood, and I stepped close to him. I took both those strong hands, and I held on. I held his gaze too, and we stood there like that, until he loosened his fists.

"Nobody plays me for an all-day sucker," I said, enunciating each word clearly. "Nobody uses me or my people for their games. I am going to find out who's doing this, and I will hand them to O'Grady. Possibly wrapped in puff pastry and slow roasted. Are you with me, Brendan?"

"Always," he answered.

I kissed him for that. I meant the gesture to be small and

soft, but it did not stay that way. Brendan is a man who enjoys a good kiss. He's thorough, and he takes his time. When we finally ran out of breath, we still stood there, just holding on to each other. Brendan brushed his mouth along the edge of my ear, and I could feel his warm, sweet breath against my skin. "Charlotte."

"I can't," I told him, as gently as possible. "Not here." As in not in his aunt's house while we were in the middle of a whole great, big honkin' heap of not knowing what was going on. Anywhere else, really, and any other time. The middle of Fifth Avenue during rush hour was not out of the question at this point.

With a sigh, Brendan rested his forehead briefly on my shoulder, but he did let go, and he stepped back.

"Sorry. I shouldn't have. It's just . . ." He cupped my cheek with his hand. "You are so damned gorgeous; you know that?"

I was beyond melting now, beyond the giggles and blushes and the warmth from a spectacular kiss. This was someplace deeper and more important, where I had to be honest, or I risked losing everything.

"I want to be sure," I said. The fact that I was echoing Anatole made me wince inside. But even that was appropriate. Because more than being in a strange house, more than being in the middle of a green and growing disaster, it was the existence of Anatole that made me hesitate. I wasn't going to play games with Brendan. I wasn't going to go back and forth between him and Anatole. I'd watched that kind of scenario play out before, and it wasn't good for anybody involved. I would make my decision and stick with it.

"Okay." Brendan shoved his hands in his back pockets. "I'd better get out of here, before I start trying to convince you you're sure now." I did not whimper at the thought of how he might go about creating my conviction, and I am proud of that. "But I want to put a warding on this room," he went on. A warding is a kind of magical security fence. It keeps out malevolent powers and, provided the warlock building it is strong enough, malevolent people. I had no doubt that Brendan was strong enough to keep out the IRS if he felt the need.

"Are we warding against vampires or against grandfathers?" I asked.

"Yes." He said it with utter seriousness. Brendan never works magic casually. In fact, the few times I'd seen him actually use his powers, either somebody'd been in immediate danger, or he'd been really cranky about it, or both.

"Is there anything I need to do?" I asked. "Or should I just head downstairs and let you, um, work?"

"Actually, I'll be able to build it more tightly if you're here, since you're ultimately what the ward's going to protect."

"So I just sit here?"

"I'm afraid so." Brendan crouched down beside the black bag he'd carried up with my suitcase, opened the catch, and pulled out a stick of chalk, and a Ziploc bag of what looked like kosher salt. Clearly we were going for the high-tech warlockery here.

"Brendan?" I settled back onto the window seat.

"Hmm?" He started sketching symbols on the floorboards in front of the threshold, and dusting salt on top of them.

"You don't like magic much."

"It's not that I don't like it; I just think it's more trouble than it's worth. Harry Potter and Hogwarts and all that sound great in theory, but when you actually give adolescent kids the power to alter other people's reality, it gets messy."

"Did you ever get messy?"

"Yes. More than once." He sat back on his heels and waited for me to ask more. I didn't, and he went back to work with the salt and chalk.

When the symbols and the seasoning were the way he wanted, Brendan stood up and pulled a box of matches out of his pocket. He'd explained to me once that magic workers tended to be sympathetic to a particular element; earth, air, fire or water. The Maddoxes were mostly attuned to fire, although every so often one of them came closer to water or air.

Brendan struck the match and turned the flame inward toward his palm, like Europeans do with lit cigarettes. He began to whisper, soft and fast, and, I was fairly sure, not in English. He walked from corner to corner across the room, his hands cupped close enough around that flame that my palms began to heat up in sympathy. The flame didn't flicker. The smell of sulfur and smoke wafted around him, too strong to be coming from one tiny match. My skin prickled and I smelled something new; something warm, familiar, and strong, like the sidewalk smell after a warm rain. There was a taste too; cinnamon and ginger, and a little bit of chili. Who knew magic came in flavors?

Brendan came to a halt in the threshold. He raised the flame high overhead and ran it down both walls and across the floor to trace the shape of the door. Then he stepped into the hall. The match winked out, taking scents and flavors with it.

I blinked, startled. "Is that it?"

Brendan held up his hand, palm toward me, as if running it over an invisible wall. "That's it. You can come out if you want."

I did, coming to stand beside him in the hallway. I didn't know what to say, so I went with the obvious. "Thanks."

"You're welcome." We stood there for another awkward minute, each trying to signal to the other the conflicting desire for another kiss and the knowledge that it was not a good idea right now, considering the circumstances.

"Talk to you tomorrow?" I asked.

"Talk to you tomorrow," he agreed.

Then we had to stand there another minute, acknowledging that the message had been received, and then for a final minute after that, because from the get-go neither one of us had ever known how to say good-bye in the middle of this kind of silence.

Finally, he started down the stairs, and I went back into my comfortable little room, changed into my favorite oversized pajamas, got into bed, and waited for the memory of Brendan's kiss to fade away enough for me to roll over and get some sleep.

I waited a very long time.

15

It was barely ten in the morning when I made my way down the back stairs, tying my bandanna around my head and wondering how long it would be before my hair got long enough to braid again. Despite the events of the previous evening, or maybe because of them, I'd slept pretty well. Now the scent of fresh-brewed coffee drew me like a mirage in the desert. I shouldered my way into the kitchen in time to see Reese standing by the fridge, clutching Hank, my line cook, by both shoulders.

"You're sure?" Reese's face lit up with a huge grin. "We really got i—"

But Reese spotted me and snapped back to attention as if he were still in the army.

"Morning, Reese. Hank." I did my best casual glide into the suddenly very quiet room. "What'd we get?"

"Bacon quiche!" squeaked Hank, shoving golden brown and delicious egg pie across the counter toward me. "We made two! But they only ate one! Not as many people to breakfast!"

"Those bridesmaids are all watching their weight," added Reese, who was suddenly very involved in pouring a cup of coffee. "Here you go, Chef. Just the way you like it." He pushed the mug to sit beside the quiche.

That I was able to leave both wonderfully fragrant breakfast items on the counter and ignore my frantic stomach for a full twenty seconds was a tribute to the level of self-control necessary to the professional chef. Or perhaps it was a tribute to the level of suspicion being around one too damned many mysteries can raise. "What's going on, guys?" I asked.

"Nothing!" Hank's throat was so tight, it was bugging his eyes out. "Gotta get back, you know? I'm helping Marie with the bread. Think maybe, like, switch over to pastry. 'Bye!" And he was gone out the side door.

I turned to Reese. "What's going on, Reese?"

"Nothing, Chef."

I won't say the penny dropped then, but it definitely rattled. "Does this have *anything* to do with a food truck?"

"No. Why? Did you change your mind about a truck for Nightlife?"

"No! We are not getting a truck!"

"'Cause I'm just saying, if we had a truck . . ."

"You're getting a truck?" Trudy pushed her way through the door from the back stairs, carrying a bucket full of spray bottles and rags. "Those new foodie trucks are just so cool."

I was truly beginning to hate all these doors. "We are not getting a truck."

"You should." Trudy pulled up a stool to the counter. "I had these Belgian waffles from this one truck the other day. Oh my God, I coulda just died and gone to heaven right there. Dibs on the coffee." She picked up my mug and downed a large gulp. I did not snatch it out of her hands. I want points for that, too.

"See, that's what I keep saying." Reese emphasized his approval by passing Trudy a slice of quiche—the one he'd originally cut for me. Not that it made any difference to me, of course. "People love a meal off a truck. And they'll line up around the block, if you just Tweet your location, and FlashNews is setting up a special food truck station for all the blogs."

I faced Reese, informing him with my eyes that we would most definitely be continuing this conversation later. "Has Mrs. Alden been asking for me?"

Trudy glanced toward the dining room door and shook her head. "No. She's been on the phone most of the morning."

"About the theft?" If she was going to take my coffee, she could darn well give me some information in return.

"Theft?" Reese paused in cutting off another slice of quiche. "They got robbed? Jesus, you'd think a place like this would be wired up its . . . butt."

"It is," said Trudy. "Whoever did this used the ICE raid for distraction."

Grim reality surged through me as the caffeine took hold. "So, you may as well know, the wedding is probably at least postponed," I told Reese. "It might be totally off. We're just waiting on the word from the clients."

Reese swore. He then sliced the rest of the way through the quiche and set the new portion on a waiting plate. "Chef, nobody said anything about it at breakfast."

"You're kidding?" I looked to Trudy for confirmation, and she nodded.

"All the girls were just going on about fittings and dye jobs and mani-pedis and what sounds like it's gonna be the Mother of All Bachelorette Parties." Reese muttered something under his breath that sounded a whole lot like "crazy effin' rich people."

"But that's imp—" Footsteps cut me off.

"Oops." Trudy swallowed her last bite of quiche. "Here it comes."

Mrs. Alden walked in from the dining room, and her gaze swept across us. As quick perusals went, this one was precise and comprehensive, noting how we were arranged and who had been talking with whom—including Trudy. Make that especially Trudy.

"Ms. Lyons, I thought you were going to take care of the guest rooms." Mrs. Alden's words carried a keenly honed edge.

Slowly, making sure her employer saw each movement, Trudy got to her feet. "I said I'd get *that* done after the foyer, Mrs. Alden." The women faced each other. No, they squared off. Except for their age, these two were direct opposites. Work had pushed Trudy's willowy body into a permanent slump, despite her legs being still long and straight. The veins and knuckles stood out on her rough hands. She wore no makeup on her puckered face, and she had allowed her braided hair to turn iron gray. Elegant Adrienne stood in front of her in a pink and apricot twin-set, probably ready for church. Her hair was dyed perfectly black, her face as smooth as the spa and Bloomingdale's cosmetics counter could make it, her hands impeccably cared for. But between these two brewed the intimate, brutal anger that can build only between very old friends, or very close family.

Mrs. Alden broke first. She turned to me, and I got to watch her pull that anger back. "Chef Caine, may I have a word?"

"Of course." I didn't bother with my notebook. I didn't care what Reese thought he'd heard. There was no way this wedding was going to happen any time soon. As I followed my soon-to-be-former client through the dining room and up the main stairs to the living room, I looked through my mental ledger to that place where I'd penciled in the two hundred K, and fondly kissed it good-bye.

"Now." Mrs. Alden took her seat in the chair by the fireplace and gestured toward the sofa. I sat. "I don't suppose you heard that, among all the other disturbances last night, this house was robbed." She looked at me very steadily as she spoke, letting me know she was giving me a chance to preserve appearances. I decided to take it.

"I'm very sorry to hear that," I answered politely. "I imagine this changes things."

"Only in that the groom's party will be smaller than was planned. Otherwise, we are moving forward."

I ran that back and played it over again. Then I added a backbeat. *Your house was robbed of an important magical artifact, possibly* the *important magical artifact during a faked ICE raid. The sire of the groom probably took it, and he has since vanished. But you're moving forward with the wedding, and you are waiting for me to give you a polite, professional response.*

This was one of those moments when I really wished I had Miss Manners on speed dial because I had no idea whatsoever how to answer this. "I . . . see."

"No, you don't, but that doesn't matter." The edge had come back to Mrs. Alden's tone. I couldn't tell whether going ahead with the wedding was her idea or not. Either way, it had pushed her very close to her personal limits. "What I need to know is, are you willing to continue as chef and caterer?"

Down to the very depths of my being, I knew staying here would be a bad idea. Just as I knew there was not enough money on the face of the earth to turn it into a good one. I should walk away. Let whatever the hell was playing out here play without me. Who cared what it was?

Unfortunately, no matter how many times I asked myself that question, one answer came back. Who cared? I did. I had a hunch I had been deliberately brought into this by person or persons unknown, and I wasn't leaving until I found out who, and why. Because there was no way it was just for my knife skills, good looks, and tapped-out bank account.

"If you want us to continue, Mrs. Alden, we are ready to do that."

She let out a long breath I'd been totally unaware she'd been holding. "Thank you, Chef Caine," she said, and I was pretty sure she meant it. "Then we'll be doing the cake tasting this afternoon as scheduled?"

I agreed and let myself be dismissed. Feeling strangely light-headed, I walked carefully down the back stairs. Either I had just witnessed the most incredible display of motherly sacrifice, or the rich really were different from the rest of us. Because nobody I hung out with on a regular basis would go ahead with a wedding when the family treasures had just been looted by the groom's relations.

"What happened, Chef?" asked Reese as I pushed my way back into the kitchen. He sat at the marble-topped island with Trudy, the coffee thermos set squarely between them. "You okay?"

"No, I'm not." I poured myself coffee and drank a big slug.

"They're not canceling, are they?" said Trudy.

I shook my head and helped myself to the lone slice of quiche they'd left behind. There are those who lose their appetites when faced with stress and mysteries. I am not one of them.

"No, of course not," Trudy said to her coffee. "That would be *sensible*."

"Are they always like this?" asked Reese.

"No. Not always. Just when it gets close to home. Then it's all to hell. Scott will do anything to keep everyone happy. Adrienne will do anything to keep everything organized, and Deanna will do everything to poke the screaming monkeys and *Karina* . . ." She stopped. "And you don't need to know any of this."

Actually I did, but this was not the time to disagree with her. If Trudy thought I was actively snooping on her employers, there was a good chance she'd close up tight.

"I take it the Renaults didn't . . . make it back last

night?" I asked, poking at the quiche to test its consistency, and carefully not looking at anything else.

"I'm told Gabriel came in just before sunrise, but the others . . ." Trudy shook her head. "I assume ICE still has them."

Or they're on the run with their haul, whatever it was. But I kept this to myself.

"So, what all went missing?" asked Reese.

I took another bite of quiche. "The thing I know about was a gun, an antique pistol off the mantel."

Trudy nodded. "If they lost anything else, they're keeping quiet about it."

"So." Reese planted his elbows on the counter. "The family got ripped off by the groom's blood relations, and we're all going to ignore it like Great Aunt Maxie's been breaking wind again?"

"Something like that, yeah," I admitted. "Listen, Reese. If you want out of this, no harm, no foul. I'll handle it." I had no idea how, but I would.

"What do I look like? I said I'd take the mission; I'm taking the mission."

"It's a catering job, not a hill."

"And your point is?"

Suddenly, Trudy was on her feet. "I'd better get to those . . . bedrooms. Adrienne's started checking up on my work." She clumped out through the door to the back stairs, but not before both of us noticed she had tears on her cheeks.

"You want me to—" Reese jerked his head to the back stairs door as it flapped shut.

"No." I drew my gaze away from the door, but slowly. "We'll figure her out later. For now, we just keep going." I downed the last of my coffee and put the mug in the sink. "I've got to hit the Terminal Market and talk with some additional suppliers. I'll be back in time for the tasting."

"Okay. I'll keep it going here."

"Thanks. And Reese?" I said as I collected my purse and notebook.

"Yes, Chef?"

I hesitated. This was not a question I wanted to ask, and the words were not lining up neatly in my head. "If something was really wrong at Nightlife, you'd tell me, wouldn't you?"

Disappointment slumped his professionally square shoulders. "You know I would."

I did, and I left there with an outsized load of guilt for even asking that question trailing along behind me.

My market business actually went more quickly than I'd expected. When you've got a big budget, suddenly the suppliers are sitting you down to their best beverages and pulling out special items that you might just happen to be interested in.

As I was leaving the market and heading for the subway, I called the house so I could make sure all remained quiet on the Alden front. Reese duly reported that Mrs. Alden had returned from church with a handful of select guests who polished off a luncheon of red snapper fillet with wild rice and a salad of summer greens. Deanna had put in a brief appearance, but she left in a cloud of bridesmaids. Mr. Alden had not been seen since breakfast, but he was expected for dinner. Otherwise, the house remained peaceful. Lloyd Maddox was nowhere to be seen, but neither, apparently was Trudy.

After I hung up with Reese, I dodged across the street while thumbing the number for Nightlife. I had no real doubt that Marie had everything in hand for the cake tasting, but the control freak in me was even stronger than my faith in my pastry chef.

"Nightlife?" Zoe picked up on the third ring.

Zoe! "Zoe?" My stride faltered, causing a student type with a backpack to have to dodge, and swear.

"Hello, Chef," said Zoe.

"What's wrong?" I demanded as I sidestepped out of the pedestrian river. "What're you doing in so early?" Panic bubbled in the pit of my stomach. It was just going on one. There was no reason for Zoe to be in the kitchen until four, three at the earliest, unless something had gone wrong.

"Nothing's wrong. Did you want to talk to Marie?"

"Yes, but . . ."

"She's right here."

"Z . . ."

"Good morning, Chef Caine." Marie's you'd-better-not-be-wasting-my-time voice said. "What can I do for you?"

"Erg-ah." I replied. Fortunately, I rallied. "I just wanted to make sure all the samples will be ready for the tasting."

"Paolo is filling them now. We will be at the Aldens' at four p.m. Was there anything else?"

"No. Yes." I squeezed my eyes shut. "Marie, is everything all right there?"

Marie's pause wasn't just pregnant; it was nine months gone. "Everything is exactly as it should be."

The sidewalk shifted underfoot. I had not heard Marie just give an evasive answer. It was not possible. Marie faced you head-on, kind of like a glacier when the ice age is coming.

"Shall I give you back to Chef Vamadev?" asked Marie.

"Yeah. Please." I sucked in a deep breath. "Zoe, you on track for opening tonight?"

"Of course. Why wouldn't we be?"

There are times when all you can do is tell the truth. "Because you're in way the hell early and you won't tell me why."

"I'm in way the hell early because I want to be sure everything's on track for opening," Zoe shot back. "If you think you need to come in and check up on us, you can do that. It's your kitchen."

I winced. I had that coming, and we both knew it. Either

I trusted Zoe, or I didn't. The big problem was, especially after Marie's nonanswer and Reese's and Hank's high-speed evasions this morning, I wasn't sure which it was. But I couldn't possibly believe Zoe was pulling some kind of fast one on me, could I?

No. I couldn't. Absolutely not. If only because if I started down that road, I'd drive myself out of what was left of my tiny little mind. And my tiny little mind had more than enough to keep it busy.

"I'm sure it'll be great. But I'll call back later for the update, all right?"

She said it was. Whether or not she meant that was between her and her conscience. We hung up, and I stuffed the phone into my purse and pulled out my notebook, stepping a little farther out of pedestrian traffic as I did. I flipped the pages open to tick off the list of suppliers I'd met with, underline the time for the cake tasting, and add a few questions about the morning-of buffet that needed answers.

I closed my book and stared at it. An outrageous thought began to slowly gel in my brain. It had the advantage of not being actively dangerous—probably. But if I got caught, there'd be a hue and cry, and I would not come out looking good. And word of what I had done would most certainly spread around, possibly to people who could make things actively dangerous for me.

I stuffed my notebook away, pulled my phone out again, and dialed Brendan.

"Charlotte. Is everything okay?" One of the things I loved about Brendan was his directness.

"I wish I knew." I told him about the nonreaction to last night's robbery. "Do you know if Henri and Jacques are actually in ICE custody?" I asked.

"Henri is, but he should be out tonight. Rafe Wallace is having a field day with this. Jacques, on the other hand, seems to have gotten away."

That one is faster than he looks. Apparently Anatole wasn't the only one to find this out. "And the gun?"

"Nothing. If the Renaults took it, either Henri ditched it or Jacques still has it."

Because clumsy as it seemed, this could all still be a way to frame the Renaults, and break up the wedding.

I sucked on the inside of my cheek. "That might explain why the wedding's going forward."

"I'm not following."

"Adrienne was awfully mad with Lloyd about the raid last night. She thought he staged it. If she thinks Lloyd stole the gun, she'd have no reason to call off the wedding, because she'd know it wasn't the Renaults who were making the trouble."

Brendan was silent for a moment. "I hadn't thought of that. You could be right."

"It'd make for a nice change," I muttered. "It'd also mean that none of this has anything to do with Oscar's death, which would make things a lot simpler."

"Wouldn't it? Okay. I've got to make some more calls, and then I'll take another run at my grandfather. We'll figure this out, Charlotte."

"Yeah," I answered, shoving my cropped hair back, "I know."

Brendan, of course, heard my hesitation. "Was there something else you were calling about?"

"Kind of." Brendan waited. "I'm going to swing by Perception."

"I thought you'd already done that."

"Yeah, but this time I'm going to try to steal Oscar's chef's notebook."

16

Sneaking into a restaurant currently holding several hundred employees plus several hundred guests may seem counterintuitive, if not utterly whacked. But, as I explained to Brendan, this was actually the perfect time. If I tried to get in on Monday when Perception would be closed, I might be seen, and remembered. Plus, by Monday, Perception might be an official crime scene. I had no doubt Detective O'Grady was currently breathing down the neck of some helpless lab tech, trying to hustle along the results on Oscar's tests. I was much more confident in my ability to tiptoe past a collection of my colleagues when they all had better things to worry about than I was in my ability to pull the same stunt with any of Linus O'Grady's hand-picked people.

Brendan, not surprisingly, also wanted to know why in the world I thought this bit of grand theft notebook was necessary. His skepticism on the point vanished when I reminded him that a chef's notebook was part appointment book, part diary, and part PDA. If Oscar had been meeting with anybody new, or receiving any new income, or plotting any big changes, the odds were good he'd have made notes about it in his book, and maybe, just maybe with what we knew about the Aldens, we could work out who had made him all dead and everything. I will not say Brendan was happy with my idea, but he did concede the point that this would be useful for us to get our hands on, as long as I was careful. I promised, three or four times.

When Brendan finally let me hang up, I found a cab and had the driver drop me off three blocks from Perception so I could walk the rest of the way. But rather than stroll right past Perception's front window, hands in my pockets, I stuck to the far side of the street, trying to look as if I were on my way somewhere else.

Perception was definitely open for business. There was a steady stream of customers crowding into the front door, and the terrace was brimming with people in their best Sunday-go-to-brunching clothes. Perception was a full-fledged "red and white" establishment. It served humans during the day and switched over to its nightblood-friendly specialties after dark. *One day Nightlife will be able to do the same,* I told myself. *One day.*

Perception's alley was a full-fledged alley too—Dumpsters, smells you really didn't want to be able to identify, bags of linen, empty milk crates, and restaurant employees standing around puffing cigarettes as fast as possible before they had to get back inside. I walked right on past the alley mouth without breaking stride, but I did get a look at the three guys standing around in their personal tobacco fog. All of them wore baseball caps—two Yankees and a Baltimore Orioles. When I got to the end of the block, I found one of the guys with a folding table full of knock-off sports paraphernalia that grace the majority of the corners in Midtown, bought myself a Yankees cap, and walked back. The alley was empty. Smoke break was over. I settled my new cap low on my forehead, grabbed a milk crate—because empty hands in a working kitchen invite suspicion—and walked in through Perception's entirely unlocked back door.

Nancy Drew, eat your heart out.

I was used to restaurant kitchens and might actually be more at home in them than I am anywhere else. But my first look at Perception knocked me back, hard. For starters, it was big. This was not a kitchen; this was a previously unknown sixth borough. The fish station was the size of my entire hot line. Prep counters stretched out for blocks, but they still looked crowded with the white coats practically elbow to elbow as they chopped and rolled and portioned. Cooks stood on step stools to stir the massive vats of stock and mashed potatoes with paddles that could have been salvaged from a Roman galley. While I watched, three guys pushed in carts of fresh bread and rolls from a separate bakery tucked out of sight somewhere, and two women in matching pink bandannas came in from the opposite direction, carrying trays of cheesecakes high over their heads to get them through the sea of bodies. An open stairway led up to a sort of loft space lined by the executive offices. All five of them had windows so management, and Oscar when he was still around, could survey their domain. There were banks of ovens, mazes of blast chillers, and a solid wall of heat and human voices. The cooks were yelling, the apprentices were yelling, the chefs were yelling, the servers streaming in and out the doors were yelling. And I was about to expire from the internal collision of sheer envy and the desire to roll up my sleeves and dive right in. I told you, chefs are not normal.

This was not my real problem, though. My real problem was those offices up in the loft, with their big, shining windows. Two of them had the blue curtains closed. But on the third set of windows, those curtains were pulled wide open, and a paunchy guy was inside at his desk, with a thin woman leaning over his shoulder so she could see whatever was on the computer screen. I'd counted on being one white coat in the crowd. But the crowd was all down here and the place I needed to be was up there, and the odds were very good its door was locked.

Somewhere, Nancy Drew was having herself a real good laugh.

My other problem was that I was now doing the one thing I absolutely under no circumstances could be caught doing—standing around. A person standing still meant something, somewhere was not getting done. A person standing was a person you could give orders to, and that meant you might notice you had no idea who the hell the person was, and that the person's particular white coat lacked the pretty blue piping and neat embroidery with the restaurant name that yours sported.

I shouldered my crate and skirted the wall, starting to perspire from heat and the sudden knowledge that maybe this had not been the best idea after all. About half a block ahead of me, I saw a stringy, graying man come round the corner, pushing a mop cart. Brushing past him and heading around that same corner, I found what I'd been hoping for—the storeroom for cleaning supplies. I ditched my empty crate, then grabbed up a towel to stuff into my pocket, as well as disposable gloves, a spray bottle, and a couple of trash bags. Restaurant kitchens generate an incredible amount of garbage. The cans are pretty much always too full, and somebody's always going around emptying them out. One look at my uniform, and another at my trash bags, and I would be instantly identifiable as somebody with a necessary job to do, but low enough on the totem pole that I was surely somebody else's problem.

I readjusted my new cap and headed out again.

Noise and heat to rival a subway platform in the August rush hour dragged me down. I kept trying to sneak glances up at the loft offices, and I kept having to pay way more attention to where I was going, ducking and dodging around the cooks, chefs, and runners. I spotted an overflowing can and emptied it out, because if I didn't, somebody might notice. This meant I had to go out to the alley and toss the bag in the Dumpster and start the whole trek across what I was coming to think of as hell's half acre over again.

"Behind!" bellowed somebody.

I ducked and twisted, but in the wrong direction. A chest slammed into my shoulder and my foot slipped on a wet patch, and I was down on my rear with a blizzard of shredded greenery descending around my head, along with a cloud of swearing, scattered applause, and a couple of whistles.

"I said behind!" A medium brown woman reared over me. "You know what behind means, you—" And she stopped, because we had both recognized each other.

"Charlotte? What the hell are you doing here?"

"Minnie?" I blinked up at her from my undignified and unsafe position in the kitchen's traffic pattern. "What are you doing here?"

"I work here." She yanked me to my feet and dragged us both over by the blast chiller. People were swearing and ducking around the fresh parsley, which was rapidly getting trodden into green slime.

"Since when do you work here?" I whispered, well, I said in a normal tone that counted as a whisper in there.

"Since yesterday. Half the staff took off when Simmons shuffled off the mortal coil. Charlotte . . ."

"Shhh!" I held up both hands. "Shhh, Minnie, please. I'm just . . ." There was no explanation short enough or good enough for what I was really doing there, so I skipped that part. "I need to get into Oscar's office."

"Jesus. Not you too."

"What?"

"Somebody get that crap cleaned up!" hollered a voice out of the crush.

"Yes, Chef!" I hollered back. "What do you mean not me too?

"Half the effin' city wants in there. Yesterday I saw Mario throwing out some little nerd-accountant type. They're saying Oscar was keeping an extra set of books and this guy . . ."

"Crap clean up *now*!" hollered that same voice. "Perez! Get your ass back to your station! Also now!"

"Yes, Chef!" we chorused. I grabbed Minnie's coat. "Help me out?"

Minnie gave me a hard look, then stuffed her side towel into my hand and pointed at the floor. "Crap clean up, now," she said, and was gone.

I bit my lip, crossed my fingers, hustled back to the supply room for a mop cart, and started cleaning. The guys at the nearest prep counter glanced at me, and away again, getting their attention back on their knives where it belonged. I scooped and mopped and dried, and took the swearing of people trying to get past me. This was bad. It could be an hour, or more, before Minnie could get away from her station again, and there was nothing I could do about that. I glanced over my shoulder at the loft offices where the man and woman were now having an argument. How in the hell did I think I was going to pull this off?

"You with the mop!" Minnie's voice rang over the kitchen roar. "Now!"

"Perez, what is your problem!" demanded another voice.

"No problem, Chef!"

I shoved my cart over to the spot at the end of the counter where Minnie was overseeing a cutting board loaded down with some truly gorgeous wild game chops. She'd also knocked her water bottle over onto the floor, and the puddle was spreading into the aisle. As I started in with the mop, Minnie's elbow joggled me hard. We both swore, and something heavy dropped into my pocket. It jingled. Keys.

"You owe me big-time, Chef C.," she breathed.

"On it, Cook M." I emptied her trash can, ditched the

mop back with the cleaning supplies, and headed up the stairs.

I didn't waste time glancing around to see that no one was watching. That really would have looked suspicious. I just let myself into Oscar's skybox of an office and closed the door behind me, making good and sure I snapped the lock shut. Thankfully, the curtains were already drawn, but that didn't necessarily buy me any time. I could still hear the raised voices next door. That pair could come storming out at any second and notice my silhouette moving around in there. Probably Oscar had several notebooks; one current and a stack of old filled ones kept for reference. If I was lucky, I'd only actually need the most recent. Hopefully I could find it and get out of there, in something approaching a New York minute.

Unsurprisingly, Oscar Simmons's office was a tribute to Oscar Simmons. The walls were covered with framed prints of the magazine covers graced by him in his whites, smiling, and artfully posed with plates of food or glasses of wine. Empty space between the prints was taken up by framed award certificates and gold medals. The bookshelves held his dozen volumes on the art of fine dining and how to translate it to the home. All of them, I happened to know, had been written by other people whose names would remain forever unknown. There was a six-top table to one side, for hosting meetings and working lunches. His desk was a marvel of space and cleanliness. You could have prepped for dinner rush on its gleaming surface, if you swapped out the pristine blotter for a cutting board. The computer was state-of-the-art. The pen set might have actually been gold.

And he was still dead. I felt very strange standing there with so many copies of his face smiling at me.

So I decided not to stand anymore. I rounded the desk and started pulling out drawers, which, fortunately, were not locked. They held paperwork, paperwork, and more paperwork. Even the great Oscar Simmons couldn't get away from it. The voices next door halted abruptly. A door opened. I ducked down and squeezed my eyes shut. A door closed. Then, there was nothing, and more nothing. I started breathing again, and as long as I was down there anyway, pulled open the very bottom drawer.

Bingo.

In this age of smartphones, PDAs, and tablet computers, a notebook can seem one step away from a clay tablet. But despite the computer industry's best efforts, it's still one of the most efficient ways to store information you'll need to find again quickly. You never run out of charge, you can do text and graphics with the same simple instrument, and it'll never show you the spinning beach ball of death.

Oscar Simmons might have existed in the restaurant equivalent of the stratosphere, but the notebooks piled in his drawer were as battered, stained, and well-thumbed as mine. If they were anything else like mine, they were filled with appointments, wish lists, memos and meeting minutes. They were also personal, if not private. I picked up the top book. This was where the work happened and the ideas blossomed. If I hadn't felt like an intruder before, I did now. I gritted my teeth, glanced at the door, and flipped the book open to the last page.

Oscar's handwriting was as terrible as I remembered it being. The book's last page, dated back in January, had some sketchy possibilities on updating Perception's appetizers, a reminder of a phone call from a new supplier, and a meeting with the sommelier; that was it.

It also wasn't the last page, or at least, it hadn't been. I frowned, running my finger down the stubble where the rest of the sheets had clearly and obviously been torn out.

Slowly, I closed the notebook. I set it back in with the others and closed the drawer. I sat there in Oscar's soft, ergonomic, leather-covered chair, and stared at the closed drawer.

I pictured sneaking in here, just as Minnie said half of Manhattan was trying to do. I pictured finding Oscar's notebooks, easy as pie. I pictured how long it would take to slip one into my purse or pocket versus how long it would take to rip out a handful of pages.

It made no sense—none whatsoever. Why risk being caught tearing out the pages when you could just take the whole book faster, and without anybody noticing for days, maybe forever? You'd only do it if (a) you were in a panic from not being used to breaking and entering or (b) you wanted to keep the rest of what was in the book, because you needed to be able to refer back to your notes.

This meant the number one candidate for ripping out those pages was Oscar himself. Oscar had been making notes that he suddenly decided he didn't want read. That meant he thought somebody somewhere might just be interested in his private notes. I thought about Minnie's description of the nerd-accountant type who'd been trying to get in there. That sure sounded like Scott Alden.

I took off my Yankees cap and ran my hand through my hair. *Okay. Okay. Say Oscar did want to get rid of some paper. What would he do? Just pitch it? Probably not. Burn it? Does anybody really do that?* Although God knew if you wanted to burn something, a kitchen was the place to do it. *Flush it?* I glanced around to see if Oscar's luxury office included a private bathroom, and my gaze fell on the industrial-strength paper shredder in the corner. *Or maybe do the effing obvious.*

I walked over to the shredder. It was little more than a knee-high, gray container with a wicked-looking bunch of blades set into the lid. The wastepaper basket beside it had been cleaned out. Of course. I bent over the machine. There followed a moment's fumbling and swearing, accompanied by a lot of glancing at the door and wondering if Minnie was wondering what I was doing up there, before I found the catch and lifted the lid. The bin was about half-full of paper confetti, proving that this was one of those high-class shredders that crosscut so you didn't have to worry about any nosy people with a lot of patience and a sizable Scotch tape budget.

I swore some more, but it didn't help. I settled the shredder lid into place. Something brushed my fingertips. I flipped the lid back over. A scrap of notebook paper had gotten jammed under the rim, probably from somebody stuffing too much, too fast into the shredder.

"Note to self: Burn or flush incriminating documents," I muttered as I fished the scrap free.

It was a list, or the bottom portion of a list, written in smeared pencil and Oscar's scrawl. I squinted at it. At first, I just thought Oscar'd been in a hurry and so had been sloppier than usual. Slowly, however, I realized whatever it was a list of wasn't written in English. Or French. Or Spanish. Or Mandarin. Or phonetic Japanese. So there I was, with a genuine, bona fide, no-mistaking-it clue in my hot little chef's hand, and I couldn't read the damned thing.

I looked up at the cover of *Bon Appétit*. Oscar raised his glass of red wine to me and winked.

17

“Chef Alamedos, these are wonderful.” Mrs. Alden said as she set down her empty cake plate. Marie, Reese, Felicity, and I were back in the Aldens’ pristine living room. Mrs. Alden sat by the fire, looking trim and perfect in her apricot twinset. Deanna and her two head bridesmaids—Lois, the blonde with the bad 1970s hang-up and Peri the skeptical redhead—occupied the love seat. Marie’s cake samples had been reduced to crumbs and thin smears of frosting in what had to be record time, but Marie’s cakes had that effect on people.

The ride back to Brooklyn Heights had felt very long. I spent the entire time alternating between checking my phone messages, calling an increasingly annoyed Zoe, and staring at the crumbled and smeared scrap of a list I’d retrieved from Oscar’s office. It stubbornly refused to morph into any language I knew. I called Brendan three times and got his voice mail, which got me wondering what kind of trouble he’d been getting himself into while I was breaking and entering and cleaning other people’s kitchens.

This was a lot to have sitting in the back of the head

while trying to concentrate on the more important subject of Marie's cake.

"I am so glad you like the selection, señora." Marie accepted Mrs. Alden's praise with her usual queen-of-the-kitchen cool. "Ms. Alden?"

"Totally fabulous!" Deanna sucked on her fork and rolled her eyes toward the ceiling. I'd watched the bride-to-be closely throughout the tasting, but what started as curiosity turned rapidly to amazement. Not one aspect of last night's raid and robbery seemed to have stuck to her. If she was repressing her trauma, she'd repressed it down flat enough that I could have made crackers to serve with the cheese course. But I didn't think it was repression. From where I sat, it honestly looked like she wouldn't have given a damn if Manhattan came off its moorings and floated out to sea, as long as her wedding was going ahead.

It was amazing. It was appalling. The only thing worse was her steely-eyed mother. Adrienne Alden watched her daughter as if she were waiting for Deanna to break.

"It's got to be the one with the raspberry." Deanna traced the tines of her fork around the plate, looking to pick up some last trace of frosting. "Lo? What do you think?"

"Definitely raspberry," agreed Lo from the 1970s. "I mean, it's like, pow! Pop! Awesome!"

"I don't know . . ." Peri poked at one of the few remaining crumbs. "I'm thinking the walnut . . ."

"You're thinking you can't *possibly* agree with anybody else." Deanna waved her away. "The vanilla with raspberry. We'll do the chocolate for a groom's cake, and you can add champagne to that sangria mix of yours, can't you, Chef? For the nightblood guests?"

"We have our head mixologist working on a nightblood-friendly champagne cocktail." I said, lying through my teeth and promoting Abe the bartender at the same time.

"Very fine," said Marie, making notes in her own book.

"We will be able to accommodate the groom's cake into our schedule. Now, as to the plated dessert . . ." She brought out a second white box from her insulated carrying case. This one held a tray with a set of little lidded cups. "We thought perhaps, given the time constraints, we might choose a set of milkshakes that can be enjoyed by the entire gathering . . ."

Marie led them expertly through the samples so they could select the three flavors for the dessert. These were most definitely adult shakes, and the tequila, rum, and brandy were all praised at least as much as the cakes.

Great for a truck, Reese mouthed at me.

It was only the presence of the clients that kept me from acting like a mature and reasonable employer and sticking my tongue out at him.

It was just as well everything was going smoothly, because my attention kept straying to the mantelpiece with its antiques. The remaining bell jars had been carefully spaced out so anyone not familiar with the room would be unable to tell anything was missing. I wondered if Mrs. Alden or Trudy had done that. I wondered again whether they could have hidden the Arall in plain sight like that. If Henri and his boys really were thieves, they would have made sure they knew the location of the thing they were stealing before they made their try, wouldn't they? That, of course, assumed they were after the Arall at all. There were any of a dozen other antiques just in this room that could probably bring in a good price, if you knew where to sell them.

And how did any of this lead to Oscar's being dead?

"Chef Caine?" said Felicity, and I shot bolt upright. Everybody was looking at me, and I felt my cheeks heat up. "You were going over the menu next?"

"Yes, yes, of course." Silently inventing some new curses for myself, I handed around copies of the event menu we'd put together. *Keep your mind on your work,* I told myself ruthlessly. *It's the one effing thing you can be sure is happening around here.*

Luckily, the menu went over as well as the cake tasting. Everything was wonderful, fabulous, and pop-pow awesomeness. Peridot did add at least ten minutes to the whole meeting by second-guessing everyone else's choice. Still, by the time we'd all stood up and shaken hands, we had the go-ahead. Orders could be placed. Additional staff could be assembled. Even more importantly, I had something I could hand Elaine West so she could decide how to strategically leak bits and pieces to the relevant media types.

"A moment if you please, Chef Caine," said Mrs. Alden as I was packing up my notes and trying to resist the urge to attempt to sidle closer to the mantelpiece. I don't know what I thought I'd find, but I wanted a closer look anyway. I probably should have been worried about that.

"Of course," I said, studiously ignoring how Felicity frowned at me. I also waved Reese away. We'd catch up down in the kitchen. But I couldn't help noticing how Deanna was looking hard over her shoulder at her mother. It was a look full of meaning and family-style telepathy. Mrs. Alden ignored her as efficiently as I ignored Felicity. Peri and Lo whispered and giggled at her, and Deanna left with her bridal peeps in tow, but reluctantly.

I sorted through my printouts and tried not to look guilty. After all, it hadn't been Mrs. Alden's office I'd snuck into.

"Some of the ladies at church were talking about Chef Simmons," Mrs. Alden said overhead. "We were all very shocked to hear about his death. I think you said you knew him?"

Had I? At this point I couldn't remember whom I'd told what. "I worked for him, once." There was no way on this earth Mrs. Alden was getting the whole story. Once a year for that particular reminiscence was more than enough.

"I'm sorry for your loss."

"Thank you." It had suddenly become vital that all my three-by-five note cards were in an orderly stack with their edges precisely lined. "It was pretty sudden."

"That was what Karina said."

"Oh." That got me to look up. Mrs. Alden's face was expressionless. I wished I had Detective O'Grady with me. He'd have known what to say to get under that perfect, polite mask. "You knew she and Oscar . . ."

"Of course. We spoke today, and she is very upset. They'd developed a close friendship. In fact, she was the one who recommended him for the wedding. I don't suppose you had a chance to see Chef Simmons after you came to us?"

It is vaguely possible that fishing line wouldn't have been as obvious if I hadn't been less than two hours from ransacking Oscar's office.

"The job has been keeping me pretty busy." I kept my gaze rigidly on my hands as I wrapped the rubber band around the card stack and laid them on top of the manila folder with my printouts. It was a complete nonanswer, and I was sure she knew it. There was only one way out of this conversation I could think of, and that was to change its direction and start heading somewhere Mrs. Alden did not want to go.

Stop. Don't do this. Quit while you're ahead. Exit stage left. But all these sensible thoughts dancing and waving their arms to try to get my attention were blocked by a single huge question in the front of my brain, and the only person who could answer it was looking calmly at me with her Maddox blue eyes.

"Mrs. Alden . . . ," I began.

"Whatever it is, you can go ahead and say it. I won't mind."

I still might have been able to turn my back if I hadn't also slowly but surely been working up a decent-sized mad at this woman for looking so calm while I was wondering how many more mental train wrecks and unanswered questions I was going to have to put up with before this wedding was over.

"Weren't you at all worried Gabriel and his family might be setting up this engagement to try to get to the Arall?"

Finally, I got a reaction. Mrs. Alden's whole frame tightened as her perfectly manicured hands clutched at each other—but only for a second. Clearly she'd learned a long time ago that surprise equaled weakness.

"Of course, Brendan told you about the Arall," she said thoughtfully. "He asked you to be part of this fiasco too, didn't he?"

"I was brought in by Felicity Garnett," I answered stonily. "Why would you think Brendan asked me to be here?"

But Mrs. Alden didn't answer, at least not directly. "Brendan's a good man. I don't know how he managed, all things considered." She straightened the copy of the menu left on the table minutely. "But no, as a matter of fact, I was not worried about the Arall being stolen. I had taken precautions against it."

"Taken precautions," I repeated slowly. "Well. That's all right then."

Mrs. Alden's jaw tightened, and I knew I'd scored a hit. I just didn't know if it had been a really good idea to take aim.

"Believe it or not, Chef Caine," she said, "I do know what kind of mess this wedding is creating."

"It'd be tough to miss."

"Yes, it would. But we must live in the world as it is, not as we want it to be. My daughter has made her choice. It will be followed through on. Was there anything else?"

There was something else. Actually, there was a whole lot of something else, but I knew a dismissal when I heard it. I thanked her and beat a strategic retreat down the back stairs.

"Everything all right, Chef?" inquired Reese as I shouldered my way into the kitchen.

I looked back out the stairway door, and then out the French doors, and the swinging door, and the side door. Then, I dropped into the stool at the kitchen island and rested my forehead on the cool, smooth marble.

"I'll take that as a no," said Reese.

"The shit may or may not be about to hit the fan." I told him without lifting my head.

"Could you be a little more vague with that?"

"Give me a couple hours and I'll try."

"If we had . . ."

"If the word 'truck' is appearing anywhere in that sentence, you can forget it."

"I'm just . . ."

"No, you're not just sayin', because I've had it up to here with this day." I raised my arm to the limit of my reach, an interesting trick when you've still got your forehead on the counter.

Reese sighed and very sensibly changed the subject. "So, what's on for tonight?"

I straightened up. What was on for tonight? Tomorrow, we had a bridesmaids' tea scheduled, plus breakfast and lunch. Tonight, though, tonight was just the family, and all the supplies were here. A new idea was forming. Considering what happened with the last one, I was ready to give it a swift kick. But there are times in your life when you know you're already in too deep to back out.

"Reese, can you cover dinner tonight? I want to drop the menu over at Nightlife so Zoe can get a look before we meet tomorrow." It was lame. It was beyond lame. There was no reason I should be heading all the way back into Manhattan to drop off a couple sheets of paper I could have read off over the phone.

"Better you than me, Chef," muttered Reese.

Of course, he thought I was going to check up on Zoe,

and I didn't blame him. But this time he was wrong. Because Mrs. Alden's dropping all that unsubtle and probably completely bogus information about Karina got me thinking. Just because mother and daughter weren't talking honestly about Oscar, there was no reason daughter and chef couldn't have a cozy little chat, especially after they'd met on the sidewalk and been so rudely interrupted by a short Irish cop.

Probably she would not want to talk to me, but I was pretty confident I could at least get my foot in her door. After all, chefs had a totally unfair advantage when it came to launching a charm offensive.

18

Normally, if I want to bribe somebody, I do the cooking myself, but I was operating under some unusual time constraints here. One of the advantages of being a chef in Manhattan, though, is you are a member of a tightly knit community of fellow professionals not averse to handing you the occasional curry hot pot to go out the back door, no questions asked.

I had to look up the address for Exclusivité. From what little I'd been told, I was expecting to arrive at a street-level shop or spa. Instead, to my surprise, the cab pulled up in front of one of Manhattan's iconic glass and steel skyscrapers just a couple blocks off Columbus Circle. It was only a guess that I'd find Karina Alden at her office, but you didn't develop and run a luxury product business without being a workaholic. Having been a badly gut-punched workaholic, I knew all about the comfort of being able to throw yourself into your job when you didn't want to think—especially if it involved not thinking about one of O'Grady's Q&A sessions.

I paid off the cabbie, grabbed the receipt (hey, it was a business expense), and climbed out onto the curb. The night was warm, and the traffic on the sidewalk and down the street was brisk. A quick check of my carrier bag showed I hadn't spilled anything yet. A quick check of my cell phone said Brendan hadn't called or texted.

A quick look where I was going showed Scott Alden on the other side of the lobby's tinted windows, striding out of the elevator.

I froze like a guilty teenager when the light snaps on, and I looked around frantically for a tourist to duck behind. But Mr. Alden was too busy texting and checking his watch at the same time to notice some random, out-of-uniform chef standing by the curb. He breezed out through the revolving door, letting the rotation point him toward Broadway, and headed down the sidewalk without once looking up.

Okay. Unexpected, I thought as I was remembering how to breathe again. It also told me two things: (1) Karina was in fact in her office; (2) I wasn't the only one feeling the need to check up on her. I did find myself wondering how that particular father-daughter conversation had gone and what kind of ground it had covered. I knew nothing about Scott Alden, except that he was rich, a T-typ, he didn't much like Lloyd Maddox, he might have tried to get access to Oscar's office, and, according to Trudy, his main goal in life was to keep everybody calm and happy.

So, who was he here to keep calm and happy? That question followed me through the revolving door and across the gleaming lobby, and I had the feeling it wasn't going away any time soon.

This was not the kind of building just anybody could wander into. I had to give my name to the guard at the desk, who in turn had to make sure somebody upstairs would agree to take charge of me before he'd agree to give me a pass and buzz me through.

That somebody turned out to be Karina Alden herself.

"Charlotte. I didn't expect to see you here," she said by way of an extremely left-handed greeting as I stepped off the elevator. But considering the last time she'd seen me was in the company of Linus O'Grady, I couldn't really blame her for the lack of warmth.

At some point, Karina had swapped out the designer dress for black slacks and a long white coat that buttoned all the way up to a high, closed neck. It looked like a cross between a lab coat and my own chef's uniform. A bitter smell hung around her, something that vaguely reminded me of the taste of AA batteries.

I must have made a face. "Sorry," said Karina. "I've been in the aromatics lab. It can get a little strong."

"You were looking kind of rough . . . before. I wanted to see if you were okay."

"You did or O'Grady did?" Karina was clearly not in the mood for any kind of verbal dance. This was a state of being I could completely respect.

"Linus O'Grady is not going to send me to ask his questions for him."

She thought about this. "No, I suppose not. I'm sorry. It's been a very bad time." Her face had that blotchy red complexion that indicated either a four-martini lunch or a recent crying jag. I was betting on the crying jag. In fact, she looked drawn tight enough to snap.

That, at least, I could help with, which helped ease any guilt I might have about coming to poke at a woman who could be guilty of nothing but lousy relatives and terrible taste in boyfriends.

"Have you had dinner?" I asked.

Karina eyed my shopping bag. "You did not bring a casserole."

"Curry hot pot."

As a trained chef, I can spot the moment when someone's stomach starts doing the thinking for them. I saw this moment blossom in Karina Alden's brown eyes, and I smiled. "Got a microwave in this place?"

Before much longer, the two of us were seated in a small lunchroom tucking into curry and rice heaped onto paper plates, and washing it down with bottles of sweet tea from the vending machine. Karina ate hungrily and steadily. I waited until her fragrant, steaming helping had shrunk by about half, before trying out the opening I'd worked out all the way across to Midtown. Now was the time to pray Felicity had been right about the breakup.

"He was a royal pain in the ass," I said.

Karina choked on a swallow of tea and regarded me warily. "Don't tell me you dated him too?"

"No. Dodged that bullet." I smiled and said a silent prayer of gratitude for accurate relationship gossip. "But I saw him in action."

"I wish I had. I don't know if it would have mattered," she added wearily. "The whole thing was stupid, and I knew it was stupid, and whenever he wasn't around, I regretted it. But when he was around"—she shook her head—"it didn't matter if it was stupid or not. It was just so much *fun*."

I let that one settle. Exclusivité took up a large chunk of this floor, which meant the rent alone would be more money than Nightlife saw in a good month. We'd passed doors labeled DEVELOPMENT LAB: AROMATICS, and RESEARCH, and ANALYSIS, as well as a half-dozen private offices. Karina had to work long and hard to keep this all going. I could understand the attraction of a little fun.

"At first it was strictly business." Karina took another sip of sweet tea. "Oscar was looking to add boutiques to his restaurants with specially branded products. He wanted a fragrance with his name on it, and he'd come to talk to us about making the juice. Things sort of went from there."

"Your mother said it was your idea to have him do the wedding."

"She said that?"

I nodded, and Karina turned her head away, but not before I saw the anger burning underneath her carefully applied blush.

"I had nothing to do with his getting the wedding job," she said grimly. "Oscar went after that all on his own. I haven't talked to Deanna since before she announced the engagement, and I don't expect we'll be talking much again in the future."

"Oh."

"Yes. Oh." Karina set her jaw. It completely changed her face. When she was just sad, she had a softness about her. But as the anger took over, that softness melted, leaving behind nothing but stone and steel. "You see, I'm not the important one. I'm not the heir to the big magical empire, so none of the Maddoxes give a damn about what I do or where I go. Deanna looks at that and sees freedom. She doesn't see that Dad and I can just be thrown overboard. It doesn't matter if I tell the Maddoxes all to go screw themselves and walk out. Nobody cares. They care about keeping Deanna happy and passing on the damned . . . magic."

"But if the . . . magic is something you inherit, wouldn't the Maddoxes be a little worried about Deanna marrying a vampire?" The list of things vampires cannot do includes making babies. It's kinda tough to pass something on to the next generation if there's not going to be a next generation.

"It's been mentioned," said Karina blandly. "Mom insists she's got the whole thing handled. I heard her telling Grandfather." Karina took a long swig of tea. "She says there's nothing for him to worry about. She says marriage or no marriage, this affair won't last, and she's got the . . . magic safe. That was before Gabriel and Deanna really went lovey-dovey, though." She added to the tea bottle with a frown.

"So, Deanna and Gabriel had been going together for a while?"

"Oh yeah. We'd been seeing Gabriel and his blood

relations around a few parties, and Deanna'd been flirting with him. Trying to cause trouble yet again. Everybody's always cleaned up after her, so nothing she could do would go really wrong, for her anyway. It was part of that whole witchy-princess thing." According to Brendan, the Maddox clan had a roughly democratic structure. If you broke too many rules, you could be voted off their particular island. But from what Karina was saying, it sounded as though the heir to the Arall got immunity from that challenge.

"Mom's tried everything to bring her in line," Karina went on. "Taking the car, cutting off her allowance, kicking her out of the house . . . When we were teenagers, I don't think a week went by without some new shouting match between them." She poked her fork into the curry, turning over pieces of lamb as though looking for more pleasant memories. "Anyway, dating a vampire was about the only thing she hadn't tried. Jumped right in with both feet. I knew she would," Karina added softly, but then she shook herself. "Anyway, she wakes up one morning and tells me she's in love. I thought it was just another part of the game. I thought we—" She cut herself off and shook her head hard. "God, this has just gotten so messed up."

That was another one of those understatements, but it wasn't going to do either of us any good if I pointed that out. "And it's family, which makes it worse."

"You have no idea."

"Yeah, I kind of do."

"No, you . . . oh." Then she clearly remembered whom she was talking to. "Well, maybe you do."

I helped myself to a little more rice so I wouldn't have to look at her while I said, "Must be hard on your dad."

"Probably. I wouldn't know." She shrugged and speared a piece of carrot with her fork. "We haven't talked much since I walked out."

In a way, it was a relief to meet somebody without a

world-class poker face. But the fact that I could read her meant I was reading yet another uncomfortable question. *Why are you lying to me, Karina? Are you trying the act out for O'Grady? Or for your mother?*

I decided then and there to go for the approach I knew best—the direct one. "Karina, the cops think Oscar might have been murdered."

"I know," she told the last of her tea, quietly, sadly. "I'm not surprised."

"Do you have any idea who might have done it?" Karina scowled at me, and I shook my head. "I'm not asking you to tell me." That was not strictly true, but there are limits to how far you can force some issues. "But, if you do have any ideas, you can trust O'Grady. He plays fair."

Karina got to her feet. She picked up her paper plate, took it over to the garbage, and pitched it. She kept her back to me for a long moment. "Anybody could have killed him," she said. "Anybody at all."

When Karina did face me again, the look I got tried to be pointed but melted quickly—and I suspect involuntarily—into pleading. "I'm sorry. I'm getting really stupid now. I need to go home." Her eyes shone bright with tears and badly suppressed anger. This woman had been crying a lot already today. She was about to start again, and she didn't want witnesses.

This was something else I could understand.

I collected my tote, said my good-byes, and left her to it. She trusted me enough to make my own way back down that long hallway, past all those doors with their neatly engraved brass plaques. I read them over, and I thought them over, all the way down in the elevator.

Here's the thing. One of the reasons I'd been able to go on at length with O'Grady about all the ways you couldn't poison someone at a restaurant is because any formally trained chef knows all kinds of ways you *can* make people sick, or even kill them. We all get extra classes at culinary school designed to make sure we don't accidentally poison our clientele, or blind them, or paralyze them, or cause massive organ failure. And believe me, if stupid enough and angry enough, I could do all of that and a little bit more.

But mine wasn't the only profession that handles potentially hazardous chemicals. My stomach clenched as I turned through the revolving door and out onto the sidewalk where the city's lights held back the dark. I liked Karina Alden. I did not want to be thinking like this about her at all.

In a blatant attempt at self-distraction, I yanked out my phone and tried Brendan's number for the umpteenth time. This time, he actually answered.

"Are you sorry?" I asked him as I ducked across Central Park West. Brendan owed me an apology for all those messages I'd left on his voice mail that he hadn't answered.

"Yes," he replied. We'd sort out exactly what he was apologizing for later. We always did. "But things have gotten a little crazy here."

"Where's here and how crazy?" I asked.

"ICE, and Henri Renault's disappeared."

"Disappeared?" I repeated. Columbus Circle was spinning. I had to stop before I staggered. A woman in a black pantsuit banged against my shoulder and brushed past, muttering about tourists.

"Oh, believe me, heads are rolling," said Brendan in a tone that made me suspect he was personally responsible for a few of the decapitations. "But it doesn't change anything. He's gone."

"But . . . but . . . how? It's barely an hour since sunset! How would he have time to break out?"

"Somebody must have stolen his body. According to my buddy here, Rafe Wallace showed up this afternoon with a writ of habeas corpus all ready to go, but somebody'd beaten him to it." Considering the term translates to "you can have the body," that was almost funny.

"Was it those two guys who staged the raid?" I asked. I didn't ask, *Was it your grandfather or your aunt?*

"It's being checked out," said Brendan tightly, and I swallowed my other questions. He didn't know, and all I would do with my prodding was remind him how much he didn't know. "They keep the nightbloods in a basement lockup until they can be processed. You need to sign in and out, and there's a bunch of other paperwork, none of which is on file for Renault." I could hear the explosion building under his voice.

"Is there anything I can do?"

"I wish. Are you okay?"

"Yeah, yeah, I'm okay," I said, which was fairly true anyhow.

"Be careful, all right, Charlotte?" he said softly. "I'm really not loving the direction this mess is going."

"I will if you will, Brendan."

"I will."

We stood there, not saying good-bye for a very long time.

19

If it hadn't meant leaving Reese in the lurch, I might not have gone back to Brooklyn that night. As it was, I didn't have a whole lot of choice.

Fortunately, I came through the side door to find Reese involved in nothing more alarming than going over his own notes and checklists, his phone wedged between his ear and his shoulder while he tried to sweet-talk a friend of a friend into signing on as an extra set of skilled hands for the advance prep work. Also fortunately, his head was so far into logistics space, he was happy to keep the conversation to the wheres and hows of the Big Day, which was fast approaching, and I was happy to let him. We synched his lists to my lists and drew up a set of questions we needed to be sure were answered about the remaining pre-event events. I heard that night's dinner had been a daybloods-only affair before. Not even Gabriel had put in an appearance.

I thought about the missing body of Henri Renault. It was a daring daylight raid, so Gabriel couldn't have pulled it off. But he might have paid somebody to do it for him—such as the two agents who had already raided the house.

I didn't say anything about this. Brendan had most

definitely already thought of that and would be following up on it. I concentrated on wrapping things up and sending Reese home before anything else out of the ordinary could happen. I locked the porch door behind him and turned around, wiping my hands on my trousers.

It was going on midnight. A normal person who kept normal hours would be exhausted, but this was the middle of my normal workday, and I was buzzing with energy. Around me the house had gone still and quiet. Adrienne and Deanna at least would be at a bridal shower that had been arranged by one of Adrienne's charities. Scott might be with them, or he might not. I pictured him coming out of Karina's building again, not looking up from his PDA.

I was able to deal with the peace and quiet for all of thirty seconds before I had to start cooking.

Deanna and her bridesmaids were expecting the full, formal English blowout for tea tomorrow—little sandwiches, cakes, the lot. Marie and her people, of course, were handling the cakes. But the sandwiches were my responsibility.

I turned the radio on low for some classic rock background noise, unrolled my knives, and started chopping up cucumbers, watercress, smoked salmon. I got some eggs on the stove to boil for a curried egg salad. Bread for finger sandwiches needs to be a little dry, so I switched knives and started slicing that up too.

My hands moved and my eyes measured and monitored mostly by instinct, leaving plenty of room in my brain to try to sort out the events of the day. I wondered how Gabriel was planning on keeping Deanna from realizing the whole ICE raid was some kind of put-up. I wondered if he knew what had happened to the gun or his sire, and if the two were currently in the same place. He must have known something, because he had tried really hard to keep her out of the way while he dealt with it—unless that was about something else altogether. Henri was old enough that he could very well be an illegal, or at least an undocumented, vampire. He might even have neglected to get himself on the official nightblood registry. I wondered about Karina and her laboratories, her affair with Oscar, and her assertion that anybody could have killed him.

Around one a.m., I heard the front door open and the sound of footsteps overhead and then on the stairs. The Aldens had returned and were heading up to bed. I wondered about Scott Alden and just how far he'd go to keep the people around him happy. I wondered if his wife knew he had seen Karina today. I thought about how Trudy believed Mrs. Alden capable of arranging a wedding with one hand and sabotaging it with the other. She also called Mrs. Alden by her first name when she wasn't being careful, had pet names for the girls, and tried to get between the family and federal agents. There was history there, and it wasn't just attached to the paycheck.

It was all just too damned weird and too damned complicated. To make things even worse, Reese had been right about the Aldens' kitchen. As I moved around it, I kept seeing what wasn't there. There was next to nothing in the pantry—no old cans of water chestnuts, or that extra can of cranberry sauce bought for last Thanksgiving. There were none of the sticky, mostly full bottles of liquor found in every house because there's always somebody who ten years ago thought blueberry schnapps sounded like the latest taste sensation. The separate wine refrigerator was also half-empty. And although Mrs. Alden said she did the cooking, she had no cookbooks, no old aprons or fraying hot pads, no battered utensils or wooden spoons with their handles worn and stained with use. This was a kitchen without a past. Where had it gone?

I couldn't find an answer for that either.

Finally the eggs finished, and I put them in a pot of water to cool so they could be peeled. While I was waiting,

I pulled a stool up to the kitchen island and spread out my notebooks on the marble. I stared at them without really seeing them. Then I pulled out that scrap of a list I'd retrieved from Oscar's office, turned the lights up full, and squinted at it.

The handwriting hadn't gotten any better. The first word could have been "actonin," "action item," or "agorium." The next word looked as though it started with a *CH*, but the next letter could have been the beginnings of a *b*, or the numeral three or a wiggly *p* for all I could tell. The last line was nothing but word salad with a lot of extra vowels sprinkled on for seasoning.

I laid the scrap down beside my notebooks. I should be peeling eggs and gathering seasonings rather than wasting time trying to decipher Oscar's shopping lists. As illegible as it was, I was sure the scrap was part of a list of some kind. Or, given that it came from a chef's notebook, a recipe.

But as I stared at the whole mess, a wave of sadness rose up from the depths of nowhere at the bottom of my brain. All those plans, all those great ideas and that enthusiasm, and they were drowning under the weight of somebody else's screwups. I swept the loose pages into a heap. I had to get away from them. I pulled open the French doors and stepped out onto the patio, breathing the night air in deep to try to clear my head.

The Alden house was a place brimming with luxury, but this was surely the greatest of them all; a private green space in the midst of one of the world's busiest cities. The night breeze swirled the aromas of herbs and fresh flowers together, completely erasing the smell of the nearby East River and any exhaust that might have been tempted to spill over from the expressway. I inhaled deeply and wandered up the central paved path, heading deeper into those lovely green scents. It would be way too easy to get used to this, although, being me, I wondered if there was enough light back there for tomatoes and zucchini.

Someone had gone through a lot of trouble to create a garden that matched the house. The place was neatly terraced, and the formal beds planted thick with carefully tended plants. Flowering vines and ivy climbed the brick walls. I passed a full-grown rosemary bush and stooped to take in the resiny scent. I wondered if there were chives, or maybe some basil, and I started mentally building compound butters for my tea sandwiches.

That was when I saw the first hole.

It was a black gap in the undergrowth big enough for both my fists. Even in the uncertain light spilling over the privacy wall, it stood out as completely incongruous among all this carefully tended shrubbery. I squatted down to look closer. Maybe somebody's cat had gotten loose and done a little digging? But no, something here had been ripped out by the roots, but the plant itself was gone. And whoever did it was in too much of a hurry to bother with the little dangly bits left behind. Plus, a couple of feet to the right, there was another hole. I turned around and pushed aside the branches on some ornamental shrub (if it didn't produce food, how would I know what it was called?), and found two more holes. One was big enough to bury a young watermelon.

Oh joy. New weirdness, fresh from the farm. I stood up slowly and dusted off my hands. *Just what I need.*

I stood there, trying to breathe deep and recover the calm I'd had such a fleeting hold of. It didn't work, mainly because the back of my neck was starting to curdle. I made myself turn slowly. If that was Henri or one of his boys drifting up behind, I was not going to let him see me freaked.

But there was nobody, just me and this garden full of holes. At least, that was what I thought, until I lifted my gaze to the patio and the French doors. There was somebody in the kitchen. It was a man—Lloyd Maddox.

He stood so the dim light filtering out from the kitchen glimmered in his stark white hair and outlined his torso, which was still powerful even though he had to be pulling seventy. My hand dove into my pocket and gripped my phone before I had a chance to even think about it. My hand wanted to call Brendan for a rescue. Fortunately, my head was still in charge. I would not retreat behind Brendan this time. Sooner or later, I was going to have to get used to dealing with this man, and, sooner or later, he was going to have to get used to dealing with me.

I strode into the kitchen. Lloyd, with an air of obvious graciousness, stood aside so I could snap on the light. The only thing worse than someone trying to loom at me is that same person trying to loom at me out of the dark.

"Hello, Mr. Maddox," I said. "Something I can do for you?" *Does your daughter know you're here? Have you got a key, or did you whammy the door?* I really needed to stop stacking up questions like that. I felt as if I were giving myself mental hives or something.

"Where was he?" Lloyd returned. "The vampire? During the raid?"

I thought about telling him to go flambé himself, but then I shrugged. If I was going to up the hostilities, I wanted there to be some point to it. "Under the sink," I said.

"Good choice." Lloyd crouched down in front of the cupboard and pulled open the door. He stared hard at the dark interior, then ran his fingertips around the edge of the door, rubbing them together as if checking for dust.

"I'm slowing down in my old age," he muttered.

"I know a whole bunch of people who will be happy to hear it." To prove I was well and truly over being impressed by him, I opened the stainless steel dishwasher and started loading bowls and knives. Thick, cold silence settled in behind me. I kept loading dishes. Lloyd kept being silent. In fact, he stayed there being silent until I closed the dishwasher and turned around. Now, he leaned against the kitchen island, watching me. It was the pose of a much younger man, and I had the sudden impression that this man very much knew his own strength. My hand suddenly itched for something to hold, preferably something sharp.

"I can see why he's taken up with you." Lloyd pushed himself away from the island, very casually putting himself between me and the door to the dining room. "You're his type."

"Cheap shot," I said. "Am I supposed to go all jealous now?"

Maddox shrugged. "Just making an observation."

"Look, how about a deal? You don't try to intimidate me, and I will stay in my kitchen, cook the food, and go away as soon as the job's done." *The job that currently includes figuring out who killed Oscar and might be trying to incriminate your daughter.*

"Except you're not going away, are you? You're going to keep dating my grandson."

Of course he'd bring it up now, when he had the home-court advantage. Everything I knew about this man said he really knew how to pick his battles. "Brendan and I are a separate issue." I struggled to keep my voice even. "It's also none of your business."

The corner of Maddox's mouth curled up in an ice-cold smile. "Am I supposed to go all contrite now?" He planted both hands on the counter. He didn't lean forward; he didn't need to. He just laid claim to all the space around him. "You have no idea what you're getting into, Ms. Caine."

"That is not only not your business; it's not your problem."

"You're wrong. It is my problem. I value human life, Ms. Caine. You are risking yours, and I don't want you to risk Brendan's."

That startled me. "I'm risking my life?" My heart froze and then hammered back to life. Did I mention I'd almost gotten killed a few months back? The experience left my adrenaline on a hair trigger.

"Yes, you are, by pretending the monsters are no threat

to us, and by coming here and helping them take over my family."

Ah. Okay. He wanted to drive us over to big-picture territory. I felt oddly disappointed. For a second, I thought I'd seen a flash of something in Lloyd Maddox that didn't show up in the sound bites—the father and grandfather underneath the mover and shaker. "I'm just here to cook," I said. "If there's anything else going on, it's none of my business."

That was a mistake. Lloyd moved forward, looking at me so hard, I could see the flecks of darkness behind his blue eyes. "He told you about the theft. Don't bother to lie. I can see the truth."

Anger started to build, and I welcomed it. Anger I could use. It would chase back the fear. "With me, that's not much of a trick," I said. "Yes, he told me. And you'll notice I'm not calling the cops, or doing anything else that will raise a fuss." *About the theft, anyway.* "I'm standing right here having a nice, civilized conversation with my employer's father." Fortunately, this once I didn't have to worry about my lack of poker face. Lloyd expected to see anger and nerves, and he was getting an eyeful.

"You have no idea what's happening here."

"You already said that, and you know what? You're right. I don't. I don't know why Deanna's marrying a vampire. I don't know why Adrienne's not telling the cops her house got robbed. I don't know why Oscar Simmons is dead, and I really don't know why Linus O'Grady is asking me about how he might have gotten poisoned on the job."

I admit it. I was hoping to piss him off enough that he might drop an unguarded word. I should have known better. Lloyd Maddox just narrowed his eyes. The air closed in around us, thick and heavy. I remembered this was a warlock in front of me, an old, powerful warlock, and I was on my own here. I'd hoped anger would burn the fear out of my brain, but fear was putting up an unexpectedly good fight. My hand slid into my pocket, and my fingers curled around my mini–spray bottle. I carried holy water for vampires, but the enhancements I'd put in might just buy me time to make it to the door if Lloyd decided to level up the menace.

"You all think you're so clever," Lloyd sneered. "So progressive and so worldly. You shake your heads at the old warriors, and you say it's such a shame we were fools for so long. You think they're not monsters anymore. But they are, and they're monsters of our making." He leaned close, and although I desperately did not want to, I saw Brendan in his eyes again; Brendan in forty years, bitter and worn down by too much death and too much change. "Maybe you'll get your own way and have all the monsters you want surrounding you. But I will protect my family. If the monsters take me down, and I have to fight my way out of hell to do it, I will come back for them all."

Each and every word hammered me into place. He was gone before I could move again. Shaking, I slowly slumped down onto the nearest stool and buried my face in my hands.

I believed Lloyd Maddox, completely and utterly. He would stop at nothing to save the lives of his family. I also believed he saw himself as a warrior. He might even value human life, like he said. But he wouldn't let that value get in the way of beating back the monsters he saw invading his city, and his family.

I also believed he hadn't staged the fake ICE raid. Lloyd Maddox would not stoop to a trick like that. He'd come down on the Renaults like the wrath of God, but they'd know where that wrath originated. This also meant it was very unlikely he'd do anything as petty as interfere with the catering, so I could cross him off the list of people who might have gotten Oscar to quit the job.

But if Oscar had discovered something that would threaten the Maddox family, would Lloyd be willing to move the chef over into the monster column? My throat closed down around my breath, because I could believe that too—easily.

Thefts and threats and weddings, oh my. I squeezed my eyes shut, trying to clamp down on the urge to laugh. But what else could I do? My life had been seesawing from the scary to the ridiculous since Felicity burst into Nightlife. Now, to add to the fun, I'd gotten Lloyd Maddox to make a personal threat. Score one for me.

My tired brain stopped there, turned around, and backtracked. I had gotten Lloyd to make a threat, right after I'd pointed out Linus O'Grady was looking into the possibility that Oscar had been poisoned.

Slowly, thoughtfully, I got out my cell phone. Finding the business card the detective had given me, I dialed the number. While it rang, I glanced around at all those doors I had no way to lock, and I headed back out into the garden.

Linus picked up in the middle of the fifth ring. "O'Grady."

"Why would Lloyd Maddox care that you were trying to figure out how somebody could be poisoned in a restaurant?" I replied.

"Chef Caine." O'Grady sighed. For a long time, he didn't say anything else. I could hear the gears turning in his finely tuned cop brain. If he answered me, he'd expect something in return. That was okay. Given everything that had been happening lately, I was more than ready to be on Linus's side. So far, he and Brendan were the only two people in this disaster who didn't seem to be operating from some hidden agenda, and I was counting myself there.

Finally, he said something. "Twenty-five years ago, before there was the separate P-Squad, I was on a team investigating the death of a design student at New York University. I was sure the kid had been poisoned, but I couldn't prove it. Then, I was told to lay off. I didn't have the clout to keep the investigation open, and I was afraid it'd be the end of my time as a cop if I tried. So, as ordered, I laid off. The death was put down to anaphylactic shock, a bad allergic reaction," he added. I was glad he couldn't see my face right then. Why, thank you, I'd never heard what anaphylactic shock is. I only cook for a living. "I not only got to keep my job; I got promoted. But I've been waiting for another sudden death to come down on somebody who's annoyed the Maddoxes ever since then," he went on softly. "Because these things never happen just once."

I may not be a trained cop, but I'm very good at putting things together. "You suspected a Maddox poisoned the NYU kid?" O'Grady said nothing, and I made a frightened and educated guess based on timeline. Twenty-five years ago, Adrienne would have been about twenty-one. "You suspected Adrienne Maddox." Calm, composed, steely Adrienne Alden, married to her number-crunching money man, living in her perfect house, lunching with her exclusive group of connected ladies, was a *murderer*?

"And her father had enough pull in Albany in those days to get the right phone calls made."

I turned in place, counting holes in the garden, smelling herbs and springtime.

"It doesn't make any sense," I tried to tell O'Grady and myself. "Why would she poison a chef? A chef who *quit*? If she was going to kill anybody, why not the vampires who were pulling a number on her daughter?"

"I don't know," Linus admitted. "Maybe I'm wrong. Maybe I've been waiting too long to prove I was right. It looks like a stroke with Chef Simmons, after all, not shock."

"But you don't believe that. You think maybe she's just gotten better over time."

O'Grady also apparently didn't feel like answering me. "How come I'm getting this call now?"

I opened my mouth. I meant to tell him. He needed to know what was going on, if only because it would look really bad if somebody else told him I'd been at Perception.

But something clicked softly behind me. I spun around. The handle on the side door was waggling back and forth, trying to turn. My brain snapped straight past fear and came up against anger. My right hand came down on top of my knife roll.

"Chef Caine?" prompted O'Grady.

"You damn well better belong here!" I shouted. "Or you're getting up close to the business end of a meat cleaver!"

"Chef?" O'Grady's voice went very, very calm. "Talk to me, Charlotte. What's happening?"

The door handle stilled. Silence followed. My fingers wrapped around the comforting curve of my chef's knife handle. I'd hunt around for the cleaver later if I needed it.

"Ah, Charlotte." Anatole Sevarin's far-too-cheerful voice vibrated through the door. "I sense you are still awake."

20

"Sorry, Detective," I croaked. "I've got to go."

"Do you need backup?" replied O'Grady in that same unhurried, even tone. "Just say good-bye if you do."

"No thanks. I'm all set," I said, although I was not sure this was entirely true. "Call you tomorrow."

I hung up on a very unhappy detective.

"This had better be good, Sevarin." I snapped the lock and tore the door open.

Anatole stood on the side porch, looking cheerful and elegant in his particular, masculine, middle-European way. One long hand rested on the shoulder of a much shorter, less elegant, and distinctly sulky vampire, who just happened to be Gabriel Renault's blood brother, Jacques.

"This says it belongs here."

Jacques's dark hair was disheveled, and his shirt was even more rumpled than it had been when he ran out of the house. The look he gave me was so sour, my skin puckered up in response.

"I thought you were on the run from ICE."

"ICE?" repeated Anatole. "ICE was here?"

"Not really." I glowered at Jacques. "But you knew that before you ran out of here."

"What are you talking about?" Jacques shot back.

"I was wondering something similar," murmured Anatole.

I ignored Anatole. "Maybe I should just go get Lloyd Maddox back here, and you can tell him what's going on."

"You wouldn't do that." There was some slight satisfaction in seeing that I'd made somebody nervous for a change, because Jacques had turned to Anatole. "She wouldn't do that?"

"She might. I sense a deep and burning anger emanating from within her."

This brought up yet another question. "Anatole, why are you even here?"

Anatole sighed, and an air of wounded dignity came over him. "That, I'm afraid, is a short and not entirely complimentary story. May I come in?"

"No," said Jacques.

"Yes," I said, and paused, squinting up at Anatole. "Can I invite you in here?"

Anatole stepped across the threshold, pushing Jacques in front of him. "Apparently you can."

"How'd you find him?" I asked, not caring particularly which of them answered.

Jacques beat Anatole to the punch, which was not something I'd seen happen a whole lot. "Sorry to disappoint, Chefy, but there's no mystery here."

"Mind your manners, Renault." Anatole's voice dropped into that deep register that makes the hind brain want to crawl away and hide. "She might not turn Lloyd Maddox onto you, but the cleaver is not out of the question."

Jacques rolled his eyes. He still smelled like onions. What kind of vampire smelled like onions?

"I was circling back to the house to find out if the coast was clear, or if I'd have to find someplace else to be for sunrise," said Jacques. "Your boyfriend was lurking on the street outside. I surprised him."

"You're *kidding.*"

Anatole was just then scrutinizing the cooling pot of eggs. I, on the other hand, was having a painful coughing fit, because it was better than outright laughing at Anatole in front of Jacques.

I shouldn't have bothered. Nobody was fooled. I just gave Anatole an excuse to do the wounded-dignity thing again. "I was distracted."

"You were blind."

The temperature surrounding the vampires dropped ten degrees, and my skin tried to do a lurch to the left and take my body with it. I dug down hard and held my ground.

"Where's Henri?" I asked Jacques.

"I don't know."

For all his refined control, I could feel Anatole's curiosity prowling the room like a cat curling around my ankles. I'd take the time to explain later—maybe—once I figured out how much I wanted him to know. Right now I wasn't going to waste the chance to get some answers out of Jacques. "He's your sire. Of course you know where he is." The connection between blood children and their sires defied distance, and time. Chet's sire, a sixteen-year-old fidget of a girl vamp, had run out on him with a pretty-boy actor years ago, and he still could have told me exactly where she was. Not that I ever asked. That was another one of my life's complexities that I tried very hard to ignore.

It was easy to do that right now, because the way Jacques was looking at me said he clearly thought I was shy several dozen IQ points. "Henri's not my sire."

"What?"

He hissed through his fangs. "You think I'd still be here if my sire had run off? Gabriel is my sire, and my mortal brother. Henri is our father, but he's only Gabriel's sire."

And here I'd thought that sort of thing happened only with certain Arkansas vampires. "But you must know where he planned to head out after the theft."

"Theft?" Jacques's jaw dropped.

"Theft?" murmured Anatole.

"Imbecile! Idiot!" shouted Jacques. He added a lot of other insults to go with the first two. Even with the French I'd garnered in bars and back kitchens, I had a hard time keeping track of them all.

I waited until he'd calmed down. "So, where'd he go?"

"I know nothing about it." Jacques ran both hands through his hair. "If I did, I'd rip his throat out for you myself." He added a whole nother string of French obscenities to bring home the point.

I waited until he was done, then turned to Anatole. "Is he telling the truth?" Anatole might joke about acute undead senses, but they were real, and he never hesitated to apply them.

Anatole contemplated the other nightblood for a long, cool moment. "I believe he is."

"Shit." I ran my hand through my too-short hair as my hopes for figuring this mess out in record time crumbled.

"And there you have it," sneered Jacques. "Now you may trust me when I also say I came back here because the one who *is* my sire has absolutely lost his mind, and someone has to look out for him before he wakes up with a stake through the heart."

All this time I'd been thinking about the vampires through Maddox eyes. I hadn't really stopped to think about the Maddoxes from the vampire point of view. What would it be like to lay yourself down at sunrise, aware that the entire vampire-hunting clan knew exactly where you were, and that there was nothing at all you could do about it? I could see how Jacques might question everybody's undead sanity in such a situation.

"So, what was up with threatening me in the alley the other night?"

"I wasn't threatening you. I was *warning* you," Jacques

shot back. "The word around is you and your brother are all right. I didn't see any reason for you to get mixed up in this *merde*. But I'm starting to wonder why I bothered."

That was most definitely and entirely not what I expected to hear. It was so much not what I expected to hear that I opened and shut my mouth a few times without getting any actual words to come out.

I don't know whether it was the whole pissed-off-vampire vibe sizzling through the air that woke somebody up, or plain old insomnia, but there was movement overhead. The vampires both noticed it too, and we were all staring at the door to the back stairs by the time Deanna Alden pushed through.

"Jacques!" she cried. "What are you doing here? Did Gabriel get you out? Where's Henri?"

"I don't know." Affecting nonchalance, Jacques reached down a wineglass from the cupboard. "I was too busy running away to keep track."

"You don't *know*?" She grabbed his arm and spun him around to face her. "You haven't heard from them? Do you even know if Henri's all right? How did you get away?"

I felt my forehead furrow up tight. Either Deanna hadn't realized yet the raid was a fake, or we were back to her being one hell of an actress. She certainly had the air of somebody who'd worked herself into what my grandmother would have called a real dither. Exhibit A: She was grabbing hold of a vampire. Exhibit B: She had a second, strange vampire in her kitchen, and she hadn't even noticed. Exhibit C: She was asking all about whether Henri, her fiancé's sire, was okay, but she hadn't said a word hinting at the theft. I wondered what Gabriel was up to that kept him too busy to call Deanna and reassure her that everything was okay. It seemed kind of a big detail to overlook when he had to be counting on her to stay put and not make things messier.

Jacques evidently noticed the misplaced emphasis and

decided to play along. "I expect I got away because I'm faster, and yes, I'm sure he's fine."

"You shouldn't even be here," Deanna went on. "Somebody could be watching the house."

"I assure you, Miss Alden, no one is watching the house." Anatole stepped forward. "I would not have accompanied Jacques here otherwise."

Deanna jumped about a foot and came down with a hard glower and a raised hand, and I put another point in the column for the really-worked-into-a-dither theory. Anatole simply cocked his head at the young witch's throwing hand and generated an air of mild regret.

Deanna lowered her hand. "I'm sorry," she said with a dignified calm she probably learned at her mother's elegant knee. "You are?"

"Anatole Sevarin, Miss Alden. I truly must apologize for intruding at this time of night."

Anatole's turning the charm on full blast is always an entertaining sight. Mischief sparked in his eyes as he gave Deanna one of his old-fashioned bows. Deanna did her best to return a penetrating glower. He remained perfectly composed under her scrutiny, and Deanna melted—slowly, but she melted. I could feel him suppressing his smile. He knew if he didn't have her in the palm of his hand yet, he could as soon as circumstances required.

For the record, that strange, uncomfortable twinge I felt way under my rib cage could not possibly have been jealousy.

"Are you a friend of Gabriel's?" Deanna asked Anatole.

"Of Chef Caine's. I was coming to see her when I met Mr. Renault." He gestured toward Jacques. In answer, Jacques rolled his eyes and poured himself a big glass of sangria from the pitcher in the fridge. Deanna, on the other hand, was clearly trying to square the fact that I had charming Russian nightbloods visiting me on the job with the other, well-publicized fact that I was dating Brendan.

I was grateful when she decided she had more

important things to deal with. "All right then, we'll leave you to it. Come on, Jacques. We need to talk."

"About time." Jacques gulped the last of the sangria, slapped the glass on the counter hard enough to make me wince, and followed her out the door and up the back stairs.

"Anatole . . . ," I began.

But Anatole had cocked his head and held up his hand. I shut my mouth. I could feel Anatole straining, and my shoulders tensed in response. His attention focused completely on the space above us, sensitive to any vibration. I had no doubt he'd be able to hear anything Deanna and Jacques whispered, even if they'd gone up to the roof.

"What're they saying?" I breathed.

"Do you really want to hear?"

I hesitated, recognizing this stood a good chance at being one of my bad ideas. But it was also a chance to get some answers to go with the mountain of questions I'd accumulated, so I nodded.

Anatole wrapped his hand around mine. I felt a quick, numbing current reverberate through my bones. Then, I heard pounding footsteps and harsh voices. It took me a second to realize that they were so rough and distorted, because I was experiencing whispers turned up to eleven. I was hearing Deanna and Jacques through Anatole's ears, and that wasn't all I was getting. I could taste Deanna's living anger, hot, gritty, and metallic.

"You should be glad Gabriel's not here. You'd be dust." She forced the words out through clenched teeth.

"And you'd be glad to tell him, wouldn't you?" Jacques's contempt was strong vinegar mixed with camphor. It leached through plaster and wood to try to tangle around me, but it couldn't get a grip. I was beyond its reach, sheltered by Anatole's *sang froid*, literally, his cold blood.

More anger. This batch was raw, green, sulfurous and hot on the tongue. "If you weren't Gabriel's brother . . ."

"We would not be having this conversation," Jacques

finished for her. "You're right. Because I would have drained you dry months ago."

"Try it." Pure heat, the taste of fire, the rasp of smoke on the back of the throat. Fear threatened, but couldn't quite reach.

"Oh, believe me, we'll get there. Compulsions fade, baby girl. They all fade." Jacques was getting closer, casting the force of his presence over her, trying to smother the flame of her nerve.

"You don't even want to be here. You keep telling everybody. Why don't you just go back to your pathetic little truck and leave us alone?"

Truck? I got an abrupt and incongruous smell of onions. But my thoughts got no further, because Jacques was talking again, and his words dug jagged edges into my palate. "Listen to me very carefully, baby girl. You've gotten your damned Maddox hooks into my brother, but it will not work with me. I've been ordered to go through with this farce, and I will, but I hope you are ready to watch your back for the rest of your pathetic little life, because I will not forget this, and I do not forgive."

Silence surrounded me—thick, cold, awful silence, broken only by the sensation of Anatole's light hand holding mine and his preternatural calm flowing through my veins. Slowly, Anatole pulled his presence back, and I sucked in a great, long whoop of air. How the hell long had I forgotten to breathe?

Anatole took no notice of my gasping for oxygen. "He's left her. Gone upstairs. The lock has turned on a door. Deanna is very angry. Jacques should be more circumspect. That baby girl has very adult protectors."

I was having a tough time focusing on Deanna and Jacques, though. I was getting my breath back and my ears were ringing, and I'd just overheard a conversation happening in whispers a floor above me, and, incidentally, I'd kind of allowed Anatole into my personal brain space.

I glowered at him. He waved me back. "You said you wanted to hear."

"You didn't say you were going to get into my head." I stopped. "How'd you do that anyway?"

"I am a vampire of many talents, and you let me in." He was looking toward the back stairs. "What do you suppose Jacques meant about Deanna's 'Maddox hooks'?"

"No idea." I slumped onto my stool. I suddenly didn't feel so good; not sick, exactly, just shaken. As though my insides had been rudely rearranged and were now trying to find their way back to their normal places. "I thought Gabriel or Henri had put the whammy on Deanna maybe to get to the Arall, but it sounds like Jacques thinks Deanna's put some kind of witch whammy on Gabriel . . ."

"The Arall?"

"Yeah, you know." I waved my hand. "The big, magical antivamp nuke that Adrienne Alden's in charge of, that might or might not be what Henri Renault ran off with the other night."

"No. I did not know."

"Oh. Shit." Brendan was going to kill me. The thought was so calm and certain, it could have come from Anatole. "I'm used to your being up on this stuff."

"You may recall the Maddoxes do not like me, and they are therefore hardly likely to share with me their deep magical secrets."

"Yeah, that would make sense." I squeezed my eyes shut. "I'm sure something else can go wrong here. I'm sure it's coming any second now."

"You may also recall," Anatole said, letting his smile creep into his voice, "that I do not like the Maddoxes and so am hardly likely to tell them when I discover their secrets."

That was cold comfort, but it was all I had. It was also very clear that I needed to stop talking. "You should go. I need to get some sleep."

"Charlotte," he said softly.

"Oh, please, Anatole . . ."

"Are you all right here?"

That stopped me, less because he asked than because he was perfectly serious. "I'm fine."

"I think you are not fine." He was right next to me. The cold that always surrounded him was reaching for me once more. It felt familiar now, which did not make me entirely happy. Neither did the way his green eyes had gone dark and contemplative. "I think you are frightened, Charlotte, and this concerns me."

"I'm not frightened." Anatole arched one eyebrow. "Okay, I'm frightened. But not for me. I'm frightened about where this mess is going and the fact that the wedding I was counting on to pay my bills is heading straight to the nether regions in a handbasket, and I don't know what's going to happen to—"

"To Brendan?"

"So?"

"So, I will clearly have to work harder. I find I am not yet ready to cede the field."

There was a whole lot I could have said to that, especially as pertained to any idea I might be a battleground, or a prize. Except the idea that Anatole felt willing to fight for what he would no doubt call my attentions was doing strange things to my brain, and the soft spot right under my rib cage. Especially since those warm promises and mischief were getting a fresh seasoning of something new. It was partly concern and partly something else—something I couldn't name, or didn't want to.

Get it together, Charlotte. I groped for the closest snark I could find. "How much of this is because I'm dating somebody else and how much is because he's a Maddox?"

Anatole chuckled. "My mathematics are terrible, but for the sake of argument, we will say it's a seventy–thirty split."

I should know better than to ask this vampire rhetorical questions. It was time to change the subject. "You never did say what you were doing lurking on the street out front."

"Ah." I expected Anatole to deny he'd been lurking, but he instead picked up the top sheet off my pile of menu notes and perused them closely. "As you know, like you, and unlike your Mr. Maddox, I must work to maintain myself . . ."

"Pity about that whole stock market crash back in 'twenty-nine."

"It was the revolution back in 'nineteen. The Bolsheviks were absolute murder on the banking system, and I had to barter a large number of diamonds to get safely out of St. Petersburg."

This one might possibly be true, or Anatole might just be waiting for me to accuse him of lying again so he could give me one of his laconic comebacks. Real vampires don't do snappy. Either way, following up wasn't going to get me anyplace I actually wanted to go. "You were saying, about work?"

Anatole sighed. "The society writer for *Circulation* has met with a most unfortunate accident. Something to do with a soon-to-be former lover, a concurrent lover, and a blunt instrument. I did not inquire closely into the details, but he is not expected back to work for some time, even after he is able to sit down again. I am filling in for him, and my editor was most interested when he heard you were taking over the catering duties for the Renault-Alden wedding."

I snatched my notes out of his fingers and slapped the page facedown on the counter. "He sent you here to get a sneak peek at the menu."

"To my shame. But, given what we've just heard between the bride and best man, I cannot say I'm entirely sorry I came." Anatole's face went still, and I had a nasty crawly sensation, the kind you get when you've seen something skitter away that second before you put the lights on. "I think Henri Renault needs to be found and reminded you are under my protection."

I could have blustered here; done the whole kick-butt-heroine shtick and insisted I didn't need his protection. But I could still feel the sharp corners of Jacques's anger in the back of my throat. He was in the house somewhere, and he wasn't any too happy with me either. Brendan might have turned my bedroom into a magical Fort Knox, but there was a whole lot of dark city out there for a pissed-off vampire to lurk in, and I worked late nights.

Of course, all of this communicated itself straight to Anatole.

"Do you wish to leave, Charlotte? I will take you home."

"No. I'll be all right." My hand strayed to my pocket, brushing the comforting weight of my spray bottle.

He nodded. If there's one thing I really do like about Anatole, it's that he has a healthy respect for my ability to defend myself.

"But you're right about one thing. Henri Renault's got to be found."

"Shall I make inquiries?"

"Can you?"

"For you, Charlotte, I can move mountains. And do not worry; I will find a way to put off my editor about the menu." Anatole took my free hand and brushed his lips against it. Then he smiled at my entirely useless attempt not to smile, or blush, and started for the door. But there was something else that needed saying before he left.

"Anatole?"

"Wait." He pressed his fingers to his forehead. "I sense . . . a threat? Perhaps something related to how my existence will come to an abrupt and dusty halt if I intrude upon your mental space again without an explicit warning?"

"You know me so well."

Anatole's eyes sparkled, and I felt those sparks dance across my skin. "Better than you realize, Charlotte."

The door closed behind him, and I stood there for a long time, thinking. I thought about Brendan and me, and how I kept teasing Anatole even though I knew it was dangerous. And how I kept not telling him to quit coming around after me.

I thought about Jacques, Henri, and Gabriel, and how neither Jacques nor Deanna seemed to know what was going on. I thought about Jacques's saying he was being ordered to go through with this farce. I thought about all the little stories Anatole liked to drop into conversation and how I had no way to know when he was kidding and when he was being straight with me. I thought about how vampires lie, especially about who they are and where they've come from. One of the attractions of becoming a vampire is it's the ultimate way to reinvent yourself. The nightblood registry was supposed to prevent identity fraud and make sure there's a public record of who's who. But there aren't a whole lot of ways to make sure what goes into the registry is accurate. Gabriel, Jacques, and Henri could be anybody, and be up to anything.

But then, so could Anatole. And I knew that, and I *still* didn't tell him to stop coming around to see me and walk me places and smile his smile full of promises at me.

At three thirty in the dark of a spring morning, I cleaned the kitchen, packed up the food I'd made, wrote the contents of the fridge and the bread box on the chalkboard glued to the stainless steel fridge, and climbed the stairs to my bedroom, trying very hard not to think anymore.

21

"You look tired," said Brendan when we'd finished a brief but pleasant greeting kiss. "Want a drink?"

"Yes. A lot."

I'd spent most of the day at Nightlife, helping Reese, Zoe, Marie, and Mel coordinate staff and deliveries. It was Monday, so the restaurant was closed. This gave us a chance to work on logistics and to use the kitchen to test and refine our Big Day recipes. Then Reese and I high-tailed it back to Brooklyn for the bridesmaids' tea. Now, those same bridesmaids, and the bride, were off at whatever bachelorette shenanigans they had planned. I could have hidden under that little brass bed upstairs. I could have gone home to Queens for fresh clothes and television. I didn't. I called Brendan. I was, as he observed with his trained security consultant eyes, tired—deeply, heavily tired. But I was also scared, angry, and confused. To top it all off, people were lying to me, which is not something I take to well even when nobody's dead. I wanted to be with Brendan. I desperately needed to tell somebody exactly how messed up things were, and he was the only one I could trust with the whole story.

Besides, this was his family. He needed to know what was going on, whether they wanted him to or not.

I followed Brendan into his living room. The first time I stepped into this gorgeous SoHo loft, the place was pristine. It featured white walls, comfortably full bookcases, blond wood floors, and the kind of clean white leather furniture that only a person without kids or pets can own. The place had looked staged for sale.

Since his paranormal security firm got the city contract, however, that had changed. Maps, blueprints, and reports had taken over Brendan's home. Papers buried the dining room table, created foot-high stacks on the spare chairs, and completely engulfed the coffee table. Schematics big enough to cover one of Nightlife's four top tables were taped to the walls above Brendan's desk, which looked like nothing more than a uniform layer of paper on four legs.

I peered at the new representations of city landmarks that had gone up since I'd last been there. "Homeland Security's going to come knocking on your door if they find out about this."

"Them? I've got them on speed dial." Brendan knows my drink preferences and had taken to stocking single malts. He poured me a healthy measure of amber liquid and handed it over as I took a seat at the far end of his butter soft leather sofa. It was the one part of the room not drowning in paper. I suspected that was because he'd taken to sleeping on it.

"Thank you." I sipped the fine scotch and let the heat of the alcohol and Brendan's presence uncurl in my veins.

Brendan touched my arm as he sat down at the other end of the sofa.

"It's been a day," I admitted. "More like a day and a half."

"I'm not surprised. Did you find anything in Oscar's office?"

"Oscar tore some pages out of his most recent notebook and shredded them." I fished out the crumpled piece of list and handed it over. "That's what's left, as near as I can tell."

Time and being carried around in my pocket had not done good things for my pathetic little scrap of a clue. Brendan gave me a meaningful look. I blushed. He went over to his paper-bound desk and switched on the lamp. He bent down under it and held the scrap up about an inch from his nose.

"What's this first one? 'Acon' . . . 'aconti'?"

"I was hoping you could tell me. Whatever it's written in, I can't read it. The second line looks like 'CH' something, but I don't think he finished it."

Brendan was quiet for a long moment, turning the paper this way and that, searching for some angle that would make Oscar's scrawl legible. "Shit," he breathed.

"What?"

"This last line. It's Old Welsh."

"You read Old Welsh?" I held up my hand before he could give me that special look. "Of course you do. What's it say?"

"I'm not sure. The guy had truly terrible handwriting. It's a smeared scrap, and he was copying something he probably couldn't read. But see," he said, turning the paper so I could in fact see. "It's got the double *f*'s and the double *l*'s and *y*'s in the middle of the words. That's almost exclusive to Welsh." He squinted at it again. "Can I keep this?"

I waved the scotch glass at him. "Go ahead. I'm not getting anywhere with it."

"How was Karina when you saw her?"

"She is not okay. She'd been crying and was about to start again. She was drifting too, as if she had too much churning around inside and she was trying to keep it all under wraps." This would make a lot of sense if she'd killed her ex-boyfriend, or if she knew who did.

"We don't know for sure it was murder," Brendan reminded me. "Let alone that it was a Maddox."

"No," I looked down into my scotch. "Except."

"Should I be sitting down for this?" inquired Brendan lightly.

"Yes."

Brendan's attempt at a smile faded, and he sank into his desk chair. Slowly, in simple words neither one of us would have to struggle to understand, I told him about my conversation with O'Grady, and the holes in the garden, and how he'd been harboring suspicions about Aunt Adrienne Alden for a quarter century.

When I'd finished, Brendan bowed his head and scrubbed at his scalp with both hands, hard. "I hate this," he muttered. "I hate this feeling of trying to choose which family member I'd rather have be a murderer."

There were no words anywhere in the language that could cover that, so I just took his hand. Brendan squeezed my fingers, hard. But I have strong hands, and I just let him hold on to me for a change.

"I'm sorry," I told him.

"Me too." Brendan's knuckles had gone white. He didn't let go, and I didn't ask him to.

"Did . . . Did O'Grady say anything else about the death of that NYU student?" he asked after a while.

I shook my head. "Maybe Oscar was trying blackmail? He was sleeping with Karina. She may have packed up on her family, but I'd bet money she knew exactly what each one of them was doing." I remembered how she lied to me about how close in touch with her father she still was. "Maybe she knew about her mother's history with O'Grady."

"Or maybe somebody in the house was worried about what Oscar might tell Karina. He was an haute noir chef, wasn't he?" I nodded. "So he would have had connections around the nightblood community. Maybe he knew something about the Renaults, and they didn't want him spreading it around."

I hadn't thought about that. I was so used to seeing

Oscar as a blowhard, I hadn't even stopped to think he might actually be a real threat on any front. "It's possible, except Oscar died during daylight hours."

"Poison doesn't have to be immediate."

Now there was a nasty idea. I could think of several ways poison could be a ticking time bomb, and I wasn't even trying hard. "There's another possibility," I said slowly.

"What?"

"That this doesn't have anything to do with the wedding. Karina's working the luxury market in a down economy. Among all the other things he was, Oscar was a tight-fisted bastard. Maybe he got her to develop a perfume for him, and then stole the recipe and broke up with her, with the intent to give the formula to somebody who would make it for cheap." New York was second only to Beijing for being able to counterfeit designer anything-you-could-ask-for. There was no reason perfume should be tougher to fake than, say, handbags. "That'd explain the list. It's a perfume formula."

Brendan picked up the crumpled scrap again. "Maybe, maybe," he muttered. "If he got it off Karina, it'd explain the Welsh. A lot of us use it as kind of a code for personal messages, since next to nobody outside the family reads it. But would that be enough to kill somebody over?"

"It'd mean the loss of some major dollars," I said. "If Karina's business had been taking a hit, it could mean the difference between life and death for her company."

Brendan nodded. "I could find out some of the financial information, but there's a risk Karina'd get word I was looking into her business."

I looked at the dregs of my scotch. "I have an idea," I told him slowly. "But you're not going to like it."

Brendan's smile was tight and humorless. "I'm braced. What is it?"

"I do know a journalist who is temporarily on the society beat."

We locked eyes, and I watched half a dozen emotions chase one another's tails behind Brendan's storm blue eyes.

"Call him," he said finally.

I pulled out my phone and hit Anatole's number before either one of us could change our minds.

"Good evening, Charlotte." Even over the phone, Anatole's voice had a silken quality that made me want to lean closer. "To what do I owe this unique pleasure?"

"Hello, Anatole. I need a favor."

"Do you indeed?" I could picture the golden sparks dancing in his green eyes. And judging by the way he was carefully not looking at me, so could Brendan.

"A professional favor," I said to both of them.

"I am most profoundly disappointed," said Anatole.

"Sorry."

"What is the nature of this favor?"

"I cannot believe I am about to say this. I need to know if there's any dish on Karina Alden."

"May I ask why you would be so suddenly interested in sordid society gossip?"

I rolled my eyes. I swear, Anatole heard the gesture. "Ah. I understand. You are intimately involved with yet more problematic Maddoxes and are looking to extricate yourself. I will, of course, be glad to help in this effort." There were way too many layers of meaning in that, but I decided to let them all go. "I will, however, expect a favor in return," Anatole went on.

"Sevarin . . ."

"A professional favor, of course."

I sighed. "I'll fax you over a copy of the wedding menu."

"Not enough."

Vamp bastard. "I'll see if I can arrange for you to be at the tasting for the new nightblood champagne cocktail."

"And we will meet privately to discuss this situation."

"Too far, Sevarin."

"Charlotte, would I ask this if it were not important?"

"I don't know. Maybe."

"That is uncomfortably close to the truth. Very well, it will not be part of the favor, but I assure you, we need to talk."

"Okay, Anatole, we'll play this your way. Why do we need to talk?"

"Because I've just had a very interesting conversation with Henri Renault."

That shattered my thoughts as effectively as a brick dropped onto plate glass. "You . . . You know where Henri is?" I said slowly, making sure Brendan heard every word.

"Alas, no. We conversed over the phone. And you may tell your Brendan if he takes this phone from you, I will not speak to him."

I looked at Brendan, who did in fact have his hand reaching straight for my phone. Scary.

"Well, what did Henri say?" I asked Anatole. "What does he want?"

"I am not at leisure to speak of it at this time." That made me wonder where Anatole was, and who he was with. Unfortunately, unlike some people, I lacked the ability to see through cell phones. "I will meet you tomorrow night, and we will discuss recent events in full then."

Okay, maybe I couldn't see through cell phones, but I could smell a rat at a hundred yards. "You're not talking because Brendan's here and you're being pissy."

"Charlotte, you cut me to the quick. I have never in all the years of my existence been 'pissy.' " But he didn't add anything else. The amused and patient silence stretched out until I couldn't take it anymore.

"Okay. I'll call you tomorrow after sundown." I very carefully did not look at Brendan.

"And I, in my turn, will see what I can find out for you about Karina Alden, Oscar Simmons, and Exclusivité."

I told him thanks, and we hung up. Brendan, as usual was making me be the one to avoid meeting eyes.

"What happened? Why'd Renault call Anatole?"

"He wouldn't tell me. He wants to meet tomorrow night," I said, then added, "I said yes, and no. I don't know what he's up to, but I expect we'll find out tomorrow. Sorry." Too much was happening too fast. I wasn't used to keeping up with this many different kinds of puzzles. That heavy wave of tiredness I'd ridden in there was looming again, and this time it might just take me all the way under.

Slowly, Brendan stood. He crossed the room until he stood directly in front of me and reached out one finger under my chin to tip my face up toward his.

"I have leftover Chinese takeout in the fridge," he said quietly.

"You are a god among men," I answered.

Unfortunately, being full of braised noodles with cloud ear mushrooms, spicy shrimp, and not-so-crispy-anymore duck with plum sauce, all washed down with hot tea and the rest of that glass of scotch, did nothing to convince my body I was not short on sleep. After about the fifteenth jaw-cracking yawn, I agreed to let Brendan drive me back to Brooklyn Heights. He tried to talk me into going back to my own apartment in Queens. Maybe that would have been smarter, but somehow that would have felt like I was retreating, and I wasn't ready to do that, not yet.

So, Brendan walked me up to my warded bedroom and kissed me at the door. We leaned together for a long moment and fumbled through one of our non-good-bye good-byes. Then I shut the door behind myself, locked it, and flopped down on my back on that brass bed. My eyes closed, and I jerked them open again. They closed again, and this time I sat up, swearing. There was another call I needed to make before I let myself fall asleep.

I pulled out my phone, hit my brother's number, and waited.

"C3?" said Chet after the fourth ring. "What's up?"

"Nothing. Too much." I'd thought I'd known what I was going to say, but now that I had Chet on the line, all my casual openings had dried up and blown away.

"Um, Charlotte? It's kinda got to be one or the other of those."

"Chet . . ." This was a mistake. I was going to regret this in the morning—later in the morning. But in my head, I kept hearing Karina Alden's contempt as she talked about her magic-wielding sister, and that got me thinking about all the arguments I'd had with Chet. That, in turn, got me thinking about how many of those arguments I had started, for no good reason at all. "Chet, the whole thing with the loan. I'm sorry."

"It's okay, C3," my vampire brother said. "Tell you what. You got time to get together tomorrow night?"

"You'll still be in town?"

"I can be."

There are moments in your life when you know it's time to just grow up, and for me, this was one of them. "I'd appreciate that. It's gotten complicated out here. Oscar's death is just part of it. Chet, I need your help."

From Chet's side of the phone came the kind of absolute silence only the waking dead can project. Finally, he said, "You need my help?"

Oh, crap. "Chet . . ."

"You. Need. My help."

"Do not make this any harder than it has to be."

"Sorry, but, who are you, and what have you done with Charlotte Caine?"

"Chet!"

The dry, snuffling sounds of my brother trying and

failing to stifle his laughter bubbled through the phone. "Okay, okay, I'm sorry."

"The hell you are."

"So, I'm not, but I will be there."

"I haven't told you where yet."

"Wherever. You're my sister."

It took a long moment for me to get my throat loose enough to say anything else. "Thanks, C4." Chet came after me, so he got to be C4 to my C3. Nobody else calls us by those names. "I'll call you tomorrow after sunset."

"I'll keep the phone on."

We said good-bye, and I hung up and laid the phone on the nightstand. My eyes stung, and my cheeks felt way too hot, the way they do right before you start crying for no reason at all. Which I was so not going to do.

I dropped onto the cushioned window seat and shoved up the sash so I could inhale a deep breath of spring. I told myself the nascent tears came from being painfully tired. It felt like a million years since Felicity had burst into the Nightlife kitchen. There was so much going wrong in so many different places, I had no idea which way to turn. I wanted rest. I wanted my life back. I wanted never to have said yes to Felicity.

I stared down into the Aldens' garden, trying to shove all this far enough into the back of my brain to open up room for sleep. My eyes adjusted slowly to the darkness, and I was able to separate the shadows into comprehensible shapes. Standing in the middle of the blobs and blurs of trees and carefully arranged flower beds were two silhouettes—a woman's and a man's. They stood close, hands on shoulders, foreheads pressed together. The wind changed direction, rustling my crisp curtains and bringing scattered words with it.

". . . Don't know why I love you . . . can't help it . . . wouldn't change it . . . just don't understand why . . ."

Well, that makes it unanimous, I thought as the man,

the nightblood, Gabriel, pulled Deanna closer into his embrace. As I was turning my eyes away, my gaze caught on something else—another silhouette. This one stood on the second-floor balcony that overlooked the garden.

Adrienne Alden watched the vampire lower his mouth to her daughter's throat. As I stared from my little window, Scott Alden came out to lead his wife back inside.

22

Despite my best intentions, my eyelids pulled themselves open at nine fifty a.m. and refused to close again. Tired as I was, sleep had been a long time coming. I kept hearing the conflicted words drifting up from the garden. *Don't know why I love you . . . can't help it . . .*

I was young once. I know what it feels like to have your hormones slam you up against the boards but not know why it's happening with this particular person. Deanna was past that stage, though. At least, she should have been. And Gabriel was undead; he didn't *have* hormones. Their romance had never made sense, but after overhearing that little scene, it was downright bewildering. I mean, the whole incomprehensible-love-stronger-than-the-both-of-us thing worked in movies like *Brokeback Vampire*, but in real life? Not so much.

Then there was Adrienne Alden, just standing on the balcony watching the show, until her husband came and got her.

It was all a little sad, and more than a little icky.

I stared at the wall for a while before rolling over and staring at my borrowed room, closed door, and the watery Tuesday morning seeping in around the curtains. It was one of those heavy, gray, humid days where you just know things are not going to get any better any time soon. I did not want to get out of this bed. But I had a job to do. My guy was down there, cooking for a flock of Aldens and whoever else barged in today. The longer I lay there, the longer he was going to be on his own.

I was on shift. I would show up. I would swear a lot and wonder what in the hell I was doing there. I might also seriously consider handing in my notice so I could go join my ex-writer friend on her chicken farm, but I would show up.

It turned out Reese was not on his own. Deanna Alden slumped on a stool at the kitchen island, downing a glass of orange juice as if it were salvation in citrus form. Her sleeveless, scarlet top had a mandarin collar, but I could still see the fresh welts on her neck. The scent of hot butter and frying batter rose from the cast-iron griddle on the cooktop where pancakes lay in two luscious golden brown rows.

"Morning. Sorry I'm in your territory," Deanna said to me. "Late night and I've got to get out to meet the girls. We're taking the out-of-towners on a shopping tour, and I haven't got my going-away luggage picked out yet . . ." She sounded considerably unperky about this bride-oriented to-do list. "Are you married?" she asked me suddenly.

"Never found anybody who could put up with me long enough." It was pure coincidence that I right then flashed on a memory of Brendan's fingertip under my chin and his invitation to leftover Chinese. I chose to ignore the smirk on Reese's face as he got busy with his spatula, flipping perfectly crisped pancakes over onto their pale bellies.

"I never thought I would either." Deanna sighed. "It's the best feeling in the world, knowing there's somebody who wants to be with you forever." That declaration would have gone over better if she hadn't been eyeing the pancakes Reese piled onto a plate as if she were planning on marrying them.

I crossed the kitchen to peer out the window to the

dining room. Scott Alden sat alone at the table with a series of what looked like reports spread out in front of him. He sipped coffee, rearranged papers, and did not look up. While I watched, Mrs. Alden came in, dressed in a neat navy blue suit. She pecked him on the cheek and he smiled. She was gone without a word, and he still didn't look up from his report pages.

At the island, Deanna was layering the pancakes with thick slices of butter. Reese set the maple syrup down beside her. Two pancakes were left on the serving plate, and they were calling my name.

I pulled one of the tall stools up to the island, bypassed the orange juice, and reached straight for the coffee thermos. "So." It was the most original opening I could manage without caffeine. "Your sister says you and Gabriel met at a charity benefit?"

This was a mistake. Deanna went from tired and starved to utterly furious in less time than it takes brandy to flare up when it hits a hot pan. "You've been talking to Karina?"

My next words needed to be spoken very, very carefully, and probably while I was concentrating on making sure I smeared my butter evenly over every cubic centimeter of pancake. "I ran into her at Perception . . ."

"She's a liar!" snapped Deanna. "Whatever she said, she's a liar!"

Whatever she said? But Deanna wasn't giving me time to get a word in.

"Always the smart one, always trying to get me to magic for her. Come on, Deanna. Just a little of the witchy-woo. Who's gonna know?" This was said in a spot-on imitation of Karina's voice. "But then *I'm* the one who gets in trouble because she'd always rat us right out to Mom."

This was something I could completely sympathize with. "My brother used to get me to filch the extra Pop-Tarts, and then he'd eat them in my bedroom, so Mom never found the crumbs in his."

"Two sisters, and a grandmother with eyes like a hawk, and I never could learn." Reese chuckled. "Oh, please, Reese! Just this one time, Reesey-Peesy. Had to go in the army to get away from them."

"Yeah, well," mumbled Deanna around a mouthful of pancake. "Except with Karina, the whole point was to get me into trouble. I mean, that was why she introduced me to Gabriel in the first place . . ."

Those words brought my train of thought to a screeching halt. "*Karina* introduced you to Gabriel?"

"Oh yeah, you didn't know? It was completely her idea. I should have known something was up when she decided to come to the Save Our Streets gala. She never does the party crap. Always says she's got business, and Mom lets her get away with it, of course, because she's not . . ." Deanna swallowed more pancake instead of finishing that sentence. But I bet the missing words were "a witch." "She was there that night, though, and she brought Gabriel right up to me. She had plans. I could see them written all over her smug little face." Deanna narrowed her eyes. "But it didn't work out her way this time."

"Because you fell in love?" I said.

"Yeah."

"So, what were the big plans?" Reese flipped a pancake onto Deanna's plate and then another onto mine. "Karina's, I mean."

Deanna shrugged and used her fork to push the fresh pancake into the center of the plate where it could soak up syrup and melted butter. "Don't even remember now. Something with a weapons contract or the NIH or something for antivamp perfume. Something stupid like that."

"Antivamp perfume?" If there was a touch of incredulity to those words, it was because I hadn't had enough coffee yet, I'm sure.

Deanna just grimaced. "Karina likes to think she's going to be the Bill Gates of the fragrance world. Got Dad to front the money for the labs and the office. I'll bet he thought she'd just go away and play. But oh no, not Karina. She's got *ambition*. She's got to think *big*." Deanna waved her knife, and caught a glimpse of the kitchen clock. "Crap, I'm late. Gotta meet the girls. Great pancakes. Don't tell Dad anything I said about Karina, will you? He'd hit the roof. Or Mom. Thanks. 'Bye."

Deanna grabbed keys and purse and was out the door before I could get my mouth shut.

"Antivamp perfume?" I said. "A weapons contract for *perfume*?" The words came out as a croak. Because in my head I was seeing that little wrinkled scrap of a clue in Brendan's fingers. The one that looked like part of a recipe, or a formula. I'd thought it was for a celebrity-branded perfume and Oscar had stolen it because he was a cheap bastard. But what if it wasn't? What if it was a weapons formula, and he'd stolen it because it was worth millions?

"Guess they figure the platoon won't mind smelling like garlic," said Reese.

"It can't be that easy." I swallowed and coughed. "It can't be. Somebody'd have done it a long time ago."

"Which would be why there's a contract out for it." Reese flipped some more pancakes off the grill to a clean plate and pushed them to me. "It's not all that easy."

"And maybe Karina got the idea to go for some defense money after Brendan signed his security contract with the city." I looked down at my pancakes and tried to remember I'd been starving a minute ago. I poured on a dollop of fresh syrup, hoping it would help.

"Maybe she's working with him," suggested Reese.

"Can't be. Brendan would have told me." I thought about that bitter, distinctly unperfumy smell Karina carried with her as we walked past all those closed laboratory doors. It was also distinctly ungarlicky. "But if Karina's working on an antivamp contract, what's that got to do with introducing her sister to Gabriel?"

"Got me, boss." Reese turned off the burners under the griddle pan and started untying his apron. He'd already moved on from the rich folks and their mysteries, and I envied him, deeply. "Can you cover here for a while? I gotta go make sure we're good to go into production." Like restaurant work, nine-tenths of catering is in the pre-prep.

There was, however, one thing my sous and I needed to go over first.

"Reesey-Peesy?" I drew the nickname out slowly, layering the syllables with import and relish. "There's really somebody out there who calls you Reesey-Peesy?"

Reese paused by the side door. "Yeah, well, there's somebody out there who calls you, and I'm quoting here, 'sweetie, darling, lamb chop chefy.' "

I winced. "Okay. Okay. I won't tell if you won't."

"Deal."

I waved Reese away, ignoring his chuckles as I set about the important business of finishing my pancakes and coffee. The pancakes were perfect—sweet and fluffy, with lovely, crispy edges. The coffee was gorgeously strong. I began to feel less sorry about having woken up this morning. Unfortunately, my returning optimism encouraged my brain to try to shunt what I'd just heard from Deanna into the ever-shifting puzzle that was the Alden family. I mean, siblings always saw things differently, especially when it came to who got whom into trouble. But Karina's insistence that Deanna was always pushing boundaries, and Deanna's insistence that Karina was the one who was pulling her into trouble—this was something beyond the ordinary sibling double-vision. Then there was the fact that the little bit of list had taken on a whole new meaning.

The house was so quiet, I could hear Mr. Alden rustling his papers out in the dining room. I wondered where Trudy was, and that got me thinking about her and Mrs. Alden, and Mrs. Alden reminding Trudy so sharply she was supposed to "take care of" the guest rooms. Then I remembered that some of those guest rooms held vampires, out cold for the day. These were vampires Karina Alden was really anxious to introduce to the family, according to Deanna, anyway. And Karina was maybe working on anti-vamp weapons contracts.

I also remembered Jacques coming and going all on his own, and how he was supposed to be spending his days in this house, but maybe wasn't.

I looked up at the ceiling. I looked at the Peg-Board by the coat hooks, with its neatly labeled keys, including the bulky ring marked HOUSEKEEPING. I forced my gaze back down to my pancakes—my warm, fluffy, syrup-soaked pancakes. There was no reason whatsoever to rush away from a good plate of pancakes, especially not to tiptoe upstairs and root around in somebody else's guest bedrooms, and especially when that somebody else could fire my ass, and probably should, for even considering that idea.

I stacked used plates and silverware and dumped the whole clattering pile into the sink. I would clean. I would not think about guest rooms anymore. I had done all the breaking and entering I needed to do. I would think about lunch, and snacks; about confirming my catering staff and my orders with my suppliers.

"Chef Caine?"

I turned, reluctantly. Scott Alden came in through the door from the dining room, a stainless travel mug in his hand. "Would you tell my wife I won't be back for dinner?" he said, refilling the mug from the thermos of coffee on the counter. "I have to get ready for the working group meeting. She'll know what I'm talking about."

"I'll tell her." I paused. "Is Trudy still here?"

"She's gone over to her sister's. One of the kids has come down with strep or something, and she's helping out."

Mr. Alden covered his mug and walked out the side door to the porch, leaving me alone in the kitchen, and in the house, because the house was empty now, except for me and whatever unconscious vampires had taken shelter in the guest rooms.

I rolled my eyes toward the ceiling again. "You're tempting me, aren't you?" I asked whatever deity looked down on fools, chefs, and women named Charlotte. "This is what temptation looks like."

Of course it was a bad idea. Of course I did it anyway—like you wouldn't have.

This was the first time I'd ventured onto the third floor of the Aldens' house, and it was beautiful. Even more than the rest of the house, though, this was the close, heavy beauty of another era. To waist height, intricately carved walnut paneling covered the corridor's walls. Above that, figured red wallpaper gleamed like silk and maybe *was* silk. If I'd pushed one of the button switches at the top of the stairs, I'd've gotten some extra light from curving brass lamps that looked as though they had been converted from gas to electric back in the day—way, way back in the day. The air hung thick and humid in that narrow hall and smelled of the rain falling outside. It was so quiet, I could hear the crunch of the Persian carpet fibers under my clogs.

There were six doors total. I stood in front of the first door on the right for a long time, waiting for a noise, or anything, to send me running back to the kitchen where I belonged. But no noise came. I pulled out Trudy's key ring, which I'd appropriated from the Peg-Board. I'd figured the nightblood guests might reasonably be expected to lock themselves in for the day. On the third try, I found the right key, and the cool, glass knob turned easily under my hand. Thick curtains covered the window on the other side, allowing through only the smallest slivers of sunlight. I stepped through and closed the door softly behind myself, then turned the lock again.

The room smelled of fresh air and lemon furniture polish, indicating Trudy had been at work in there recently. As my eyes adjusted, I could see the furniture was a match for the corridor—thick and heavy and distinctly Victorian. Twin beds took up most of the space to my right. Matching dressers stood to the left. The beds, with clean white spreads on them, looked as pristine and innocent as if they'd just come off the set of a fifties sitcom. They were also totally unoccupied. In fact, the whole room looked unoccupied.

I drifted over to the nearest dresser and pulled open the top drawer. It was empty. So was the drawer under it, and the one under that. I checked the second dresser, and the closet—all empty. I turned slowly, fingering the keys in my pocket. So, okay, the Aldens had a lot of spare bedrooms, and they weren't using this one. Except, I kept remembering Mrs. Alden ordering Trudy to "take care" of the bedrooms and breathed in the chemical tang of fresh fake-lemon polish. Trudy had been in there, taking care of something. It might have been only the dust bunnies, but somehow I didn't think so.

Did Mrs. Alden want something destroyed or hidden? And just from whom was she hiding it?

For a brief moment, I regretted I wasn't really Nancy Drew. Especially with the dim light, this place looked perfect for hiding incriminating evidence. It ought to have secret panels or concealed compartments under the floorboards. But they didn't cover finding hidden clues in culinary school, and I didn't even know what I was looking for evidence *of*. The only genuine law-breaking I knew about for sure was the theft of that gun off the living room mantel. Maybe Little Linus had planted suspicions in my brain about Oscar's death, but even if Oscar had been poisoned, I was hardly going to find an empty bottle under the bed with a label saying DON'T DRINK ME.

I did check under the bed, just in case. I didn't find a bottle, or anything else—not so much as the smallest footprint of a dust bunny. From this I concluded that however much the Aldens were paying Trudy, it wasn't enough.

The knob on the next door I tried turned without the key. This had to be a family room. I told myself I should back away. It was one thing to be snooping on guests suspected of stealing. Snooping on the family was completely leveling up the whole plucky-girl-detective fetish.

No, I didn't listen to this very good self-referential advice either.

The Victorian Age had been banished from this second room. When at home, the occupant went in for black iron frames, glass tables, and white gauze curtains, both on the queen-sized bed and the window. The carpet was modern beige, and my clogs sank in deep.

Either Trudy hadn't had a chance to get in there yet today, or this room was off limits. Clothes draped over all the chairs and the bed; mostly designer jeans and brightly colored tops. The dressing table was a battlefield of cosmetics paraphernalia, perfumes, and used tissues. I couldn't picture either Mrs. Alden or Karina making a mess like that, let alone leaving it behind them, so this had to be Deanna's room.

This realization drove me to a moment of pure, girly curiosity. I opened the closet, and there, on a hook on the door, hung the wedding gown. It was a strapless sheath of pure white, trimmed around the waist and hem with silver filigree and clear sparkling stones that would match her engagement ring. Deanna would look like a million breezing down the aisle in that. The longer I looked at that lovely gown, the more depressed I felt, and I could not for the life of me figure out why. I should be angry, not sad. Add one more thing to the Makes No Sense pile.

I left Deanna's room and in the hall stopped once more to listen. The quiet remained unbroken, except for my fishing the key ring back out. The next door on the left was also locked, and the second key I tried opened it soundlessly.

This time, I'd found Gabriel's room. I could tell, because he was lying on the bed, in a pair of dark pajamas.

When you see them on TV, vampires during the day just look asleep. When you see them in reality, they look like what they are—dead. The blue stone in the ring on Gabriel's hand had more life than his open eyes. His jaw hung loose, and his hands and feet were completely limp. His skin had gone slack against his bones and had turned dull and waxy yellow. I knew from experience it wouldn't matter how many times I told myself that body was going to get up and walk. Right now, it was a corpse, and I reacted to it as I would to a corpse—with fear, revulsion, sadness and an immediate desire to get the hell away from it. But I couldn't, because I had to see what the corpse's room had to tell me. Probably nothing. Hopefully nothing. Please, let there be nothing.

It is possible there are creepier ways to spend your time than searching a vampire's bedroom while that vampire is staring at you with day-dead eyes. Cleaning out an Old Country werewolf den, for example, or going for a midnight row in the Black Lagoon. After a while, though, the whole enterprise started to feel more than a little silly. Honestly, nothing says overreaction like poking around through somebody else's sock drawer. Gabriel owned several pairs of black and gray socks and a few matching black and gray silk handkerchiefs. I lifted the silk carefully aside, and found nothing. Going through the other drawers, I found shirts, and ties, and jeans, and nothing. I went through the bathroom and found men's toiletries. I went through the closet and found slacks hanging up neatly and a classic black tux, all ready for the Big Day. The shoes were lined up underneath, and had nothing in them but arch supports.

But there was also a shoe box. With the feeling of

having nothing left to lose, I opened it. In a nest of tissue paper waited the black patent-leather footgear obviously meant to go with the tux. I closed the box again, and was about to put it back, but I moved a little too fast, and something went *clink*.

I shook the box. *Clink.* I tore off the lid, pulled out the black shoes, and a slither of gold spilled onto the closet floor, clattering loudly enough to wake the dead. I looked over my shoulder. The dead stayed still. So, thankfully, did the door.

I poked at the glittering pile carefully, as if it might bite me. When I realized what it was, I sucked in a sharp breath as if it *had* bitten me, because in that pile were a monocle on a gold chain, a gold pocket watch, and a watch chain with all kinds of gold dangly bits hanging off it, like charms from a charm bracelet. There was a heavy gold signet ring too.

All Henri Renault's old-school bling had been hidden away with Gabriel Renault's wedding day shoes. I lifted up the tissue paper to check under the shoes. There was a slim leather wallet. Inside were a state nightblood registry ID and an ATM card, both with the name Henri Renault on them.

I put the gold and the wallet back where I'd found them, closed the closet, and turned away.

"Gabriel, what have you done?" I whispered. Gabriel, of course, didn't answer. His dead eyes stayed still, and the blue gem in the carved gold ring on his hand glittered dully in the rain-filtered light. I meant to head for the door and get out of there before someone could catch me being an idiot. But my eyes wouldn't come along with the rest of me. They had picked up some very uncomfortable ideas from looking at Henri's jewelry hidden in the closet, and now kept staring at that ring on Gabriel's limp hand. I gave up and moved to the bedside, my heart thumping and my mouth dry. I bent close and took a good look.

Gabriel Renault, who was supposed to be from the "Gay Paree" of at least a century ago, had a class ring on his withered hand: New York University, 1987.

That was when I heard the footsteps in the hall outside.

My brain froze, but my body kicked into high gear, and I dove for the nearest hiding place—straight under the bed. My head cracked against the mattress rail. The world spun, and Gabriel's loose arm shook down to smack me in the butt. I gave a squeak I was extremely glad no one else was around to hear. I was also suddenly flat on my stomach under the bed without quite knowing how I'd gotten there.

The door clicked and the hinges sighed and I held my breath, noticing vaguely that Trudy had been busy in here too. As with that empty double room, it was nowhere near as dusty under Gabriel's bed as it should have been.

A pair of well-polished men's dress shoes with pressed blue trouser cuffs walked to the foot of the bed and paused. They turned their toes toward the dresser. I bit my lip as I heard the drawer scrape open and the rustle of cloth. The man grunted, and the shoes turned again, and then went still. I slid my hand over my mouth and tried to muffle the sound of my breathing with my palm.

The man in the polished shoes was more methodical than I had been, and much, much slower. Those shoes traveled back and forth across that room at least a dozen times, while I went from terrified, to embarrassed, to impatient, to needing to pee really badly, and back to terrified, because the polished shoes walked right up to the edge of the bed, and their owner grunted again. There was more rustling cloth, and at last the shoes retreated toward the door. I went limp and pressed my forehead against the floorboards. The door opened. The shoes paused in the threshold.

"You can come out now, Chef Caine," said Lloyd Maddox. "Neither one of us will be talking about this."

And he shut the door behind him.

23

First, I ran for the bathroom. Then, I came back and checked Gabriel's hand. Yes, the ring was gone. Lloyd Maddox had thought it was important too, and he'd taken it. But I also checked the shoe box. The monocle, watch, chain and wallet were all in place. I don't know if Lloyd didn't understand the significance, didn't find them, or just didn't care.

There was, however, the possibility he had gotten hold of the same thought that had crawled into my head—that against the odds, Gabriel had killed Henri sometime after Henri had called Anatole. Maybe *because* Henri had called Anatole.

But probably Gabriel didn't kill Henri. It was somewhere between horrendously difficult and impossible for vampires to break from their sires, let alone actively rebel against them. My brother's sire had waltzed out on him years ago, and he still wore the ring she gave him. Also, Gabriel probably wouldn't commit murder and then just stuff the evidence in a shoe box while he was out cold for the day. Probably. Unless he hadn't had time to do anything else with it before the sun came up. But probably I was being paranoid. Probably.

I started down the back stairs. This was going to be a

very long day, and I could tell already that even a good bout of cooking was not going to settle my jangled nerves. I needed to get out of this house. I needed to be on familiar ground, even if just for a little while. I'd slip the keys I'd borrowed back into place on the Peg-Board, leave a note for Mrs. Alden, and catch a cab back to Manhattan. I'd spend a few hours in my own kitchen, bossing around my own people. When the sun went down, I'd find out what Anatole had to tell me. I'd save thinking about how I was going to ask a major favor from Chet for later.

But as I was formulating this grand plan, a new sound drifted up the back stairs. Below me, a woman was swearing. It was the tight, forceful kind of cursing done by someone who really didn't want to be overheard. So, of course, I pushed immediately through the kitchen door to see what was going on.

What was going on was Trudy was slumped against the French doors, cradling her head in her hands and swearing a blue streak. She saw me and straightened up before I had to say anything stupid such as, *Are you okay?*

"What happened?" I asked instead. I figured this was somewhat less stupid.

"I'm fired," Trudy croaked, letting her hands flop to her sides.

"*What?* Who . . . how . . ." My stammering stopped as quickly as it started. "Lloyd Maddox."

"I got back in time to meet him on his way out. He said he'd be telling Adrienne I wasn't to be trusted anymore, and he didn't even tell me *why*. He's going to get her to fire me, and she'll do it too." I started to say that wouldn't happen, but the words never made it out, because she was right. Mrs. Alden would do it.

"Jesus, Trudy, I'm sorry."

"Twenty-five goddamned years," Trudy spat. "Thrown it all away. I thought I *knew* them. I thought I understood . . ." She pulled a tight face and shook her head.

I pulled out a stool from by the kitchen island. Trudy climbed onto it and sat there, running her hands across her face, and across her smooth gray hair. I couldn't put an arm around her; we weren't on those kinds of terms. Setting down a box of Kleenex within easy reach, I then did the only other thing I could think of. I opened the fridge. Marie had sent over a blueberry coffee cake, so I cut a generous slice and set that down next to the tissues.

"You don't have to . . . ," started Trudy.

"Yes, I do. I'm incapable of offering sympathy without food. It's a chef thing." I pulled out the coffee beans and the filtered-water pitcher.

Trudy's puckered mouth twitched into a fleeting smile. "When my sister had her first kid, I went over every night for two weeks and just . . . cleaned. It was how I could take care of her." She made another face. "We take care of our own. What a crock."

"The Aldens?" I started the coffee brewing and came to sit down beside her.

Trudy nodded, staring out the French doors at the garden. "Twenty-five years, can you believe it? Twenty-five years I've been cleaning up after them. I came to the city to come out, and here I am . . ."

Twenty-five years ago was the Change Time, when the paranormals started to open the coffin, or the broom closet. Trudy had just said she'd come to the city to come out. That meant either she was gay, or . . .

"Trudy, are you a witch?"

"Of course I'm a witch!" Trudy stared at me as if I'd started shedding IQ points on her clean floor. "You don't think Adrienne and Lloyd would let anybody in their house they didn't have a hold over, do you? Don't know how you got in," she added with a frown.

"You'd be surprised." I pulled the coffeepot off its burner and poured us both cups, even though Trudy hadn't so much as looked at her cake. "Okay, maybe you wouldn't. Did your family know the Maddoxes?"

"Pffft." Trudy lifted the cup, looked at the black liquid, and put it down again. "We're so far down the ladder, we can't even see the rung the Maddoxes stand on. No. I just ran away from home." She picked up the coffee cake and bit into it. Marie's own brand of magic was at work again. "I'd spent my life up until then being told I had to hide what I was," she mumbled around her mouthful. "But everybody knew what was happening. Vampires were coming out into the open, and the witches and the weres and all the rest were being hauled out too—either to stand with them or fight them. Of course, it was happening in the cities first. I thought, New York, that's the place for me. I'll be a dancer and a witch, and I'll have my own place and . . ." She shook her head. "I got here just in time for the Five Points Riot."

"Jesus," I whispered. As a neighborhood, Five Points doesn't actually exist anymore. Once, it had been a gang-ruled slum. Now it's just another set of Manhattan streets. But for some reason, back in the mid-1980s, the area became the big hangout for the newly outed but still legally nonhuman paranormals, and the name was revived. Then, one day, somebody decided to go in and clean Five Points' nonhuman residents out. Vigilante gangs armed with stakes and knives started going house to house, "laying to rest" every nightblood they could find. Some witches and weres joined the vigilantes. Some lined up to try to stop them, and found themselves fighting hand to hand and spell to spell with their own kind. The cops stayed away in droves, and the riot went on until sundown. Then, the vampires that the vigilantes hadn't finished off woke up, and the real fun started.

But toward morning, the vampires seemed to go crazy. They started attacking their own side, and each other, in a mindless fury. No one knew quite why it happened.

Vampires do not cooperate well with their own kind. Some people thought that natural enmity combined with a mob mentality in some kind of bad feedback loop. Other people thought one of the witches in the crowd had gotten off some kind of nuke-level antivamp spell and driven them all insane, although no one had ever admitted to anything. If Maddoxes had been in the fight, that theory suddenly sounded a whole lot more likely.

I didn't ask which side Trudy had been on. I didn't ask what she'd seen or done, although given how little she'd seemed to know about vampires, and the fact that she was working for the Maddoxes, I thought I could guess. But I just let her eat coffee cake until she was ready to start talking again.

"Adrienne got the Maddoxes to take me in afterward," she went on finally. "I didn't have a degree, and I'd busted up my knees during the fighting, so the dancing was out . . . I wound up taking whatever cleaning jobs I could get to make ends meet. When Adrienne married Scott Alden, she asked me to come work for them. I was so grateful. I had my own kids by then, and their father was a bum and . . ." She swigged some coffee. "Anyway, it was fine. I could study magic if I wanted, and I had steady work and my schedule was flexible enough that I could take care of my own kids, and then here comes this thing between Deanna and Gabriel and"—Trudy made an exploding gesture with her free hand—"poof! Suddenly I'm working for the Wicked Witch of Brooklyn Heights, and being told to keep my mouth shut and to remember I can be shoved out the door anytime. And Grandpa Lloyd has decided the time is now. Take care of our own," she repeated to her empty plate. "Yeah, right, as long as I remember my place and don't ask for a raise."

"Why the change? I would have thought . . . after everything . . . that you and Adrienne were friends."

"Yeah, you'd think, wouldn't you? By the way, this coffee cake's terrific."

"I'll tell Marie. She's brilliant on a regular basis." I waited.

"Adrienne and I were friends," Trudy said softly. "Until I told her she shouldn't let Deanna get away with the crap she was pulling with this vampire 'boyfriend.' I *told* her those girls didn't give a damn about the family and they would not stop until they'd really broken something, and that something might just be her." Trudy paused. "But she wouldn't listen to me. She never did. She was the responsible one. The fixer. She was going to fix this, and I was going to stay where I belonged." She shook her head hard. "I gave up. I just gave up. You can't blame me, can you?"

"No," I said. And I really couldn't. In the back of my head, though, I was thinking, *So, Adrienne Alden is another control freak. I should have recognized it, even under all that poise and calm. Maybe because of all that poise and calm.*

"Adrienne married a man who needed her, badly. She raised two kids so they'd know exactly who and what they were. Karina was there to be family for Scott, and they were supposed to stay together in their T-typ box. Deanna was supposed to be family and heir for Lloyd and the Maddoxes and stay in the witch box. There," Trudy said, miming dusting her hands. "All nice and even, as long as everybody stayed put."

Except when it came down to it, Adrienne couldn't control her branch of the family any more than Lloyd Maddox could. That thought must have showed, because Trudy nodded.

"There was that thing with Dylan Maddox last year, and then Brendan went public with a way to make real money and a new reputation by working with the city and the vampires rather than against them . . . You have no idea what that's done to the family."

"He doesn't talk about it," I murmured.

"Well, it ain't been pretty," said Trudy. "Especially since Deanna started seeing Gabriel. Now we've got Lloyd Maddox coming in every day and browbeating Adrienne about not being able to control her own daughters, and how she doesn't understand how important she is. And . . . well, today I'm coming in and Lloyd's going out, and he decides to start in on me about not taking proper care of the woman who saved my skinny white ass all those years ago, took me in, and gave me a home and a job. And so, I'm fired."

"I'm sorry," I said again, but at the same time I noticed Trudy's eyes were completely dry, and while she was picking at coffee cake crumbs, she hadn't once reached for the Kleenex.

"It's okay," she said. "It's my own fault really, and . . . well, and I'd actually made up my mind I needed to get out of here a while ago. But . . . well, I thought I'd have at least a little more time, but it's all hit the fan and . . . What am I going to do?" she demanded suddenly. "My one girl's in California and the other's in Texas, and they've both got full houses and mortgages, and I've got nothing except years of maid service and a pair of bum knees. My savings won't last a week, and who's gonna hire me?"

"I would."

Trudy shook her head. "Don't."

But I wasn't listening. Finally, here was something I could help with. "Have you got any supervisory experience?"

"At the Roosevelt Hotel, but that was ages ago . . ."

"You've worked hotels? Great." There was a notepad by the phone. I pulled out my phone, opened the address book and scribbled down a name and number. "Here. Call this, ask for Peter, and tell him Chef Caine sent you. Their hotel's head housekeeper just quit. The manager's a good guy, but you've got to have backbone to deal with him."

Trudy stared at the paper as though it might burst into

flame; around this house, you never knew. "You're serious?"

"Yes, and I know it's not legal for them to ask, but find a way to slip in that you're a witch. Apparently, they have real problems with out-of-towners leaving little half-used Viagra amulets around . . ."

Her eyes narrowed as the despairing housekeeper was rolled under by the hard-bitten survivor. "What do you want for this?"

"I want to know why, if Lloyd Maddox has enough influence with Adrienne Alden to get you fired, he hasn't stopped Deanna's wedding," I told her. "If you don't want to tell me, that's all right. The number's good either way."

Slowly Trudy folded the paper and tucked it into the pocket of her work dress. I watched hard mental calculations chase one another around behind her eyes for a long moment. I also abruptly remembered the tears in her eyes when she'd watched Reese standing by me even as the mess got itself piled higher and deeper.

"He hasn't seriously tried to stop the wedding," she said softly. "He's making a lot of noise, but he's not really doing anything."

I sucked on my cheek, then asked the other question—the one I'd asked Mrs. Alden but gotten no good answer to. "Why wasn't Adrienne worried about Gabriel and company stealing the Arall?"

Trudy frowned. "Because you can't steal the Arall," she said. "It's not a thing; it's a formula."

"Formula?" I repeated slowly. "Like a recipe?"

Trudy nodded. "Adrienne's specialty is potions. She's what's called a Macbeth worker, after the three witches in the play. You know, 'eye of newt, toe of frog . . .' "

This time the penny didn't just drop. A whole shower of coins rained down inside my skull. I was also an idiot—a total and complete idiot. Because I'd been staring at a big-ass clue every time I looked into that beautiful, herb-filled garden. And that was even before I'd gotten my hands on that recipe in Oscar's office.

Karina had an antivamp perfume contract? What could be better than basing it on her family's own secret recipe?

"Mrs. Alden, Adrienne, ripped the ingredients out of the garden so no one would be able to figure the formula out by coming in and having a look around." She'd cleaned out her kitchen for the same reason, throwing away everything and anything that might be a hint as to how she brewed up her potions, any potions, not just the Arall. She'd taken precautions, all right. Only they weren't against the Renaults. They were against her own daughter.

"Deanna knew she'd done it, of course," Trudy went on. "I'm sure she's told Gabriel. Whether he told the other two . . . I don't know."

So, Henri might not have known the Arall was a concept, not an artifact. He even might have thought it was being hidden in plain sight on the mantelpiece, just like I had. "What does the Arall do?"

Trudy hesitated. "I don't know. It's a family secret."

You're lying. I carefully kept my eyes on my coffee. I waited. A lot of times people will talk too much, just to cover a silence. But Trudy was better than that. We both sat there, watching steam curl in our cups, and thinking our own thoughts. I thought about the Last Resort and the Five Points Riot for a while as I stared out at the back garden. But I also thought about Adrienne Alden being a potion worker and a control freak. Would she kill Oscar if she found out he'd gotten hold of the Arall formula? She might. But would she let her daughter take the blame, even if her daughter had betrayed the family?

She might. She was a Maddox after all.

I remembered her watching Deanna and Gabriel out in the dark, declaring their love, and the fact that they didn't know why they loved.

Oh. No. She didn't. She wouldn't.

"Trudy?" I whispered.

"Yeah?"

"Could Adrienne make a love potion?"

Trudy met my gaze, and I watched the pennies raining down behind her eyes.

"Would she make a love potion and feed it to Gabriel?" I asked. "Or maybe to him and Deanna?"

"Oh no. She wouldn't."

"Are you sure? Because it seems to me it'd be a hell of a way to keep Deanna safe from his blood family and to control them both at the same time. Deanna would become very, very cooperative, because she'd need her mother's help to stay together with her true love, and a magically induced love would be strong enough to crack Gabriel's bond with his sire. Wouldn't it?" I added. Just in case the Renaults were planning something like, say, just for argument's sake, theft or blackmail, Gabriel would now be both willing and able to side with Deanna and her family, splitting apart the nightblood forces—and possibly splitting them apart far enough that he would be able to kill his sire if Henri continued to threaten his true love and her family. Adrienne Alden was covering all the bases.

Trudy's face screwed up painfully tight, and she drummed her fingers against the marble countertop. "Maybe. Maybe. Oh, blessed mother and father, she just might have. That would explain it. And she's been putting Lloyd off, telling him she's got it under control . . ."

More ideas dropped into place for me, a whole summer shower of them. "Trudy, can you work potions?"

"A little." She shrugged. "I'm a water witch, so I have an affinity to brewing."

"Could you do up an antidote to a love potion?"

Trudy was very quiet for a long moment. "Yes." She spoke to the bottom of her coffee cup. "Probably, anyway. Breaking a spell is usually easier than setting it." She paused. "What are you thinking?"

"I'm thinking it's not fair." That was why looking at that gorgeous white dress had made me sad. On some level, I'd already known Deanna and Gabriel were being used. "I don't care what else is going on; it's not right." It's not right to play with other people's existence, even if they're your own kids—especially if they're your own kids. I suddenly found I had lost my ability to sit still. "I have to get out of here." I grabbed my knife roll and my chef's coat and headed for the side door.

"Are you going to tell Brendan Maddox?" Trudy asked behind me.

"Yes." I had to. This was so huge, I couldn't even consider keeping it secret, even though my throat tightened painfully at the thought of how this new wrinkle to his family mess would hurt him. "But . . . I don't want him to be the one who has to break the spell. He's taking enough heat as it is."

Trudy nodded, her gray eyes sad. There was so much going on inside her. I couldn't even begin to guess at half of it, but the regret was plain to see. "Okay. This all might take a day or so. I'll call as soon as I can."

"Thank you. My number's on that paper too." I paused. "I'm really sorry, Trudy."

"Me too, Charlotte. Me too." She stood up, smoothing down her dress. "In case I don't get the chance later . . . thank you for everything."

She headed upstairs, I assumed to pack something or leave official notice, or maybe key the Scarlett O'Hara staircase. I took my stuff and headed out the door. As soon as I was clear of the house, I had my phone in my hand. I'd thought I'd be going to Nightlife first, but my conversation with Trudy had changed my mind. I needed to get hold of Brendan, now. He had to hear what I knew, whether he wanted to or not. Because it was his family, and because he trusted me.

I just wished that one day I could deliver the closest thing I had to a boyfriend some good news for a change.

24

But Brendan wasn't answering his phone, again. I left a voice message asking him to call, and telling him I'd be at Nightlife instead of Brooklyn Heights. As I did, another one of those bad feelings crawled slowly up my spine. After unearthing Henri Renault's jewelry in Gabriel's bedroom, and spotting an NYU class ring that might just have belonged to a kid murdered right around the time the Five Points Riot was going down and that also might be the center of a blackmail scheme, I found I really did not like not knowing where Brendan was.

I could have caught a cab back to Manhattan, but I needed time. I had to think about what I was going to tell my people. I had to give Brendan time to get my message and call back. So, I sat on the subway train, watched the lights and stations flicker past, and tried and failed to think. And then tried some more. And then failed some more.

Because I was about to put a halt to the wedding of the decade, deliberately and with malice aforethought. That meant the money was never going to materialize. Not to mention that Felicity was never going to speak to me again. Elaine was going to quit for sure this time. Mel might just possibly forgive me, after a while. At least I could put off telling those three what had happened until after I'd gotten Trudy's antidote to Gabriel and Deanna. But I had to tell Reese and Zoe today, just like I had to tell Brendan. They deserved to know. Besides, there was no way I was letting any of my people walk back into that double-width, Italianate mansion with its so thoroughly messed-up residents. Zoe and Reese would be all right, though. They had plans, and by now, I was pretty sure I knew what those plans were. I just didn't know how I was going to manage without them.

I had to tell Marie too. I rested my head against the train window. I was a dead chef walking.

I let myself in through the back door of Nightlife and was greeted by a kitchen full of silence. The lights were all on. Pans of perfect golden brown chiffon cake occupied the cooling racks by the pastry oven and filled the air with sweetness and warmth. But they were unattended, as were the prep stations, the cooktop, and the grill. I dropped my purse on my desk and put my hands on my hips. I'd been working myself into my own particular dither only to walk in on an empty kitchen? It seemed like a waste of effort.

Then I heard the voices coming in from the dining room.

"We *can't*, not while Alden week is going on," Zoe was saying. "You both know it. She'll have a total, control-freak meltdown."

"It does not matter," answered Marie in full Cakeinator mode. "It is up to her how she will react. It is up to you to act like grown-ups, not naughty children."

I drifted to the door and leaned in close. I might have qualms about eavesdropping on clients, but those were *my* people out there.

"Zoe," said Reese, "that meltdown you're worried about is already on the way. She *knows* we're keeping something from her. Hell, the whole kitchen knows what's happening.

I had to ban Hank from coming out to Brooklyn anymore. He almost gave it up last time."

"I know, I know. But we need her focused on the Alden wedding, for Nightlife, and for her sake as well. As soon as the wedding's over, I'll tell her myself, I swear."

It's not often in life you get to time your own entrance. "What are you going to tell me?" I asked, pushing through into the dining room.

The looks on my sous-chefs' faces as they jumped back would stay with me for a long time. Marie, of course, did not jump back. She just turned smoothly, so I could see her mouth was set in a thin straight line.

"Chef Caine . . . ," began Zoe.

I held up my hand. "I know." There's a space between calm and numb that you get to when you're already aware the worst has arrived. It's surprisingly peaceful there. "You're quitting. You've gotten the truck, and you're setting up on your own." Zoe opened her mouth, but I didn't let her finish. "I don't blame you. If it makes things any easier, the Alden wedding really is off now. I'll be settling up with Felicity Garnett as soon as it's official, but our kill fee isn't going to come to even a quarter of what we would have made on the catering. So right now, I don't know how Nightlife's going to make it through next year. If you're going, this is a very good time."

Reese folded his arms and looked to Zoe. Zoe responded by rolling her eyes. "Told you, didn't I? Control-freak meltdown."

"This is not a meltdown." Zoe had seen me melt down, and I would have expected her to be able to tell the difference.

"Of course it is not," said Marie. "You only melt down when you cannot be the martyr."

I stared. I couldn't help it. Marie waved my stare away. "*Madre de Dios.* You think none of us know you by now? You believe you have an answer you do not in fact have, and you are answering to nothing but your imagination. Again." She added that last word, looking at me over the rims of her glasses. "No one is leaving. Nightlife is going to be reviewed by the *New York Times*."

Those words sank in and set off a very strange reaction in my brain. A sort of *whump* sound, like when you turn a gas burner on high.

"The *New York Times*?" I said, just to make sure I'd heard properly. Because there now seemed to be a ringing in my ears. Zoe was trying to stare daggers at Marie, but she was hopelessly outclassed. No one was answering me. "Nightlife is going to be reviewed by the *New York Times*?" I said, louder this time.

"Probably not for a month or so," said Reese. "Zoe's contact's not completely sure . . . but we're on the critic's target list."

Zoe sighed and shrugged in surrender. "That's what we haven't been telling you. I got a call from a friend after you took the wedding on. I didn't want to tell you because you would have . . ."

"Had a total control-freak blowout?"

"She said meltdown," Reese jerked his thumb at Zoe. "Now, I personally, think a blowout is much more your style."

They were all looking at me, waiting to find out which noun was going to show up. Pride elbowed anger, and both turned around to face my staff. I could let them have it. I should let them have it. This was not a small secret, or the discovery somebody had described me as having a frowny face. This was massive. The *Times* was the gold standard. There were thousands of restaurants in New York, and the *Times* chose only a handful each year to visit. Even with the proliferation of online review sites, the opinion of their dining critic could still completely make a restaurant. Or completely break it. This could be the most important thing to happen to Nightlife to date, and my staff had kept it from me, because they thought I couldn't handle myself. They thought I was as bad as Oscar and had to be *managed* . . .

But Marie's words loomed up in my brain. *You are answering to nothing but your imagination.*

I stomped hard on the brakes of my runaway thoughts, because if I didn't, I was just proving all three of them right, and not in a good way.

"Okay." I made my shoulders square themselves. These were my people. I owed them my best. What was happening with the Aldens was not their fault. "I was serious about the wedding being off. Before the end of the week, our bacon will officially need saving, and a good *NYT* review could at least help. Is there a current picture of the critic up in the kitchen?" The *Times* critic was supposed to visit restaurants anonymously. Maybe that happened the first time or two. After that, everybody had the picture posted.

Zoe nodded. "And Robert and Suchai are on red alert."

"They'll spot him. Thanks for handling this, Zoe."

She blinked. "You're welcome, Chef."

Reese was controlling himself, manfully, but it wasn't going to last much longer. I clenched my jaw and crossed my arms to conceal that I was also clenching my fists. There was something else that needed to be taken care of right now.

"Zoe? Marie?" I said.

"Yes, Chef?" replied Zoe. Marie just waited with exaggerated patience to hear what I had to say, but she clearly did not hold out great hopes for it.

"As you may know, Reese has been thinking we should consider a food truck . . ."

Zoe didn't let me get any further. "Now's a bad time to launch a truck. The trend's already peaking." She said this directly to Reese. Clearly, there'd been more than one conversation going on behind my back. "But if we were going to think about expanding, we should consider a café."

"Café?"

"Quick and casual after-sunset dining," said Zoe. "No one's really going after the nighttime equivalent of the lunch crowd. We could have a take-out counter with Marie's milkshakes leading the list. It'll have to be fast, smooth service, very tight logistics. Reese would be just the one to run it."

I felt my eyebrows rise. "You don't want the job?"

Zoe shook her head and said matter-of-factly, "I want your job."

"It's a nice idea," cut in Reese. "And I do like being Just the One. But start-up costs would be a mint and a half. That's the whole point of getting a truck. Start-up's nothing, even with the permits. We'll be turning a profit at the end of the first month. And," he added as Zoe drew a deep breath, "it won't matter if the 'trend's already peaking.'" I never met anybody who could pack more attitude into a pair of air quotes than Reese. "It's not peaking for haute noir food. That trend's barely even started."

Marie threw up her hands. "Children. I am surrounded by children. I am going back to my cakes."

"Um, about the cake, Marie . . ."

She waved me off without even bothering to turn back around. "I already knew this was not happening. Those cakes are for my niece's *quinciñera*."

I was surprised, and aware I should not have been. This was Marie. She was different from the rest of us. Witness how I wasn't chewing her out for using the restaurant kitchen for personal business. "How'd you know?"

"No one who would choose raspberry and vanilla over my apricot walnut is in her right mind."

Marie vanished into the kitchen, leaving me with Zoe and Reese and the grand schemes they still hoped could rise from the ashes of this latest disaster. They were talented, and impatient, and, whether I wanted them to be or not, they were right. Yes, money was an issue—a hulking eight-hundred-pound gorilla of an issue. But I knew this much—if Nightlife stood still, it would die. We had to grow. The only question was how.

Now was a chance to show what I was really made of. I needed to make a decision, and for a change, I knew just what it should be.

"I want business plans on my desk," I said. "For the café and the truck. Cost projections, revenue projections, menu outlines—the works. We get a good review from the *Times*, and we'll implement the best proposal."

At this, my sous didn't just look at each other; they sized each other up, gleefully.

"So, get on it," I told them both. "We're on the clock."

"Yes, Chef," said Zoe calmly.

Reese's eyes gleamed. "Oh yeah. I can work with this."

I watched them as they headed for the kitchen, ornery pride and ornery affection jockeying for position inside me. Then, a thought smacked me in the back of my head, reminding me what was going on outside, and that I'd better fight my way out of the current mess before diving headfirst into the next one.

"Reese? One sec."

"Yes, Chef?" Reese tried to turn toward me while still keeping a wary eye on Zoe as she vanished into the kitchen.

"You said there're only a couple trucks out there doing haute noir? Are any of them actually operated by vampires?"

"Don't know offhand, but I can find out."

"I'd appreciate it."

He paused. "Why am I finding this out?"

"Because I think one of those vampires might be Jacques Renault, and I want a little word with him about the behavior of his relatives."

"Just you, or you and Chet?" Reese slowly rubbed his hands together. Translation: You'd better have backup on this or I'm not moving off this spot.

But for once, having it hinted that I might possibly need help for any given enterprise failed to raise my hackles. "Chet, and a certain vampire journalist who both just happen to be due to come around here tonight." Or they would be as soon as I made a couple of phone calls.

Reese thoughtfully cracked the knuckles of his tattooed hands. "I'll see what I can find out, Chef."

He also headed into the dining room. I slumped onto one of the bar stools and tried to suppress the urge to pour myself a scotch. Alcohol was not the answer. It was never going to be. I hopped off the stool and circled round the bar. The fridge back there held bottled water, like just about every fridge in the place did. I cracked one open and chugged down a healthy portion.

Slowly, I set the bottle down on the bar. Alcohol was not the answer. You could overdo it on alcohol. It could even kill you.

It was also, in its pure form, a colorless liquid. I looked at the water bottle; I looked at the rows of liquor bottles on the shelf behind the bar. I thought about that scrap of a clue from Oscar's office, and the second line, the one that looked like "CH" and a squiggle that I'd thought looked like a numeral three. CH3 couldn't be a word, but it could be a chemical.

I yanked my smartphone out of my pocket and fired up Google. I entered CH3 into the little white oval, and hit Search. I waited. I drank more water. I listened to the voices drifting from the kitchen. I didn't want to be right. I didn't want to be right.

The little Search window cleared, and I got my list of answers. The first was an online encyclopedia article about methane. The second was a Web page for Channel 3. But the third was an entry for methyl alcohol.

Methyl alcohol, also called methanol, or wood alcohol, was colorless and when ingested, could produce dizziness, blindness, and death. These sounded a lot like the symptoms of a stroke.

It was easy to get, and widely traded. You could dissolve all kinds of things in it, I read, which was why it was used as a base for everything, such as paint thinner, and even perfume—or maybe even antivampire potions.

I closed the Search window, and hit REDIAL on O'Grady's number.

"Chef Caine," he answered immediately. "What is it this time?"

"Oscar was poisoned," I said, looking at my water bottle, which was just like the one I had at my station, and just like the one I left open on my desk almost every night. I thought about how I could easily knock back half a bottle before I noticed something smelled funny, because at this point I was never paying attention. I pictured Oscar realizing he'd stepped over the line in his dealings with the Aldens and staggering around his office as he tried to stuff incriminating evidence into the shredder before calling 911, and not quite making it. "And I know how they did it."

25

Of course, O'Grady did not rush off with the crime scene tape. He made me repeat everything I suspected, and I knew he was writing it all down. He thanked me and hung up. Now, it was a waiting game, yet again.

Fortunately, the sun was setting and Nightlife was gearing up, so I had plenty to keep me busy. I also had one or two little agenda items of my own I fully intended to complete before the night was over.

I left messages for Anatole and for Chet to meet me at the restaurant at closing time. Neither one would be thrilled to see the other, but I'd deal with that later. I also geared up my most carefully neutral voice and called the Aldens, saying that I was needed in Manhattan to continue to work on event coordination and that I would be calling them with updates in the morning.

The real problem was Brendan still wasn't answering his phone, and for the first time in my adult life, I felt almost too keyed up to cook. Fortunately, word had spread among my staff that I was in on the news about the *Times*. So, instead of a jumpy, worried line crew looking over their shoulders at me, I had a bunch of pros intent on testing themselves. Zoe and Reese cracked the whip for me in the kitchen. Suchai was on the case in the front of the house, and the dining room was full to the brim. No matter what happened tomorrow, today we were doing great.

Despite all this, I couldn't relax into my work. I'd slipped my phone in my pocket next to my spray bottle, and I couldn't ignore its weight jiggling around in there as I moved from the pass to the hot line and back again. I also couldn't ignore the way it wasn't ringing, and wasn't ringing. For the first nonringing hour, I silently cursed warlocks and not-quite-boyfriends in my head. Then, I started praying to whoever looked after warlocks and chefs that Brendan was okay wherever he'd gotten to. Then I swore I was going to kick his ass up and down Tenth Avenue, and then break up with him. Oscar was dead, and Adrienne Alden was maybe a poisoner who was framing her daughter, or maybe Scott Alden was doing the framing, or maybe Karina was the poisoner and was getting help covering up from her father. Gabriel had maybe murdered his sire, and how *dare* Brendan not call me with all these maybe's going on?

Then I started promising that I'd never, ever, forget to call him again, if he'd just call me now. Just one little call.

But that wasn't the real agony. The real agony came at ten twenty when I felt my phone buzz against my hip, and I didn't have hands free to answer it. It was a full ten minutes before I could snatch it out of my pocket and read the text message.

am fine on lead call l8tr. bm

I just about dissolved into a little puddle right there on the line, but I recovered myself and stuffed the phone back in my pocket. "I'm going to kill him," I told Zoe.

"Yes, Chef," she said. "Marty! Pick up twenty!"

The next message came at twelve fifteen: *still fine lead playing out*

"So very dead." I shoved the phone back in my pocket. "Eighty-six the tuna! We're out of tuna!"

The next one came at one thirty-three: *still fine staking out my guy wish u wr here.*

"Dead, dead, dead." I grabbed the squeeze bottle of white truffle oil.

"I wish he'd send you some bad news so you'd quit wanting to kill him," said Reese. "The boy just plain don't know how to treat his lady."

"Gimme two pumpkin soups!" I hollered, tearing a ticket off the machine and shoving it onto the dupe slide. "And where the hell's my duck for fifteen? Oh, and Reese? Shut up!"

"Working, Chef!"

Chet and Anatole showed up right at two a.m., just as Robert was locking the front door. And I'd been right. They were not happy to see each other. At least, Chet was not happy to see Anatole. Anatole just bowed to my brother and gave his annoying and inscrutable smile some extra airtime.

"Yes, Chet," I said with a sigh as my brother opened his mouth. "I will tell you what the hell he's doing here." I hadn't had a new message from Brendan for the last twenty-seven minutes, and my shoulder blades were going all twitchy trying to stop my hand from reaching for my phone yet again. "But upstairs, okay?"

"Good evening, Charlotte. Caine," said Anatole, cool and absolutely unruffled. "Upstairs?"

"You'll see."

I don't have space at Nightlife for a private office, and there are times, such as during closing, when the dining room's as full of staff as the kitchen. Although you might not have guessed it, I do also just plain get tired of hanging around the back alley. So, over the course of the past few months, I had manufactured a place where I could get a little privacy. I led Anatole and Chet up three flights of underlit stairs that smelled of various kinds of smoke, out onto the roof, and into to my own private garden.

The wind gusted hard, ruffling my too-short hair and carrying with it the smells of exhaust and impending summer. It rattled the plastic sheeting over beds of baby lettuce and microgreens. The herbs, bush beans, and, most importantly, the tomatoes, stood in their own boxes, waiting for sunlight to replace the tarnished silver of streetlight that reflected off the glass skyscrapers rising all around us.

"What's all this?" asked Chet, gesturing at my greenery.

"This is what I've been up to since you left." It wasn't anything close to what the Aldens had, but I'd nailed together the frames for those boxes, helped to haul bags of soil up those three flights of stairs, and set up the blue compost bin by the air duct. This garden was as much mine as the kitchen downstairs.

"This is you breaking about fifty municipal codes," Chet shot back. "Good going, Charlotte."

Sensing an impending and possibly lengthy sibling-only digression, Anatole intervened. "Enchanting," he murmured. "What else have you been keeping secret from me? Us?" he corrected himself as Chet narrowed his eyes.

Sharing is not something I do naturally. But that had to stop. If I was to put an end to the mess the Aldens had gotten me and Brendan into, I needed both Chet and Anatole, whether I wanted to need them or not.

So, I told them how O'Grady suspected Oscar's death might be murder. I told them he suspected it might have something to do with Adrienne Alden, because of the death of an NYU student that happened around the time of the Five Points Riot. I pointed out that Adrienne Alden and Trudy Lyons had been close friends, except not permanent ones, because Trudy had been trying to warn Adrienne that her daughters were out of control and was chafing at being underpaid. Then there was the fact that Adrienne was probably trying to control Deanna, the important magical heiress daughter, using a love potion. Except it was Karina, the smart, successful T-typ daughter who introduced the Renaults to Deanna and who had access to a poisonous substance that could mimic the disorientation and blindness that accompanied a stroke. Add to this the detail that Gabriel Renault had an NYU class ring on his hand, or at least he had before Lloyd Maddox stole it. But although he stole the ring, Lloyd left Gabriel lying in peace, near a shoe box full of Henri's accessories. Oh, and Lloyd had fired Trudy, who was revenging herself by making me a love potion antidote.

When I finally ran out of breath, Anatole had both eyebrows raised. Chet, on the other hand, whistled.

"Wow. Charlotte, that all makes no kind of sense whatsoever."

"I beg to differ," said Anatole.

"There's a surprise," muttered Chet.

Anatole ignored him. "It explains a great deal about a phone call I received from Henri Renault."

"Renault called you?" Chet said this to me, as if he couldn't believe I had left out this detail from my story. Maybe I shouldn't have, but it was already getting to be one hell of a long story, and I wanted to find out what Anatole had to add to it.

"Renault claims he has the legendary *Popeth Arall*, and he has offered to sell it to me."

"I thought you didn't know what the Arall was."

"I never said that," Anatole reminded me with gentle smugness. "I said I didn't know it belonged to the Maddoxes. The legend of the weapon itself has been around for centuries."

Chet gestured impatiently. "And Henri said he'd sell it to you. And . . . ?"

"Actually, he said he was going to auction it off, but if I wanted it, I could have first chance."

"What did you say to him?" asked Chet.

"I told him I would consider it."

"Does he know you don't actually have any money?" I put in.

Anatole's shrug was perfectly noncommittal. "He does not believe it. Anyone as old as I must have amassed a considerable fortune."

"He's supposed to be pretty old himself. Why is he shilling for money?"

"This is one among many questions I asked myself. Henri is not as subtle as he thinks he is, but neither is he stupid. In the past, he has run some very long games, and he has used his pretty children as major players."

A hard laugh burst out of me as I pictured the monocled little vampire, who couldn't keep his hands off the help, trying to go head to head with Anatole. "Henri Renault thinks he can con *you*?"

That earned me a small smile. "Your faith in my judgment is most flattering, Charlotte. But no, I don't think Henri believes he can con—to use your word—me. I am certain he *believes* he has the Arall. He heard it was a weapon, he stole a weapon, and he is trying to sell it. Which leaves me with the question, should I try to buy it?"

Chet shoved his hair back, only to have the wind plaster it right back across his forehead, and glowered at us both. He'd been working on that glower. I could feel its cold pricking against my skin. It was an odd reminder that my baby brother was growing up, in a nightblood kind of way. "Will one of you explain to me why we're standing up here and not sharing any of this priceless info with O'Grady and the Paranormal Squadron?" And that was another one. Six months ago, he never would have suggested going to the police for something like this. It was, I had to admit, a damned good question.

"To begin with," said Anatole, "I avoid talking to O'Grady if at all possible. Also, because what will make

Charlotte's life easier is much more important to me than what will make his life easier." Anatole had a highly personalized code of conduct. I suppose it was a good thing to see it skewing in my favor, but I couldn't shake the sensation it gave me of the roof shifting underfoot. "What will make Charlotte's life easier is finding out what this thing Henri has actually is, and quietly returning the stolen property to the Maddoxes."

"She's set to ruin the wedding, so how is this going to help her?"

"Lloyd Maddox wants the wedding ruined, so that is not an issue. If she also quietly returns the Arall, he will be more than ready to see that she is left alone so she will have no reason to go talking to the police about any little behavior problems on the part of his grandchildren. A state of affairs I am also happy to help facilitate."

"Try again, Sevarin," I said so Chet wouldn't have to. "You just want to know what Henri's got."

Anatole shrugged. Clearly, this little difference of interpretation was of no importance. "I told Henri I would meet with him tomorrow night and we would bargain then. It is my intent to get whatever he has, and allow you, Charlotte, to hand it back to the Maddox clan. You will, I hope, tell them who helped retrieve their property."

My mouth opened before I had any words. I closed it again. There still weren't any words. There was something else going on behind those impenetrable green eyes. No one can do enigmatic like an old vampire, and Anatole was pouring all he had into the act. He stood there smiling just enough to show the tiniest corner of a fang. And all at once, I understood.

"Oh, em effing gee," I whispered. "You're doing this to get to Lloyd Maddox. If you find out what's going on with the Renaults, he'll owe you a favor!"

"I've been at his throat, and I've been a thorn in his side. I decided to try a new tactic. It is a new age, after all."

"You're going to kill him with kindness," Chet said, and for the first time I heard admiration creep into his tone.

Anatole's smile broadened, and smug satisfaction radiated from him like heat off a flat-top grill. "And there is not one thing he can do about it."

"So where are you going to pull off this fast shuffle you've got planned?" Because even to a hardened control freak such as myself, it seemed the best place to be for such an encounter was well out of the way.

Anatole, however, was not going to give me the option. "I thought Nightlife after closing would make an excellent location for an exchange of this nature. Neither too private nor too public."

"Nightlife?" I stared at him. "You want me to leave you and a thieving nightblood in my restaurant while he's trying to use you as a fence for stolen magic?"

"Actually, I was hoping you would both be there. I prefer backup for such operations."

Skepticism strong enough to wilt my lettuces oozed out of Chet. "You don't think Henri's going to get suspicious to see me and my sister at your little bargaining session?"

"I think he's rather expecting it." Anatole smiled, waiting for me to catch up. He didn't have to wait long.

"You told him I was your girlfriend, didn't you?"

"That is an approximate translation of what I told him, yes."

Chet was giving me a look so pointed, I could have staked him with it. I waved him back. I could handle this one, and turned my best you're-late-for-your-shift glower onto the senior nightblood. "Anatole . . ."

"It was necessary to impress upon him you were not to be interfered with. I am afraid our Henri Renault is woefully behind the times. There are only a few connections between nightblood and dayblood that he recognizes, and those are all proprietary."

That might even have been the truth, but it didn't make

me back down on my glower at all, even though I sensed that it wasn't quite getting through to Anatole. I gave it up. I ran my hand through my hair and stared out at the city. We had to get to Henri. We, I, had to find out what he'd actually stolen, as well as what he knew about Adrienne Alden and all the rest of it. At the same time, if I let Henri into Nightlife, there could be real trouble. The last time I'd gotten mixed up in a showdown with nightbloods, there'd been fire involved.

"I'm there the whole time," said Chet to Anatole.

"*What!*" I answered with what was apparently an expected level of calm, because Chet just shrugged.

"You were going to do it anyway."

"I was not!"

This declaration was not only less than strictly true; it left me with the feeling that I'd suddenly reverted to being six years old. And, for the record? It was no fun at all being six years old with two vampires looking down at you in amused disbelief.

Chet turned back to Anatole. "Brendan's going to want in too. She'll tell him."

"That had occurred to me."

I was going to have to get some more girlfriends. I'd had it about up to here with the testosterone squad.

"Do I actually need to be here for this?" I demanded. "Because if you two have important man talk, I'll just go back to my knitting."

Anatole looked at his watch. "I believe we are finished. Renault will be contacting me later tonight. I'll tell him we will meet here tomorrow."

"Not here," I said. "I'm not risking Nightlife, or any of my people over this."

Anatole waved, conceding the point. "Where would you suggest?"

"I've got a friend with a little place in Midtown." I was even fairly sure I could talk Mel into going along with the operation. His sense of drama and gallantry would rise to the occasion, as long as he didn't have any events planned.

"I will trust you to make the arrangements then," said Anatole. "Will nine p.m. suit?"

"Would it actually matter if I said no?"

"Of course it would. But I do not anticipate it becoming an issue."

My answer was cut off by the roof door opening. Zoe leaned out of the stairwell with the air of somebody ready to beat a fast retreat. Smart woman.

"Chef?" she called from her safe distance.

"What's going on, Zoe?"

"We're ready to lock up, and Reese says the truck you're looking for is the Bite Mobile, and it'll be on the corner of Sixth and Grand for another half hour."

"Great. Thanks. Tell everybody they can head out."

Zoe started to pull the door shut but stopped halfway, obviously steeling her nerves. "Is there something I need to know, Chef?" There were claws unsheathing behind those words.

"Not yet, I promise."

Zoe, however, did not seem to be in a trusting mood. She looked at Anatole, and at Chet, and then back to me. "If the place is burned down tomorrow morning, I'm going to find your ass and hand it to you."

"You'll be first on the list," I promised. Zoe nodded, satisfied, and left us there, closing the door solidly behind her.

"What're you looking at the Bite Mobile for?" asked Chet, displaying an unprecedented level of tact by changing the subject.

"Jacques Renault's working there—I think, anyway—and I want to talk to him."

Anatole's eyebrows inched up a fraction. "Jacques Renault, who has been making his living robbing rich houses with his blood family for a century or so, is now working a food truck for minimum wage? Do you not think that would be rather a comedown?"

"You were there, Anatole. Jacques's tired of being a parasite, and he thinks his blood family's lost their minds and, thanks to the Equal Humanity Acts, he's got a choice as to how he makes his living."

Chet shook his head. "Charlotte . . ."

"This is what I needed your help for, Chet," I said, cutting him off. "Jacques needs to know it's possible to get away from his sire. That is, if he still wants to once he's heard about the love potion."

A whole set of possible replies came and went behind my brother's dry eyes. At last, he dropped his gaze to the heavy gold ring on the third finger of his left hand. "Yeah," he agreed. "It's possible to get away. But now I've got to ask you, why are you doing this?"

I remembered how Jacques looked at me and said the word was my little brother and I were okay. "Because against the odds, I think he might actually be a decent guy. And"—I ground my teeth together—"because it's his family and he deserves to know what's really going on and have his chance to do something about it."

Chet tilted his head as if he needed to look at me from a whole new angle. "This is a change, coming from you."

"Yeah, I know. Would you help me talk to him? Both of you?"

Anatole smiled, and, to my surprise, bowed out. "As delighted as I am to be included in this party, I'm sure your brother is capable of handling Jacques Renault."

"I am too," I said. "But I don't know who Jacques's going to have with him."

Anatole faced Chet. Chet faced Anatole.

"Hungry?" asked Chet, showing his fang.

Anatole flashed his right back. "I find I am. Shall we?"

Guys. I rolled my eyes and pulled out my cell. Nothing new from Brendan. I shoved my phone back into my pocket but kept my hand curled around it as I led the nightbloods down to the street. I hoped they couldn't tell I was really doing this to keep busy. If I stood still measuring the amount of time it had been without hearing from Brendan, I was going to get really scared.

Oh, and just so you know? Any night where your best option is to track down a vampire to try to make him talk to you about his illegal activities is automatically a bad night.

26

It shouldn't surprise anybody that a food truck calling itself the Bite Mobile would be painted a shiny black with scarlet accents and signage. I did (reluctantly) like the retro-Airstream shape, but whoever had the idea to fit it with outsized fins on the back needed to be taken out and lectured, sternly.

To prove we were not entirely slow learners, Anatole, Chet, and I not only worked out ahead of time what we'd do when we found the truck; we split up before we were within the line of site of the take-out window. So, it was only Anatole and I who walked up to the window. And sure enough, there was Jacques, manning a bank of blenders while a shorter nightblood girl was frying onions on the compact flattop.

"Bon soir." Jacques turned the French on full from his station at the miniature prep counter. "What can I . . . Shit!"

Having successfully grasped the essentials of the situation, Jacques Renault slid past the grilling nightblood and bolted out the rear door, which was where—per our simple yet elegant plan—Chet had stationed himself. As Jacques tried to dive for the commuter lane, Chet grabbed him around the waist and swung him onto the curb.

Jacques swore in outraged French fit to burn our ears off. The grilling nightblood hissed hard and grabbed a cell phone off the shelf overhead.

"I'm with them." Chet nodded toward me and Anatole as he knotted his fist into Jacques's collar to keep him from trying another escape. Jacques responded by balling up a fist and swinging it straight into Chet's outstretched palm. Chet grunted and held on. Score one for my little brother.

"We need to talk to Jacques," Anatole informed the grilling nightblood. A stout woman when she was alive, she was now somewhat withered and saggy, with fading tattoos on her arms and two long braids of brown hair hanging down her back.

She squinted over her shoulder at her simmering onions. "This gonna take long?"

"That depends entirely on him. We will attempt to have him back to you shortly."

"In one piece, 'kay?"

"That also depends entirely on him."

She shrugged and waved the spatula, then went back to stirring her onions. Running a nightblood food cart on the mean streets must be a lot more exciting than running a restaurant, because if someone had caused one of my staff to bolt out of my kitchen, I would have at least asked for ID.

However, this was her business, not mine. I nodded in a friendly way, one food pro to another. I admit I did also cast a glance at the chalkboard menu. It was heavy on the organic and locally sourced blood, and it had a whole range of sandwiches for the daybloods that looked as if they'd be really tasty if executed decently. Maybe this truck idea wasn't as tacky as it seemed.

There was no time for an exchange of views, though. Anatole and Chet were already walking Jacques around the corner and into the shadows between an alley and a black SUV that I was pretty sure was illegally parked. I hurried to catch up.

"Hi, Jacques," I said, feeling more than a little as if I should be wearing a trench coat and a fedora. Chet had let him go, but I did notice that my brother had also stationed himself in the mouth of the alley at Jacques's back, while Anatole was on guard in the front. Jacques would have to be faster than both of them if he wanted to make a break for it, and I didn't think even he could be. He also didn't look at all happy. I couldn't find it in me to blame him for that one.

"Now what?" Jacques was doing his best to project annoyance, but I could feel the fear seeping out under the bluster.

"I wanted to talk to you about Henri and Gabriel," I said.

"Well, I do not want to talk to you."

"You do, because you want to know how Deanna Alden got her—what did you call it—'Maddox hooks' into Gabriel."

Jacques started forward, and Chet, who I strongly suspected was enjoying a chance to play the heavy, clamped a warning hand on his shoulder. "What do you know?" demanded Jacques.

I put my hand in my pocket. Of course I had my spray bottle. I trusted Chet and Anatole to do their best, but you never knew who might be sneaking up behind you or charging you from the front. "I think Adrienne Alden gave Gabriel a love potion."

Vampires, even Vampires of Color, are already pale, so when one blanches, it's really impressive. Jacques's skin went so white, I could see the mottling on his bones. "Not possible."

"These are the Maddoxes we are speaking of," Anatole reminded him. "When it comes to working against our kind, they are very good at what they do."

"But a love potion for a nightblood? It cannot be done. We are not affected by the magics that work on daybloods."

Anatole shrugged. "I would not put it past them to have done some very careful research down the generations, and possibly some very unpleasant experiments."

Jacques's attempt at menace dissolved along with the last of the color in his cheeks. "I knew those bastards had done something," he muttered. "There was no reason for it. One minute, Gabriel is going on about the plan; the next, he's telling Henri he's out of the game . . ."

"What was the plan?" I asked.

In general, I'm a fan of the direct approach. Unfortunately, this time it just reminded Jacques whom he was talking to. "Why should I tell you anything?"

It was Chet who answered. "Because when this mess is over, you might need somewhere to go, and I can help you, if you show me you're a straight-up guy."

Jacques reared back and looked at my brother down that long Gallic nose with an attitude that was almost in Anatole's class of old-school snobbery. "Why would I need your help, Caine, is it? *Chet* Caine?"

"Yeah, it is." Chet remained admirably unimpressed. "You need my help because you don't know squat about getting along in the open. If you did, you wouldn't be mixing blood smoothies in some half-assed food truck."

"It is a free country, and it is my choice."

"Riiiiight," sneered Chet. "You mean, it annoys the crap out of your sire, but Gabriel considers it harmless, so he lets you get away with it. This isn't what you want; you're just stretching out the chain. The second he snaps his fingers, though, you'll be back."

"What do you know about it, little boy?"

My hand tightened around my spray bottle, but Anatole laid his fingertips on my arm, signaling me to keep still.

Chet held up his hand, displaying his ring. "Six years," he said softly. "That's what I know. My sire was a girl named Melody. She ran off with one of her other blood children without even saying good-bye to me, and I haven't heard from her since. Every night I come back up, and I feel how she's gone. Every night, I want to go after her."

"But you don't." Jacques stared at Chet's gold ring.

"No, I don't, and you don't have to follow your sire either. You can have a separate existence."

"You're lying," Jacques whispered. "It cannot be done. You're lying to get me to talk to your sister."

"He is telling the truth," said Anatole. "I have known him for some time now, and he is entirely separate from his sire."

I've never seen a look like the one that crossed Jacques Renault's face on a vampire that wasn't starving. He didn't dare to believe what Chet was telling him. He couldn't believe anybody was that strong.

As for me, I was just impressed. I hadn't seen this side of my brother before. But then, if I was being honest, I hadn't looked for it. Jacques wasn't the only one learning something new tonight.

"Come on, Jacques." Chet didn't move closer. He didn't reach out a hand. He just stood there, giving Jacques plenty of room and plenty of time. "Give it up. All you've got to do is be straight with us now. Then, I'll help you. There are others who will too, but you gotta prove you're ready to live in this world, in this time."

Jacques was struggling. His mouth and hands twitched as he fought with instinct and anger to stand his ground. "What . . ." The word dragged itself out slowly between his fangs. "What do you want to know?"

That was my cue. "How come Gabriel had a class ring from NYU?"

"It isn't his. Henri got it as part of the extortion plan," Jacques answered. "This whole disaster started as black-mail. It was going to be another one of Henri's elegant little schemes. We were going to get close to Adrienne Alden and let her know we had information about the exploits of her college days. She would pay to keep it quiet, and we would agree to a reasonable price for our silence. Or at least something Henri considered reasonable."

"Attempted blackmail against a Maddox?" This merited a double-eyebrow lift from Anatole. "That takes . . . What's the word I'm looking for . . . ?"

"Chutzpah?" I suggested.

"That will do, yes."

"Henri said the time was right," Jacques said softly. "They're more exposed than they used to be. Lloyd Maddox is losing influence. The grandson needs to keep his reputation intact if he's to keep his city contract. Plus, Linus O'Grady has shown himself perfectly willing to pursue convictions at all levels, something that has already made certain highly placed paranormals with long pasts very uncomfortable."

I pictured Linus sitting across from me with his well-thumbed notebook and his heavy, scarred hands. He might even smile at this description of his reputation.

"Besides," Jacques went on, looking at the alley over Chet's shoulder with something like longing, "if it didn't work, we could just disappear again."

"What changed?" I asked.

Outrage and confusion slammed out of Jacques into me. I would have reeled back a step if Anatole hadn't put a steadying hand on my back. "They won't tell me! All I know is Henri comes back one morning close to sunrise and says the plan has changed. He says Gabriel is setting up the Alden daughters, and if all goes well, we're moving into the house. 'Just like the good old days,' he says. Moving in with the Maddoxes! Just like the good old days! I tried to tell them both it was suicide, but do they listen to me?"

"I gather they do not," replied Anatole blandly. "Why did you go with them?"

"Gabriel is my sire! He dragged me out of the mud at

the Somme, and he gave me his blood when I would have died!" Jacques twisted his hands together as if he wanted to tear apart the air between them. Desperation, memory, fear and hope all knotted together in that air. I retreated. Believe me, you would have too. But while my erratic survival instincts were kicking in, my thoughts were sticking on something Jacques said.

Henri said they were setting up the Alden daughters? Daughters, plural?

"Yes, yes," said Anatole impatiently. "Which came first, the change in Henri's plan or the change in Gabriel's attitude?"

"But what about Oscar?" said Chet. "He's dead, and O'Grady's giving the Aldens the eyeball. Why take the risk of murdering him?"

"It's starting to look like Oscar found out something he wasn't supposed to," I said. "Given all the plans flying around, that might not have been too hard either."

"And that fake ICE raid?" Chet added unhelpfully. "How's that work into it?"

"They're going to get us all killed!" snapped Jacques, whose own set of priorities did not include the death of random chefs. "Maddox won't let me go when he's killed Henri and Gabriel. They'll call me back. They will. I'll have to go, and I'll die right beside them."

"Except you don't have to go back," said Chet. "You can come with me. I've got a guest room you can use for the day. Then, tomorrow night you're going to meet some friends of mine. We'll help, I promise."

Jacques gaped at him. He was shaking. I haven't felt sorry for a whole lot of nightbloods before, but I felt sorry for Jacques right then. I was pretty sure he had told us what he knew of the truth, and I was pretty sure none of this was his idea.

"I'm on shift . . . ," he said, which only made me feel better about him.

"You just quit." Chet shot me a quelling glance, and this once I decided to let myself be quelled. "It's a new night. Come on." My brother put his arm around Jacques's slumped shoulders and started leading him away.

"Chet?" I said to his back, and he grinned over his shoulder at me.

"U-hwos meetings," he said.

"You-whos . . . Huh?"

"UHWOS. Undead Healthy Without Sires. It's a support group for vamps who have lost their sires or are trying to leave dysfunctional blood-family situations. We meet every Tuesday. Jacques's going to need a sponsor." He tipped me a salute and walked Jacques up the street.

Anatole, on the other hand, laughed, long, loud, and hard. He spun away from me and spread his arms wide. "I love you!" he cried to the city at large. "Do you hear, New York? I love you!"

"Love you too!" came back the city echo. "Now shut the hell up!"

I found myself genuinely and honestly not knowing what to think.

"Considering a serving of humble pie, elder sister?" inquired Anatole, stepping up beside me.

"Crow," I said. "Maybe pan-seared, with a red wine reduction."

He smiled, mischief and humor sparking in his green and gold eyes. It felt comfortable standing beside him for that moment—way more comfortable than it should have. Worse, in the middle of talk of murder and blackmail and Maddoxes behaving badly, it felt safe. And I was looking in his eyes and seeing the secrets waiting there again, the secrets he would share if I moved a little closer.

My phone buzzed against my hip and I swore, but I wasn't sure whether I was annoyed or relieved. I yanked it out and hit the button. It was a text message, and it was from Brendan.

home now news call l8tr

Yeah, right. I stuffed the phone in my pocket and faced Anatole. He had stepped away and folded his hands behind his back. The warmth around him was gone, replaced by a heavy, autumnal chill.

"Once again, I see I am too slow. Go to your Brendan, Charlotte. We will talk later."

I laid a hand on his arm and then charged toward Sixth. "Taxi!"

27

I worked the old Jedi mind trick of promising a substantial cash tip to the cab driver. This got me to Brendan's place in fifteen minutes. The elevator felt slower than Midtown traffic, and I was banging on the door and having a hard time breathing by the time Brendan opened it.

"Charlotte?" He peered sleepily at me and shoved his bangs back from his forehead.

"I get four text messages all night, and you expect me to wait for 'call u later'?" I demanded. At the same time I noticed how he looked okay—as if I'd woken him up, but otherwise okay.

"Yes," he said simply. "What's the problem?"

"I . . ." I swallowed. "I don't know. But you could have . . ." Lloyd Maddox was cleaning up loose ends, and Henri was running around without a keeper, and Oscar was so very dead and . . . and . . .

"Come in." Brendan took me by the hand and led me into the living room where he sat me on the sofa. The papers, I noticed, had started encroaching there too. "And it's okay. I know."

He was trying to be soothing, and I found, as upset as I was, I wasn't in the mood. "I'm glad it's okay," I said, but most of my concentration went into pulling myself together. "What do you know?"

"I know Uncle Scott financed that fake ICE raid."

"Scott?" I pictured the high-priced nerd at his dining room table with his papers and his coffee and his self-deprecating smile. "Scott Alden? Karina and Deanna's father?" The man I'd been told just wanted everybody to be happy.

"I don't know that many Scott Aldens," Brendan answered, shoving his hair back again. I'd definitely woken him up. Another time I would have said something about payback, but now was not the time. I would say something, later, when the force of his being okay wore off, and when I understood why nerdy Scott Alden had helped commit what I was pretty sure was a major fraud of some kind.

"I finally ran down the agents who pulled it off," Brendan said. "He paid them fifty thousand to stage the raid and plant the appropriate paperwork in the ICE databases. They got another fifty if they, and any spare Renaults, vanished afterward. Unfortunately, one of my guys knows the guy who set up their new IDs for them."

Scott Alden shelled out a hundred thousand for only one night's work? I should have held out for more for the catering. "But *why*?"

Brendan gave a jaw-cracking yawn and scrubbed at his face. "Believe me, I spent a long time trying to find out. Unfortunately, Uncle Scott's never been much of a talker. He just told them what needed to happen, and they just did it. I'm guessing it was so the theft could happen in the confusion."

"But why would *Scott* Alden pay ICE to stage a raid so a vampire could steal something off the mantel? It makes no sense." Especially when that little gun wasn't even the Arall. Even if Scott didn't know exactly what the Arall was, he'd have known what it *wasn't*. Had Henri screwed up and grabbed the wrong thing? "Was it his idea, or did somebody talk him into it?" Like Adrienne, or Karina? He'd been coming out of Karina's office. Was that to warn her Brendan was on their trail? Or was it just to make sure she was on track with whatever antivamp formula she was developing? A defense contract, especially one for Homeland Security, could cover the amount shelled out for the fake raid a hundred times over.

Brendan cocked his head toward me. "I take it this wasn't what you were going to tell me."

"No. I'd found out something . . . really different." Brendan waited for me to get it back together. I really didn't want to. He liked his aunt. He didn't like a lot of people in the family he spent so much time trying to pull out of the Dark Ages. I did not want to be the one to have to tell him this. I wanted to retreat, or lie. But that would be even worse. "I think your aunt Adrienne gave Deanna and Gabriel a love potion."

Brendan didn't do anything immediately. Then his eyes went distant, and he shifted his weight, straightening his back and getting ready for action. "A love potion?" he asked quietly. "Are you sure?"

I told him about the conversation I'd overheard in the garden last night, about hiding under the bed while Lloyd Maddox removed the class ring from Gabriel's hand, and about the conversation I'd had with Trudy afterward. I also told him about how Jacques had essentially confirmed all my suspicions, conclusions, and nagging little fears.

Abruptly Brendan stood, but not with his usual grace. Jerkily, as if his gears had rusted, he stalked over to his paper-strewn desk and stood staring at a blueprint taped to his clean white walls. In one motion he tore it down and balled it up tight, tossed it away, and reached for the next one.

"Don't!" I leapt across the room to grab his arm. "Don't let them do this to you." He wasn't just tearing paper. He was giving up.

"You've got no idea," Brendan's voice rasped in his throat. "No idea at all how hard I've worked, how hard I've *tried*. I've smiled and cajoled and bargained and compromised. I've put up with more of Grandfather's everlasting shit than I ever thought I'd be able to. And it never stops." He dropped into the desk chair and ran his fingers through his hair, as if trying to comb his thoughts back into his head. "It could have been great, Charlotte. I could have made this work."

"You still can. Nothing's . . ."

"Charlotte! My family is manipulating and murdering people using magic! You think people freak out about the vamp whammy? You wait until *this* hits the FlashNews. 'City contract given to warlock embroiled in murder investigation.' "

"You didn't do anything."

"Doesn't matter. I'm the one getting the city money, and I'm related. I'm not surprised Grandfather's trying to keep this quiet." He thumped his fist hard against the chair arm. "What the hell did she think she was doing?" He didn't wait for me to answer. "Just when I think my family couldn't get any stupider, they pull something like this. I'm going to renounce my loyalty oath, I swear. Let them all go to hell on their own."

"Brendan . . ." I crouched down so we'd be at eye level, but he held up his hand.

"Don't, Charlotte. Just . . . don't."

"Okay." I eased back onto my heels. "But you ought to know, I'll be hearing from Trudy soon. She said she'd do up an antidote for the love potion."

Slowly, Brendan turned his face toward me, and it was rock hard. "You went to Trudy before you came to me?"

My mouth went dry, and I realized I was afraid. But the fear bled quickly away, leaving behind a bedrock of anger. Nobody talked to me like that—not even Brendan. "I didn't think potions were your thing."

"You don't know what my thing is!"

"No. Because you don't talk about it."

"Pot. Kettle. Sooty."

I straightened up and faced him squarely. I was not one of his whining, bratty cousins, and he did not get to treat me like it. "You want to fight, Brendan Maddox?" My voice was soft and tight, and my fists were clenching the air. "We can fight, but I'm not doing this halfway." I'd seen the Maddoxes polite, backstabbing arguments. That was definitely not how we Caines did things. "If you start with me now, we're going to really get into it. Screaming, throwing things, the whole nine yards. You just say the word."

Now I saw something new in his eyes, and my heart swelled painfully. Because Brendan looked confused. "Charlotte, what are you doing?"

"Trying not to scream, Brendan. Because if I've got to have an argument with you, that's what's going to happen."

"I'm sorry," he whispered. "I shouldn't . . . I don't . . ." He buried his face in his hands.

I stood there, watching the strongest man I'd ever met within an inch of breaking down, and I didn't know what to do. It was true. We never talked about this stuff. I didn't want to talk about it. I'd wanted him to be just Brendan when he was with me, not Brendan of the Maddox witch clan. I didn't want there to be things in his life bigger than I was. And I'd believed that was what Brendan wanted too. Because of that, I had no idea what he was really going through, or what to do about it now that it had all hit the fan.

There are times in your life you really don't want to find out you've been a selfish brat. They tend to be accompanied by wishing the ground would open up and swallow you whole.

"No, it's my fault," I said, gulping down pride and air. "What are we going to do?"

Brendan flopped back in the chair, letting his hands dangle between his knees. His face twisted up as if he weren't sure whether to laugh or yell. "You cannot tell me you did not have some kind of plan coming in here."

"I did, but you're going to say you don't like it." And I told him about the meeting with Henri that Anatole and Chet and I had agreed to on Nightlife's roof, making sure I emphasized Sevarin's offer to set up the sting, and Chet's willingness to play backup, something I had to admit he was surprisingly good at.

"Charlotte . . . ," began Brendan as I stopped to draw breath.

"I know, I know. I don't like it either, but I don't know what else to do."

"Charlotte . . ."

"I can't let you be there, Brendan. You get that right? Henri will be able to sense you, and he'll balk. If we're going to find out what he's got, we need to . . . What?"

Brendan had laced his fingers behind his head and crossed one leg over the other. "Just waiting until you're done talking to yourself."

I swallowed my snappy comeback. This really wasn't the time.

"You're right; I don't like it," Brendan went on. "But I also think you're right that it's the best idea we've got. It also covers the two areas I'd trust Sevarin absolutely on."

"Two?"

His smile was small and it vanished quickly, but the light lingered in his eyes. "Sticking it to my grandfather and protecting you."

He had a point. That this point made me squirm a little was really not Brendan's fault.

"So, are you going to ask me to make sure my grandfather's kept busy tomorrow night, or am I going to volunteer?"

"I'd rather you volunteered, because I'm already feeling pretty low right now."

Brendan stood and crossed the short distance between

us so he could take both my hands. He ran his calloused thumbs over the backs and looked me right in the eye. "Charlotte, I think it'd be a good idea for me to make sure I know where my grandfather is tomorrow night while you, Chet, and Anatole are meeting with Henri. Besides, I've got a whole lot to talk to him about."

"Okay. But, Brendan . . . you'll be careful?"

"I know you don't like him, Charlotte, but you don't really believe my grandfather would hurt one of his own, do you?"

I thought about the cold menace that surrounded Lloyd Maddox when he spoke of protecting his family. He was a man used to power, and to making calculations that got people killed for what he considered just causes. He was also very used to deciding whom he considered human, and whom he considered a monster. I thought about what Jacques and Brendan both said about his fading power. "I don't know," I admitted. "So, promise me?"

"I promise, but you be careful too, Charlotte."

"Brendan, my restaurant's going to be reviewed by the *New York Times*. There is no way I'm missing that."

We kissed, and he did that thing where he cupped my cheek and looked into my eyes. I did that thing where I got melty and scared at the same time. But it was totally worth it.

28

I like exhaustion. Exhaustion is a bully that shoves all other considerations out of its way and lets you fall straight into sleep. That I was in my own bed in my own apartment for the first time in what felt like forever only served to back Exhaustion up. I slept like a vampire at high noon.

Sometime after sunup, I stumbled out of my room and headed to the bathroom. I stumbled out again, with no thought in my head except dropping back into my bed and finding out where I'd left that last bit of sleep.

"Hold it right there!"

Of course it was Jessie, standing at the living room end of the hall, her arms folded. She was wearing an expression on her perfect face that could only have been inherited from an Old World nana seen on one too many bad days.

I could not begin to count the ways I didn't need her or her inherited glowers just then.

"Don't you have faces to paint?" I growled.

"It's a slow week, and my roommate's gotten herself tied up in a murder. Oh, wait, that would be *another* murder!" Jessie brandished her smartphone at me, and I saw the Flash-News app was open. The headlines glowed in screaming red, indicating vital updates of personal interest.

Of course, my name was going to be all over whatever those articles and videos were. I grabbed the phone out of her hand and thumbed the screen.

Celebrity Chef Oscar Simmons had been murdered. This was the word from an "anonymous source," inside the Paranormal Squadron. I winced. Either Linus had a leak, or he had let that out to make the Aldens nervous. I knew which I'd bet on. But, of course, buried down below these facts was a bio on Oscar, and that bio included the tidbit that he'd recently "turned down" a lucrative appointment as catering chef for the upcoming Alden-Renault wedding. It also pointed out that the job Oscar turned down had been taken over by the infamous "Vampire Chef," Charlotte Caine. From there, the links branched back to Nightlife, and all the news that we generated last year.

I sighed and handed Jess her phone back. I did not need to read a recap of how I got to be infamous. I'd been there and done that. My head was throbbing. I needed more sleep, and coffee, and possibly to turn myself over to witness protection. "I'm not tied up in it," I told her firmly. "I'm just in close proximity to it."

"Same thing."

"It is not!" Damn. That six-year-old was just not going away. Fortunately, Jessie decided to ignore my feeble attempts at denial.

"Charlotte, this is serious!"

"I noticed, Jess." I dropped onto our sagging green sofa. "Believe me, I've spent the better part of a week noticing how serious this is." I looked around. "Where's Trish? She hates to be left out of these conversations."

"New client, early meeting." Jess tucked her skirt under her as she sat in the wingback chair she'd inherited from her grandmother. "What are you going to do?"

"Try to keep Elaine from quitting on me, for starters," I said. The rest, she did not need to know. I looked thoughtfully at my roomie. Jessie was a good person. She just lived in another world, a bright daytime world that involved pretty colors and pretty smells.

Smells. I straightened up. "Jess. Tell me about perfume."

I'm not sure what she saw in my face just then, but it made her shrink back a little. "What? Why?"

"How's it made? What do you need to do?"

"I'm a cosmetics consultant. What do I know about perfume?"

"It's the beauty industry—you must know *something.*"

"And PepsiCo is the food industry, but you couldn't tell me how to make a snack chip," she shot back.

"I could probably get you close." Not that I made a habit of eating prefab snack chips where anybody could see, but that was a separate issue.

"Really? How?"

"I'd taste it, look at it, take it apart . . . Jess, this has nothing to do with perfume."

"Actually, it kind of does. I've got a friend; she's setting up as a private aromatherapist . . ."

"That's a thing?" My forehead wrinkled. I should not be trying to talk about this stuff before coffee. I headed for the kitchen.

"Expanding market too," said Jess as she got up to follow me. "But she worked for Estée Lauder for a while. She says that when a new perfume comes out, the first, like, twenty bottles are all bought by the competition so they can take the fragrance apart and analyze it."

This was not what I was expecting to hear. I was expecting to hear about chemicals and formulae, and stuff like that. This was way different, and it was leading my brain down all kinds of uncomfortable paths, all of which were leading to Karina Alden's door at Exclusivité.

I made coffee, and then because I was, however reluctantly, awake enough for my stomach to complain about it, I found the eggs and cream in the fridge and set a pan on the stove to get hot.

Assume Karina had in fact wanted to get hold of the Arall so she could mass produce it. If that truly was the case, whether that production was for the military or the general market didn't really matter. Assume her father had offered to pay to help get it for her . . . Assume Oscar had found out what she was doing and was taking meetings to decide which side of this disaster would pay him more money, depending on the information he'd acquired . . . and that was what had been in the notebook pages he'd shredded.

Except Karina wasn't a witch. Even if she could have gotten hold of the Arall poison and taken apart the chemical component, she couldn't have reproduced the actual potion. Her mother had destroyed the formula ingredients and clues before that faked ICE raid and the theft. But it wasn't Karina who stole the gun. It was Henri, and he was busy with blackmail for an old murder, not new murders or weaponizing perfumes.

Except he also talked about setting up the Alden daughters—daughters plural. What if Henri had planned on framing Karina for the theft of the Arall? Maybe she was the one who'd wanted to talk to her father. Maybe she knew about Henri's involvement with the theft. That was a real possibility. That left the question, though, of what Scott Alden was actually doing and what Oscar had really known that got him killed . . .

I whisked cream into eggs, and considered my pots of herbs on the windowsill.

"Incidentally, Charlotte?" said Jess.

"Yeah?"

"If you're trying to distract me with breakfast, it's not going to work. You need to figure out what you're going to do."

I knew what I was going to do. I also knew I wasn't going to tell Jess, because I didn't want to deal with the fit that would follow after. This meant I really was going to have to distract her with breakfast. I rolled up my pajama sleeves and got to work.

Twenty minutes later we were both sitting down to fluffy piles of eggs laced with fresh basil and mozzarella and nicely crisped hash browns. Jessie forgot to ask me any more questions, and I was more than happy to let the food and trivial conversation reign.

At least it reigned until the door buzzer sounded. "Cripes," muttered Jess around a last mouthful as she jumped up. "That's Sheryl. We've got a meet-up. She's early."

But it wasn't Sheryl. "I'm looking for Charlotte Caine?" Trudy's voice crackled through the speaker grille.

"Right here, Trudy." I came up behind Jess. "I'll buzz you in."

"What's this?" Jess asked, and I instantly regretted not being dressed. I should have said I'd meet her in the lobby.

"Jess, if I swear I'll tell you everything later, will you not ask any questions now?"

"No," she said, "because you'll put me off until I've forgotten what we were talking about. Or you'll feed me. So, what's up?"

"Jess," I began slowly, "I really, really don't want to lie to you."

"So don't."

"Thanks, I won't. I . . ."

Proving that sometimes the universe has excellent timing, Trudy knocked on the door right then, and I was able to turn away to let her in.

"Trudy, thanks for coming." This was the first time I had seen Trudy out of uniform. Even off-duty, though, she wore black; black leggings and black slip-on flats and an oversized black shirt. Her hair was knotted at the back of her head, and her face was bare of makeup but full of worry.

I introduced Trudy to Jess. "We were just finishing breakfast," I said. "Come on. I'll get you a cup of coffee."

Fortunately, Trudy was quick on the uptake and followed me into the apartment's tiny kitchen. Jessie might be nosy, but she hated to be seen looking nosy, in front of strangers anyway. So there was no way she could follow us. Her glare let me know she was conceding the round, but not for long.

"Here's . . . what you asked for." Trudy pulled a bottle out of her purse and set it on the counter.

"Thanks." It was one of those travel-sized plastic containers for putting shampoo in to get it through security at airports. I tucked it into my bathrobe pocket and traded Trudy for a cup of coffee, feeling vaguely as if I'd just done a drug deal. In a way, I guess we had. I had no idea what the legality around possession of a love potion was. O'Grady probably could have told me. Now, why, oh, why didn't that make me feel any better?

"Did you get hold of Pete?" I asked to get my mind off that thought.

"Who? Oh, your friend with the job. Um, not yet. I wanted to get this done first." Trudy sipped her coffee, but was clearly not interested in it. "You'll . . . You'll be careful with that, won't you? It's the magic version of prescription meds. You shouldn't take it if you don't need to."

"Got it."

"Sorry, I can't stay." She put her mug in the sink, a reflexive reaction on the part of the professionally tidy. "I just . . . Look, thank you again," she said. "For what you've tried to do. I do appreciate it."

This sounded way more like a permanent good-bye than I was comfortable with. I shifted my weight a little, suddenly very sorry I didn't know this woman better. "Trudy, are you okay?"

She smiled tightly across at me and lied. "Yeah. At least, I will be. I've got to go. Remember what I said about the potion."

And she all but ran out of the apartment, straight past Jess without saying a word.

"Charlotte?" said Jess. "What was that about?"

"Swear to God, Jess," I said, fingering the bottle in my pocket as if the answer might be written in braille on the side, "I really don't know."

Fortunately for me, Jess's friend Sheryl showed up a few minutes later, and my roommate had no choice but to leave me alone. I showered and dressed, and I drank another cup of coffee. Then, I called the Alden house, and, thankfully, got the voice mail. I put on my perky voice, such as it was, for the recording, saying Reese and I would be spending most of the day at Nightlife supervising the catering prep, and that I could be reached at this number if I was needed, and I'd be back on duty tonight. Somehow, with word of Oscar's murder circulating on the Web, I didn't think Adrienne Alden was going to squawk too loud about my not being there to make lunch. She very probably had other things on her mind right now.

I took out the bottle Trudy had given me and held it up to the light. The liquid inside was the pale amber color of weak tea. I tipped it back and forth. It was thick, a little thicker than maple syrup but not as thick as honey. I uncapped it and waved my hand over it, wafting some fumes toward me. I smelled . . . reality. It bit hard in the back of my nasal cavity, a startling feeling, like being shocked awake. If you wanted to sneak this past somebody, you'd need something strong to mask it, like scotch, or espresso or . . .

My thoughts stopped dead in their tracks, and I stared at the bottle—the one, lonely little bottle. Something was wrong here. Jacques and Anatole both had talked about how vampires weren't vulnerable to the same magics humans were. If that was true, there should be two antidotes, shouldn't there? One for Deanna and one for Gabriel.

Could Trudy not know about the different . . . call them tolerances? After all, she wasn't a topflight witch, like Brendan and the Maddoxes.

Or maybe she didn't expect me to know two antidotes would be required. She could be pulling a fast one. But why? Didn't she want to undo Adrienne's spell? She had certainly seemed shocked enough about it. On the other hand, they had been friends and allies for a long time. What if she'd cracked and told Adrienne what was going on? What if what she was holding wasn't an antidote? What if it was poison?

Couldn't be. Adrienne Alden wouldn't poison her own daughter.

But she might poison her daughter's fiancé. Because if vampires were immune to the magics that worked on humans, humans might just be immune to the magics that worked on vampires. That had been one of our big theories last night, hadn't it? That Adrienne Alden would kill Gabriel when she was ready. And here was a way to commit a murder without getting her hands messy. She could give the murder weapon to the stupid chef who had gotten into the middle of her family's business and who was most unwisely dating an important member of the clan.

Oh. I closed my hand around the bottle. *Shit.*

29

I didn't tell Brendan about the bottle Trudy gave me. Maybe I should have, but I figured what with trying to deal with his grandfather, he had enough on his plate for one day. We'd all get through tonight, and I'd tell him in the morning. I sealed the bottle up in a Ziploc bag and tucked it deep in the bottom of my purse.

Then I pulled on my big-girl panties and called Elaine. I got her voice mail. I left a message. I cleaned the kitchen, called Elaine again, and again got her voice mail. I went grocery shopping and checked my e-mail. I called Marie to find out how the *quinciñera* was shaping up and whether she had everything she needed. Then I checked the Flash-News gossip about Oscar's death. My name remained blessedly way, way down on the bottom, and the links and threads to the old news about last year were already fraying.

I called Elaine again.

"I know you don't want to talk to me," I told her voice mail. "I don't blame you. There's just one thing." And I told her about the impending *Times* review.

There were a couple of abrupt clicks. "You had better be serious about this," said Elaine.

"Cross my heart," I told her. I did not hope to die. Considering what was coming tonight, there'd be too much genuine opportunity for that after sunset.

The silence on Elaine's side spoke volumes, mostly about being at the very tiny crisply burnt end of her patience with her most troublesome, poorest paying client.

"I know, I know," I said. "Just . . . please don't quit yet, okay?"

"I'll think about it." She answered with enough heat to give me hope. It was when she went frosty that I really had to watch out.

She hung up. I hung up and faced my empty apartment. It had just gone on four, still way too early to head out for Nightlife. Except I had nothing left to do but hang around and think about that bottle in the bottom of my purse and wonder what else I was getting myself into. This was a nonstarter. So, I grabbed my stuff and headed out.

Mel, as I had suspected, had loved the idea of his great marble and gilt hall being used for a sting operation against some bad-guy vamps. I swore him to secrecy, of course, but I strongly suspected he had called up three talk hosts and at least two reality show producers while he was in his office getting me the spare keys. So, I spent the day at Nightlife, with those keys in my purse, waiting for sunset and immersing myself in all the paperwork that did not deal with bookkeeping. There was a surprising amount of it, mostly involving scheduling and ordering. We were heading into vacation season, and I had to work the puzzle of keeping my place up and running and yet give my people their much needed time off.

I'd just gotten the last two weeks in June mostly worked out when my phone rang. I checked the number, saw it was Brendan, and answered immediately.

"How's it going there, Charlotte?" Brendan's voice sounded strained. Or maybe it was too carefully casual.

"Waiting to set up the sting," I told him as I felt my eyes narrow. "What's up?"

"I have Trudy here with me. She's in a bad way. Seems Deanna'd gotten word that her family's done some extra interfering with her and Gabriel. She started questioning Trudy, and Trudy spilled the beans."

My narrowed eyes clamped shut and squeezed tight. I pictured Deanna with her fireball in her hand and static electricity crackling in her eyes. "This is not good."

"No," agreed Brendan. But there was no relaxation in his voice. He was trying to tell me something, something important. I could hear it, but I couldn't understand it. "Deanna knows you've got the antidote, and she wants you to bring it over to the house tonight. Have you got it?" he asked.

"Yeah, yeah, I've got it."

"Okay, look, I know you've got this . . . thing going down, and I've got to go calm down Grandfather. God knows what he's heard. Can you meet me tonight at the Aldens' house? And . . ." He hesitated. "You might want to bring Chet with you."

Yeah, and a small army. Because something was going badly wrong over there. My hand tightened around my phone, and it took all my strength not to demand what was happening. If Brendan had Trudy beside him, there was only so much he could say without getting her suspicious.

"Okay," I told him slowly. "It'll be late, after the . . . thing. And . . . don't say anything yet." I dropped my voice and actively thanked heaven for my association with Linus O'Grady. "If you want me to call the cops, or just not show up at the Aldens' tonight, Brendan, just say okay right now. That's all."

"No, it's all right," he said. I should have been relieved, but something inside me refused to let go.

"There's something else you ought to know." And I told

him how Trudy had only given me one bottle of antidote. "We still good?"

He took his time answering. "Should be. But I'll tell you the whole story when you get out there."

I didn't like it. Something was wrong. I did trust Brendan, but I also trusted my own sense of trouble. There was, however, nothing at all I could think to do. "Call me if anything changes," I said.

"You too. 'Bye."

I said good-bye and stuck the phone in my pocket.

"Right. Okay," I breathed to my empty kitchen. "Boyfriend being enigmatic and vampire sting on deck. This is definitely going to be one of those fun nights."

I'll give Henri Renault this: he was punctual. At nine o'clock, the phone rang, and I opened Carriger Hall's front door. We'd decided to use the front lobby because there was a view of the street. I was betting that the possibility of a passing pedestrian witness would slow down any murderous impulses not held in check by the presence of my undead bodyguards.

At first glance, though, I would have sworn I'd never before seen the nightblood waiting outside. At second glance, I knew why I'd found all that jewelry in Gabriel's shoe box.

The vampire who stepped into the echoing gold and marble hall wore khakis and a yellow polo shirt. The only bling on him was a heavy, gold wrist watch. His hair was cut in a flattop, and he smelled of Ivory Soap and truffles.

In addition to making him look thoroughly modern, the new style took about twenty years off his physical age. His lack of height helped. If I hadn't known better, I would have thought I was looking at a relatively new vampire, who'd been maybe seventeen or eighteen when he was turned.

Henri Renault wasn't disguised; he'd taken the disguise off and left it with his blood child.

"Oh, you're good," I breathed as I stood back to let him in.

"So I tried to tell you, my dear." Henri moved close, looking up into my eyes, but I nodded toward the sweeping staircase. Henri turned to see both Anatole and Chet standing a couple steps up, giving him matching hard looks. You could have used the cold between them as a blast chiller.

Proving he wasn't all that stupid, Henri instantly dropped the flirtation. I wondered if he'd told Gabriel he was going on the run first, or had just left the gold in the bedroom for him to find. Or had Gabriel, under the influence of Adrienne's love potion, told his sire it was time to get out of Dodge? Whichever it had been, here and now, Renault walked warily forward, glancing this way and that. But it was just the four of us. I'd sent Chet and Anatole around in search of the hall when we got there to make sure.

"Renault," said Anatole by way of greeting.

"Sevarin. Monsieur Caine."

I shoved my hands into my pockets to find my phone and my spray bottle, but otherwise I held still. *I will stay in the background,* I told myself with every ounce of strength I had. *I will let Anatole do the talking. And if Renault so much as looks at me sideways, I will get him right between the beady little vamp eyes.*

Anatole evidently sensed my impatience and walked down the last couple of steps to come level with Henri. "Well, Renault, it is your play," he said. "Have you brought the item, or are we simply supposed to trust you and move straight to negotiations?"

"You sound as if you've done this before, Sevarin." Renault oozed smugness. I glanced at Chet. My brother shook his head.

"I have, and with far more powerful and frightening creatures than you," replied Anatole. "Charlotte, remind me to tell you about the time I spent in Chicago . . . but that is for another night. For now, Renault, you can tell us what you want."

"*Bien.* I want only what I have always wanted—the Arall."

"But you said you have it."

"I do. However, I am not a fool, Sevarin. You are not buying the Arall for your own sake. Your lady here has asked you to help retrieve it, and you have agreed. It matters not a bit to me, as long as we can reach an equitable price."

You know all that chefly self-discipline I've talked about? It deserted me right then and there. "Wait a minute," I said, loud enough to raise a hollow echo from the marble walls around us. "You went through all the trouble to steal the . . . thing from the Aldens, and you expect me to believe you don't care if Anatole's going to give it right back?"

Anatole turned toward me. I could feel him wondering how this little interruption was working with my agreement to let him do the talking. I was wondering that myself.

Henri shrugged. "The world has very much changed, and"—he glanced down at his polo and khakis, and I felt the twinge of regret—"I find I must as well. My sons . . . well . . . alas, poor Gabriel so betrayed. And Jacques, he courts change and the love he has found in this city is not for the glamor and the game such as I tried to teach him."

Chet opened his mouth. I shook my head hard, and he closed it again. "Kids these days," I said.

"Just so." Henri sighed. "As a result, I am left to make my lonely way in a world that is in so many ways more dangerous than the one I am accustomed to. My recent experiences with the Aldens have shown me it is time to retire as an adventurer. But I must have money. So, I must have something to sell. The information I had hoped would serve . . ." He shrugged. "What is the saying about best laid plans?

Enfin. So, instead, there is the Arall and the question of who will offer the best price for it. I personally am interested in how much Sevarin will pay to discomfort his old enemy." He looked at Anatole expectantly.

"You've really thought about this, haven't you?" I said.

"I do try to be thorough."

Yes. Yes you do. I felt my forehead bunching up as I tried to keep my thoughts from showing on my face. It wasn't going to work, but my forehead tried anyway. *You're debating the merits of selling the Arall versus keeping it for yourself as if you've been having this argument for a while. But who would you have been arguing with? And if you were on the side of keeping it for yourself, who was on the side of selling it to . . . who? Who would pay a lot of money for a surefire antivamp weapon? Let me rephrase. Who wouldn't pay a lot of money for a surefire antivamp weapon?*

But, of course, if you were a vampire, you might not see the money as being worth it. You might pretend to go along, all the while scheming how to keep the Arall for yourself.

But a double cross required a patron. That patron had to want the Arall, either to keep, or to sell to the highest bidder. Scott Alden might want to do it, especially if Scott had gotten involved in one of the recent spate of banking disasters like so many other high-flying money managers. Karina Alden might want to do it, if her own very exclusive business had taken a hit from the whims of fashion or the bad economy or both. Lloyd Maddox might want to do it to very, very quietly get around centuries of family tradition, and really take the fight to the nightbloods.

Scott, Karina, and Lloyd. Which of them are you double-crossing here, Henri?

Anatole gestured impatiently. "I need to see what you have, Renault. Then we will discuss price."

"*Bien sûr.* And I must know you are capable of meeting

my price. As I am about to enter retirement, I am afraid it will be high."

Without breaking eye contact, Anatole reached into his jacket pocket and brought out a small black velvet bag. Gently, he tipped it up over his palm and out dropped a single white diamond the size of my thumb.

"Oh. Em. Effin'. Gee," whispered Chet as he trotted down the stairs to get a better look. I had to agree with him. The diamond was one of the most beautiful things I had ever seen. This was crystallized perfection that begged you to pick it up, look at it closely, and lay claim to it, because it was such a pretty, pretty thing.

"Ahhhhh . . ." Henri sighed like Reese confronted with a really good steak. He plucked the diamond up to hold between his thumb and index finger and brought it close to his eye. The stone caught the lobby's warm light and reflected it back as brilliant rainbows.

"There are twelve more just like it." Anatole smiled a very little. He also watched Henri very, very closely. Tension radiated from every inch of him, wrapping around me and making it hard to breathe.

"Really, Sevarin?" Henri—reluctantly I thought—returned the stone to Anatole's palm. I didn't even see Anatole snatch it away, until his hand was pulling back out of his pocket. "Don't tell me you picked over some Romanov bones in your time."

"Certainly not. Let us say there was a certain aristo lady who wished to keep her head more than she wished to keep her jewels."

Oh, for heaven's sake, was Anatole going to try to snow him with one of his stories? Except from the sparkle in Henri's eyes, it seemed to be working.

Henri fingered his chin thoughtfully. "I find I am in a mood to be generous, Sevarin. I will take eleven of the diamonds for the Arall."

"And I find your generosity does not set me at ease,

Renault. You will get six. Three now, and the rest when I have confirmed it is indeed the Arall you are selling me."

"Pah. You see what he does to me, your lover?" Henri waved his hands in a gesture somewhere between dismissal and despair. I pressed my fists against my thighs to remind myself not to start swinging for the "your lover" crack, although it was an even bet whether my first target would be Henri, Anatole, or Chet. Because I could feel my brother trying not to laugh. "I could have ten times the worth of these jewels from Maddox to give his precious family secret back to him, and years of blackmail besides. Ten."

"And you would for all that time be a target to him as you never had before. Seven stones."

I was starting to get itchy, and not just because of the tension bleed-over from Anatole. I didn't like Henri's delaying tactics. They gave me the nasty feeling that while he stalled us all here, something else might be going on.

"What've you got?" I said.

Both Henri and Anatole turned toward me. The weight of the sudden attention of all three nightbloods threatened to squash my thoughts flat, but I pushed it aside. "This is all kind of pointless if he hasn't got the Arall, isn't it?"

"If you were a man, *ma chérie*, I would have to call you out for that."

"Wouldn't be my first brawl," I shot back before Chet had time to start getting all manly. "What about it?"

Henri sighed, rolled his eyes, and shook his head at the heavens. "Sevarin. Can you not . . ."

Anatole's fangs gleamed in the lobby light, and this time it wasn't because he was smiling. "As Charlotte herself would say, Renault, you really do not want to finish that sentence."

"Very well." Henri reached into his jacket's side pocket and brought out a pair of leather gloves. "What I am going to bring out looks very like a pistol. Please do not overreact."

Henri put the gloves on and then pulled a handkerchief-wrapped bundle out of his pocket. He peeled the cloth back carefully to reveal the little silver pistol I had last seen on the mantel of the Aldens' living room.

Anatole stretched his hand out toward the gun. His face tightened, and he withdrew, slowly.

"Charlotte, if I could prevail upon you?"

I took the pistol out of Henri's hand. It was light, way too light, and too smooth. I tilted the barrel away from me. The gun sloshed.

And I started to laugh. I laughed in great big whoops that doubled me over so hard I couldn't breathe. I couldn't help it. Because the Arall was a potion, and it had been sitting on the mantelpiece the whole time, and Henri really had stolen it, despite all the precautions Adrienne wanted to make sure everybody watched her take.

"Charlotte, what the hell's the matter with you?" demanded Chet.

"It's a squirt gun!" I howled. "The most powerful anti-vamp weapon the Maddoxes could come up with, and they put it in a squirt gun!"

Chet stared, and then he chuckled, and then he threw back his head and shouted. "Hands up, nightblood! Squirt! Squirt!" He mimed shooting with two fingers. "And there's Lloyd Maddox staring down the barrel. Squirt!"

"If you two are quite finished," drawled Anatole, "you might recall that is a squirt gun full of poison."

"Yeah, yeah, sorry." I wiped my eyes, and Chet bit his lip, which is something you should be careful about when you have fangs. I held the squirt gun up again. Actually, like Henri's little Old World dandy act, it was a terrific disguise. Even if someone would believe you'd keep the family's secret weapon on the mantel, they'd never believe you'd put it in a kid's toy.

All at once, my urge to laugh dried up and blew away. Because if this was the Arall, that meant Henri had known what he was stealing before he'd taken it, which meant someone had told him what to look for. That someone knew a secret even Brendan didn't know. Slowly, I raised the barrel of the pistol. All three vampires moved away from me. But I just turned the little squirt gun over to find the plug for the reservoir and popped the cap. A bitter, unpleasant smell wafted out, one that was like the taste of AA batteries.

Of all the senses, smell is the most evocative. It wakes up memories you didn't know your brain had kept. And in that moment, I knew what exactly had happened, and how and why. Carefully, I fixed the stopper back into place.

"Did you offer to sell it to her, or did she pay you to steal it?" I whispered.

"Who, Charlotte?" asked Anatole.

"Karina Alden."

Right then, Henri charged.

30

He never had a chance.

I threw myself sideways, and the next thing I knew, Anatole's rock-hard arms were around me. The world spun, and we were up the stairs and on the landing. Back on the main floor, Chet had Henri straight-armed over his head, held by belt and collar. All he needed was a mask and my brother would have been ready for Pro-Wrestling: Nightblood Xtreme.

"Let me go!" screamed Henri.

"You tried to jump my sister!" shot back Chet. "You're lucky I don't take your head off!"

"Are you all right, Charlotte?" asked Anatole, calmly but slowly loosening his hold on me.

I meant to answer yes. But now that I was sure the whole great honkin' mess surrounding the Arall did originate with Karina Alden, I was sure about several other things too.

"No! *No!* Anatole! Brendan!" The string of unwelcome realizations flooding my brain also swamped coherent speech. "He's going over there! Phone! Where's my phone!" I didn't wait for an answer. I stuffed the squirt gun in my pocket and bolted down the stairs to the coat check counter where I'd left my purse and jammed both hands in. Chet shuffled sideways, keeping Henri held over his head. I punched Brendan's number.

"Uh, Charlotte?" said Chet gently. "This guy's getting wiggly."

"One second." The phone rang. "Come on. Come on. Comeoncomeoncomeon."

"Put him down, Caine," said Anatole. "I think Henri knows better than to try that again."

Out of the corner of my eye, I saw Chet swing Henri down and set him on his feet, bend him over the marble coat check counter, and press his hand down on the back of Henri's neck. But all I really paid attention to was how my phone rang, and rang, until it sent me to voice mail.

I swore and hung up, then punched Brendan's number again. Henri struggled against Chet's grip.

"Hold still," ordered Chet.

"Or one of us will most certainly break your neck," said Anatole calmly. Henri froze, his cheek pressed flat against the counter. "It's all a matter of appealing to reason, you see."

Brendan's phone rang and rang, and I got sent to voice mail again. "Damn it!"

"What's happened?" asked Anatole.

"Brendan. He's gone to the Aldens' house. Trudy asked him to go. She told him that Deanna had found out what had happened with the love potion and wanted the antidote." Karina would kill him. Everything was on the line for her now, including her freedom once O'Grady got the whole story, and then there was whatever the Maddoxes would do to her when they found out what she'd done to them. "I've got to get out there."

Anatole's face went absolutely still.

"I'll take you," said Chet quickly, stepping around Henri.

"No," said Anatole. "I will go with her."

"I'm not going to argue this one, Anatole," Chet began, but Henri seemed to think this was a good time to bolt for the exit. My brother reached out almost casually and snagged him by the collar, jerking him off his feet. He choked and flopped down next to Chet, glaring up at him. Chet ignored this, but he also kept hold of Henri's collar.

Anatole faced Chet, serious as the grave. "Someone has to confine this creature and fetch O'Grady out to Brooklyn."

"You . . ."

But I'd had enough. We were wasting time. "Figure it out!" I snapped. "Or I'm going on my own!" I would. I had to. I couldn't stand there. She'd kill him. She might have already killed him. It'd been hours since I got that last phone call. Anything could have happened.

No, no, it didn't. Don't think it. He's alive. We'll be in time.

"Caine," said Anatole, "are you strong enough to protect Charlotte from the Maddoxes if they go on the attack? Be very, very sure of your answer."

"Shit," hissed Chet through his fangs.

I dug into my purse again and tossed Chet O'Grady's card. Vampire that he was, he snatched it out of the air with his free hand. "Tell him everything," I said. "And make sure you put this"—I dropped the squirt gun on the counter—"someplace safe."

Chet nodded. "Go," he said to me before he turned his hard, dry eyes to Anatole. "If she gets hurt, I'm coming after you, Sevarin."

"If she gets hurt, I'll deserve it."

Running out the front door with Anatole right behind me, I charged into traffic. A yellow cab squealed its brakes and came up with the bumper brushing my knees.

"Brooklyn Heights!" I shouted as I hauled the door open.

"You crazy?" said the bearded, coffee-skinned man behind the wheel. "Get out of my cab! I'm off duty!"

But Anatole pushed his way in beside me and dropped

the diamond in the cash drawer. "Get her there alive," he said. "Beyond that, we don't care."

There aren't a lot of times I've regretted not having a car. That ride, though, was one of them. I closed my eyes, gripping the hang strap with one hand and Anatole's cold, hard fingers with the other, while the cab slid and skittered through traffic, its horn blaring in one continuous blast of sound.

He's not dead, I told myself. *He can't be dead. He isn't dead. We'll be in time. He's not dead.*

But Karina Alden was already a murderer. She'd killed Oscar. She'd used poison so Linus would waste his time chasing after Adrienne rather than looking at Karina and what Karina was up to. What Karina was up to was getting her hands on the Arall so she could analyze it and reproduce it in her lab to sell it to the military, or whoever else might be buying. Once Karina made the sale, she'd be able to pay her father back for the money he'd fronted for her to start Exclusivité. Or maybe they would just split the profits and finally get the hell away from the Maddoxes, because it was really hard to be the T-typ in a magical family.

But it was being the T-typ that gave Karina the ultimate cover with her relatives. Nobody paid attention to her. She said it herself. She didn't matter. She could be thrown overboard. She'd been given her perfume company by her father who just wanted her to be happy. None of her magic-wielding relatives had so much as raised an eyebrow. They probably didn't even realize how much she knew about their magical secrets. Why would they care? Even though she'd dedicated herself to building up a profession where she could analyze and reproduce complicated chemical formulae, she couldn't *do* anything with them, could she? Not anything important. Not anything magical. And even if she could hire an outside witch, how would she get the formula for the Arall, or anything else? Adrienne certainly wouldn't tell her, and neither would Deanna, because Deanna hated her.

Enter Gabriel Renault, two-hundred-year-old professional party guest. Karina figured out the blackmail he planned, but she had a better idea, and she invited him over to her office one night. They'd had a friendly little chat, and she thought she had enlisted him for her purposes and that he drafted his blood children to help.

But then it all went wrong because Deanna and Gabriel fell in love. They now wanted to look after each other, and this lover's impulse left both Henri and Karina high and dry, just as Adrienne Alden had planned when she administered the potion. In love, Gabriel and Deanna wouldn't want anything to do with stealing and selling the Arall. Deanna wouldn't want such a powerful antivampire weapon out where anybody could use it, and Gabriel would be sensitive to Deanna's wish to stay alive with a chance to fulfill her dynastic obligations, which included keeping the Arall's secret in family hands.

And they would stay in love until Adrienne had taken care of the rest of the blackmail and the rest of Gabriel's blood family, and was ready to do him in. Except she hadn't known Karina and Henri were working together. And no one had predicted that Henri would try to run, or that Jacques would find a support group courtesy of my brother, Chet.

"Brendan's smart," I whispered. "If I put it together, he can. He's set something up. It's already over. He's a security specialist. He'll have already figured it out. He did. He had to. He's okay. He's okay. He's okay."

Something cold settled into my veins. My frantic thoughts stilled and receded back from my consciousness. This was Anatole, I realized with a disturbing level of calm. Anatole had reached into my mind without permission. He was sharing his calm, distancing me from my own fear.

And God help me, I sat there and I let him do it.

Anatole made the cabbie stop a block from the Aldens' house. We climbed out, and the driver gunned the engine and was gone, leaving us alone beneath the streetlights. It was that dead time of the night, between everybody who had to get up in the morning being home in bed or in front of the TV and everybody else still being out and about. We had the street to ourselves.

Anatole had withdrawn his chill presence, and my thoughts were my own again. Fortunately, they'd decided to calm down and get serious.

"You saw the wall around the Aldens' back garden?" I said to him. "Can you get over it?"

Anatole considered. "You are thinking you will go in and distract Karina while I sneak in the back?"

"You can find Brendan if they've got him hidden, and get him out."

"I can find Brendan, but you must realize neither one of us is going to leave you with Karina Alden."

"You can do all the macho heroics you want, as soon as you've got Brendan with you."

I could feel Anatole forcing the cold distant air he carried with him to wrap around his emotions like a cloak. He was shielding me from him, and himself from me.

"I'm sorry," I whispered, shaken. "I'm sorry, Anatole. Please, don't . . ."

Anatole waved his hand carelessly, but he also turned away. "I knew what I was doing when I offered to accompany you. Give me five minutes; then make your entrance."

And like that, he was gone, and I was alone. I bit back a curse and started walking. The curtains had been drawn on the brownstones so no one could see me go by. My clogs sounded too loud on the concrete. This wasn't normal. I was in the middle of Brooklyn, and the world around me felt utterly empty. I couldn't even hear the traffic, let alone any voices. A black town car trundled slowly down the middle of the street, and I pulled my shoulders up to my ears, trying to huddle in on myself. Fear simmered in my veins, working its way up to a full boil.

Five minutes. Five minutes. I chanted silently. I measured my steps. I counted seconds in heartbeats and slow, steadying breaths. I resisted the urge to try to reach my thoughts out to Anatole. I couldn't tell, though, if I was afraid I wouldn't find him, or that I would.

The Aldens' house loomed up in front of me. Anger turned up the heat inside me, burning straight through the fear. I was ready to march straight up to that front door and bang on it—hard. Make a racket, wake the neighbors, force somebody in this ritzy neighborhood to pay attention to what was going on around them. But I stopped myself. If I tried to get in the front door, somebody might just wonder what gave me so much confidence. I had to put on at least some kind of show of sneaking in.

So I ducked down the path between the houses. I'd hop the back gate to the garden and get into the kitchen through the French doors. Half the time I'd been working there, those were left unlocked. I curled my finger around the cool wrought-iron gate and lifted one foot.

The gate squeaked and swung open. I bit my lip and backed up a step. But it was too late.

"Come in, Charlotte," called Karina.

My mouth went dry. My heart tried to duck under my ribs. But where was I going to go? I put my hand in my pocket and my thumb on the trigger of my ridiculous little spray bottle. Fat lot of good it would do me if she had a gun or a witch with her. But for the moment, it was all I had.

I moved slowly forward, shuffling down the flagstone path, trying not to jump at the shadows stirring in the warm breeze. Slowly, I eased myself around the corner of the brownstone mansion. There on the patio, Karina Alden sat at a little glass-topped table. Trudy was just emerging from the kitchen, carrying two steaming mugs with her.

And there was the final piece of the puzzle. Karina couldn't reproduce the Arall without somebody who could reproduce the magic that went into it. There was only one person who might know that part; someone Karina could trust, and someone, not a Maddox, who needed the money.

"Hello, Trudy," I said.

"Hello, Charlotte." She set the mugs down on the table; one in front of Karina, one in front of an empty chair.

"Thanks." Karina wrapped her hands around her mug. "Looks like you were right. She would come right away if she thought Brendan was here."

My heart wobbled, tipped, and fell. I glanced up at the curving stairs to the balcony, and at the dark windows and the silent house. "It was a bluff." And I'd fallen for it. I knew you could work magic with a cell phone. I'd seen Brendan do it. I knew Trudy was a witch, one of many in this whole cluster of double-crossing who could have been working with Karina. Despite this, I didn't do anything to confirm where Brendan actually was. I didn't call Lloyd, or Linus. I didn't go to Brendan's apartment, or even sneak Anatole up to the side of the house to see if he could sense him. I'd thought Brendan was walking into a trap, and I panicked; now I was the one trapped.

Karina smiled and nudged the empty chair out. "Sit down?"

I walked down the steps to the patio. I focused on Trudy and Karina. I did not look at the garden wall. "So," I said to Trudy, "I take it you never did get around to calling Pete?"

"I am sorry," she said. "I didn't have any choice."

"There's always a choice."

"Yeah, but it's not always a good one," Karina said with a sigh. "Especially not when it involves going to prison for murder, right, Trudy?" Trudy turned her face away.

"This is about that NYU kid, isn't it?" I said. "It wasn't Adrienne who killed him. It was you."

"It was an accident," Trudy murmured. "That's all."

"She got hold of the wrong bottle." Karina shook her head in a mock sympathy creepy enough to stand the hairs on the back of my neck on end. "Back in the day, my mother was more willing to help friends out with her potions. Trudy wanted a love potion, but she got it mixed up with the store of the Arall she had left over from the Five Points Riot. At least, that's the story and they're sticking to it." She gazed at the steam rising from her mug. "For what it's worth, Mom says it was an accident too. Trudy says she gave the boy the potion in good faith. The problem is, she's not sure Linus O'Grady would believe that. Neither was I."

"You've been working on this a long time, haven't you?"

Karina shrugged. "Not this specifically. I knew I'd find some way to make the family pay what they owed me. Sit down, Chef. Trudy's made coffee." She pushed the mug across the glass.

I ignored her. "I know Linus O'Grady, Trudy. He'd listen." I put all the conviction I had into that, and got exactly nowhere. Trudy just shook her head, her mouth drawn tight. She thought it was too late. I could see it in the set of her shoulders and the way she refused to catch my eye. She'd thrown in with Karina, and there was no way back.

"You can go now, Trudy," said Karina. "I know you've got a flight to catch."

Trudy nodded, then headed for the French doors. Pausing, she turned and lifted her eyes to mine. "I am sorry," she told me again.

I just shook my head. She might be telling the truth, but it was way past mattering to me. Trudy turned away fast, then vanished into the kitchen. I let out a long breath and took a couple of steps forward. I couldn't worry about her anymore. Anatole was out there in the dark. He was listening, and by now he knew it was all a trap. But he'd be waiting for a chance to come get me out. I had to keep Karina talking and make sure that chance showed up.

"So, where're your folks?" I asked.

She shrugged. "Oh, you know, out and about. Wedding business."

"Your dad's keeping your mom out of the way, isn't he?" I'd reached the table. I could have grabbed her. This didn't seem to bother her at all. "He knows what you're up to."

"Some of it," Karina admitted. "Except he thinks it's all a frame-up to keep Henri from being able to blackmail Mom."

"Didn't think he'd go for the profit motive?"

"No. Surprising coming from a man who spends his days making money for other people, isn't it?" She shrugged. "That's all right. Once Mom's in jail, the Maddoxes will just leave him by the wayside, and it'll be over." She had her fingers wrapped loosely around her mug, but she wasn't drinking.

"You hope." I felt a gentle stirring, not in the air, but in the back of my mind. It was Anatole, and he was getting closer. I did not let myself turn. I circled the table, as if intending to sit down in the empty chair. Karina tracked me with her gaze.

"Look, Charlotte. I'm sorry about the phone call, but I needed to get you out here. There's no reason we can't work out a deal."

"What kind of deal did you work out with Oscar?" I shot back.

Her face twisted up tight and her eyes brightened. It took a couple of tries before she could form a new sentence. "That was a mistake."

"Which part? Trusting him or killing him?"

"Both," she whispered. But then she shook herself and her calm certainty returned. "I really never thought he'd try to steal the Arall out from under me."

Tears glittered in her hard eyes. She cared about Oscar; I was sure about it. She might have murdered him, but she cared about him on some level anyway. It was just the witches she didn't give a damn about.

It hit me. "You think they're monsters, don't you?" I said. "Not just the vampires. You took your grandfather's ideas a step further. You think all the paranormals are monsters, including the witches."

"Well, they're sure as hell not human," she snapped. "Prick them, they don't bleed. Poison them, they don't die. Come on, Charlotte, sit down. Have some coffee."

I reached out and picked up the mug. Karina smiled, and, I swear, she licked her lips. But then, I knew she had no poker face. I brought the mug closer to me, letting the steam waft against my face. There it was again, that faint, bad, metallic smell. Probably she'd thought it would be masked by the bitter odor of the fresh, hot coffee, and for just about anybody else it might have worked.

I dumped the whole thing into the nearest planter.

"Hey!" Karina started to her feet.

"You didn't really expect me to drink that, did you?"

"No, not really."

Karina tossed the contents of her own mug right in my face. I shouted and stumbled backward, trying to knuckle hot coffee out of my eyes and wipe it off my cheeks. A cold wind blew past me. Karina laughed, and then she choked. I blinked hard, and my vision cleared.

Anatole stood on the patio. He had one of Karina's arms twisted behind her back, and he had his hand around the back of her neck. But she was just grinning, and both of them were staring at me.

"What?" I shook coffee droplets off my fingers. The metallic smell was all around me, getting deep into my nose, and tingling on the back of my throat and the insides of my cheek. I must have swallowed some of the stuff. I coughed and spat, and it didn't help.

"What is that?" whispered Anatole. "What have you

done to her?" His mouth was open, as if he were trying to swallow the steam as it dispersed on the breeze.

Oh. Shit.

"It's the Arall," I said. "Anatole, she's got the poison working. You need to get out of here."

"Oh yes, Anatole," said Karina brightly. "You really should get out of here."

But Anatole wasn't retreating. He swayed on his feet, hard, almost losing his balance. He lifted his hands away from Karina, who obligingly stepped aside, so he could move toward me with a slow, predatory grace. I could feel the cold that surrounded him shifting and changing. I could feel his fascination reach out to rivet me in place—fascination and hunger.

"It's a complex little formula," Karina said. "It renders humans irresistible to vampires. It's also extremely corrosive. Even if they just bite through the skin, it rots out their mouths and fangs, generally past their ability to heal before they die of starvation. Of course, it's not too good for human skin either, and when ingested, it's poison, what with the methyl alcohol and so forth. That's why it's the last resort. You see, it kills the human as well as the vampire."

"Bet it blisters like hell," I croaked. Maybe it raised hives, so that somebody who died of it might look as though he'd had a really bad allergic reaction.

She nodded. "We're going to have to work on that. You should be starting to feel it right about now."

She was right. My throat and mouth had started to itch. So had my eyelids, and my eyeballs—not just my eyeballs, but the sockets underneath, and my face, and my neck, and the backs of my hands. And none of that mattered, because Anatole was coming toward me, and his hunger was worming its way into the pit of my own stomach.

"Run, Charlotte," Anatole croaked. "Please. Run away."

Karina laughed, and that bright, brittle sound kicked me into gear.

I lunged sideways and snatched up the nearest wrought-iron chair. Karina jumped back, and it whistled as I swung it past her and ran toward the house. Anatole hissed hard behind me, and I felt hope warring with the hunger. He thought I was running away.

I, on the other hand, was thinking that if the Aldens had splashed out for safety glass, I was hosed. I screwed my eyes shut and swung the chair against the French doors. Glass crashed all around me as the window shattered, and the burglar alarm screamed blue murder.

"Nice try, Charlotte," said Karina. "But it's too late."

There was no time to answer her. I leapt through the shattered window and hit the tiles running. Glass grazed my skin, and it drew blood. Swell. That'd just be fuel for the fire inside Anatole. Plus it was going to hurt like hell in a minute. I slammed through the door to the back stairs and started up as fast as I could move my feet. I had to get to my room—my warded room; the place Brendan had made safe for me.

Cold and hunger crawled against my back. Anatole was right behind me. I threw myself up the steps, two at a time. Survival put my systems on overload, and every portion of my body was focused on running toward safety. The burglar alarm screamed and whistled and clanged. I rounded the landing, dragging air into my burning lungs. I couldn't breathe. My vision swam. My throat was way too tight, and my tongue filled my mouth. The itch spread down from my eyes across my face and down my arms.

My feet shot out from under me. My chin slammed against the stair tread, banging my teeth together and missing my tongue by a hair. I screamed as I felt Anatole's iron grip around my ankle.

"Charlotte . . . ," he whispered. It was almost his lover's

voice; that warm, seductive voice that made me want to come close—almost but not quite.

I grabbed at the stair rail, but my hands were thick and clumsy as if I were wearing oven mitts. And they itched. Oh God, they itched. "Anatole, stop," I croaked. "You don't have to do this."

"The hunger's going to kill me," he grated. "I cannot die. I *cannot*!"

I made myself twist around. Anatole was on his knees, holding my ankle. His face was ghost white, and his eyes were flat and dead.

"No," I made myself say. "This isn't you, Anatole. This is the Arall. It's making you crazy!"

"Exactly."

Karina's voice came up from the landing below us. My vision was blurred from the swelling in my eyes, but I could still see her grinning. If I hadn't hated her before, I did now; she was just like her grandfather at his very worst. She'd decided who the monsters were, and now she was going to clear them out of her way.

One finger at a time, Anatole released his hold on my ankle. I tried to pull away, but pain screamed up my leg. Something had broken in there. I was dead. I was so dead. I pulled myself up one stair—and another.

"You did this." Anatole bared his fangs at Karina. They were long, thin, and curved like a cobra's. "You're waiting for me to kill her."

Karina faced him and all the anger pouring off him in ocean waves, and she smiled. "Well, you could go ahead and try to drain me. My mother will save me, or Grandfather will. Blood's thicker, even when you're just the T-typ. And after that, Granddad will take the gloves off and you'll be dead anyway."

Anatole staggered to his feet. "It would be worth it to meet you again in hell." He started down toward her.

"No, Anatole!" I couldn't stand. My ankle couldn't take

it. My ears rang, and my vision was closing in. I shoved myself feet-first down those stairs, sliding down on my belly. Anatole ducked sideways, and I slammed to a stop on the landing. Karina stepped neatly to one side.

I pushed myself to my knees and, with my burning, swollen fingers, groped in my pocket for my spray bottle. "I can't let you," I croaked. "You'd be killing yourself."

"Charlotte, get out of the way."

"No." I pulled out the bottle. The itch was digging through my skin down to my bones. I wanted to stab my nails into my skin and tear it off. Wood snapped under Anatole's fingers as he tried to keep from moving off the stair where he stood.

"You'll have to kill him," said Karina calmly. "And then you'll die anyway. It's what we call a win-win."

"Charlotte, save yourself." Anatole staggered down one step. He was starvation. He was terror. He was trying to shield me from the riot of need pouring out from him, but it wasn't doing any good. I hurt; I burned. I was going to die. Karina Alden was giggling.

"Charlotte." Anatole stumbled down one more stair. He was losing to the hunger. If he made it to the landing, he was going to drain me dry, and we both knew it.

"I'm sorry, Anatole."

I took aim with my bottle.

And I got him square in the kneecap with a load of holy water and garlic oil.

Anatole screamed in pain and toppled sideways over the railing, down to the main floor. The noise he made landing was the worst sound I'd ever heard.

"Bitch!" shrieked Karina.

"So's payback!" I turned the bottle on her and got her right in the face, same as she'd gotten me. I didn't have any magic poisons. I'd just added cayenne pepper to my mix, because not everybody who sneaks up on you in alleys is undead.

Karina screamed as the garlic and pepper hit her eyes. She staggered and fell back, and down, and I heard something go snap before my eyes swelled all the way shut, and I started screaming too.

"Charlotte!"

"Freeze! Police!"

Brendan. That was Brendan and Linus O'Grady. But all I could do was wheeze and cough. Well, okay not quite all. As Brendan bolted up the stairs toward me, I discovered I could pass out too.

31

When I woke up again, I was in the hospital. It was the same wing I'd been in after last year's fire. My favorite nurses, Dawn and Gordon, were still on duty. They gave me a fair amount of crap for taking up their bed space again, but that was okay; I was alive to take it and that, at least, felt really good.

Plus, this time I didn't have to get my head shaved, and healing up after a bad case of hives and blisters hurt a lot less than healing up after a bad case of second-degree burns and smoke inhalation, even when you added in the busted ankle.

I had a steady stream of visitors too. Zoe, Reese, and Marie stopped by to keep the staff around me well fed and to let me know that the *Times* critic hadn't shown up at Nightlife yet. Felicity came by to tell me that the kill fee was already in Nightlife's bank account and that she and Mel were teaming up to coordinate a blowout charity bridal show. Brendan held my hand and let me in on the latest on his meetings with the city council. Of course, as soon as the ambulance took away what was left of Karina and as soon as O'Grady arrested Adrienne in the middle of intermission at the Met, Brendan had gone straight to city hall and offered to leave the job. They were deciding the question now.

O'Grady came by too. Lots. I made what felt like a year's worth of statements, and I signed reams of paper. I'd be testifying in court against Adrienne, Henri, and Trudy too when they caught her, if he had anything to say about it. Apparently, Scott Alden had three law firms on retainer trying to make sure he didn't. My money was on Little Linus.

Chet came by on the night shift. Jacques did too. Jacques was hurting and a little shaky, having made the break with his blood family, but Chet said he was doing okay, and I found myself in the very unusual position of being willing to take my brother's word for it.

The person who did not visit was Anatole. My second night in the hospital, though, the aide brought in a bouquet of red roses with a note printed in clear, tidy letters.

I leave you in capable hands. Yours, Anatole

I swore until I ran out of modifiers, and I fumbled with my smartphone. It's no small trick to get one of those things to work with bandaged hands. But I did finally get Anatole's number punched up. For all that, what I got was a recording.

The number you are trying to reach is unavailable or has been disconnected. Please. . . .

I hung up, and I discovered a store of adjectives and insults inside me that I hadn't yet tapped. Because it wasn't his fault. It was the poison and the Maddox magic that had made him turn on me. He ought to know that.

Except he did know that. And the reason he'd been there at all was because he'd thought he could protect me. Instead, he'd wound up endangering me. He would have killed me. Because of that, he was gone, and I wouldn't have the chance to tell him to stuff the pride and undead testosterone. The only part of what had happened that was his fault was what was happening now, because he was being a stiff-fanged idiot.

I wiped the tears out of my eyes before anybody could see them.

Getting out of the hospital is a long, uncertain process, even if you are able to stand on your own two feet. You have to be checked out by a half-dozen people, and they all have to hand you different sets of papers and instructions. I was sitting on the edge of the bed, kicking my one working heel and wondering what would happen if I tried sneaking out my window with the bulky boot I had to wear on my broken and still-throbbing ankle, when the door opened. I turned, praying for the doctor with my final release papers.

But it was Brendan, smiling a little grimly. He stepped aside so Deanna could walk past him. I stood, slowly.

She looked pale and thin, as though she hadn't been eating. She was rubbing her arms and not looking at me. Her T-shirt had a scoop neck, and I could see the scars on her neck, almost but not quite healed up.

"Hi," she said, and swallowed.

"Hi."

"I . . . um . . . I wanted to say . . . Brendan told me you tried to help. Thank you."

"You're welcome." I met Brendan's eyes. He shook his head. She saw the gesture and grimaced.

"I've had the antidote," she told me. "So has Gabriel. He's seen O'Grady and he's . . ." She bit her lip. "He's gone. I don't know where."

I tried to imagine what was going on inside her. She'd been head over heels in love, only to find out it was the result of magical manipulation on the part of her mother, to break up a scam her now-dead sister had been using her for. And then the guy who'd gone through it all with her had proven his true worth by running away.

I suddenly felt a lot less sorry for myself. I had a home to go to. I still knew who I was and what my life was, and that, if I stopped to think about it, was a whole hell of a lot.

"I'm sorry," I said. She shrugged. "Do you know what you're going to do?"

She glanced up at Brendan. "She's going to stay with me for a while," he said. "We'll figure something out."

"What's your grandfather say?" I was prodding, and I probably shouldn't have been. There are some things you just can't help.

The question did raise a little smirk from Deanna. "Not much he can say. I'm still heir to the Arall, and he's got a whole lot of damage control to take care of before he can even get round to me." She wandered over to my bouquet of roses and touched the petals gently. I couldn't tell what she was thinking. I reached out and took Brendan's hand and squeezed it. He returned an answering pressure, and the tension inside me eased a little.

"I feel like this is my fault," Deanna said to the flowers. "I don't even know why."

"You got used," I told her. "It's the kind of thing that makes you feel really stupid. But it's *not* your fault. You were just convenient."

"I guess. Maybe." She took a deep breath and lifted her head. "But, it's over now, right? Here's where we get to start over."

"Yes, that's exactly what happens now." I said, and I meant it.

She said her good-byes and left us there. Brendan closed the door behind her and came to sit next to me on the bed.

"I got a message from Anatole," he said.

"You're kidding."

"Nope. He told me to take good care of you."

"Or he'd come find you?"

"It was a little more graphic than that, but yes." Brendan ran his thumb over my bandages, very, very gently. "Are you okay?"

I knew what he was asking. He wanted to know if I was

okay with Anatole's leaving. I decided I would misunderstand, because I had no answer for that.

"Mostly." I trapped his restless thumb under the palm of my other hand and held it there for a moment, feeling his warmth and strength and understanding. It was too much. I had to set it aside. "I'll be better when I can get out of here."

The twist Brendan gave to his smile said he knew exactly what I was doing, but he was going to let me get away with it. "As soon as you're cleared, I'll take you home," he said.

"I'd rather you took me to Nightlife."

Slowly, Brendan bowed his head into his hand. "You'll go anyway, won't you?"

"Do you need me to lie? For plausible deniability or anything?"

"No, don't bother," he said with a sigh. "I'll take you."

He did too. Brendan had a regular car service, and the driver knew the shortcuts to Nightlife's back alley. I felt like Frankenstein's monster limping in the stupid boot, but Brendan walked me in the door at five o'clock, straight into the steam and the shouting and the thudding of the knives.

"Heads up!" shouted Zoe from the expediter's station. "Chef in the house!"

All my people turned and faced me. All of them cheered and whooped and applauded and swore, raising a cacophony that rattled the dishes on their racks. Suchai and Robert came through the doors from the dining room, leading the wait staff to add to the noise.

I couldn't see straight. My eyes had gone into open rebellion, and the tears were already trickling down my cheeks. "Yeah, yeah, all right," I said. "Back to work, all of you!"

"Yes, Chef!" chorused my people, and I knew I was well and truly home.

"I'll be round at ten to pick you up," said Brendan as my people settled back to work. I opened my mouth. He tucked his hand under my chin and shut it for me. "Ten," he repeated, holding my bandaged hand up in front of my face to emphasize exactly how little I was going to be able to do in terms of cooking tonight. "Or I will drag you out of here straight back to the hospital."

"I'd like to see you try," I muttered through clenched teeth.

He just grinned and kissed me, and left me there without trying to say good-bye. I let him go, because I knew he'd be back at ten. And he'd take me back to my apartment, and we'd talk, and whatever happened after that . . . it would happen and it would be okay.

I dropped my purse on my desk and my butt in the chair. There was a stack of mail, mostly bills, of course. I gritted my teeth as I sorted through them. But in the middle of the stack was a yellow envelope with a handwritten address in tidy, printed letters.

Anatole? I tore the envelope open and pulled out a card decorated by an artsy watercolor of a rustic cabin surrounded by a field of daisies. Inside someone had scrawled a brief note.

We're coming back. Save us a table.

Love ya,

Melody

The card toppled slowly out of my bandaged fingers. I knew only one person in the whole world named Melody. A little fidget of a sixteen-year-old girl, she was the one responsible for my brother's extreme reactions to things such as sunlight and garlic.

Oh.

Shit.

ABOUT THE AUTHOR

Sarah Zettel is the award-winning author of over twenty novels spanning a whole range of genres: science fiction, fantasy, romance, and now mystery. When not writing, she's practicing yoga, playing the fiddle, cooking, and reading, although generally not all at once. She lives in Michigan with her rapidly growing son and her husband, Tim, who is a lecturer and aerospace engineer at a certain large public university.

Also Available

from

Sarah Zettel

A Taste of the Nightlife

A Vampire Chef Mystery

Charlotte Caine isn't called "the Vampire Chef" because she's a member of New York's undead community—she just cooks for them. Her restaurant, Nightlife, is poised to take the top slot in the world of "haute noir" cuisine.

But when a drunk customer causes a scene, a glowing review from the city's top food critic doesn't seem likely—especially when that customer winds up dead on Nightlife's doorstep. Now, with her brother under suspicion for the murder, Charlotte has to re-open her restaurant and clear her brother's name—before they both become dinner.

Available wherever books are sold or at penguin.com

OM0065